DARK CORNER

<u>BOOK YOUR PLACE ON OUR WEBSITE</u> <u>AND MAKE THE</u> <u>READING CONNECTION!</u>

We've created a customized website just for our very special readers, where you can get the inside scoop on everything that's going on with Zebra, Pinnacle and Kensington books.

When you come online, you'll have the exciting opportunity to:

- View covers of upcoming books
- Read sample chapters
- Learn about our future publishing schedule (listed by publication month *and author*)
- Find out when your favorite authors will be visiting a city near you
- Search for and order backlist books from our online catalog
- Check out author bios and background information
- Send e-mail to your favorite authors
- Meet the Kensington staff online
- Join us in weekly chats with authors, readers and other guests
- Get writing guidelines
- AND MUCH MORE!

Visit our website at
http://www.kensingtonbooks.com

DARK CORNER

BRANDON MASSEY

KENSINGTON PUBLISHING CORP.
http://www.kensingtonbooks.com

DAFINA BOOKS are published by

Kensington Publishing Corp.
850 Third Avenue
New York, NY 10022

All Kensington Titles, Imprints, and Distributed Lines are
available at special quantity discounts for bulk purchases for
sales promotions, premiums, fund-raising, and educational or
institutional use.

Special book excerpts or customized printings can also be
created to fit specific needs. For details, write or phone the
office of the Kensington special sales manager: Kensington
Publishing Corp., 850 Third Avenue, New York, NY 10022,
attn: Special Sales Department, Phone: 1-800-221-2647.

Dafina Books and the Dafina logo Reg. U.S. Pat. & TM Off.

First Trade Paperback Printing: January 2004
First Mass Market Paperback Printing: January 2005
10 9 8 7 6 5 4 3 2 1

Printed in the United States of America

To my mother, who made it possible—
in more ways than one.

In the Beginning

Although William Hunter had lived his entire life as a slave on a plantation in the Mississippi Delta, he had never experienced anything like the horror he was about to face.

His muscles ached. His hands were sore and dark with gunpowder. Blood—not his own—soiled his ragged shirt and pants.

Killing was hard work.

But they weren't done yet. The worst was still ahead of them.

He was part of a group of four men. One was a black man, a slave from the same cotton fields on which William had once toiled; one was a young white man, their slave master's son; the last man was a warrior from a Chickasaw Indian tribe.

They were an unlikely team, drawn together to battle a common enemy. Only an hour ago, there had been seven of them. Two had been killed; the other, unable to endure the terror, had run away.

"We don't have much time till dusk," William said, looking to the edge of the forest, where the orange-red sun steadily sank into the horizon. "We must finish what we've begun."

The men grunted. Their faces, sweaty and spattered with blood, were grim with resolve.

William knew that every one of them was as frightened as he was, but they were determined to conceal their anxiety. True courage was doing what you had to do—without giving in to fear.

Almost as one, they shifted to confront the cave. The ragged mouth was large enough to admit three men. Sharp stones jutted from the ridge of the maw, like teeth.

Like fangs, William thought. A shiver rattled down his spine.

The fading sunlight did not penetrate the thick blackness that lay beyond the entrance. Stepping inside the cavern would be like plunging into a deep Mississippi night.

He hoped that their weapons would be sufficient. He was armed with a rifle. The Indian warrior had arrows, the heads wrapped in kerosene-soaked cloth. The other black man gripped a shotgun, and the white man had a revolver—and a supply of dynamite powerful enough to shatter the cavern walls, if need be.

All of them carried whiskey bottles full of kerosene. A cotton rag dangled from each lip, a poor man's fuse.

They'd done the best they could with the wreckage they discovered at the ravaged plantation, the place that, only yesterday, had been his home.

William had fashioned a torch from a broken broom and a towel. He struck a match and lit the makeshift wick. The fire sputtered, then strengthened into a healthy flame.

He advanced to the front of the group. Holding the torch aloft, he looked at each man.

They were brave men. He did not understand how he'd become their leader. He did not understand much of anything that had happened since his old life had ended last night. He walked on instinct—and faith.

"One day, our children will thank us for this," he said. "Let us pray that they never have to follow in our footsteps."

The men nodded and murmured their agreement.

William Hunter turned to face the cave's mouth. This close, the stench of death wafted from inside like a dense fog.

He whispered a prayer, for himself and his men.

Then, he led them into the darkness.

Part One

HOMECOMING

Evil knows where evil sleeps.
—Ethiopian proverb

One who enters the forest does not listen to the breaking of the twigs in the brush.
—Zambian proverb

Not to know is bad; not to wish to know is worse.
—Nigerian proverb

Chapter 1

At sunrise on Friday, August 23, David Hunter drove away from his town house in Atlanta with a U-Haul trailer hitched to his Nissan Pathfinder. The trailer contained clothes, two computers, books, small pieces of furniture, and other assorted items that held sentimental or practical value. He had left behind everything else at the town house, which, in his absence, would be occupied by his younger sister and her roommate.

In the SUV, David had a road map, a thermos full of strong black coffee, a vinyl CD case full of hip-hop, R&B, gospel, and jazz discs, and his four-year-old German shepherd, King. King lay on the passenger seat, looking out the window as they rolled across the highway. David tended to drive with one hand resting on the canine's flank.

They made excellent time. Traveling Interstate 20 West, they swept through Georgia and entered Alabama within a couple of hours. It was a fine day for a road trip. The morning sunlight was golden, and the cloudless sky was a tranquil ocean blue. Traffic was light and flowed smoothly.

After three hours on the road, sixteen miles outside

Tuscaloosa, Alabama, David pulled into a rest area. He kept King on a leash as they walked along the grassy sward of the designated pet walk, but the dog was well behaved and didn't wrestle against the leash or try to force David into a run. King handled his business near a tree with the solemn dignity that befitted his name.

David was returning to the truck, planning to let the dog inside so he could go back and use the rest room himself, when he saw the man.

He leaned against a white Cadillac DeVille. Slender and brown-skinned, perhaps in his mid-fifties, he wore a green shirt and tan slacks. He talked on a cell phone, checked his watch.

From a distance of about thirty feet, the man looked like David's father.

David stiffened and stopped. King, brought to a halt, looked at David questioningly.

Although the day was warm and humid, a chill fell over David.

As if sensing David's attention, the man turned. He met David's eyes briefly, then looked away, continuing to chat on the phone.

The man was not Richard Hunter, his father. Of course it wasn't him. His father had died five months ago.

David sighed, went to the SUV, and let King climb inside.

I need to stop this, David thought, as he walked to the rest area washrooms. *I'll never see my father again. I have to accept it.*

He used the rest room, then returned to the parking lot. The man who resembled his father was gone. Whoever he had been.

David got behind the wheel of the SUV.

His cell phone chirped.

"Hey, it's your mama. Where are you?"

It was just like his mother to call the moment after he experienced an episode of weirdness.

"Hey, Mom. I'm right outside Tuscaloosa, Alabama. I passed the big Mercedes-Benz plant a little while ago."

"You're driving too fast. You shouldn't be that far already."

Although David was twenty-nine years old and had traveled extensively throughout the country, by air and by car, Mom never hesitated to dole out travel tips and cautions.

"I've been cruising at seventy-five. Traffic has been light." He paused, then added, "I'm at a rest area. I just saw a man who looked like Dad."

"Oh," Mom said. A note of melancholy crept into her voice. "Remember how the same thing happened to both of us, when your granddad passed? For a while, it seemed that once a month we'd see a man who looked exactly like him."

"I remember. But I feel different about this. Because there's always a chance . . ."

"David, honey, it's not good for you to think about that. I know it's painful for you, but you need to try to let it go. Your father is gone."

David swallowed. A monarch butterfly landed on the windshield, its colorful wings gilded with sunlight. It seemed to peer inside the truck at David.

His mother was right. He had told himself the same thing many times. His father, Richard Hunter, was dead and gone forever. Any stranger who looked like him was just that—a stranger.

But the circumstances of his father's death stirred a naïve hope that he might be alive.

Richard Hunter had not been an ordinary man. He was a writer, not merely good but brilliant; a Pulitzer Prize winner who evoked favorable comparison to the revered literary lions in the canon of African-American literature: Ellison, Hurston, Wright, Morrison. Richard Hunter had lived an adventurous, colorful life that matched his literary accomplishments. After a brief, disastrous marriage to David's mother that produced only one child, Hunter moved to Paris

to write his first novel, an immediate best-seller, and there-
after embarked on a series of journeys that took him from
Morocco to China, from South Africa to Nepal, from
Australia to Indonesia, from Brazil to Denmark . . . his father's travels could've filled a dozen issues of *National
Geographic.* Writing and publishing one best-selling novel
after another, publishing essays in *The New Yorker,* crafting
stage plays that opened on Broadway, and penning the script
of an Oscar award–winning film, Richard Hunter had the
proverbial Midas touch in the literary world. But his ability
to sustain meaningful, long-term relationships seemed to be
directly inverse to his writing talent.

David hardly knew his father. Throughout his dad's endless globetrotting, it was a rare event to receive so much as a
postcard from him, to say nothing of a birthday or Christmas
gift. He called or wrote David every few years, and visited
less often. Although Hunter married three more times, and
entertained countless girlfriends and mistresses, he never
had another child. Often, David had thought that being
Hunter's only child would have meant something to his father, but their relationship never developed beyond a superficial, awkward friendliness. David had learned more about
Richard Hunter by reading about him in magazines than he
had through direct contact with his dad.

But in March of that year, his father had been on a boat in
the Gulf of Mexico, deep-sea fishing, when a storm swept
him off the deck and into the ocean. An extensive search by
the coast guard failed to recover his body. At the coroner's
inquest, he was declared legally dead.

Richard Hunter's will revealed that he had bequeathed his
money, property, and belongings to David—the total value
of which equaled over four million dollars.

David was suddenly rich, granted a fortune by a man who
was a relative stranger to him.

Nagging questions circled David's thoughts. Why did his
father ignore him for his entire life and then will him every-

thing he had owned? Had his father loved him, but been unable to express his feelings? What kind of man had Richard Hunter been, outside his literary exploits?

And the question that haunted David most of all remained: Was his father really dead? His body had never been recovered, which gave David a fragile hope that, somehow, his father had survived the accident. But if Richard Hunter had survived, then where was he? Why hadn't he resurfaced to reclaim his life?

It was hard to speculate about stuff like that. One bewildering question led to a slew of others even more puzzling.

"I hope you learn a lot about your dad while you're in Mississippi," Mom said. "Like I've told you before, I don't think you need to make this trip, but I know you won't be happy otherwise."

Although his father had been a world traveler, between his journeys, he always returned to his hometown: Mason's Corner, Mississippi. There, he lived in a modest house that had been in the Hunter family for generations. The home had been vacant since his father's death.

"Well, like I've said, I'll be there for a year," David said. "Maybe not that long. It depends on how things go, and what I find out."

"What do you expect to find out, David?" Mom said. Mom had asked him the same question before, but there was a desperation in her voice that he hadn't heard previously. "It's a tiny town with three traffic lights. What do you think you're going to learn there?"

David turned the key in the ignition. The engine hummed to life.

"I don't know, Mom," David said. "Maybe . . . the truth."

At a quarter past three o'clock in the afternoon, driving north on Interstate 55, David passed a road sign that announced the upcoming exit for Mason's Corner.

Anticipation tingled in his gut.

It had been about fifteen years since he had visited Mississippi. He had purposefully taken a longer route to Mason's Corner, traveling Interstate 20 West into Jackson, at the center of the state, where he then connected with Interstate 55 North, which would take him up to the northwest region, at the edge of the delta. He wanted to absorb the sounds and sights, and immerse himself in this place where his father's family had lived for so long.

Mostly, the land was covered with verdant hills that appeared to stretch to the edge of the world. At other times, maple trees and pine trees crowded the highway, their trunks festooned with kudzu. In many of the open stretches, he saw vast fields of soybean and cotton.

It was easy to imagine that this had once been a land in which cotton plantations had sustained the economy. The earth was so fertile it seemed anything might thrive in the rich soil. North of Jackson, David had stopped to refuel, and the warm, humid air was like the inside of a greenhouse.

The exit ramp for Mason's Corner came into view. He turned onto the winding lane, and entered a tunnel of trees that blanketed the road in dense shadows. Then, the trees thinned out and gave way to a suspension bridge. A sunlight-spangled river rushed in the chasm below. Two black children stood along the sandy bank, working fishing poles.

The bridge, about forty feet long, rattled and clinked as he drove across it. King poked his nose out the half-open window. He whined.

David stroked the dog's neck. "We're almost there, boy. I know you're fed up with riding in here."

Ahead, a blue sign read in white letters: Welcome to Mason's Corner, the Jewel of Mississippi. Pop. 3,200.

The town limits were marked only by small, erratically spaced homes. Rusty cars sitting on concrete blocks filled front yards, and clotheslines heavy with garments snapped in the summer breeze. People—everyone David saw was black—sat on porches and lawn chairs. They watched him drive by, and he thought he could hear what they were thinking: "Who's that guy moving here?" This wasn't like Atlanta. In a small town like Mason's Corner, a new resident would be noteworthy.

The road, Main Street, cut through the center of downtown—though calling the tiny business district "downtown" was being generous. While he waited at a traffic light, he looked around. Faded storefronts lined the road: a diner, a clothing shop, a florist, a furniture store. Old black men sat in chairs in front of a barbershop, talking and watching anyone of interest—all of them looked his way, their gazes lingering over the trailer. A scattering of cars and trucks were parked diagonally along the curb; a lot of people owned pickup trucks.

The light switched to green. He rolled forward.

He spotted other buildings: a People's Bank branch office, an elementary school, a library, the police station, a Baptist church, a BP gas station, a barbecue joint, a pool hall with a Coors beer sign in the window. Farther ahead, there was a large park that had basketball and tennis courts, a baseball diamond, a playground, benches, and a pond that sparkled like quicksilver.

Everywhere, when he passed people, they looked his way and appeared to take note of the trailer. He could only smile. "Welcome to Mississippi," he said to himself. King chuffed.

David consulted his directions. The family home was located on Hunter Drive, which was coming up. He made a right turn, and found himself in a peaceful neighborhood of mature, leafy elms and modest houses.

The place was half a block down, on the left. A black mailbox at the curb had the name "Hunter" written in fancy script.

He pulled into the asphalt driveway.

Sitting in the idling truck, David stared at his new home. A sensation of unreality washed over him. He had really done it. He had left behind his life in Atlanta and moved here, to the land of his father.

"My new home," he whispered.

It was a two-story house, painted eggshell white, with clapboard siding and forest-green shutters. According to Earvin Williams, his father's estate attorney, the home was almost eighty years old and had been constructed by a team of men that included David's great-grandfather. The place looked as though it had been kept in good repair. It had a screened-in porch, a two-car garage, and a tool shed, too.

The lawn, however, badly needed to be mowed. Earvin had said that he'd hired someone to cut the grass, but that was a few weeks ago. The property had been undisturbed since his father's death. The lawyer had paid the utility bills, in the meantime, and promised David that he only needed to bring his belongings, and move right in. "There's no telling what you might find in there," Earvin had said. "Your father lived the last few months of his life in that house, may his soul rest in peace."

That's perfect, David had thought. *Maybe I can figure out what Dad was doing before the accident. . . .*

King clawed the glass, jarring David out of his reverie.

"All right, boy, we're getting out." David cut the engine. "We're here."

King looked at him as if to say, *It's about time, man. You've kept me cooped up in this thing forever. Let me outta here!*

David opened his door, and King, normally patient, didn't wait for David to walk around and open the passenger door. The dog scrambled over the seats and leaped outside. He roved across the yard, sniffing.

"Don't run off," David said. He raised his arms and stretched.

At a brick home across the street, a grandmotherly woman tended a bed of flowers. She waved at him. He returned the greeting.

He could get used to having friendly neighbors. At his town house community in Atlanta, he and his neighbors had rarely spoken to one another.

He had a lot of unloading and unpacking to do, but he'd take care of it later.

The screen door was unlocked, and opened silently.

Thick waves of humid air churned in the porch. Three lawn chairs stood inside, ranked beside one another. A copy of the *Chester County Ledger* lay on an end table, beside a glass ashtray filled with a cigar butt. His father had loved cigars.

David picked up the newspaper. It was dated March 9th. Two days before his father had vanished.

A chill zapped through him, like an electric shock. He dropped the paper.

There was something eerie about touching an item that had been last handled by a dead man. But he would have to get used to it, if he was going to live in this house.

King bolted inside the porch. Tongue wagging, the dog bumped against David, eager to go inside.

David opened the door.

The first thing that struck David was the smell: a stale odor hung within, as though the house had been sealed for years and not only for a few months. He found the thermostat in the entry hall, and switched on the fan. He'd open windows, too, as he encountered them, then turn on the air-conditioner later.

King set off down the hallway, sniffing eagerly.

As he stood in the foyer, David had the distinct feeling that he had walked into a dream. Like a place in a dream, the house felt familiar, yet foreign. The last time he had visited, he was fourteen. He'd spent two weeks there during the summer, entertained by his two cousins (whose names escaped him) and, less often, by his father. He'd left convinced that it was the most boring place in the world—they had none of the cool stuff they had in Atlanta—and vowing that he'd never visit again, no matter how badly he wanted to spend time with his dad.

Funny how time could change a person's mind.

A staircase twisted up to the second floor. Four doorways were in the first-floor hall. David slowly walked past each room. The living room was the first room he passed, a spacious area full of overstuffed furniture, a grandfather clock, framed family photos, a television, a fireplace, and a rocking chair. Next was the dining room: a large oak table stood in the center, circled by matching oak chairs. On his right, a bathroom. A familiar slurping sound came from within.

"King!" He opened the door. The dog had its snout in the toilet, lapping up water.

"I'll get some water for you." David went through the doorway at the end of the hall, into the kitchen. He found a large bowl in a cabinet, filled it with tap water, and set it on the tile floor. King drank greedily.

The kitchen was basic: it had a gas range, Formica countertops, a pine dinette table. A Polaroid photo was pinned against the refrigerator with a magnet: his father, clad in fishing gear and standing on the deck of a boat, showing off his catch of the day, a large, gleaming bass.

Dad died on a fishing trip like that . . .

David's breath caught in his throat. He left the kitchen to explore the rest of the house.

On the second level, there were five rooms: a master bedroom, a guest room, another bedroom, another bathroom, and an office. One look inside the office confirmed that this was where Richard Hunter had spent most of his time, because the other rooms lacked any distinctive mark of his personality.

Two large windows, veiled with half-open venetian blinds, admitted afternoon sunshine. Oak bookcases lined the walls; the shelves were packed with tomes—his father's works, and many others. A large oak desk stood along the far wall, a black leather chair in front.

From his research, David learned that his father had written at least three of his novels while sitting at this desk. An IBM Selectric typewriter sat in the middle of the desk, like a museum relic. His father had composed his work only on typewriters, never on computers. A jar full of sharp pencils stood to the left of the typewriter, and a rubber coaster lay on the right, marred with a coffee stain. His father would drink coffee continuously as he hammered out his prose.

At David's town house in Atlanta, he had arranged his desk similarly: writing implements on the left, a coaster on the right, and a computer, instead of a typewriter, in the center.

He settled into the chair. He was the same height as his father, six-foot-one, and he found the angle of the chair and desk comfortable. Perhaps he would set up his own computer in this room, right here.

"This is where the great man worked," David said. His voice seemed loud, and he laughed, uneasily. The office was so quiet and still that he might have been sealed inside an airtight cell.

He noticed that a framed photograph lay on the corner of the desk, facedown. He picked it up. It was an old picture of David, at maybe three years of age, his mother, and his father. All of them had afros, and wide grins.

He was shocked to find that his father had kept this family photo close at hand. This gave him something new to think about. Had his father missed the family life he had once had?

He looked around. No additional clues jumped out at him—yet.

David yawned. He'd driven over nine hours and needed to take a nap. Thinking about this stuff was tiring him out.

Before leaving, he opened the blinds of the window nearest the desk, to see what kind of view the office provided. He saw a vista of rolling green hills, deep forests, and, perched on a hilltop in the distance, a sprawling antebellum mansion, a remnant of the old South.

Coldness tapped the base of his spine.

He didn't understand why looking at the house made him feel cold. He could not remember ever seeing the mansion, though surely it had been there when he'd visited the town as a teenager.

Someone should tear down that place, he thought, suddenly and irrationally. *It should be demolished—*

The door burst open, and David almost screamed.

It was only King. The dog dashed inside and leapt onto David, tail wagging.

"Okay, okay, I know, your bladder is full now and you need to pee." David stroked the dog's neck. "Come on, let's go outside."

David looked out the window one last time. The chill returned, skipping along his spine like an icy finger.

Hurriedly, he left and shut the door.

Outside, while King cavorted across the yard, David began to unload the trailer. Although he was exhausted, he worried that if he dared to sleep he would not wake until late in the evening. He didn't want to leave his possessions in the trailer overnight. He likely had no need to fear thieves in this town, but years of city living had made him cautious.

He had opened the trailer door and gripped a cardboard box full of books when the grandmotherly woman who had waved at him earlier walked across the street. She was accompanied by a tall, lean man who appeared to be her husband.

"Good afternoon," the man said. He had a crisp, deep voice. "Are you our new neighbor?"

"That I am." David placed the box on the ground. "My name is David Hunter."

"A pleasure to meet you," the man said. "My name is Franklin Bennett. This is my wife, Ruby."

David and Franklin shook hands. Franklin had a strong, dry grip. David immediately had a good feeling about him. One of the few things his father had taught him was how a trustworthy man will always have a firm handshake.

Franklin and Ruby looked to be in their mid-sixties. Ruby was dark-skinned and petite, with large, clear eyes. She wore jeans, tennis shoes, a United Negro College Fund T-shirt, and a cap that covered a full head of salt-and-pepper hair. Franklin was bespectacled and balding, with a trimmed gray beard. He wore a white dress shirt, slacks, and suspenders. He had a scholarly demeanor. David was willing to wager that he was a teacher.

King came over and snuffled the Bennetts' legs. David introduced the dog, and the couple smiled and petted King. They were obviously dog lovers.

"So you're a Hunter?" Franklin said. "Was Richard Hunter your . . ."

"He was my father," David said.

"We're so sorry to hear about what happened," Ruby said. "What an awful accident."

"Your father was a good man," Franklin said.

"Thank you," David said. "I moved here from Atlanta. Someone has to take care of the house for a while. It's been in our family for a long time."

"That is most certainly true," Franklin said. "Since nineteen twenty-seven, in fact."

"Really?" David said. "I didn't know that."

Franklin chuckled. "I'm a bit of a history buff, David. One of my long-standing hobbies has been exploring the history of our fine town."

"Don't get Professor Bennett started." Ruby grinned. "Will you be living here permanently, David?"

"Maybe for a year. After that, we'll see. I've never lived in a small town, so I'll see how I like it."

"It's a markedly slower pace of life than what you're likely accustomed to," Franklin said. "But we love it. We grew up here, moved away to Washington, D.C., to have our careers and raise our family, then decided to come back here for our retirement."

"What's the age range of the people here?" David said.

"It's not a town full of old folks, sugar," Ruby said. She chuckled. "We've got retired folks, like us, stable, working families, then some kids your age, and younger. We've got our share of young, pretty women, too. Are you single?"

"Ruby, don't pry—" Franklin started.

"It's no problem." David laughed. "I'm single."

"Keep your eyes peeled, then," Ruby said. She winked. David laughed again.

"We could talk your ears off all day," Franklin said. "But I see that you were in the process of unloading this trailer. Why don't I assist you?"

"Thanks, but that's okay. I don't have that much to take inside."

"Frank only wants an excuse to keep asking you questions," Ruby said. "David, please let him help you, or else he'll talk me to sleep *wondering* about you."

Franklin scowled. "Woman, you do not know my mind at all." Then he laughed.

"Since you put it that way, I could use a hand." David smiled. These were the nicest people he had met in ages. Although he could have unloaded the trailer on his own, he *was* interested in continuing his discussion with Franklin. The old man claimed to be a history buff, and he might know a great deal about David's own family history as it related to the town.

Most of all, David wanted to ask him about his father.

They chatted as they conveyed boxes inside. David learned that Franklin really was a retired history professor. He had taught at Howard University for over thirty years. In his life as a retiree, he spent his time pursuing his lifelong passion—history—and had become the town's official historian. The historian position had never been formally conferred upon him by town authorities—they didn't have an official post for such a person. It was official, Franklin said, because everyone, including the mayor, approached him whenever a question about history arose.

"Are you a writer, like your father was?" Franklin said as they hefted boxes full of books into the house. "You've got quite a few titles here."

"I'm an avid reader. Outside of English classes in college, the only writing I've ever done is in computer code. I worked as a programmer for a consulting firm before I started my Web design business two years ago."

"Ah, so you're an entrepreneur!" Franklin set down the box he'd been carrying beside the staircase. Sweat glistened on his face. He pulled out a handkerchief and blotted his skin dry.

"Listen, you don't have to help me with all of this moving," David said. "I can finish the rest on my own."

"Nonsense. I need the exercise. Don't be concerned, I won't have a heart attack on you."

It took half an hour for them to finish lugging everything inside. Ruby returned to bring them tall, icy glasses of sweet tea. David sipped the tea gratefully; King looked at him with sad eyes, as if expecting him to share. "None for you," David said, and stuck out his tongue at the dog. King barked.

Exhausted, David and Franklin took seats at the dinette table in the kitchen. David thanked Franklin again for his assistance, and Franklin waved it off.

"The only physical exercise I pursue these days is riding my bicycle around town," Franklin said. "I'm happy to do some weight lifting."

David nodded. "You know, since you live across the street, I was wondering, did you know my father?"

Franklin pursed his lips. "Interesting question. Although I was Richard's neighbor for seven years, and though he was often present during that time, I'd have to say that we were acquaintances, not genuine friends. This is the first time I've set foot within this house."

"So my dad wasn't very friendly."

"He was friendly, but he was a private man—rightly so considering his public persona. I think when he was here, in his home, he wanted to be left alone, to enjoy life like an ordinary man. He was famous here, understand. Tourists came from hundreds of miles away to drive by this house and gawk, or they hoped to spy him as he made one of his brooding walks throughout the town.

"That said, I don't think Richard had many friends in Mason's Corner. But of course, absolutely everyone knew him."

"I didn't," David said. When he realized what he'd blurted out, he blushed.

Franklin arched his eyebrows.

"I might as well tell you," David said. "My father and I didn't exactly have a good relationship. He was a stranger to me, to be honest." He swept his arm across the kitchen. "Then, when he passed, he gave it all to me. Everything he'd owned."

"Which perplexes you, and understandably so," Franklin said. He shook his head. "I'm sorry, David. Richard Hunter was an enigma to me. I don't pretend to understand his motivations."

"Neither do I, and that's why I'm here. I want to piece everything together—as much as I can, anyway. I won't be satisfied until I get some answers."

David was surprised by how openly he spoke to Franklin. He'd told his mother, and no one else, about his purpose for moving to Mason's Corner. His family and friends believed that he was there because he wanted a temporary break from Atlanta.

"I wish you Godspeed in your mission," Franklin said. "I suspect you'll find life in Dark Corner to be an enjoyable change of pace."

"Dark Corner?"

"The locals call the town Dark Corner. Do you think you know why?"

"I've no clue."

"Because the town is over ninety percent African-American, and has been for generations. Dark Corner was originally a slanderous name, actually—think of the derogatory term, 'darkie'—but over time, it acquired a certain charm and became part of the shared language of the residents. I suspect Edward Mason would be aghast if he were alive today to see what had become of his lovely corner of the South. The Negroes have taken over the plantation!" Franklin laughed.

David laughed, too. "Was Edward Mason the town founder?"

"Correct. Around eighteen forty-one, Mason established an immense cotton plantation here. Have you seen his estate, Jubilee?"

David thought about the mansion he had spotted from the window upstairs. The place that had given him a chill.

"Is it one of those antebellum houses, with columns out front?"

"That's the one, you can't miss it. It's perched on a hill at the eastern edge of town, like a castle. Edward Mason liked to stand on the veranda of Jubilee and survey his cotton kingdom, and glory in his achievements."

"Does anyone live there today?"

"Certainly not. Jubilee is reputed to be haunted. Townsfolk won't go near it."

David's hand was curled around the cold glass of tea; the iciness in the glass traveled up the length of his arm, and spread throughout his body.

"Haunted?" David said. "Are you serious?"

Franklin shrugged. "That is what the stories claim. I've

never seen evidence of it myself, but then, like other towns-people, I avoid Jubilee, too. It has an aura about it that . . . well, it disturbs me, to be frank."

"I felt the same thing when I saw the house earlier. A chill."

"Trust your instincts," Franklin said. "I'm a man of reason and logic, but the more I learn, the more I realize that there is much in our world that resists easy classification."

"I don't plan to visit the place anytime soon," David said.

"Wise choice." Franklin nodded. "One of these evenings, you must join Ruby and me for dinner. I'll share some of the tales with you. There are many. Mason's Corner is a small town, yet claims a colorful history."

"I'd like that," David said. A yawn escaped him.

Franklin hastily pushed away from the table.

"You need your rest, you've had a long day," Franklin said. He retrieved the empty glasses. "We'll talk more soon. And you're welcome to come over anytime."

"Thank you again for your help." David accompanied Franklin to the door. Franklin crossed the street, a bounce in his step.

David smiled. What a guy. He had made his first friend in Mason's Corner.

But he'd had enough activity for one day. Tomorrow, he'd finish getting settled in and would begin exploring the town.

He dragged himself upstairs. In the master bedroom, King lay across the bed, snoring loudly.

"King, I think that's my spot."

The dog raised its head, groggy.

"On the floor, buddy," David said. "The rules haven't changed."

Groaning, King hopped onto the floor, and slumped on the rug.

David lay on the mattress and sank into a deep sleep.

* * *

"Now David seems like a nice young man," Ruby said to Franklin. She was in the kitchen preparing dinner. "He's a spitting image of his daddy, too."

"That's the first thing I noticed." Franklin put the empty glasses in the sink. "For a moment, I thought I was seeing a ghost."

"I hope you invited him to dinner."

"I extended a dinner invitation for the near future, but I'll wait a few days before I mention it to him again," he said, thinking of David's purpose for moving to Mason's Corner. The boy was on a mission to learn about his father, and Franklin didn't want to hound him, though he would like to spend more time in the Hunter house, exploring.

"He's a friendly kid, quite open, not at all like his father," Franklin said. "We'll be spending more time together, chatting."

"Don't you go digging through his family's possessions," Ruby said.

"The Hunters have lived in Dark Corner for generations. They must have books, photos, relics—"

"Like I said, Professor Bennett. Respect the young man's privacy."

"Am I that intrusive, my dear?"

She smiled. "Sugar, when you've got something you want to find out, only God Himself can hold you back."

Franklin leaned against the counter. He stroked his chin.

"Ruby, as much as I've learned about this town, I feel as if I'm missing something. I know all about Edward Mason and his vile plantation; I know sordid tales about many of the families here; I could draw a timeline of every major incident that's occurred in this town over the past one hundred and sixty years. But my intuition tells me that I am missing an integral piece of the puzzle. The Hunters always have been a private clan. I believe that there's a reason why."

Ruby clucked her tongue. She opened the oven and checked the progress of the roast beef.

"I'm not befriending David only because I want to discover his family's secrets," he said. "You know me much better than that. I genuinely enjoyed speaking with him and hope to develop a friendship. However, if I can discreetly uncover a few historical gems in the process, that would please me immensely."

"You know how I feel about digging into people's business," Ruby said. "But I know your ways. You won't be satisfied until you find the dirt."

"It's not dirt. It's only data."

She smiled. "What do the kids say these days? Whatever, man."

He kissed her on the cheek. "I'm going to feed the hound."

"Dinner will be ready in ten minutes," she said.

A large bag of Purina dog food stood near the back door. Franklin took the big scoop that lay on top of the bag and dug it inside, filling the cup with the brownish nuggets.

The dog waited for him at the foot of the steps. It was a mutt, a mix of a collie and another breed he couldn't place. He'd discovered the hound rooting through his garbage one day, and he had adopted it as his own. He never brought the canine inside the house or threw a leash around its neck. He let the dog roam throughout the town as it wished. It came to him when it was hungry and wanted to be petted, normally at the same time every day.

He'd named the mutt Malcolm, because on the day he found the dog he'd been re-reading the autobiography of the famous civil rights leader.

"Hey, how're you doing, Malcolm?" Franklin scratched the dog behind the ears. It whined in pleasure. He poured the food into the large bowl that rested at the base of the steps. He refilled the water bowl, too.

As he watched Malcolm eat, he considered what he and Ruby had discussed. He had been honest with his wife—after being married for over forty years, he'd learned that it was simply easier to be honest. He was convinced that the Hunter family possessed information that could deepen his knowledge of the town's historical background. After living across the street from the notoriously taciturn Richard Hunter for seven years, Franklin had almost given up hope of learning what secrets the Hunters might be guarding. But David—now he was a nice young man. And Franklin suspected that David did not know his family's history himself. The two of them could, if David allowed it, learn together. Indeed, he might very well be a great help to David.

Life in Dark Corner, normally predictable and quiet, was going to become a lot more interesting, very soon.

Chapter 2

Kyle Coiraut could not relax on the airplane.

Although he sat in the first-class section of the Boeing aircraft, in a comfortable leather seat, and though the seat beside him was vacant, ensuring abundant elbow room, since he had boarded the plane at Charles de Gaulle, in Paris, he had been fidgeting. He tried to read the book he'd brought along, a Mississippi travelogue, but he could not focus on it for any longer than a few minutes. Attempting to read the airline magazine and the *Wall Street Journal* brought the same disappointing result. When he slipped on headphones and switched on the portable CD player to listen to one of Rachmaninoff's peerless piano concertos—music which usually turned his thoughts away from his troubles—the notes drew his nerves as taut as piano wire.

He drummed his long fingers against the armrests. He understood the source of his unease, of course: he could not tolerate sacrificing control of his safety. The fact that he had placed responsibility for his welfare in the hands of a human, the pilot, tortured him. Humans were fallible and accident prone. Airline crashes were not common, but they happened with enough frequency for this transcontinental voyage to thoroughly unsettle him.

A window was beside him, and he'd pulled down the plastic shutter, shutting out his view of the clouds. He did not ordinarily fear heights, but looking through the portal made it frightfully easy to imagine a fatal plummet to the earth.

The flight attendant, a striking blond woman, strolled along the aisle, checking on passengers. She smiled at him and asked, for perhaps the third time, whether he required anything else to enhance his flight experience. He smiled briefly and responded that he was fine. He had not eaten anything and had drunk only water, and had asked her for nothing. She continually approached him, he suspected, because she believed him to be a celebrity.

His clothing might partly explain her curiosity. His entire wardrobe was black: boots, slacks, shirt, leather jacket, and hat. He wore tight, black leather gloves and aviator sunglasses, too.

His skin was a rich chocolate-brown, and he was tall, about six-feet-five, with the build of a track runner. Draped in his elegant, ebony garments, he cut an impressive figure.

The flight attendant likely thought he was a professional athlete; perhaps a famous basketball player seeking to avoid attention. Or maybe a famed fashion model. He routinely encountered similar assumptions whenever he swam through the pool of humanity during daylight hours. In actuality, his heavy, dark clothing was a matter of necessity: vampires did not endure sunlight well.

Sun rays did not affect vampires as dramatically as the popular media portrayed. He wouldn't catch fire, or melt as though he were made of wax. But exposure to ultraviolet light caused his skin to itch terribly. According to Mother, a vampire who habitually courted daylight would accelerate the aging process, too. Needless to say, vampires only ventured outdoors during the day when it was essential.

His journey to the United States was essential. He had been waiting for this trip for his entire life—one hundred and sixty-eight years.

He shifted in his seat. They had been airborne for only thirty minutes. He had at least eleven more hours in the sky and a connecting flight ahead of him. An eternity.

This was not his first airline trip. Throughout the past few decades, he had traveled the globe via air. But he had taken his previous journeys in Mother's private jet, piloted by an especially gifted human agent. He regretted that he had refused Mother's offer of taking the family aircraft to the United States. Now, he paid for his arrogant refusal with extreme discomfort.

His black leather bag lay on the seat beside him. He unzipped the top compartment, and retrieved a cool aluminum packet.

The silver vacuum-sealed packet contained sixteen ounces of human blood—though no one watching could discern the precious fluid contained therein. When enjoying a meal in the company of humans, discretion was vital.

He and Mother procured all of the blood they required from blood banks, as did many vampires these days. He had not fed on a living creature in ages. Mother, ever concerned about risk and attracting dangerous attention, had insisted that they learn to sustain themselves through safe, nonviolent means. The emergence of blood banks was a boon for vampires; the wealthy ones had forged confidential arrangements with a small, trusted network of blood banks throughout the world.

There was no need to ever hunt for food again. Indeed, hunting human prey seemed primitive to him, an activity pursued only by uncivilized vampires, or those who were poor and had no alternative. The few prosperous vampires who chose to hunt did so for sport, under carefully controlled conditions—the vampire equivalent of game preserves.

Kyle removed the black straw from the back of the carton. It took three stabs at the perforated hole for him to puncture the surface and slide the straw inside.

He restrained himself from sucking dry the entire packet in a greedy gulp. He had fed only a few hours ago, and was not genuinely hungry. He sipped only to soothe his nerves.

The cool, thick blood flowed over his tongue: delicious.

He leaned back in the seat, sighed.

A pleasurable warmth spread through his body.

The blond flight attendant appeared at his shoulder and asked if he would like a pillow. He accepted her offer.

Smiling flirtatiously, she asked him to bend his head forward. She slipped the pillow behind him and gently pushed him back against the cushion.

"Let me know if you need anything else, sir." Her fingers brushed across his shoulder. Her tongue flickered briefly between her glossy red lips.

He smiled. "Thank you. I certainly will."

He watched her walk away, her tight hips undulating under her skirt. He loved human women, and they invariably found him irresistibly attractive. Some of the fictions about vampires were true: vampires were considered to be sexy.

His head resting against the pillow, Kyle closed his eyes. For the first time since he had boarded the airplane, his thoughts unwound, and his muscles relaxed.

Not surprisingly, as his mind drifted, he thought about his last encounter with Mother . . .

Silvery beads of afternoon rain streamed down the tinted parlor window as Kyle gazed outside at the green hills of their country estate.

Behind him, Mother said, "I do not approve of this trip. I understand why you wish to leave, but I do not approve."

Kyle turned. Mother reclined on a chaise lounge, frowning. Even in her distress, she was indescribably beautiful. Her skin was dark and flawless; her lustrous, midnight-black hair cascaded to her shoulders. Six feet tall, she possessed a lean, exquisitely proportioned figure. She was dressed in a silky lavender wrap, and matching shoes.

Mother's true name was Lisha, but amongst humans she used many aliases, to maintain her privacy. To a human, at first glance, she would appear to be no older than forty. In truth, Mother was the oldest living vampire in the world—and the original mother of their race. Her true age was a mystery, even to Kyle.

One look into her eyes confirmed that she was far older than she appeared to be. Almond-shaped, obsidian, and gleaming, her eyes reflected a depth of knowledge and wisdom that few living beings would ever attain. She had mesmerized countless creatures with her compelling gaze, including him.

Meeting her eyes and voicing his decision to disobey her wishes was one of the most difficult steps Kyle had ever taken. Perspiration coated his face.

"Mother, I must go. When you told me the truth, you foresaw what I would decide to do, didn't you? You should not be surprised."

A month ago, Kyle had resolved to leave his mother's French estate and establish a home of his own in another region, perhaps in western Africa. His resolution was born of a restlessness that had plagued him for years. Like a child, he had spent his life under the protective arm of his mother, and though he lived in luxury and absorbed her endless store of knowledge about vampires and mankind, he yearned to break away, to live his own life. Mother had known that he would want to leave one day, and she was not startled. But what startled him was when she told him the truth of his father.

Before, she always had led him to believe that his father was dead and had died before Kyle was born. She finally revealed that his father was in the United States, entombed in a cave in a rural town in the state of Mississippi, alive, but submerged in a Sleep that had, so far, endured for over a century and a half.

His father was alive. Throughout his life, he had wondered about his father, his male co-creator. Although, as Mother tried to explain, most vampires lived happily without full knowledge of both their parents, Kyle did not believe that he was like other vampires. His gift—and perhaps his burden—was his capacity to feel emotion. He was not a cold-blooded predator, a heartless creature of the night. He was capable of a vast range of feeling that surely rivaled what any human could experience.

He wanted to understand his place in the world. He wanted to be guided and taught by one who could understand him in a way that Mother could not. He had yearned for a connection to his father, and had thirsted for knowledge about him, even though Mother had deceived him into believing that his father was dead. And in Mother's opinion, one who was dead was not worth discussion; she'd told him little about his own father.

Mother had lied to "protect" him, she claimed. It was only when she realized that he was going to leave her, to live his own life, that she confessed. He hated her for lying to him, though he understood her intentions in concealing the truth. She knew what he would decide to do once he had learned the truth. *She knew.*

"You are correct, I am not surprised at your intentions," Mother said. "I told you the truth at last because I had hoped you would handle the knowledge wisely. I warn you to leave the past alone, my son. Let your father rest, in peace."

"You ask the impossible," he said. "All my life I've wondered about what he was like, how it would have been to know him. Do you think I could ever rest, knowing that he's alive?"

"How do you think I feel?" she said. "He was my companion. I loved him deeply—more than you could ever understand." She closed her eyes for a moment, drew a breath to compose herself. "Leaving your father to follow his unfortunate fate was one of the most difficult decisions I've ever made."

"But that was almost a hundred seventy years ago!" Kyle said. He slammed his fist against the back of a chair, and it creaked under the impact. Mother watched him, patiently enduring his tantrum. But a tall figure swathed in black appeared across the room, at the door.

"Is everything all right, madam?" the vampire said.

Kyle hissed. This vampire was his mother's newest companion. He annoyed Kyle, but then, virtually all of her companions annoyed him. Kyle had sufficient self-awareness to admit that he was jealous of the attention that Mother lavished on her lovers.

"Mother and I are having a private discussion," Kyle said. He raised his hand, and the parlor door, propelled by an invisible force, swung shut in the vampire's face. Kyle glimpsed surprise in the creature's eyes before the door slammed; his mother's companion was a new vampire and had yet to learn the extent of a vampire's talents.

Mother had calmly watched the brief exchange.

Kyle paced across the hardwood floor. "As I was about to say, times are different now. The American slave trade has long since ended. There is no Civil War. My father could live in peace."

"Child, those points are irrelevant. Diallo was born and raised as a warrior. When he was taken to the United States as a slave, his taste for violence only grew more intense. If I had not intervened, he would have died at the hands of his slave master."

"You've told me all this. But that was so long ago."

"I'm telling you again because you must listen to me. For Diallo's entire life, as both a man and a vampire, his hunger for violence has been insatiable. After he left me in New Orleans, when I was pregnant with you, he roamed the countryside and murdered hundreds—not for food, not for vengeance, but because he *enjoyed* it." She gave him a level gaze. "Do you understand me, Kyle? Your father was a monster. A Sleep of a thousand years would never diminish the bloodlust that rages in his soul."

Kyle stopped pacing and slumped in a chair across from his mother. His hands trembled.

"I can change him," Kyle said. "When he learns that I am his son, his heart will change."

Mother laughed bitterly. "Change Diallo? Even I could not change Diallo. He is more iron-willed than you can fathom. It is fortunate for us that the humans imprisoned him. He had awesome potential as a vampire. If he had been allowed to cause mayhem much longer, he would have tapped the range of his gifts, and in the end, brought destruction on us all."

Kyle could not bear to look at her. She was so keenly perceptive, and he hated it. She had lived so long and learned so much about the paths that life followed that she could predict what would happen long before such events came to pass. "Life is a Byzantine labyrinth," she had told him once. "But after you have lived as long as I have, you no longer dwell in the maze. You hover above it, and regarding it below you, can discern each twist and turn, far in advance."

Mother reached across the distance that separated them and put her hand on his arm. Her long, slender fingers were warm.

"Let your father sleep, Kyle. It is better for all of us for you to let him be. He is at peace."

He shrugged off her hand.

"I can't," he said. "I have to know him, and see him. I *have* to."

She folded her arms across her chest. "You are too human, just as he was."

"Excuse me?"

She spat out the words: "Stubborn, short-sighted, emotional. Too much like a human. It was your father's undoing. Unfortunately, it may be yours as well."

"Mother, I don't wish to offend you—but you don't know everything."

Her eyes were not angry, only melancholy. "If you pursue this endeavor, I cannot assist you, or intervene. You can take our aircraft, but that is all the assistance I will offer."

"I'm not taking our airplane," he said. "I'll get there myself. Mamu and I will do everything. I don't need you."

Mother flinched as if slapped, and he felt sorry for what he had said. Then his regret faded. He wasn't sorry, not really. He was tired of her dictating his life, offering her sage advice about everything. He wanted to choose his own course of action, and if it proved to be wrong, then that was his burden to bear, and he would learn from the experience.

He realized one reason why he wanted to leave Mother and seek out his father: Living with an ancient being like her robbed him of experiencing the peaks and valleys that were a part of life. Life with Mother was smooth, predictable, safe. She lived in a heavily fortified compound, her every need provided for, her global network of connections ensuring her prosperity, her wisdom shielding her from making mistakes that would cause dangerous conflict. Life with her was, in a word, *boring*.

But as he thought about his unknown father, the mighty vampire whom Mother had failed to tame, his heart throbbed with excitement.

"You seek to be free of me," Mother said. "You desire to

learn on your own, to taste trial and error. I know your heart, my son."

"Then you know that you can't change my mind. I am going to do this, without your help."

She nodded, slowly. He rose and kissed her cheek.

"I am leaving in the morning," he said. "Good-bye, Mother."

A tear coursed down her face. It gave him pause. He could not recall the last time he had seen her cry.

"You've been a wonderful son," she said. "I've had many sons, but I've loved you the most, Kyle. Please, remember that, always."

He took her hand in his and squeezed it. "You talk as if I'm going to my death. I'll come to visit on occasion. You'll see me again."

Mother did not reply immediately, and as he walked out of the chamber, he heard her words, which she spoke in a whisper.

"No. I never will."

After an hour and a half in the air, the airplane touched down in Amsterdam. Kyle was grateful for the opportunity to stretch his legs. He sipped another packet of blood before getting on the next aircraft, which carried him on a tedious, ten-hour voyage to Memphis, Tennessee.

It was late evening when he finally met Mamuwalde—or "Mamu," his preferred nickname—his personal agent, at the terminal gate.

"How was the flight, sir?" Mamu asked in French. He took Kyle's bag and carried it over his broad shoulder.

Kyle responded in English, a subtle signal that they would not speak French here.

"Absolutely awful. I'll never fly commercially again. We will charter a private jet when we depart. We can discuss the details later."

It was Friday, August 23rd. The terminal was only sparely populated. They did not need to wait at baggage claim. Kyle had sent all his necessary clothes and items in advance. They walked out of the airport.

"It's humid here," Kyle said. He felt as though he had wandered into a suffocating cloud of heat. He had read about the summer climate in the American South, but experiencing it firsthand was a different matter altogether. He slid off his gloves, unbuttoned his jacket.

"It is warm, indeed," Mamu said. He was attired in navy-blue slacks, a tailored white shirt, a somber Italian tie, and polished black wingtips. Mamu dressed for his work as an agent with the same attention to detail as an executive laboring in a corporation. Kyle believed Mamu would've been wearing his suit jacket if not for the stifling humidity.

Mamu led the way to the parking lot. He was a stout man, in his thirties, bald-headed and clean-shaven. Born in Paris, of African lineage, he was a member of a family that had been quietly serving as agents to vampires for generations. Mamu and his sister had been in the employ of Kyle and his mother since they were teenagers; before them, his parents had served the family.

The relationship between a vampire and his agent was one of the most important relationships a vampire could establish. An agent could handle matters during daylight hours: business transactions, errands, and the endless, miscellaneous details of daily living. Traditionally, an agent was assigned to a single vampire for much of the agent's life, from adolescence through late middle age.

For their devotion to the care of vampires, agents were rewarded with comfortable, prosperous lives, and, more compelling, the opportunity to learn ancient secrets to which few humans throughout history have ever been privy.

On rare occasion, a vampire decided to take an agent as a companion—and made them a vampire. But the practice was frowned upon because it disrupted the balance between vampires and the available pool of agents. If all vampires took their agents as companions, they would have to acquire new agents, and it required years to select and train a capable agent. Agents volunteered for the role with the understanding that they would never become vampires.

Kyle trusted Mamu implicitly, in a way he would never dare to trust another human. He had told Mamu of his plan to find his father before he had told Mother about his mission. Mamu enthusiastically supported him, though it did not matter whether he agreed with Kyle's wishes or not. An agent was sworn to obey a vampire's commands. Still, Kyle was relieved to have Mamu's earnest assistance. He regarded the man as a friend, not an obsequious servant.

In the parking lot, Mamu headed toward a silver Lexus sport utility vehicle.

"Excellent taste," Kyle said. "Of course, I would expect nothing less from you, my friend."

Mamu smiled. He placed Kyle's bag in the vehicle's cargo area.

They settled inside the cabin.

"How far are we from the town?" Kyle said.

"Approximately forty minutes," Mamu said in his precise English.

Although, after being conscious throughout the day Kyle needed to sleep, he was too excited to doze. He was going to find his father. Butterflies fluttered in his stomach.

"What do you think of the town?" Kyle said. "Mason's Corner?"

Mamu shrugged, his dark eyes scanning the highway. "It is not much of a town. Small, rural, working class. We would be wise to maintain a low profile. The residents appear to pay undue attention to strangers."

"I see. Any incidents?"

"When I was in the hardware store acquiring supplies, the

clerk, an elderly man, asked me where I lived, and I indicated the estate that we are renting. He regarded me as if I were insane. 'The Mason place?' he said. 'It's haunted, man, don't you know that?' "

"Haunted? What do you think of that?" Kyle watched his friend closely.

Mamu's fingers tightened on the steering wheel. Mamu, though he had lived around vampires for his entire life, was deeply superstitious and frightened of the world of the unseen.

"Monsieur, you know me well. I am not one who is easily disturbed. Yet I have found it difficult to sleep in the house."

"Because you believe it to be haunted?"

"I do not know. It is beyond my ability to investigate. Perhaps you will be able to discover why."

"I'll check it out when we arrive," Kyle said. He did not doubt that the mansion was haunted; he had seen tormented, restless spirits before. They did not particularly interest him or trouble him. What harm could a ghost cause to an immortal being?

But Mamu was only a man. Kyle patted his friend's shoulder.

"Do not fear, my friend. Besides, the residents' belief that the house is haunted could benefit us. The people will leave us alone and allow us to perform our work undisturbed."

"That is an excellent point, *monsieur.* I had not considered it."

Kyle smiled. "Can we have some traveling music?"

Mamu found a contemporary jazz radio station on the stereo. The lulling voice of a saxophone hummed from the speakers.

Kyle reclined in the seat and looked out the glass, watching the wooded countryside race past. A fat, pale moon cast milky light on the land. Kyle sensed the creatures of the night roving through the thick forests: predator and prey, engaged in their ageless game.

Father, I am coming to free you, Kyle thought. When he regarded the deep night, it was easy to believe that his father would receive his telepathic message. *Your son has arrived, and I will save you . . . from yourself, if I must.*

The Lexus shot like a silver bullet through the darkness.

Chapter 3

The next day, Saturday, began as a busy one for David. In the morning, he dropped off the trailer at the U-Haul center in Hernando, fifteen minutes north of Mason's Corner. Upon returning home, he finished unpacking.

He spent a couple of hours opening boxes, sorting through items, and placing them in rooms throughout the house. King awoke from a nap and trailed him, whining. David ignored the hound for a while, then finally relented.

"Okay, I know you're bored," David said to the dog. "How about we go to the park?"

King barked his approval.

The town park was located off Main Street. It was eleven o'clock. The sun rays sizzled mercilessly, and the humidity was cotton-thick. He was thankful that he had brought a cold bottle of water with him.

He clipped the leash to King's collar, and they walked across the grass at a brisk pace. Magnolia trees bloomed, waxy and lush, their flowers emitting a sweet aroma. In the distance, a small lake gleamed in the sunlight, and a red sign warned "No Swimming."

David didn't see anyone there—most natives probably stayed inside at that hour to avoid the heat—but then a black Labrador darted around a maple tree ahead. David was so startled that he let go of the leash. King, thrilled to see another canine, took off after the Labrador, barking.

"King, come back here!" David chased after the dogs.

Moments later, he found the hounds playing in the grass, near a young black woman who lounged in the shade of an oak tree. Sitting Indian-style on a blanket, she didn't seem troubled by the dogs. She watched them, giggling, as if viewing a funny cartoon.

David approached, panting. He was in good shape, but the humidity sapped his strength.

The woman turned and smiled at him. He suddenly found it even harder to breathe. She had the most beautiful smile he had ever seen, with dimples so deep his fingers could disappear in them.

"Come enjoy the show," she said, and indicated the dogs. King was striving mightily to sniff the Labrador's rear end, and the Labrador nimbly eluded him. "Is he yours?"

It took David a second to realize that she had spoken to him. In addition to her smile, she possessed sparkling, honey-brown eyes. He easily could have looked at them for hours.

What's wrong with me? he thought. *I never act like this when meeting a woman.*

"Uh, yeah, he's mine," David said. "King, uh . . . hasn't had any female company in a while. I didn't mean to let him escape the leash. Your dog startled me."

She favored him with another dazzling smile. "Sorry about that. I usually let Princess run loose when I'm here. She doesn't bite."

"So she's named Princess? That's kinda funny. King, meet Princess." He thought he sounded corny, but no other witty comments came to mind.

Smiling again, the woman unwound from her cross-legged sitting position and stretched her legs in front of her. He tried to avoid staring at her, but it was impossible. She was lovely. Dressed in denim shorts and a yellow tank top, she had mahogany skin and a toned, shapely figure—a physique like an aerobics instructor or a track runner. Her dark brown hair was tied into a ponytail that dangled to the middle of her back.

Best of all, she didn't wear a wedding band on her ring finger. Thank you, God.

There was a moment of silence, in which he realized, with some surprise, that she was checking him out as openly as he was admiring her.

"Our dogs have introduced themselves," she said, and he caught her soft Mississippi accent. "How about we introduce ourselves to each other?"

He knelt on the grass and extended his hand. "I'm David Hunter."

"Nice meeting you, David. I'm Nia James."

He thought he felt electricity when their hands touched, but maybe that was wishful thinking on his part. However, their handshake did last a second or two longer than was customary.

"I haven't seen you in town before," she said. "I would've remembered seeing you."

Heat flushed his face. She was flirting with him, shamelessly. He felt as shocked as the class nerd who learned that the school's most popular cheerleader had a crush on him.

"I only moved here yesterday," he said. "I live on Hunter Drive, and in the Hunter house, actually."

She blinked. "You're related to Richard Hunter?"

"He was my father."

"Oh, my God." She put her hands to her mouth, blushing. She grabbed the hardcover book beside her and showed him the front cover. It was one of his father's controversial, best-selling novels, entitled *Coloreds Only*.

"I've read all his books, many of them twice," she said.

"He was brilliant, an amazing writer." She put her hand on her chest and appeared to regain her bearings. "I'm so sorry about what happened to him. That was a terrible accident."

He nodded somberly. "Did you know my father?"

"Not really. I saw him around town all the time, of course, but I only spoke to him once or twice. He signed my book." She cracked open the cover. He read the inscription on the fly page, "To Nia, the prettiest girl in town, who has great taste in literature." It seemed a typical comment for his father to make. His dad had been a notorious ladies' man, though Nia was surely no older than twenty-six or twenty-seven, young enough to be his daughter.

"You favor him, you know," she said. "I've seen photos of Mr. Hunter when he was in his twenties. You could be his twin."

"So I've heard. To be honest, I didn't know my father well. He was pretty much a stranger to me." He was rarely so open with a new acquaintance, but something made it easy for him to trust this woman. She radiated a comforting aura.

"I'm sorry. I know how that feels, sort of. My father died when I was a little girl. I only have these vague memories of what he was like."

"How long have you lived here?" he said.

She laughed. "I'm a homegirl, David. I've been here all my life, mostly. I grew up here, went away for college at Jackson State, then moved to Houston for a few years . . . but that didn't work out—long story, there." She shrugged. "I've been staying with my mom for the past year that I've been back."

"Do you plan to stay here for a while?"

"Maybe another year or two. Mason's Corner is a nice, quiet town, but I think it's obvious that there isn't much to do here, socially or otherwise. I've been thinking of moving to Atlanta."

"Really? I'm from Atlanta."

"And you gave up the ATL to live here?" She reached forward and placed her warm palm against his forehead. "Are you sick?" She laughed.

He chuckled. "It's a long story. Maybe I'll tell you later. How about . . . over lunch?"

"I'd like that," she said, and wriggled her toes in the grass. Her bare feet were smooth, with crimson, pedicured toenails. A gold anklet glittered around her slender ankle.

Talk about a stroke of good luck. He could hardly believe that a routine walk in the park had brought him face-to-face with such a fine woman. But he had an inexplicable feeling that he and Nia were *meant* to meet; intuition told him that it was destiny.

His rational mind, however, told him that he was only infatuated.

Still, he decided to push his luck one step further. "Cool, so are you free for lunch this afternoon?"

A dimpled smile curved across her face.

"One o'clock," she said.

As was his habit on Saturday mornings, Franklin Bennett rode his Schwinn bicycle downtown. He enjoyed the exercise, and, even better, catching the latest gossip.

Franklin loved Dark Corner on summer mornings. On such mornings, the town moved at a slower pace than usual (which was really slow), folks sitting on their porches, sipping coffee and reading the *Chester County Ledger.* Others were busy with yard work. Children played in the streets. Many people, children and adults alike, waved at Franklin as he zipped past. He returned the greetings. Riding his bicycle made him feel like a youth again, cruising throughout town.

When he reached Main Street, he pedaled to Shirley's Diner.

"Morning, folks," Franklin said. A scattered chorus of "Morning, Doc," greeted him. Shirley's was a simple place: a ceramic counter wound along one side of the restaurant, with about ten stools in front of it. Throughout the middle, a row of tables stood; along the opposite wall, there were vinyl booths.

The delicious aroma of eggs, hash browns, sizzling meat, and coffee wafted through the air.

Every customer there was a regular, mostly men, who breakfasted there so often the waitresses didn't need to ask what they were ordering, because they always requested the same meal. One of the waitresses on duty, a busty woman named Gloria, brushed past Franklin balancing three plates in her hands. "Scrambleds and ham coming right up, sugar," she said to him, and winked.

Franklin looked for a seat. Typically, he liked to eat with a different person each time he visited. Everyone had a unique, fascinating story to tell, and all of it was a piece of town history, in one way or another. He had become an expert on the history of Mason's Corner, not from reading books, but from talking to a vast array of people.

He spotted Van Jackson, the police chief, in a corner booth, sipping coffee and reading the paper.

"Mind if I sit with you a spell, Chief?" Franklin said.

"Sure, Doc. Have a seat."

Van Jackson had been the police chief for eleven years. Before him, his father had been the chief. Balding and in his forties, Jackson had a long face that always seemed to be stretched into a sad expression, as if he had recently received bad news. Some of the folks called him "Sad" Jackson. He was a somber man, but he had a sharp mind. Franklin enjoyed talking to him.

Gloria slapped down a glass of orange juice in front of Franklin, then refreshed Jackson's coffee. Jackson folded his paper.

"How are things?" Franklin said.

Jackson added cream to his coffee. "Things are things, Doc. Ain't nothing much happening here. The usual mess."

"I have a new neighbor," Franklin said. "David Hunter. He moved into his father's house."

"Is that so?" Jackson raised his eyebrows. "Knew Hunter had a boy, but I ain't never seen him. Moved into his family's place, did he?"

"He arrived yesterday. He's a nice young man, friendly."

"Wife, kids?"

"He's a bachelor."

"Oh, Lord. Ruby's gonna hound him to death. She's a sweetheart."

Van Jackson's wife had died of cancer two years ago, leaving him to raise his teenage son by himself. Ruby, convinced that a single man was a dead loss in the kitchen, had constantly nagged Jackson about joining them for dinner. Jackson had accepted her offer a handful of times, but he didn't need Ruby to cook for him anymore. Word was that the chief was dating Belinda Moss, the town librarian.

"I'll stop by to say hello to the Hunter boy," Jackson said. "He's the kid of the only celebrity this town's ever had. Reckon that merits a welcoming party from the chief."

"That would be good of you," Franklin said. A minute later, Gloria appeared and placed a plate heaped with scrambled eggs, country ham, hash browns, and buttermilk biscuits in front of Franklin. Franklin began to butter a biscuit.

"The Hunter boy ain't the only new resident we have," Jackson said. He sipped his coffee. "Someone's moved into the Mason place."

Franklin dropped his butter knife. It clanged against the plate.

"Yeah, I 'bout spilled my coffee when Wilson told me," Jackson said.

Roseber Wilson was a real estate agent who handled transactions for most of the properties in town, including Jubilee, the Mason estate.

"Who moved there?" Franklin picked up his knife again.

"Black man with a funny accent, Wilson said. Sounded like he was from France. Can you imagine that? Ain't never heard a black man with a French accent, though I know we got black folk over there."

"Have you seen this Frenchman?"

"Seen him driving around. Got one of them big Lexus SUVs. I ain't talked to him, though, or seen anyone with him."

"Odd." Franklin dug into his eggs. "I wonder why he chose the Mason place."

"He ain't buying it, Wilson said. Said he was only gonna rent it for a few months. He was real secretive, wouldn't tell Wilson much about his business."

"Strange, indeed," Franklin said. "Renting an enormous, dilapidated property like that for only a few months. I wonder if this fellow is aware of Jubilee's reputation."

Jackson shrugged. He looked out the plate-glass window. He glanced at Franklin and nodded, indicating that Franklin should check outside.

Across the street, a silver Lexus sport utility parked in front of the hardware store. A broad-shouldered, dark-skinned man with a shiny bald head climbed out of the vehicle. He was sharply dressed in a gray suit. He strode purposefully into the store.

Franklin frowned. Hearing this news about the Mason place and seeing the mysterious new resident made him uneasy, though he could not place his finger on why. Maybe because it didn't make sense. A foreigner renting an antebellum mansion in rural Mississippi? Either he was planning to refurbish the place and turn it into a tour destination, or he was up to something he had no business doing.

I should not leap to such conclusions, Franklin admonished himself. The fellow could be an upstanding gentleman with a legitimate interest in the property and the town. He was allowing small-town xenophobia to color his thoughts.

However, Van Jackson was frowning, too.

"Excuse me, Doc," Jackson said. He put on his hat. "I've

fiddled away enough of the town's money this morning. Got to get back to work."

"See you around, Chief." Franklin watched him leave. He noticed that the chief kept his attention riveted on the hardware store across the street.

Franklin could not help himself. The chief was suspicious. Now, so was he.

What was the man doing at the Mason place?

At one o'clock sharp, David parked in front of MacDaddy's Barbecue. As he climbed out of the Pathfinder, a green Honda Civic pulled into the parking spot near him. Nia stepped out.

"Right on time," she said.

She had changed into a pink blouse, khaki shorts, and sandals. She had let down her hair, too. It flowed to her shoulders in curly waves.

"My father was right," David said. "You *are* the prettiest girl in town."

She smiled. He opened the restaurant's glass door for her, and they went inside.

It was a small, neat place, with lots of windows. From the size of the take-out counter it appeared that they did a lot of carry-out business, but there were tables spaced throughout the dining area. The mouthwatering aroma of barbecue spiced the air.

The restaurant was busy. People were lined up at the carry-out counter, and all the tables except one were full. David and Nia grabbed the only vacant table, in the corner.

David picked up the single-page menus that lay nestled between the salt-and-pepper shakers.

"I already know what I'm going to eat," she said. "The catfish sandwich is delicious. I grew up on them."

"Then I'll get the same," he said.

A waitress came to take their orders. They asked for the

catfish sandwiches, and sweet tea. The server returned quickly with the drinks.

As they sipped tea, their gazes met. They watched each other for a long, quiet moment, a pleasant tingling building in David's stomach.

He felt as though he were in a movie, one of those sappy romantic comedies like *Sleepless in Seattle*. He had never had an experience like this with a woman, and it frightened and thrilled him all at once.

Then, at the same time, they smiled—in unspoken acknowledgment of the rare chemistry that coursed between them like electrical current.

"So," Nia said. "You were going to tell me why you moved to Mason's Corner."

He put down the glass of tea. "Well, it's because of my father. I mentioned before that I never knew him that well. I decided to come here and get to know him, I guess. By living in the same house and being in the town where he spent so much of his life, I'm hoping to . . ." He made a grasping motion with his hand, straining to find the right words to express himself.

"Understand him?" she said.

"That's part of it. Understand him—and understand *myself*. Because I'm his son, I think I've picked up certain habits, talents, and quirks from my dad. For example, he used to drink strong, black coffee, never adding sugar or cream. When I was a kid, I used to think it was disgusting. Now, guess how I always drink my coffee?"

"Strong, no sugar, no cream?"

He snapped his fingers. "Exactly. I never thought I'd like coffee that way, but it's the only way I like to drink it now. And there're a bunch of other things I think I've picked up from my father, subconsciously. I'll never learn everything about him, but if I can just learn *more* . . . it's important to me, Nia. I can't explain it any other way."

"I understand what you mean," she said. "I really admire you for having the self-awareness and the guts to come here and sort of absorb yourself in his life. That says a lot about you."

"I didn't have anything pinning me down in Atlanta. My mom and my sister live there, but they're doing fine. I'm self-employed and can do my work from anywhere. If there was ever a time to do some exploring, this is it."

"What kind of work do you do?"

"I design Web sites. I majored in computer science at Georgia Tech, then worked for a few years at a technology consulting firm, but corporate America wasn't for me. I started my business two years ago and haven't looked back. What do you do?"

"I have a graphic design company. Run it out of my house."

"So you own a business, too? That's cool. How long have you been doing it?"

"For almost a year," she said. "I went to Jackson State on a track scholarship, ran track on the pro circuit for a minute after I graduated, then injured my knee and had to retire. I taught high school for a little while, first in Houston, then here, then took the plunge and started my own company. And I haven't looked back, either." She smiled.

He smiled, too, genuinely impressed. "That's too bad that you had to quit running track. But you've definitely kept yourself in great shape."

"Thanks, I run and work out just about every day. But I don't miss track competition that much. I love being my own boss, building something of my own from the ground up. I know you understand what I'm saying."

"Oh, yeah, I hear ya. People are surprised when they find out that I'm not a writer, though. They always expect me to follow in my dad's footsteps."

"Do you plan to write, someday?"

He laughed. "Are you kidding? I love to read, but I can't

write worth a lick. That's definitely something that I did *not* inherit from my dad."

The waitress delivered their meals: catfish sandwiches, with coleslaw and french fries on the side. Before leaving, the waitress peered closely at David.

"You any kin to Richard Hunter?" she said in a thick Mississippi accent.

"He was my father."

"Willie, I told you!" she shouted at someone behind the counter. "This here's the Hunter boy!"

David blushed. People turned to look his way. Many of them nodded and smiled, or only stared as if trying to see the resemblance between him and his dad.

The waitress clutched his shoulder. "I was awful sorry to hear about what happened to your daddy. I'm praying for your family."

"Thanks," David said.

He blew out a pent-up breath when the waitress left and people looked away.

Nia smiled, amused. "Get used to the attention, sweetie. Your dad was the only celebrity who ever came from this town. Everyone is gonna want to check you out."

"Seems like it." He picked up his sandwich and began to eat. As Nia promised, it was delicious. "What was it like growing up here?"

She popped a french fry into her mouth. "Wonderful, really. Quiet, safe. Lots of the people who live here have been here for a long time, so mostly everyone knows one another. It was a fun place to grow up. I have two older brothers—neither of them live here anymore—and they let me join them on all kinds of adventures. Fishing, hunting, catching snakes—"

"Snakes?"

"Sure. Not poisonous snakes, silly—though we did trap a water moccasin once. My mama would've had a fit if she'd known. I still haven't told her." She laughed.

"Growing up in Atlanta wasn't anything like that. The closest I came to a snake was in the city zoo."

"There's nothing like living in the country, but I love big cities, too."

"Why did you leave Houston to come back home?"

"I'll tell you, David, another time, I promise. It's something I don't like to talk about. I'd hate to ruin the good time that we're having."

"Tell me whenever you're ready." *We all have issues,* he thought. *I'm not baggage-free, either. Shoot, this move to Mason's Corner is so I can work out my problems.*

He took another bite of the sandwich. "A couple of people have mentioned the walks that my father would take around town. Would he go anywhere in particular?"

"He walked through the park a lot, and some of the trails. He walked Main Street all the time, too."

"He never talked to anyone while he was walking? I read somewhere that he'd bite your head off if you said anything to him."

"He kept to himself. I only had a real conversation with him once, and that was in over twenty years of seeing him around. But he'd usually say hi to me and people like Vicky Queen—girls he thought were pretty. Your father was a flirt. But he was charming about it, not like some nasty old man."

"Did he have any friends here?"

She sipped her tea. "Hmm . . . he'd go to church pretty often. He went to New Life Baptist, here in town. I think he was good friends with the senior pastor, Reverend Brown. I've been going to the church since I was little, and I'd see them talking sometimes."

David made a mental note. "I might visit the church tomorrow morning."

The waitress returned. She placed a dish of peach cobbler on the table, and two spoons.

"I hope y'all saved room for some dessert," the waitress said. "Willie says this is on the house, 'cuz the Hunter boy's new in town, and y'all make such a pretty couple, too."

"Ooh, that's so sweet," Nia said. She called out across the room, "Thank you, Willie!"

David couldn't wipe the embarrassed grin off his face.

"I might as well tell you," Nia said, dipping a spoon into the cobbler, "in a tiny town like this, an unattached young man and woman having lunch is big news. By this evening, they'll be speculating about when we'll get married and what we'll name our kids."

"You are too much." He laughed. "Speaking of this evening, are you doing anything?"

"Oh, yeah. There's so much going on in Mason's Corner. I run into fine, available young men all the time here, you know. My social calendar is kicking."

He grinned. "How about dinner and a movie?"

"We'll have to drive to Southaven. They don't have a theater here in town. Is that okay?"

"That's fine with me."

"Okay, pick me up at—wait a minute. You don't have a girlfriend waiting for you in Atlanta, do you? Or a wife?"

"I'm an unrestricted free agent. No girlfriend, no wife. What about you?"

"*Nada.* I date here and there, but like I was saying, Mason's Corner doesn't exactly have it going on socially."

He was more relieved than he dared to let on. "So when should I pick you up? Seven?"

"Seven sounds good."

"Cool. That gives me time to go home and cut the grass. The lawn hasn't been cut in weeks."

"Wait a couple hours, until it cools off some. I don't want you to have a heatstroke."

"Good point. It gets hot in Atlanta, too, but this is a whole new level of heat."

"Ain't nothing like summer in Mississippi, honey," she said, exaggerating her southern twang.

They finished eating. After he paid the bill, he walked Nia to her car. They hugged, and she felt wonderful against him—warm and firm, yet as soft and inviting as a favorite pillow. Her clean, feminine scent filled his nostrils and made him dizzy.

She gave him her phone number and directions to her house.

"See you tonight," she said.

Smiling, he watched her drive away. What a beautiful, intelligent woman. He could not wait to see her again that evening.

His gaze traveled across the blue horizon and stopped at the old, antebellum mansion. Jubilee. Sitting on the hill, it overlooked the town, like a forbidden castle.

His smile fell away.

Junior Hodges had been working all day.

Every Saturday throughout the spring, summer, and fall, Junior awoke at sunrise, and if it wasn't raining, went to the tool shed behind their trailer home, unlocked it, and rolled out his old John Deere lawn mower.

He'd push his mower across town, making stops at each house on his list.

There was good money in cutting grass. He'd earn anywhere from ten to twenty-five bucks per yard. When he reached the end of his list, he'd usually made over a hundred dollars, sometimes as much as a hundred and fifty, depending on how generous people were feeling and if he could squeeze in some extra lawns or quick jobs.

Sometimes, kids made fun of him, calling him dumb, teasing him for being a thirty-year-old man who made a living doing odd jobs like lawn mowing. Junior didn't let their mean words stop him. He'd push his mower through town cutting grass until he was an old man, God willing. He didn't dare tell those youngsters how much money he was making. He didn't want any competition.

Still, sometimes the teasing hurt. He wondered whether they were right about him being dumb. Mama, when she was alive, used to say that he was "special," and Junior had liked that—but Pa was one of the people who called him dumb. He'd never done well in school, and had pretty much dropped out in the tenth grade. He could read a bit, and write things, too, especially the names of people who were going to hire him for work, and jobs that he had to do. As far as math, he could add up how much money he'd made and subtract the cost of gas and other stuff, to get at his profit. Mama had taught him how to do that—she called it "business math." She'd run a hair salon out of their house, back in the day.

But Junior knew that he could never be as smart as a guy like Doc Bennett, for instance. That old guy was a walking, talking book. He cut Doc Bennett's grass every Saturday, and afterward, if Doc was around and Junior had time to spare, Junior liked to talk to him and soak up everything he said, and learn new words.

He wasn't sure whether he was really dumb, and he figured he shouldn't worry about it too much, though it bothered him every now and then. All he knew for sure was that he loved to work. One Sunday, Reverend Brown had spoken on how God respected the man who put in an honest day's work. Junior thought about that sermon whenever he felt bad about himself. He'd rather have the respect of God than a bunch of sassy kids.

Around three o'clock that afternoon, Junior was rolling his mower along the sidewalk. He was a bull of a man, six-foot-three, and coal-black, with a large, flat nose. He wore his favorite work overalls, a T-shirt, and work boots. His giant hands, curled around the push-handle of the mower, were padded with calluses.

It had been a steaming day, but he was used to the heat, having lived in Mississippi all his life. He couldn't afford to be lazy and stay in, waiting until it cooled off to cut his lawns. There was too much money to be made. Sometimes when it was especially hot, he imagined that he could see crisp dollar bills wedged between the blades of grass, and the image kept him motivated to suffer through the heat.

He was saving money to buy himself a truck. He'd seen a black Ford pickup sitting in the parking lot of Earl's Used Autos, and how he wanted it! With a truck of his own, he could get around to his jobs faster, and have time to do more work, and more work meant more money. The truck cost three thousand dollars, and Junior had saved two thousand so far. He'd only been able to save the money by putting it in a secret place in the trailer, otherwise, Pa laid his hands on his money to borrow it. Pa never paid him back.

Ahead, Junior saw the last house on his list for today: Vicky Queen's place.

He always made her yard last, on purpose. Not only because it was on the way to the basketball court at the park, where he planned to go when he was done working, but because he liked to take his time at her place, too.

Her white Cadillac was parked in the driveway. She was home.

His heart beat a little faster.

He pushed the mower into the driveway, beside the Cadillac. He went up the steps to the front door, knocked.

"That you, Junior?" a soft voice said from within.

"Yes, ma'am," Junior said. He wiped sweat from his forehead with a ragged handkerchief. "I'm here to cut the grass."

The door opened. Vicky Queen was so pretty it hurt to look at her. She wore a white blouse that showcased her ample cleavage, a tight black skirt that rose well above her knees, and heels. The sweet scent of her perfume enveloped him like a mist.

Her big eyes were precious gems. They sparkled.

Junior smiled. "You look real nice. You going to work today?"

"I sure am, Junior. A queen has to work, too, sometimes." She cracked a smile. "You want some ice water, honey?"

"Ice water sure would hit the spot."

"Come on in, then."

He stood just inside the door while she sashayed into the kitchen.

Her place was full of nice stuff—leather furniture and expensive-looking vases and artwork everywhere. Folks said that Vicky Queen got mostly everything she owned—from the new Cadillac to her clothes, to the plush things in the house—from the rich men she met while working at the casinos in Tunica. Junior didn't believe it was true until he rode his bike past the house one morning (on the way to doing a paint job) and saw a white limousine parked out front.

But seeing it didn't change the way he felt about her. He'd been in love with Vicky ever since they had lived next door to each other, as kids. She was pretty, but she had always been so sweet to him, too. What she did with her life was none of his business. She was one of the nicest people he knew.

Vicky came out of the kitchen with a dripping glass of ice water. She walked right up to him, never letting her lovely eyes leave his.

His mouth got dry. He needed that water badly now.

"I can't stand to let a man go thirsty." She handed him the glass.

"Thank you, ma'am."

She watched him closely as he drank. Sometimes, he wondered if Vicky liked him, as more than a friend. There was something about the way she looked at him . . .

Naw, he was fooling himself. Vicky liked those high roller guys. He couldn't compete with them. He'd never be rich.

He finished off the water and handed her the glass. "Thank you for the water, ma'am."

"How many times I got to ask you to stop calling me 'ma'am'? I'm the same age as you, Junior." She smiled.

Although she smiled, he couldn't tell if she was serious or not. He stammered, "Uh, I'm sorry, ma'am—I mean, Miss Queen—"

"Vicky."

"Vicky," he said, and the name sounded foreign rolling off his tongue. He never called her by her first name, and his heart beat a little faster. "Well, uh, Vicky, I better get to work."

"You're welcome, Junior. You let me know if you need anything else." She batted her long eyelashes. "Anything at all."

"I sure will." He felt her watching him as he went outside and started up the lawn mower.

She acted funny sometimes. He wondered, again, if she liked him. But it seemed like a crazy thought. He'd only get his feelings hurt if he kept thinking about it. A beautiful, classy lady like her would never want him.

But as he mowed the lawn, he imagined himself driving that shiny black pickup . . . with Vicky Queen sitting by his side.

David was finishing the lawn when the police cruiser parked in front of the house.

Although it was a quarter past four and the day had cooled by a few degrees, it was still the most intense humidity he had ever experienced. He'd worn an old Nike T-shirt and ragged denim shorts, and in short time, sweat had glued the clothes against his skin. He'd drunk two bottles of water, too, and seemed to sweat it through his pores so quickly his skin might have only been a sieve.

While David worked in the yard, King watched him from the front window. The dog wanted to come outside, but it was too hot for the furry canine to spend much time out-doors. He'd take King for a walk later.

David switched off the mower. The blades thumped into silence.

A stout officer stepped out of the vehicle. David crossed the yard to meet him, severed blades of grass clinging to his boots.

"Good afternoon," David said. "How can I help you?"

The officer inclined his head to indicate Franklin Bennett's home across the street.

"Doc Bennett told me you'd moved here. Figured I'd stop by to welcome you to the town. My name's Van Jackson. I'm the chief of police." He extended his hand.

The chief had a strong grip. "Pleasure to meet you, Chief. I'm David Hunter, but you probably know that already. Everyone else here does."

"News travels quickly in a small town, buddy." Jackson hooked his thumbs through the loops of his belt. "With you being the boy of the only celebrity this town's ever produced, well, I thought that deserved a personal visit."

"I appreciate that," David said. "As you can see, I'm getting things in order here. The grass hadn't been cut in a few weeks."

"You moving here for good, or you just here to put things in order?"

"I might be here for a year or so. I visited the town a long time ago, but I've never lived in the country. I grew up in Atlanta."

"Is that so? Nice city. Been there myself to see the King center and catch some Braves games," Jackson said. "What kind of work you do?"

"I design Web sites. I'm self-employed, so I'll be working out of the house."

"Nothing like being your own boss." Jackson nodded with approval. "I hope you like our town, and stay a while.

We ain't got enough young folks here. Lot of 'em split soon as they graduate from high school."

"How long have you lived here?"

"Me? All my life, buddy. My pa was chief before me, too. I ain't never wanted to live anywhere else."

"Did you know my father?"

Jackson leaned against the side of the cruiser. "Nah, not that well. We chatted here and there, but Hunter, he liked his privacy, and I respected that. He had enough folks hounding him as it was."

"Like who?"

"Oh, tourists, mainly. They'd drive past the house here or try to catch him when he was walking. Nosy folks like that."

"I've seen a couple of cars cruise past the house since I've been here," David said.

"I ain't surprised. Kind of unfortunate way Hunter went, that's bound to draw more snoops than usual. You be sure to let me know if anybody causes you a problem."

"I sure will," he said. "Is there much crime here?"

Jackson shrugged. "Incidents here and there. Vandalism, shoplifting, breaking up fights at the pool hall. And drugs. Drugs more than anything. Ain't just a big city problem anymore, they're everywhere." He sighed. His face, which already appeared perpetually sad, looked even more melancholy.

"Franklin says this town has a colorful history. Such as the haunted house—"

"You mean the Mason place?" Jackson's eyebrows arched. "Someone moved in there."

"Are you serious? That old, run-down house on the hill?"

Jackson folded his arms. "Sure did. Couldn't believe it myself. I ain't stopped by to chat with the new resident, yet. I might do that."

"I wonder who moved in there? And why? I mean, if it really is haunted."

"Can't speculate," Jackson said, and David had the distinct impression that Jackson could speculate all right, but he wasn't going to share his ideas with a guy he'd only met five minutes ago, no matter whose son he was.

"Doc Bennett's quite a man," Jackson said. "But he's got some tales in that big brain of his. Folks love to swap stories, but that doesn't mean they're all true."

"I'll keep that in mind."

"Nice meeting you, Hunter. You take care, and holler if you need anything."

"Thanks for stopping by," David said, but Jackson had already hustled into his car. He roared away down the road.

David pushed the lawn mower to the tool shed, behind the house. After he stored the machine inside, he stood in the middle of the backyard. Insects buzzed around him, reveling in the freshly cut grass. He waved them away.

From where he stood, he had a glimpse of Jubilee. Sunshine glimmered on a window.

Who would move into a place like that? The house was a wreck, and it was creepy as hell.

Was it truly haunted, or had Franklin only been sharing a fabled piece of town lore?

He was not sure he wanted to know the answers to his questions.

Chapter 4

Jahlil Jackson was scheduled to work at Mac's Meat and Foods that afternoon. The store was located in a brick building, next door to a Laundromat, on the corner of Davis and Taylor. When he was younger, Jahlil and his friends used to love stopping by Mac's on the way home from school, to buy ice cream and candy. Now, the sight of the store's big red-and-white sign made him want to punch someone.

"You're late again!" Old Mac barked, the minute Jahlil walked inside. Old Mac stood behind the gleaming meat counter, wearing a crisp white apron. He was a short, bald, white man, in his sixties, with faded tattoos on his wiry forearms. He raised his watch and tapped it. "What time are you supposed to be here to work?"

"Four, I guess," Jahlil said.

"Four? It's four-twenty, little Jackson!"

"I got held up by some things," Jahlil said. This guy was a trip. What difference did it make if he was twenty minutes late? There was nothing going on there that demanded Jahlil's attention. He was only a stock boy, he didn't own the stupid store.

Old Mac grunted. "Mop the aisles. There are some boxes

in the back that need to be broken down and disposed of too. And pick up the lot. You forgot to do that yesterday, little Jackson."

"Fine. And my name's Jahlil." He stormed away into the back room.

Jahlil was sixteen, and this was the third job he'd held in the past four months. First, he'd worked for the town grounds crew, cutting grass and weeds, and cleaning up litter, and he hated that job and quit. Then his father got him a job at Shirley's Diner, as a busboy, and that lasted only a week, because there was no way he was going to clean up after folks. His dad had lined up his latest gig, too, here at Mac's Meat and Foods, and he'd been there about a month. He hated it there. Old Mac was a mean bastard who ran the place as though he were a sergeant and the employees were his soldiers. A Vietnam war veteran, Old Mac seemed to have forgotten that the war had ended a long time ago.

The only reason Jahlil had kept the job so far was because he was sick of Dad hounding him. To be honest, he didn't understand why he had to work at all. The fellas he hung out with didn't work, and their folks didn't harass them about it. Dad was always riding him about being responsible and earning his own money. Jahlil understood all that responsibility shit, but he didn't think it was something for him to be concerned about right now. He was only in high school. Why couldn't he enjoy being a teenager?

When Jahlil raised that argument, Dad would cite his low grades, the same reason he gave for not allowing Jahlil to drive. Dad was full of explanations and excuses. It was impossible to win an argument with him.

He wished his mother were alive. Things would be different if she were here. She never would have forced him to work. . . .

He had to stop thinking about how much he missed her. His chest had gotten tight, a sure sign that tears would follow soon.

He was outside picking up the lot—collecting trash, in other words—when the fellas came through. T-Bone was driving his mama's old blue Oldsmobile Ninety-Eight, and Poke was riding shotgun. A hip-hop joint rumbled from the car stereo, the latest song by the gangsta crew from Jackson, Jacktown. T-Bone had been playing the album so much lately that Jahlil was convinced he would soon wear down the tracks on the CD.

The plate-glass windows of the store—plastered with handwritten signs advertising sales on ribs and chicken—vibrated in unison with the heavy bass booming from the speakers.

Jahlil set his broom and dustpan against the store's brick wall, and went to see his boys. T-Bone lowered the music's volume a few notches.

Jahlil had grown up with T-Bone and Poke. They were the same age and in the same grade, but they looked as though they lived in different worlds. Both T-Bone and Poke sported a gold tooth and earrings, and they had tattoos on their arms and chests. Fake platinum hung around their necks. T-Bone's hair was braided in cornrows, and Poke had a puffy, wild afro.

Jahlil's father would not allow him to get a gold tooth, wear an earring, get a tattoo, rock more than one gold chain, or sport a hairstyle other than a low-cut fade. Dad was too damn strict. When Jahlil argued with him about it, Dad would say, "Why you wanna look like those 'hood rats, boy? They ain't even gonna graduate from high school." Although Jahlil didn't like Dad's 'hood rats comment, he had to admit that he was right about his boys dropping out. Both T-Bone and Poke promised that they weren't going back to school this fall.

"Hey," T-Bone said. Jahlil smelled beer on his breath: a bottle of Coors, wrapped in a paper bag, was wedged between T-Bone's thighs. "What's up with you?"

"Working this tired-ass job," Jahlil said. "That fool Old Mac's getting on my nerves."

"We 'bout to play ball," Poke said. "You comin'?"

Jahlil chewed his lip. He really wanted to play ball and hang with the crew. But if he ditched his job, Old Mac would tell Dad, and Dad would never shut up about it. It would be one more thing he'd hold over Jahlil's head to explain why he wouldn't allow him to do something, like drive a car.

"Let Old Mac pick up his own trash, man," T-Bone said. "We been picking up white folks' trash for centuries."

Jahlil didn't bother to mention that almost everyone who lived in Mason's Corner was black, and chances were, any trash littering the parking lot had been dropped there by black people. But T-Bone was forever talking some quasi-militant shit.

"We cruised by the court, man," Poke said. "Andre's there."

"For real?" Jahlil said. Andre, though he didn't actually deal dope, always had weed on him, and he was cool about sharing with them, probably because he lived with T-Bone's sister.

"Yep," T-Bone said. "So what's up? You gonna hang, or you gonna slave for the white man?"

Jahlil looked toward the store. Old Mac stood beside the front entrance, arms folded across his chest, glowering at Jahlil.

The decision was easier than Jahlil had imagined.

I ain't working for you no more, Jahlil thought. *Tell my dad, I don't care. I hate you and your stupid store.*

"Let's roll," Jahlil said.

T-Bone laughed. "That's my nigga."

Jahlil didn't bother to look back as they rolled away.

Chief Jackson got a call he loathed almost as much as notification of a crime: Old Mac, calling to say his son had ditched work.

"I've got to let go of your boy, Chief," Old Mac said. Jackson heard genuine regret in his voice. "I've given him a chance, but he doesn't want to work. His attitude stinks, and I can't depend on him."

Jackson paced the floor of the small office at headquarters, the phone pressed against his ear. Across the room, Deputy Ray Dudu glanced up from the tabloid he was reading.

Jackson settled into his swivel chair, turned to face the calendar on the wall. He didn't like to let folks see him upset.

"Okay, buddy," Jackson said. "I get you. Thanks for giving my boy a shot. Apologize for the trouble he's caused you."

"I don't want to tell you how to raise your son, Chief, but he's headed down a dangerous path. Those hoodlums he hangs out with—"

"Mac, I've got to go." Jackson did not want to let Old Mac get started about the "hoodlums" that were Jahlil's friends, because then Old Mac would start complaining about people loitering in the parking lot of his store, and then he'd begin to rant about crime in general in Mason's Corner—he would go on and on. "I'll stop by and chat with you later, hear?"

Jackson hung up. He checked himself from throwing the phone across the room. His son . . . he did not understand him. He just didn't.

"Jahlil having problems at work?" Deputy Dudu said.

"Something like that," Jackson said, turning around. He didn't like to discuss family business with outsiders, especially with someone like his deputy. Deputy Dudu was a good guy and a top-notch cop, but he was an odd one.

Deputy Dudu unfolded himself from the seat behind the desk, and it was like watching a praying mantis maneuver out of a crevice. Light-skinned, Dudu was tall and lanky, with a small head that seemed out of proportion to the rest of his body. He was fastidiously neat, clean shaven, with big white teeth. His uniform was spotless and pressed, the creases of his slacks almost as sharp as blades. His shoes were so shiny that Jackson half believed the deputy wore a new pair each day of the week.

Dudu leaned on the edge of his desk. In his gigantic, bony hand, he held an issue of one of those wacky tabloids. Dudu read the tabloids zealously, the same way Jackson's deceased wife used to devour paperback romance novels.

"You know what the problem could be?" Dudu said. He tapped the cover of the publication. "Extraterrestrials from Venus. It says in here that Venusians—aliens from Venus— are beaming signals to Earth, to scramble brain waves, and that our youth are especially vulnerable. It could explain your boy's erratic behavior, Chief."

Jackson only stared at him. Dudu was serious, that was the worst part. He believed all of that alien crap. Heck, Dudu believed everything he read—the more bizarre, the better. Dudu's fascination with all things weird ranged from the tabloids to the lurid horror novels that he kept stacked on his desk.

At times like this, Jackson was astounded that he had hired this man as his deputy. Perhaps *his* brain waves had been scrambled when he'd given Dudu the job three years ago.

Jackson stood and hitched his belt. "I got to make a run. Hold it down, hear?"

"Let me know if you want more details about how the aliens—"

"Later, Deputy."

Jackson pushed Dudu's madness out of his thoughts, and focused on his son. He needed to find him, and he had a good idea where Jahlil had gone. There weren't many places in town where youths could hang out.

He drove down Main Street, made a right on Pine Lane, and pulled his cruiser up to the basketball court. A group of young men, most of them bare-chested, played ball. Onlookers leaned against the fence.

Jahlil was on the court playing. He spotted Jackson's car, and Jackson could see his son mouthing the words, *Oh shit, my dad's here.*

Jackson didn't climb out of the cruiser. He wanted to avoid causing a scene and embarrassing the kid in front of his buddies. Doing something like that would only make Jahlil resent him more than he already did.

Though I don't understand why the boy resents me at all, he thought.

He tapped the horn.

Jahlil sauntered to the car, looking cool, putting on a show for his friends, as if to say, *No problem, everything's all right, fellas, I can handle my dad.* Finally, he got in and slammed the door.

Silent, Jackson pulled away.

As he drove, Jackson watched his boy from the corner of his eye. Jahlil looked so damn much like Paulette, his mother, that Jackson's heart kicked. Jahlil had his mother's chin, eyes, nose, and lips. He had inherited Jackson's sturdy build and low, even voice. Sometimes, when Jahlil talked, Jackson thought he was listening to a recording of himself from twenty or so years ago.

Jackson took them to a quiet area on the outskirts of the town. He parked on a bluff that overlooked the Coldwater River. Years ago, Jackson would bring Jahlil here, to fish. Those were happier times.

"Got a call from Old Mac today," Jackson said. "Said you up and left with your buddies when you were supposed to be working."

"I'm not working at that stupid store anymore," Jahlil said. "Old Mac's racist. He treats me like I'm his slave."

"Old Mac ain't racist, and you know it. I've known him twenty-some years. He's a good man. He did me a favor, giving you a job at his store."

Jahlil shrugged. That so-what shrug was the boy's response to many of Jackson's points. It infuriated him. Why couldn't they have an ordinary, two-way conversation?

"I can't keep getting you jobs, son," Jackson said. "I'm using up all my goodwill with the business folk in town."

"I don't wanna work, anyway."

"If you're living with me, you've gotta have a job. You got to learn to be responsible, earn your own paycheck. That's the way the world is."

Another so-what shrug.

Jackson flexed his thick fingers on the steering wheel. He wanted to seize Jahlil by the shoulders and shake him, to rattle some common sense into his head. Did the boy think that life was only hanging out with his lazy buddies, playing ball, and chasing girls? Jackson didn't know what Jahlil was thinking. That was the most frustrating—and frightening—thing about his relationship with his son. He had no idea what his son was thinking, and the unknown terrified him.

"What do you want from me?" Jackson said. He was surprised to hear himself speak the words.

For the first time since Jahlil had climbed in the car, he turned and looked at his father.

"Huh?" Jahlil said.

Jackson cleared his throat. "You heard me right. What do you want from me? I can't figure it out at all, so now I'm asking you direct."

Jahlil shrugged. But then he said, "Stop riding me about having a job. I want to enjoy being a teenager. I got my whole life to work. That's what Mama would say. She wouldn't want me to work."

Jackson's breath snagged in his chest. If he drew in another breath, he felt that his lungs just might burst like balloons.

He could not believe that Jahlil had reached into their shared tragedy—Paulette's death—and thrown it into his face like this, to justify his unwillingness to hold a simple job. It was like a desecration of Paulette's memory. The boy could not possibly know what he was saying.

But I asked him what he wanted, and he told me.

Jackson slammed the car into gear and screamed back into town. He didn't slow until they reached their house. They rocked to a halt in front of their ranch home.

"Go in, and stay put," Jackson said. "We'll talk about this later."

"Whatever, man." Jahlil got out and strutted away.

Jackson watched his son go inside. He may as well have been watching a stranger, someone else's child. This mule-headed, lazy kid could not possibly be his own son.

But Jackson could not shake the feeling that, somehow, he was to blame for what had happened to his kid. The problem was that he couldn't figure out what he'd done wrong and how he could work out of this mess.

Some chief he was. He was supposed to keep the town in order, and he couldn't keep his own family in line.

Shaking his head, he went back to work.

Shortly after Chief Jackson left the basketball court with Jahlil, a silver Lexus SUV cruised to the curb. Junior, who was driving to the hoop when he spotted the vehicle, stumbled and lost the ball.

"Look at that!" Junior said.

The other players and the guys hanging out around the court turned. Most of them only shrugged. But not Junior. From his lawn-cutting jobs, he knew what kind of car just about everyone in town owned. This one didn't belong to anyone he'd seen before.

He drifted off the court to look at the Lexus more closely. Someone shouted at him to come back to the game, but Junior ignored him. The silver truck had mesmerized him.

Andre, his cousin, leaned against the chain-link fence, smoking a cigarette. He was a big guy, around Junior's size.

He had a black do-rag wrapped around his head, the end of it trailing down his neck like a ponytail.

Andre nodded at Junior.

"That ride goes for about sixty grand," Andre said, coming to stand beside Junior. "You'd have to cut grass for twenty years to save up enough to get that one, cuz."

"You ain't lying," Junior said.

The Lexus truck hummed, idling. The windows were tinted with a weird sort of reflective glass, so Junior couldn't tell who was sitting inside.

The passenger-side window slid downward.

A bald-headed black man wearing shades and a gray suit sat behind the steering wheel. He was real sharp and rich looking, the kind of man Vicky Queen liked, Junior thought.

Classical music piped out of the vehicle. Junior had never known anyone to listen to music like that, for fun. This guy was kinda different.

"Good afternoon, gentlemen!" the man said. He had a booming voice, and the strangest accent Junior had ever heard. "May I speak with you for a moment?"

Junior pointed at himself and Andre. "Us?"

"Approach the vehicle, please."

Junior looked at Andre. Andre shrugged, took another pull of his cigarette. Both of them stepped closer to the Lexus.

The guy turned down his music.

"What you want, man?" Andre said.

The man smiled. He had teeth like someone in a Colgate commercial—they were a perfect, shiny white. The contrast of his teeth and his dark skin was striking.

"Would you be interested in a job?" the man said. "It would be for one night only. It will be hard work, manual labor, and that is why I am seeking the services of two strong young men such as yourselves."

At the mention of a job, Junior leaned closer. "What kinda work you want us to do, mister?"

"Digging," the man said. "As I stated, difficult manual labor."

"Digging for what?" Andre said.

"You will be compensated well for your efforts," the man said. As though by magic, a gold money clip that held a thick wad of bills appeared in his fingers. "Each of you will be paid two hundred fifty dollars."

"Two hundred fifty dollars!" Junior said. It would take him a week to earn that much money. "Just for doing some digging?"

"That is correct, gentlemen. I will require your services this evening, at nine o'clock. Are you familiar with the residence named Jubilee?"

"Oh, uh, yeah," Junior said. "Up on the hill."

"Shit, that crib is haunted," Andre said. But he kept his eyes on the dollars that the man casually held. "And you ain't answer my question. What we gonna be digging for?"

The man sighed. The money vanished. He looked away from them.

Junior's heart clutched. He could feel two hundred fifty dollars about to slip out of his grasp.

He pushed Andre aside and stuck his head inside the truck.

"Mister, we'll do the work. Don't mind my cousin."

The man flashed his dazzling smile. "It is good that you are so industrious, young man. Please arrive at the gates of Jubilee promptly at nine o'clock tonight. Make certain that you are wearing boots and work clothing. I will supply everything else that you will require."

"Yes, sir." Junior bobbed his head. "We'll be there."

"Until this evening, gentlemen." The passenger-side window came up. He cruised away, the Lexus purring like a panther.

Andre watched the truck leave, frowning.

"Junior, I don't know, man. Folks be saying that place is

haunted. And that nigga still didn't say what we was gonna be digging for."

Junior scratched his head. It was kinda funny, wasn't it? He'd heard stories about the Mason place being haunted, but he'd never set foot inside the house himself. And Andre was right: the man hadn't said what they'd be digging for.

But two hundred fifty dollars was a lot of money. Andre didn't have a job, but he had two kids and was living with a woman, so he needed the money as much as Junior did.

"That is a lot of cash, though." Andre threw his cigarette on the ground and stubbed it out with his foot. "All right, cuz. I'll pick you up at a quarter to nine. Then we'll go check out this gig."

"I'll be ready." Junior smiled. Already, he was thinking about how, with two-fifty in his hands, he would be much closer to buying his pickup truck.

Kyle awoke at sunset.

Contrary to popular perception, vampires did not sleep in coffins. They preferred beds with mattresses—the more comfortable, the better. What sane creature slumbered in a wooden box intended for the dead? Myths amused him sometimes.

He was in the master bedroom suite of Jubilee. The shutters—a custom design that guaranteed protection against daylight—were tightly closed, allowing deep shadows to dwell inside. But his vision was perfectly attuned to the darkness.

There wasn't much in there worth seeing. Like the rest of the residence, this room ached for a renovation. Mamu had done a commendable job of cleaning the house to make it somewhat livable, but this was, by far, the most wretched room in which Kyle had ever slept. Numerous wooden planks were missing from the decaying hardwood floor. The walls, riddled with peeling paint, appeared leprous. The ceiling fan had lost at least two blades, giving it the look of a junked propeller. Cracks veined the windows.

Although Kyle had the means to renovate the property, he would not waste money on the effort. They planned to live in this town for only a few weeks. He had instructed Mamu to purchase new beds, linens, special blinds, and necessary appliances and furniture, but to leave most of the mansion in its present, dilapidated condition. For Kyle, it was a welcome change from the opulence in which he had lived all his life.

He rose from the king-size bed. He wore black silk nightclothes. He slid on a matching pair of house slippers that awaited beside the bed.

There was a knock at the door.

"Come in," Kyle said.

Mamu stepped inside. "The sun has set, *monsieur.*"

"I've noticed." Vampires had a biological clock that synchronized their bodies to the rising and setting of the sun. Mamu was aware of this, yet believed that he had to notify Kyle each day. Kyle did not mind. Mamu was a man of rigid habit.

"How did you sleep?" Mamu said.

"Wonderfully. The bed was comfortable. Thank you."

Mamu smiled, but Kyle sensed that his friend's question had another meaning.

"I sensed a haunting spirit, though I did not see it," Kyle said. He smiled. "It was afraid of me."

"Ah," Mamu said. "It knew that you are not a man."

"You are safe as long as I am here, my friend," Kyle said. He clasped his hands and strolled across the room. "I'm hungry. Come with me and tell me of your progress."

As they left the room and descended the spiral staircase, Mamu filled him in on what he had accomplished that day. Everything was prepared for the work they were to begin in a few hours.

Flickering white candles illuminated the hallway and rooms. Kyle despised electric light.

In the kitchen, Kyle retrieved a packet of blood from the refrigerator. Mamu had procured two new refrigerators. He stored his own human food in the other one.

Sipping blood, Kyle opened the door to the basement and navigated the stone steps, Mamu following behind him.

Candles burned in the cellar, too.

"Ah," Kyle said, pleased.

A large bed occupied the middle of the area. It appeared to have come from a hospital, as it had railings along the side to prevent one from rolling off the mattress. An IV rack stood beside the bed, though no bag of fluids hung from the hook—yet.

A big pine entertainment center stood several feet in front of the bed. It contained a twenty-five-inch television, a combination DVD/ VCR player, a stereo system, and a collection of films and audio recordings. The media library was composed mostly of documentaries on historical topics, though a handful of popular films and programs were included: *Dracula,* starring Bela Lugosi, *Interview with the Vampire,* featuring Tom Cruise, and the best of *Dark Shadows,* the TV show with the fascinating vampire, Barnabas Collins.

"Is this what you had wished for, sir?" Mamu said.

"This is excellent. You've outdone yourself." Kyle approached the bed. He smoothed the crisp linens, fluffed the thick pillows. He was as giddy as a child, his nerves crackling with energy.

Laughing, he suddenly leapt across the cellar to a short staircase that led to a set of wide, wooden doors.

"Where do these lead?" Kyle said.

"Outside," Mamu said. "They are storm doors. I have placed a new padlock upon them."

"You are too much, my friend." Kyle noted that there were no windows in the chamber. Splendid.

Kyle had learned patience in his long life, but for once, he could not wait. He could not wait until later tonight, when he would, finally, meet his father.

David could not remember ever having such an enjoyable first date.

He'd picked Nia up at seven, and they had driven to Southaven, twenty minutes north of Mason's Corner. They had dinner at a Southwestern-style restaurant, then visited the multiplex cinema to see a movie.

After the film—a typical summer action flick full of explosions and one-liners—they stopped by a café for dessert.

"We had peach cobbler at lunch, and now we're eating cheesecake," Nia said. She giggled, dangling her fork. "Are you trying to put some weight on me, or what?"

"You are a little skinny."

She threw a napkin at him. "Hey, you said I was in great shape."

"I was only trying to make a good first impression." He laughed, then grew serious. "I wouldn't change one thing about you."

She gave him the full effect of her lovely eyes.

It had been that kind of evening—filled with meaningful gazes and flirtatious, yet profound, compliments. Only once in his life had David been similarly at ease with a woman, and that had been two years ago, with his ex-girlfriend, whom he'd thought he would marry. When they broke up, he'd been shattered. She had been his first genuine, mature love. He'd doubted that he'd ever meet a woman like her again. Lightning never struck twice.

But now, he had met Nia.

He was a practical guy. He wrote goals in a journal, and executed them. He never attempted anything of importance without thinking it through from beginning to end. He liked an orderly—even predictable—life, in which he could maintain control at all times. When he had come to Mason's Corner, the possibility of meeting a woman had never crossed his thoughts.

But now, Nia.

Although he had known her for only a day, he could not deny the sense of rightness that he felt in her company. Was it love at first sight? He hesitated to slap a clichéd label like that on it. But it was something special, something worth growing and exploring.

Nia was watching him. He had the feeling that she knew exactly what he was thinking, and instead of making him nervous, he felt warm, accepted.

"I want to tell you why I left Houston and came back home," Nia said.

He put down his fork. "Okay. If you feel comfortable sharing that with me."

"I do," she said firmly, as though reaffirming it to herself. "In Houston, I was stalked."

He listened. She would share the story at her own pace.

"This happened after my knee injury forced me to stop running track," she said. "I was teaching at a high school. One of my colleagues, Mr. Morgan, a math teacher, asked me out on a date. He was a good-looking guy, in his thirties, never married, and he seemed really nice, intelligent, and thoughtful. So I went out with him.

"Talk about the date from hell. The minute he picked me up, he started talking about all of our colleagues. He had strong, negative views of everyone. Mr. So-and-So is a homosexual, he'd say, and we should keep him away from the boys in his class. Ms. This-or-That is a bitch and always has been, and I can't wait until she leaves. He went on and on like that throughout dinner. He was a totally different person in private than he was at school.

"Our plan was to catch a movie after dinner, but I already had a headache from listening to his nasty attitude. I told him I had to get in early to grade some papers, and asked him to drop me off. He drove me back to my place, and he made a couple comments about how I was rude for ending our date early. I let it pass. I only wanted to get away from him. But I could've given him a piece of my mind, because if anyone had been rude, it was him.

"The harassment started the following week. He asked me when we could get together again, and I said I was busy. 'Then when is your schedule open?' he said. I told him I didn't know, hoping he'd get the hint. He didn't.

"He started to leave vulgar notes in my mailbox. Stuff like, 'Baby, can I have a private tutoring session with you?' and 'You're too damn sexy to be teaching here, you're gonna make me lose my mind.' He never signed these notes, but I knew it was him. No one else had any reason to write them. The messages got cruder and more frequent. I complained to the principal, and she said she was going to talk to Mr. Morgan. She took my complaint seriously, which was something I'd worried about. I thought my complaint might be laughed off. But apparently, this wasn't the first time that this guy had done something like this. He'd been forced to leave his last teaching position because of the same kind of thing.

"But the principal must not have been all that frightening to Mr. Morgan, because he stepped up his harassment. He called my place at all hours of the night, never saying anything, just breathing hard on the phone. He'd leave a rose under the windshield wiper of my car. And he started showing up at the gym where I worked out. He'd find a spot where he could watch me run around the track, and he would stare at me the entire time.

"I finally confronted him and told him that I wanted him to leave me alone, or I was going to call the police. He laughed it off and acted like I was the one tripping. 'I only want to spend time with you, get to know you better,' he said. 'I'm a good man, and I want to prove it to you.' He wasn't worried about my threat to go to the cops. Maybe he didn't believe me, maybe he didn't care. I don't know what he was thinking, really.

"This harassment went on for weeks. Then, one night I came home and found that someone had been in my apartment. Clothes were all over the place, but my lingerie was missing. I knew who'd done it, though I had no idea how he got into my place. He had a sick, cunning mind.

"I was scared to death then. I called the police. They talked to him and warned him to stay away from me, and they gave me advice on how to handle the situation. I hoped they'd thrown a scare into him. They hadn't. He only got worse. He called more frequently, he followed me to and from work, and tailed me when I ran errands. There was no escape from him. He promised me that I would be his, no matter how long it took.

"I was a nervous wreck. I was afraid to leave the house, pick up the phone—to do anything. Mr. Morgan was everywhere, like he had cloned himself a dozen times. I called the police again, and I got a restraining order. Instead of cooling him off, it drove him over the edge.

"When I was alone in the teacher's lounge one afternoon, he assaulted me. I've always been a fitness nut, trying out new sports, and when I was in college I'd started learning tae kwon do and had gotten as far as a blue belt. The training came in handy, and it probably helped, too, that Mr. Morgan isn't that much bigger than I am. He's about five-nine and pretty lean, and I'm five-seven. Anyway, we tangled in there, and I busted his lip. It might've gone further if a couple other teachers hadn't walked into the room. Mr. Morgan ran out, and I called the cops again.

"Now, you'd think that after I had kicked his butt, he'd leave me alone, right? Nope. First of all, the cops didn't find him at home. They couldn't find him anywhere. That night, I stayed at a friend's house, 'cause I was afraid to go to my place alone. She lived with her boyfriend, so there were three of us there, and she had a rottweiler, too. I thought I would be safe, if only for that night.

"Late, around one in the morning, Mr. Morgan broke into the house. He had a gun this time. He shot my friend's dog, then he pistol-whipped my friend's fiancé. I heard all of this happening while I was in the guest bedroom, and let me tell you, never in my life have I been so scared. I pushed the dresser against the door and hid in the closet. Mr. Morgan tried to break down the door, and he kept chanting 'Going to get my baby, Nia; she belongs to me. Nia's all mine, all mine, all mine.' He had gone crazy. I was convinced that he would break in and blow me away. I was praying just as much as he was chanting.

"The police got there before Mr. Morgan could get me. He gave himself up peacefully. He was sentenced to two years in prison for assault and other charges."

"Only two years?" David said. "That guy was going to kill you!"

She smiled bitterly. "He could get paroled sooner, for good behavior."

"That's crazy," he said. "Damn, I'm so sorry you had to go through something like that."

"I had to leave Houston," she said. "I used to love the city, but it held too many painful memories for me. Even though Mr. Morgan was in prison, I imagined that I saw his face everywhere I went. I had nightmares—and still do sometimes—about him escaping and coming to finish me off. Mama asked me to come back home. It didn't take much convincing on her part. I was ready to live in a place where I felt safe."

"And this Morgan guy is still in jail, right?"

"He's been locked up for a little over a year. But like I said, he could get out early. I'm praying that whenever he's released, he won't come after me. I hope he forgets about me."

"You think he could find you here?"

Her eyes were haunted. "Definitely. He's slick, smart. He could track me down. Some women who've been stalked have actually needed to change their names and move far away, to where no one knows them—like they're in a witness protection program. But I never want to do that. I can't leave behind everything I know and love."

He reached across the table and took her hands in his. Her skin was cool, her palms moist, and he realized how much reliving her terror had shaken her.

"I picked up tae kwon do again, after I moved back home," she said. "I take classes at a dojo in Memphis. I've got a black belt now. I've bought a gun, too. And I know how to use it. If Mr. Morgan comes again, I'll be ready for him."

"You've got another weapon, too," he said.

"What's that?"

"Me. I'm not letting anything happen to you. You've got a bodyguard, girl."

She smiled, squeezed his hands. "You're so sweet. How did I ever meet such a nice guy at the park in little, boring Mason's Corner?"

The words came out of him before he could think about the meaning of what he was saying.

"Maybe it was destiny."

Andre pulled up in his car at ten minutes past nine o'-clock.

Junior had been sitting on the rickety front steps of the trailer. He had been fidgeting, restlessly counting the stars in the clear night sky. He never liked to show up late for a job. Andre was supposed to pick him up at a quarter to nine, and as the minutes ticked away, Junior grew more agitated. The bald-headed, rich man in the Lexus was offering them good money for a few hours' work, and they were going to blow it by showing up late. What if the guy hired someone else? They'd miss out on all that money.

At times like this, Junior felt an aching need for his own pickup truck. With his own ride, he'd never arrive late to work, anywhere.

When Andre arrived in his battered white Chevy, Junior raced to the car.

"Man, we're late!" Junior hustled inside. "We was s'-posed to be up there at nine. It's ten minutes after!"

"Chill out, cuz," Andre said. A toothpick dangled from his lips. From the pungent smell inside the car, Junior could tell that Andre had been smoking, and not cigarettes, either. Andre had that lazy look in his eyes that let Junior know his cousin was as high as a kite.

"You been smokin'," Junior said. "We got to be ready to work, Andre."

Swiveling the steering wheel with one hand, Andre made a dismissive motion. "You worry too much, cuz. It's cool."

"That man's gonna be mad that we late," Junior said. Andre cruised, slowly, and Junior gritted his teeth. With the passing of each minute, he could feel dollar bills slipping out of his fingers.

"What I wanna know is," Andre said, "what this cat gonna have us diggin' up? I told you they say the Mason crib is haunted."

"I don't know," Junior said. He had avoided thinking about the scary tales of the Mason place, preferring to focus on the money he was going to earn.

"I been asking around 'bout that cat," Andre said. "I heard he was from France; that's why he got that funny accent."

"Oh," Junior said. He didn't know exactly where France was, only that it was far away and that he'd never go there. Not unless they had some good-paying jobs he could do that would be worth the trip.

"It just don't make any damn sense. A nigga from France living in that big-assed, haunted crib, and now he want us to do some digging—at night. I got a bad feeling about it, cuz."

"We gotta go, Andre. That's a lot of money—"

"I know, you wanna make some money. I need the money too, that's the only reason I'm going with you. My girl's been on my case 'bout working a job."

They drove up the steep country road that led to the Mason house. Junior hadn't been up here in . . . well, he couldn't remember the last time. No one lived up this way, so there was no reason for him to ever swing through this part of town.

The mansion came into view. It sat far back from the road, up on a peak. Soft lights gleamed through the windows.

A tall, wrought-iron gate restricted access to the long dirt lane that led to the house. Andre parked in front of the entrance.

They got out of the car. Towering trees, cloaked in darkness, flanked the fence. A cool breeze whistled through the branches.

Other than the wind, the night was silent, as though they stood on a hill at the top of the world.

Andre approached the gate. "Damn, this place is creepy as hell."

Junior ignored Andre. He peered through the fence bars, looking for the black Frenchman. "We too late. I bet he left us and got someone else. We ain't gonna make any money."

"Stop tripping." Andre banged the gate with his fist. It creaked open on rusty hinges. "Come on."

Junior followed Andre inside. Across the lawn, a moving shadow appeared.

"Gentlemen!" It was the Frenchman. He shined a flashlight in their direction. "Only the two of you have come?"

"Yeah," Andre said. "We didn't bring nobody else."

"We apologize for being late, mister," Junior said.

"That is acceptable," the man said. "My name is Mamuwalde."

"Mamma-what?" Andre said.

"Simply call me Mamu," he said, as if annoyed.

Mamu, Junior thought. Figured he'd have a crazy name like that.

The fella had changed into a new suit, too, Junior noticed. This one was navy blue, just as sharp as the other one. The guy probably had a closetful of nice clothes.

Mamu gave them a once-over. "I earnestly hope that you are prepared to work, gentlemen, and to work hard. We have a great deal of labor ahead of us tonight."

"Diggin' for what?" Andre said.

Mamu only smiled. "We are behind schedule. Follow me, please."

Andre mumbled something under his breath, but he followed. Junior followed his cousin.

They walked toward the mansion, but as they got closer, Mamu cut a path along the side. Junior realized that they weren't going inside the house. They were going somewhere else on the property.

But the house held his attention as they walked past it. He looked at the soft light that flickered in the windows, but blinds prevented him from seeing through the glass and figuring out what was going on inside.

He thought he saw a dark face peering at him through a dimly lit window on the second floor. But when he blinked, the face was gone—if it was ever there to begin with.

A chill rattled down his spine. He wasn't going to pay any more attention to the house. He kept his attention on the ground.

They walked along the side of the mansion, then across the huge backyard, and finally entered the woods that bordered the lawn. Mamu led the way with the flashlight, but it was so dark out there that when Junior turned away from the light, he couldn't see his own hand in front of his face.

He quickly turned back to the spray of light cast by Mamu's flashlight. The darkness gave him the creeps. Shoot, this whole place creeped him out.

No wonder folks said the place was haunted.

They had trudged through the woods for several minutes when they reached a clearing near a huge tree. At the edge of the meadow, a gigantic, kudzu-covered hill rose high into the sky. It looked like the side of a mountain.

"I didn't know they had all this back here," Andre said to Junior.

"Me, neither."

Mamu turned on another light. It was one of those big circular lights that stood on a stand.

Equipment was spread out on the grass. Junior saw shovels, sledgehammers, a gas lamp, a hammer drill, a yellow canister that had the word "gunpowder" written on the side, several empty buckets, a heap of blankets piled on what looked like a stretcher, and more stuff he couldn't name.

"This is our work site," Mamu said. He tossed a shovel to each of them, and gave each of them a pair of gloves, too.

Mamu walked to the vine-covered hill. He pointed.

"We will begin digging here," he said.

"We gonna be digging into this mountain?" Andre said.

"It is not a mountain," Mamu said. His lips curved into a mysterious smile. "It is a cave."

Chapter 5

Around half-past midnight, David parked in front of Nia's house.

"Want to take a walk?" Nia said. "I'm not ready to go in yet."

"Sure. But you know, people in Atlanta don't walk around the neighborhood at this hour."

"Let go of that big city paranoia, sweetie," she said. She pinched his cheek. "It's safe here."

They climbed out of the truck. David glanced at the front windows of her house. A curtain dropped, as if someone was spying on them and didn't want to be seen.

"Your mother, huh?" he said. "She's up late."

"Oh, yeah. Mama won't go to bed until I come in. That's how she is."

"Are you and your mother close?"

"We are," Nia said. "Maybe too close. I love Mama, but she can be overprotective. She's always been like that with me, her only girl, and what happened in Houston only makes her worry more."

They took each other's hand—it felt like a natural gesture they had been doing for years—and strolled along the sidewalk.

The neighborhood was quiet and peaceful. Lights shone in the windows of many homes, but almost as many other houses were dark. Cicadas, crickets, and other night creatures sang their timeless songs. A balmy breeze riffled the trees.

"Have you mentioned anything to your mother about me?" he said.

"Are you kidding?" Nia said. "She'd tie me to a chair to keep me from leaving unless I told her who you were."

"What did she say?"

"You don't want to know."

"Why?"

"Let's just say that Mama knew your father's reputation for being a player, back in the day. In her opinion, 'the fruit doesn't fall far from the tree.' I'm putting it more nicely than she did."

"Great. So your mother doesn't trust me."

"Don't worry, I'll take care of it. You just be your normal, sweet self."

Ahead, there was a small playground with swings, a slide, monkey bars, and a couple of wooden benches. Nia sat on the bench and pulled him down beside her. A street lamp cast golden light over them.

They turned to face one another. David could feel the desire building between them. He stroked the back of her neck. She put her soft hand against his cheek.

They kissed, lightly at first, then, more deeply.

"Do you realize," she said, "that we've spent almost the entire day together?"

"And the day has passed way too quickly," he said, and kissed her again. Moaning softly, she ran her fingers through his short hair. She shifted her body to mesh into his.

He placed his hand on her thigh, stroked her smooth skin. She felt so good against him that he never wanted to move. The scent of her perfume enveloped him like a sweet fog.

What a fine, fine woman. Feminine and sexy, yet independent and strong. A perfect blend of every quality he had ever dreamed of finding in a woman. If Nia were a drink, he would've drunk himself into a stupor.

He didn't know how long they kissed—time stood motionless as their lips and tongues flowed together—but at some point, when his eyes were open for an instant, he glimpsed the Mason place in the distance, between the tree branches. Light glowed faintly at the windows.

His stomach heaved, as though he had swallowed something sour. Reluctantly, he broke off their kiss.

"What's wrong?" she said. "You look like you've bitten into a rotten apple."

"That house." He pointed behind her. "Something about it really bothers me."

Frowning, she looked over her shoulder. "The Mason place?"

"I get a bad feeling every time I look at it. A feeling that something isn't quite right there."

Her voice lowered. "It's supposed to be haunted, did you know that?"

"I've heard. Someone just moved in there, too."

"What? Who?"

"I don't know who, but when Chief Jackson stopped by, he said someone had moved into the place. He didn't say much else about it. What do you know about the house?"

"Only the basics. I know that the man who founded the town, Ed Mason, ran his plantation from there. He was known for being cruel to his slaves. Around the time of the Civil War, his slaves revolted and killed him—they hung him from a tree. But many of the slaves who took part in the insurrection were then killed themselves by the authorities. A lot of bloodshed happened up there."

"What about these tales of the house being haunted?"

She smiled, but it was a nervous smile. "Are you sure you want to hear this?"

"Definitely, now that you've got me curious."

"Okay," she said. She drew a breath. "My brothers and I went up there, once. I was nine, I think . . . they would've been eleven and thirteen. Like I told you earlier, the three of us were always into stuff we had no business doing. We got the bright idea in our heads that we'd see if the Mason place was really haunted.

"We rode our bikes up there one summer afternoon. Eric, the eldest, led the way, I was in the middle, and Robert brought up the rear. We left our bikes at the gate, then climbed the fence. There were so many tall, old trees up there, throwing deep shadows everywhere. And it was so still, too, like the quiet before a storm.

"We walked down the path, to the mansion. We were bunched so closely together I'm surprised we didn't stumble over one another's shoes.

"We'd decided that we were just going to look in a window. But we had to get close to do it. We had to go onto the veranda. We climbed the steps and walked across the veranda, trying to keep from tripping on all the vines that covered everything. We went up to one of the front windows. It was covered with dirt, so Eric cleaned a spot with his shirt. Then we looked inside."

"What did you see?" David said. Although she was telling the story, his own heart hammered.

"We saw a gray-haired white man, dressed in a black suit. He sat in a rocking chair in the living room. I could see every detail about him—it was Edward Mason. For real. I recognized him from pictures. His face was bluish, and his eyes bulged. He looked like someone who had been cut from the noose after he'd been hanging for a while. He turned and looked right at us.

"I think all of our hearts froze. We were paralyzed. The

man rose up out of that chair—floated out of the chair, really—and started to come toward us. He levitated through the air, walking, but his feet weren't touching the floor.

"We snapped out of our daze and ran away from the house, screaming. I was as fast as my brothers, and I don't ever remember running so fast. But as we were bolting across the yard, there were people watching us from the shadows under the trees. Black people dressed in work clothes, like slaves on a plantation. I couldn't see them clearly—they flickered, sort of, like images cast by a film projector. But they were there. All of us saw them.

"My brothers and I hurdled that fence like it was only two feet high instead of six. Got on our bikes and *zoomed* away from there. I've never been back since, and never will if I can help it."

Finished speaking, she hugged herself. He put his arm around her, drew her closer.

He didn't need to ask her whether, in hindsight, she believed the incident had truly happened or was only the creation of a child's overactive imagination. Her reactions in recounting the story made it clear that she believed what she had seen, even nearly two decades afterward. He had no choice but to accept the reality of her experience. Although accepting the existence of ghosts was a stretch for him.

But I can't deny the feeling I get in the pit of my stomach when I look at that house.

"I need to stop asking so many questions," he said. "You ever heard that line, 'Don't ask a question if you aren't prepared for the answer'? I wasn't ready for your answer."

"I've never shared the story with anyone," she said. "I don't think my brothers have, either. After it happened, we never talked about it."

"I appreciate you sharing it with me, but I doubt that I'll bring it up again, anytime soon."

"Learn to do what I do, David: don't look at the Mason place. You'll feel better."

They rose from the bench and began to walk back to her house. She wrapped her arm around his waist and nestled her head against his shoulder. He held her protectively within the span of his arm.

When they reached the narrow walk that led to her front door, they faced each other, hands clasped together.

"I want to see you tomorrow," he said. Under normal circumstances, he'd never ask a woman out two days in a row. But nothing about their situation seemed normal to him. This was one of those rare times when all of the standard rules of dating were worthless.

"I was hoping you'd say that," she said. "I want to see you, too."

"I'm going to the church in the morning, New Life Baptist. How about you join me?"

"Oh, David, I would, but I have to meet a client tomorrow morning for a really big project." She tapped her lip. "How does dinner sound? I'll cook. Do you like lasagna?"

"Love it. So you can cook, too?"

"I'm Superwoman, baby, didn't you know that?"

He laughed. "What time?"

"Around three," she said. "We'll have dinner at my place, okay?"

"I'm there." He looked toward the house. A silhouetted shape waited behind the window. "Guess I'll meet your mother, too."

"Don't worry, David. She'll like you. She better, because I like you."

They melted into each other's arms and shared a fiery kiss.

"We better quit," he said. "Your mother's gonna come out here and beat me off of you with a broom."

"I'm a grown woman, sweetheart. Mama might make a comment, but that doesn't mean I have to listen to her." Her tongue darted across his neck. Then she bit his tender flesh there, lightly, and a shiver of pleasure rippled through him.

"Nia, Nia, Nia." He pulled her within his arms. "Who would've thought a walk in the park . . ."

"I know," she said, her head buried against his chest. "I know."

They kissed again, and then she went inside, waving before she closed the door.

Without her presence, the night was dull. He realized how tired he was. He had been floating on an adrenaline high while in Nia's company, and in her absence, fatigue hit him.

But he wasn't too tired to remember to avoid looking at Jubilee as he drove home.

Nia's mother was waiting for her when she came inside.

"I thought I was going have to come out there and separate you two," Mama said. "It's not proper for a young woman to be kissing and carrying on outdoors, where everyone can see."

Nia dropped her purse on an end table, and sighed. She had hoped to make it to her bedroom with fielding only a minimum number of questions and comments about David, thinking that her mother would be too tired for much conversation. But one look at Mama swept away those hopes.

Sitting on the couch, Mama was wrapped in a green house robe and slippers. She had rollers in her hair, and a mug of coffee at her side. A crossword puzzle and a pencil lay across her lap, and she was wearing her glasses. Mama's eyes were alert, ready to probe.

I wish she'd get a life, Nia thought. Her mother had never remarried after Nia's father died twenty years ago, deciding to focus her energies on raising her three children. Nia and her brothers all graduated from college and established successful lives—but the downside of them growing up was that Mama hadn't had anything to occupy her time, outside of work and church. When Nia moved back in, however, Mama regressed into serious mothering mode.

"Mama, please," Nia said. "I'm tired."

"Don't Mama, please, me, Miss Nia James. You know better. Did you lose all your good sense while you were living in that evil, immoral city?"

In her mother's opinion, any city with a population greater than twenty thousand—in other words, most cities in the world—deserved two labels: evil and immoral. But Mama had never lived outside of Mason's Corner. Her distasteful opinion of cities was formed by the unending series of sensational TV news and cop shows that she consumed for hours a day—programs that exhibited crime, filth, immorality, and everything else that Mama found worthy of loathing.

"I'm twenty-seven," Nia said. "Not seventeen."

"I know how old you are, young lady. You're old enough to know better. I can see that this Hunter boy is going to be a bad influence on you. But considering his father, I would've expected nothing less."

Nia folded her arms across her chest. "David's a nice guy. You can't condemn him because of his father."

"Like father, like son," Mama said, with the familiar, Mama-knows-best tone that always set Nia's nerves on edge. "You don't know anything about this boy. You've known him for one day and already you're swooning over him."

"No, I'm not. We went to lunch and dinner; we had a good time. It's not like I'm having his baby."

"Not yet," Mama said. "The way that you and him were carrying on outside, it won't be long before you'll be announcing that you're pregnant. And he'll leave you then, yes he will, like his father left his mother. The fruit doesn't fall far from the tree."

"Why do you keep bringing David's father into this?" Nia said. "They are two completely different people."

"The man was a whore," Mama said. "An immoral, whorish man who used his fame to manipulate women."

"Like you?" The words spilled out of Nia.

Her mother's face darkened. "That's none of your business."

"So why are you in my business?"

Her mother spread her arms. "Because you don't know any better, Nia. Look at what happened in Houston—"

"Okay, I'm going to bed," Nia said. She spun and marched down the hall, toward her bedroom.

"I'm only trying to help you!" Mama pleaded.

Nia rushed inside the room, slammed the door. She dropped onto the bed. Heart pounding, she stared at the ceiling.

She felt as though she were in high school again. This was crazy. What had she been thinking when she had accepted Mama's invitation to move back home? When she had told David that she and her mother were close, she was telling the truth. But she had gotten along much better with Mama when she had lived in Houston.

I have to get out of here, she thought. *Mama is going to drive me nuts.*

But where would she go? Atlanta? Charlotte? She had plenty of friends in both cities, which would help ease the transition, but what if she moved away from home and something bad happened again, like it had in Houston? Her friends couldn't save her from *that.* Mason's Corner was dull, but safe. She was one of the town's golden girls: everyone respected her, admired her, looked out for her. Respect, admiration, and neighborly concern were tough to come by in a big city.

One of the worst aftereffects of her stalking experience was her damaged self-confidence. She used to possess an adventurous, easygoing spirit. Not anymore. Although it had been over a year since the madman had terrorized her, he visited her when she slept, his leering face creeping into her dreams with upsetting frequency. Sometimes, she took sleeping pills in order to achieve a peaceful rest.

Considering how deeply Mr. Morgan had shaken her, it surprised her how quickly and willingly she had opened up to David. A distrust of men had kept her on guard. But David was different. He was special. No matter what Mama said about his father.

I will not let Mama ruin this for me, Nia thought. *She will have to get with the program.*

Before she turned in for the night, she checked on her mother. Mama was finishing a crossword puzzle.

"I invited David to dinner tomorrow," Nia said. "I'm cooking. I want you to meet him, Mama."

"Hmph. I'll meet him," Mama said. "I'll give you my opinion, too. One of us has to show some good sense in this house."

Nia let the comment pass. She kissed her mother on the cheek and went to bed.

She slept without nightmares.

Junior had never worked so hard in his life.

For over four grueling hours, Junior and Andre plunged the shovels into the earthen wall. The dirt was hard and packed tight. At times, it was like trying to dig into concrete.

Junior had a strong, work-toughened body, but he thought his muscles would be plenty sore come tomorrow morning.

Mamu did not help them. He walked around, occasionally pointing out an area in which he wanted them to dig. Sometimes he tinkered with the equipment that lay nearby.

Mamu did not allow them to take a break for any longer than a minute or two, which was hard for Andre. Andre hardly ever worked outdoors, and he smoked all the time, so he kept breathing hard and taking a long time to lift his shovel. During one of their breaks, Andre complained that he was thirsty, and Mamu tossed them bottles of water and went back to fiddling with the equipment.

When Mamu was out of earshot, Andre leaned close to Junior.

"I bet we diggin' for treasure, cuz."

"Huh?" Junior took measured sips of the water, knowing from past experience that drinking too quickly would give him muscle cramps. "What kinda treasure?"

"Gold, jewels, something like that, man." Andre nodded toward Mamu. "Look at this operation, cuz. That cat is gonna blow a hole to get in this cave when we done diggin'. You don't go through all this trouble unless you gonna get some loot."

"You think so?" Junior said. He turned over the idea in his mind. Gold. It made sense. No wonder Mamu could afford to pay them so much money. It was nothing for him to pay them five hundred dollars if they were gonna help him dig up a treasure chest of gold.

"I bet that Ed Mason cat buried some stuff in here." Andre tapped the side of the cave with his shovel. "He was rich, man. Rich folks always hiding money and shit."

"Heck, you just might be right, Andre. I ain't never thought about that."

Andre winked. "Watch and see, cuz. If we can stay around long enough, maybe we can lay our hands on somethin' when French boy ain't lookin'."

"Gentlemen, please resume working!" Mamu said.

Andre smiled at Junior, his gold tooth glimmering. They went back to work.

Junior couldn't get Andre's idea out of his head. As he slammed the shovel into the ground, he stayed on the lookout for anything that sparkled in the dirt. It wouldn't do for him to hit gold and miss it.

After they had been digging for about another half hour, they hit a wall of solid rock.

"Yo, man!" Andre said to Mamu. "We can't dig no more. We done hit some rock."

"Excellent!" Mamu said. He had taken off his suit jacket

and rolled up the sleeves of his fancy white shirt. He wore a yellow hard hat, goggles, and gloves. "Gentlemen, stand back, at least ten feet. I will begin microshaving."

"Huh?" Andre said, but he moved away, and so did Junior.

The French guy looked liked he knew what he was doing. Using a hammer drill, he bore a hole in the rock. He stuck a long soda straw in the gap, a thin wire trailing from the tube to a small device he held in his hand. Then he stepped backward several feet and pressed a button on that handheld gadget. The stones broke apart with a loud crack.

"Ain't that something," Junior said.

"Load the crushed rocks into the buckets," Mamu said crisply.

They did as he ordered. After they had cleared away the crumbled stones, he commanded them to stand back again. He set about drilling another hole so he could blow up more rock.

As Junior watched, he became aware of another presence nearby. He turned, looked in the darkness beyond the circle of light.

A tall, slender man, draped in black, stepped out of the shadows. He was dark-skinned, like Junior, but he was a couple of inches taller than Junior, who stood six-three. The man wore a black shirt, black slacks, and shiny black boots with silver buckles.

Junior's first thought was that the guy was some kinda star. He acted cool and in control. When he walked, he seemed to glide. It was weird.

The man floated past Junior and Andre, saying nothing to either of them, only nodding. He approached Mamu, and he and the Frenchman spoke too softly for Junior to understand what they were saying. But it was plain that the man in black was the one in charge. Mamu looked like a servant.

When they finished chatting, Mamu stood back, and exploded another rock.

Junior realized that the guy in black had vanished.

One second he was standing beside Mamu; the next, he was gone.

Junior had never looked away from the men. He had only blinked. The man had disappeared, literally, in the blink of an eye.

No one could move that fast. It was impossible.

Coldness seeped into Junior's bones. And this cave digging, that scared him, too. All of it was too strange and scary. Who were these people, and what was in the cave?

His cousin's eyes were as wide as hubcaps.

"Where'd that man go?" Junior whispered. "I feel like somethin' bad's going on, Andre."

"I'm ready to get out of here, cuz," Andre said. "Don't know if I want that gold no more."

"Ain't no gold," Junior said, and he could tell that Andre believed him. "Somethin' else is in there."

"But what the hell is it?" Andre said.

Mamu approached them. "We are not finished yet, gentlemen. We must continue to displace the stones."

"Aww, shit," Andre said. "Man, when you gonna let us go?"

"Soon. Come now."

"What happened to the dude dressed in black?" Andre asked. "He cut out of here with the quickness. I ain't never seen nobody move that fast."

Mamu gave them another of his strange smiles. "My employer will be returning soon."

It took all of Junior's courage for him to drag himself forward. His stomach was in knots.

They spent another hour watching Mamu blow up stones, then coming behind him to load the junk into buckets. Finally, Mamu said that he felt cool air coming from inside the cave—a sign that they were almost done—and ordered them to pick up the sledgehammers and start whacking away.

Swinging the hammer at the rocks, Junior's arms felt as if they were ready to fall off. He could not wait to get home and go to bed. In spite of the good money he was going to earn, he didn't ever want to do something like this again.

They chiseled open a good-size doorway in the cave. Using the shovels, they cleared away the crumbled stones. Mamu actually helped them this time.

A terrible smell drifted from inside the cavern: an old, rotten stench. Junior couldn't see what was in there because it was dark, and he wasn't sure he wanted to know what lay within. He only wanted to get his money and go home.

At last, Mamu set down his shovel. He dug his hand into the pocket of his slacks and retrieved the money clip.

"Your work is done, gentlemen," Mamu said. He peeled off several crisp bills. He handed Andre a portion, then gave Junior his share. "You are free to go."

"I must impress something upon you before you leave us," a deep voice said, and Junior jumped as if someone had thrown water in his face. The man in black was suddenly beside them; he was the one who had spoken.

Junior's legs were watery. How had this man gotten there so quickly, without making a sound?

It ain't natural, Junior thought. *This man, I don't know who he is, but what he does ain't natural.*

The thought came to him, unbidden, that maybe the man in black wasn't a man at all.

"You must not tell anyone in town what you have done this night," the man said. "Give me your word that you will keep it secret."

Andre looked at the bills, then stuffed them into his pocket. His voice was shaky. "All right. I ain't saying nothing."

"Me, neither," Junior said. He shook his head adamantly. "Nothing."

The guy in black nodded. "You may go." He flowed past them and slipped inside the cave, as swiftly as a shadow.

Mamu winked at them, then picked up the lamp that lay on the ground. He switched it on and entered the cavern's dark mouth.

Andre looked at Junior. "Cuz, what the fuck is happening?"

"I . . . I don't know. I ain't sure I *want* to know. I want to go home."

Andre's eyes narrowed. "These cats is up to no good, man. Come on."

"Where you going?"

"I want to look inside and see what they doing."

"Andre, get back here!" Junior grabbed his shoulder.

Andre brushed away his hand. "Only wanna take a quick peek. I done busted my ass helping these cats. I wanna know what they doing."

Junior groaned. His legs trembled. But he followed Andre. Both of them moved quietly and lowered their heads as they stepped underneath the jagged ridge of the entrance.

It was dark inside, and the awful smell made Junior want to vomit. He covered his mouth with his shirt.

Mamu was ahead of them, out of sight around a corner. The backsplash of his lamp gave them a little light as they picked their way forward. Junior and Andre moved forward, in step with one another.

They reached the corner of the cavern tunnel. Junior heard Mamu and the other guy speaking in hushed tones.

Andre put his finger to his lips. He and Junior leaned forward and peeked around the corner.

What they saw made them drop to the ground in stupefied shock.

Human skeletons. Dozens of them, piled one atop the other across the ground. Many of the corpses were swaddled in old rags.

Junior's stomach flip-flopped. He vomited.

Through his teary eyes, he saw the guy in black and

Mamu, standing at the far end of the mass of skeletons. They saw him.

"Get out of here!" the man in black said, his voice like thunder. He pointed in Junior's direction, and Junior felt himself lifted in the air by an unseen power. He was flung against the wall with tremendous force, the breath *whooshing* out of his lungs, pain cracking across his back. He collapsed on a warm cushion underneath him, and realized that his cushion was actually Andre.

Weak and dazed, but filled with a terror that he had never known, Junior grabbed Andre by the scruff of his neck. Andre got his legs under him, and the two of them broke out of there.

They ran all the way to Andre's car.

Kyle was relieved when the two men fled. He regretted that it had been necessary to use force against them. But he was close to achieving his goal and would allow nothing to impede his progress.

Mamu bowed his head. "I selected our laborers poorly. I apologize, *monsieur.*"

"I accept your apology. Let us hope the men remember their vow to remain silent about what they witnessed. Perhaps their fear will ensure obedience."

Kyle, too, had been surprised to discover so many fire-blackened corpses. From Mother's tale of his father's demise, he had known that his father had recruited a number of vampiric warriors, but he had not expected to find so many. He had counted twenty-one bodies. How powerful his father must have been to command such a horde to follow him on his murderous mission!

The air in the cavern was thick with stale, pent-up air— and latent energy. Kyle sensed his father's presence; it was like a coolness in the ether. It raised the hairs at the nape of Kyle's neck. He shivered with a thrill of anticipation.

He hated that Mother had lied to him for so long about his father, but he was grateful that when she finally revealed the truth, she had spared no details. Mother had given him the precise location of this cave, though she never had seen it with her own eyes.

Indeed, Mother had told him everything—except for where he would find his father sleeping within the earthen tomb. She rightfully expected that Kyle would be able to discover his father's resting place on his own.

"When we are finished tonight, I would like for you to return here and dispose of the bodies." Kyle swept his arm across the heap of fallen vampires. "Burn them to ashes, and bury them. I don't wish to leave behind any evidence."

"It will be done."

Deeper in the tunnel, Kyle saw symbols engraved on the wall. He moved closer.

The symbols were a language that Kyle could not interpret.

"Can you read this?" he said to Mamu. Mamu was fluent in nine languages.

Mamu brought the lamp closer. The words had been chiseled into the rock.

"I am sorry," Mamu said. "It is an African tongue, I believe, but I cannot decipher the meaning. I can research it—"

"He lies here." Kyle tapped his boot on the ground beneath the inscription. "I sense it. My father lies here!"

Kyle dropped to his knees. He traced his fingertips across the smooth, cool cavern floor.

"I feel him, underneath us," Kyle said in a trembling voice. "Ah, the power."

He plunged his hands into the earth. Mamu set down the lamp and came forward to help him, but Kyle shoved him aside.

"I will do this alone. I have waited all my life for this moment!"

He tore great plugs of dirt out of the ground. He worked with machinelike speed. Dust plumed through the air, coated his face and his hands. But he did not slow.

After he had dug about three feet beneath the surface, he touched something: cloth. Cotton overalls.

He furiously ripped away chunks of earth.

Dusty, dark skin became visible. Cool to the touch.

Kyle heard someone shouting. He initially thought it was Mamu, but it was him. He cried, "I am here, Father!" in a delirious chant.

He uncovered large hands, long arms, a wide torso, broad shoulders. Then a face.

Even though his father's face was slack and crusted with dirt, the resemblance to his own features was clear.

My father.

Tears tracked down Kyle's cheeks.

But his father's eyes did not open. He continued to float in the depths of Sleep.

Kyle dug away more dirt, freed his father's legs.

"Extraordinary," Mamu whispered. "He is so well preserved, as if he had slept only a day."

"Help me, Mamu!" Kyle gently hooked his hands under his father's armpits. "Lift his legs!"

Together, they removed Diallo from the grave. Kyle carefully cradled his father's head in his arms.

He felt as if he might explode from the impact of the emotion that rushed through him. He was crying, trembling.

He rested his fingers against Diallo's neck. The flesh was cool. But there came, slowly, the throb of a pulse.

"He is alive," Kyle said.

Awe widened Mamu's eyes. "I will help you transport him inside, *monsieur*."

"I will do it myself." Kyle placed his arm under his father's back, then slid his other arm in the bend at the back of Diallo's knees.

His father was enormous. He had to be at least seven feet tall, and weighed well over two hundred pounds.

Nevertheless, Kyle carried him. Weeping, Kyle carried him all by himself, toward the house.

Toward a new life.

Chapter 6

Sunday morning, David attended worship service at New Life Baptist Church, on Main Street. Nia had mentioned that his father had attended the church regularly and counted the pastor as a friend. David hoped to speak to Reverend Brown after the service, to learn more about his dad.

The church was a large, simple brick building with stained glass windows and a gleaming white cross atop the roof. Inside, dozens of polished oak pews filled the sanctuary. The pews were lined with plush, royal blue cushions that matched the carpeting. White lamps that resembled small globes hung from the ceiling, showering the chapel in golden light.

David arrived early for the eight o'clock service. At a quarter to eight, the church was nearly full. He sat near the back. A chorus of six men and women arrived at the altar and launched into a familiar song of praise. He tapped his foot in rhythm with the beat. Although New Life was smaller than the church he attended in Atlanta, a comforting atmosphere filled the place.

When he was a child, David's mother had dragged him and his sister to church every Sunday, forcing him to attend

Sunday school and participate in activities such as the youth choir. David had learned a great deal and mostly enjoyed going, but he grew to resent his mother's pushing him to attend, yanking him out of bed when he wanted to sleep in, demanding that he go to choir practice when he'd rather hang out with his friends. He vowed that as soon as he moved out of her house, he would go to church if he felt like it—and if he didn't feel like it, he wouldn't go. When he moved out to attend college, he went through a period of eight years during which he slipped into church no more than four times a year.

But two years ago, one of his high school friends died in a car accident. David suddenly decided to begin attending church again. There was nothing like a shattering realization of your own mortality to awaken a yearning for Divine guidance.

Worship service began promptly at eight. Reverend Brown made his way to the altar. He was a bear of a man, middle-aged, with glasses and a somber demeanor. He was dressed in a conservative blue suit, and the only piece of jewelry he wore was a wedding ring.

A choir of about twenty-five people led the congregation through several stirring songs. People clapped, sang, shouted, and danced. David smiled. Baptist churches were the same across the South.

After the choir finished singing, a slim woman in a yellow dress read the announcements, and then asked the visitors to stand to be welcomed. David hesitated, then rose.

"What is your name, young man?" the woman said.

"David Hunter."

A murmur rolled through the crowd. *That's Richard Hunter's boy,* many people whispered. *Looks just like his daddy.* Reverend Brown raised his head from his notes and made eye contact with David. David nodded at him, and the reverend nodded in return.

Now that he had made his presence known, he was certain that the pastor would make it a point to speak to him after the service. He sat, palms sweating in anticipation.

The reverend delivered a sermon about seeking the truth and being prepared for the answer you might receive. He spoke in a clear baritone, sprinkling his speech with precise references to Bible scriptures. "'Ask, and it shall be opened to you,'" he said. "But to this I'll add, you better know what you're asking for and *be ready* for the answer! Don't go knocking on God's door till you got your act together! Can I get an amen, friends?"

A chorus of *amens!* erupted from the congregation.

When the service concluded, exit doors along the sides of the building opened. People filed out into the steaming morning, buzzing with conversation. David had seen the pastor stride into the lobby, so that was where he headed.

On his way, many people approached him to ask if he was, indeed, the son of Richard Hunter, and he confirmed that he was. "Boy, you a spittin' image of your daddy!" was the most common response. Then they offered their condolences. David thanked them, and moved on.

He found Reverend Brown in the lobby, greeting church members with handshakes and hugs. David awaited his turn, and when he finally came face-to-face with the pastor, he was startled when the man pulled him into an embrace.

"I prayed that you'd come to the service, David," he whispered. "I have to speak to you."

"Okay," David wheezed, his chest constricted by the reverend's bear hug.

Reverend Brown relinquished his hold. He put his meaty hands on David's shoulders and sized him up, grinning.

"I know you've heard this many times, son, but you look exactly like your father did as a young man."

David smiled. "Yes, I've heard it before."

The pastor's smile faded. "I want to speak to you in my

office. It's at the end of the hallway. Please wait in there, and I'll be with you in a few minutes. I have to finish greeting the church family."

What's this all about? David wondered, walking away. At the end of the hall, a sign beside a door read "Reverend Brown."

It was a small but comfortable office, with a large oak desk, a leather chair, and two padded chairs flanking the desk. Photographs hung on the walls. The pastor had two framed degrees, one from Hampton University, the other from Alcorn State. An attractive family photo—the pastor, his wife, and two teenaged boys—stood on the desk. A window gave a view of the meadow behind the church.

Reverend Brown entered the office five minutes later. He settled into his chair and removed his glasses. He massaged the bridge of his nose.

"That was a powerful sermon you preached this morning," David said.

"Thank you," Reverend Brown said. "I also found it appropriate that you happened to be in attendance the morning I delivered that particular sermon. It proves the hand of God in our lives."

"I'm afraid I don't follow you," David said.

Reverend Brown tapped the desk with his thick index finger. "Seeking truth, son. You've come to Mason's Corner because you're seeking the truth about your father. Is that right?"

"How did you know?"

"I knew your father well. Probably better than anyone in this town. He told me that he hadn't done right by you. But when he passed on, he left you . . . everything." Reverend Brown spread his hands to emphasize his point. "Yes, he told me that he was going to bequeath his fortune to you. It was bound to make you curious and eager to learn more about Richard."

David was stunned at the pastor's insight.

"I'll interpret your silence as confirmation that I'm correct," Reverend Brown said.

David leaned forward. "What can you tell me about my dad?"

Reverend Brown steepled his hands. "There's no simple way to summarize the character of a man like Richard Hunter. He was a complex individual, driven by motivations that I think he didn't often understand himself. Just as one cannot easily reach a conclusion about what kind of man he was, likewise did Richard distrust easy, obvious answers."

"Like what? Break it down for me, if you don't mind."

The pastor rotated slowly in his chair. "Richard loved to debate theology with me. He was a Christian and had been for all of his life, but toward the end, I think he grew dissatisfied with the answers that the Bible supplies about achieving everlasting life, Divine mercy, and a place in heaven— weighty subjects of that nature. Richard began to study other religions: Buddhism, Islam, Hinduism, all of the other 'isms' you can think of. He was seeking answers to questions that had puzzled him for his entire adult life."

"I did notice a lot of books about religion in his library."

"Of course. He didn't stop with the books, either. He began to hold discussions with a young woman named Pearl. She lives on the outskirts of town, and a lot of folks believe that she's psychic. Your father was relentless in his search and would leave no stone unturned."

"Pearl." David made a mental note to follow up on her later. "Still, I don't get it. What was he obsessed about?"

The pastor tapped his lip with a pencil. "Have you read your father's work?"

"I've read all of his books. Many of them twice."

"What common theme runs through them? Consider it carefully."

David leaned back in the chair. "The plight of the black man in America?"

"Probe deeper."

"I guess he . . . he seemed kind of obsessed with death."

"Close, very close. But what, exactly, about death interested him? Think about one of his last books, *Prodigal Son*."

"Okay. The story was about a man who fakes his death."

The pastor smiled, but it was a rueful expression. "There you go."

Shock ejected David out of his chair.

"Are you serious? You think my dad faked his death?"

"I'm convinced that he did, David."

"But . . ." David couldn't finish the sentence. He collapsed into the chair. He felt dizzy.

Reverend Brown turned, reached into a mini refrigerator beside the desk, and withdrew a bottle of water. He handed it to David. David thanked him and took deep gulps of the water. His nausea faded.

Reverend Brown raised his index finger. "Please understand now, I wasn't an accomplice in Richard's plot. He shared nothing with me about his plan to disappear. I'd never go to the police or anyone else to voice my opinion, as it's just based on my knowledge of his character and recollections of our discussions. I'm only sharing this with you because you're his son, and you wanted the truth. I've given you the truth as I see it."

David shook his head. "I don't want to believe it, but I've wondered . . . you've just validated what I've suspected all along."

Reverend Brown came around the desk and put his hand on David's shoulder. "I'm sorry. But remember that when you ask a question, you have to be prepared for the answer."

"So where is he?" David said. "If he isn't dead, where did he go?"

The pastor clasped his hands, sighed. "I don't know. I tell you, I've racked my brains thinking of where Richard might've gone, what he's doing. He's traveled the world, you know, and is comfortable in a wide range of cultures. He could be anywhere."

"Why?" David said. "Why fake his death?"

"Think about it. If the world believed you were dead, you would, in a sense, get a picture of how life on earth would be if you had genuinely passed on. Consider all of the articles that have been written about Richard since his supposed death. Think of all the tributes and outpourings of love, compassion, and admiration, by friends and foes alike. I imagine that Richard is soaking up all of it, reveling in his secret knowledge, savoring his victory. He has, in effect, cheated death, from a worldly perspective."

"Too much." David dragged his hand down his sweaty face. "This is too much for me. I came all the way here from Atlanta and moved into his house, for nothing. I'm not going to learn anything about him. He's gone to who-knows-where, and that's it."

Reverend Brown returned to his chair. "I disagree. Coming to Mason's Corner was the best step you could've possibly taken. I'm convinced that, in his home, you'll find clues that will tell you what's happened to him."

"Clues?" David said. "Like what?"

"I don't know. Books, papers, correspondence, photographs, artwork—you can search through his belongings and piece together the puzzle. To a large degree, a man's thoughts can be divined from his surroundings. I don't think it'll be easy, but with the grace of God, you'll discover the complete truth."

"I'd be lying if I said that I was ready for this," David said. "But thank you for being honest with me. It means more than you can know."

"Please keep what I've told you in the strictest confidence. If you have to share my theory with a friend, don't let them know who gave you the idea. It wouldn't look good for the pastor of the largest church in town to be responsible for spreading a controversial rumor like this."

"Understood." David was wrung out, ready to go home and crash on the bed.

Reverend Brown stood, signaling that their conversation was over. He folded David into another hug.

"May God bless you, David. I'm praying for you. And your father."

Still numb with shock following his conversation with Reverend Brown, David returned to the house.

When he walked through the front door, he saw the place as though with a new set of eyes.

I'm convinced that, in his home, you'll find clues that will tell you what's happened to him.

His discussion with the pastor felt as if it had been part of a dream. A dream he wanted to forget.

In the living room, he settled onto the sofa. King trotted toward him and slapped his paws on David's lap, wanting to be petted.

"Not now, King," he said. "Go lie down."

King looked at him pitifully, then lay on the floor near David's feet.

David stared at the ceiling. The fan rotated slowly.

So my father might be alive. Might be, remember. Reverend Brown could be wrong and has no proof to support his theory. But what should I do next?

How about traveling? With the fortune his father had given him he could travel the globe searching for his dad. But where would he go? He didn't have the vaguest idea.

As the pastor had advised, the search would have to begin in this house.

A recent black-and-white photograph of his father stood on the coffee table. His father leaned against the vine covered column of a large, antebellum-style house. He wore a gray sport coat and a white shirt. His arms were folded across his chest, and his famous cigar jutted from his fingers.

David thought that his dad's confident, the-world-is-my-oyster smile held a hint of mystery.

He looked into his father's piercing eyes, as though he could communicate telepathically with him, wherever he was in the world.

Where are you, Dad? Why have you done this?

He traced his finger across the picture frame.

Maybe he shouldn't try to find his father. Maybe his father did not want to be found by anyone, including his son. His father, who had been photographed publicly for decades, would have needed to alter his appearance in order to live his new life in anonymity. What if he acted like a different man, too?

Concentrating on the photo, David felt a realization stirring. He walked through the house, gripping the picture in his hands.

He climbed the stairs to the second floor. He walked into the office and stopped beside the window.

He raised the blinds.

In the distance, Jubilee loomed, as ominous as ever.

David studied the photograph, looked out the window again.

It looked like his dad had taken the photo in front of the Mason house.

For Sunday dinner, Nia prepared a fresh salad, lasagna, garlic bread, and for dessert, peach cobbler.

Nia worried about how her mother would receive David. When she returned home after her meeting with a client in Memphis, Mama talked about how, at church, David had stood when visitors had been asked to rise. "You could see that the boy was eating up the attention, *glorifying* in it," Mama said. "Just like his father." She was determined to find fault in David, and Nia was beginning to think that her mother's dislike for David had nothing to do with David—and everything to do with a troubled relationship her mother must have had with David's father.

David arrived at three o'clock. He was casually dressed in tan slacks and a white, button-down shirt. He looked handsome.

He presented her with a bouquet of fresh tulips and lilies. "This is for the ladies of the house."

"Ooh, thank you. That's so sweet of you. Come on, I'll introduce you to my mother." She took him by the hand.

Mama sat in the recliner, a crossword puzzle on her lap. She peered over the edge of her glasses.

"Mama, I'd like you to meet David."

David stepped forward to shake her mother's hand.

"Hmph," Mama said, allowing her hand to be held briefly. "I saw you at church this morning."

"Did you? I enjoyed the service."

"Were you paying attention?"

Oh, Lord, Nia thought. *Here we go.*

"I was." David's smile had frozen.

Mama twisted her lips. "I hope so. Because I sure was. I have a few things I want to learn *the truth* about. Know what I mean?"

"Uh, sure." David's eyes shifted around the room.

Nia broke in. "Hey, dinner's ready. Let's eat."

Dinner was equally strained. David tried valiantly to engage her mother in conversation, asking about their family, sharing details about his own family and background, commenting on things he had seen and people he had met in town, and touching on current events, but Mama would not be charmed. She gave him curt responses and narrow, distrustful looks.

Nia was embarrassed. She rarely brought men home to meet her mother, but her mother had never behaved like this.

When Nia began to serve the peach cobbler for dessert, Mama got up.

"All right, being civil has worn me out," Mama said. "Nia, I'm going to take a nap. Make sure you clean up what you messed up. David, take care of yourself."

Stunned, holding the spatula in her hand, Nia watched Mama leave.

"Well," David said. "Looks like I blew it."

"I'm so sorry, David. Mama doesn't usually act like that."

"I don't get it. What did I do wrong?"

"Nothing, you were a sweetheart," she said. "I don't think the way Mama acted has anything to do with you. She hasn't told me so, but I think she's bitter about something related to your dad."

"That explains it, I guess. Doesn't help me much, though. I can't change my bloodlines."

"Don't worry, she'll get over it." Nia put down the spatula. "I need to get out of this house for a while. Want to take a walk? We can have the peach cobbler later."

Outdoors, they strolled along the sidewalk, hand-in-hand, following the same path they had taken last night. It was a warm, gorgeous summer afternoon. The earth was vibrant, bursting with life and possibilities.

They walked into the park, where they had settled on a bench the night before. They followed a hiking trail that curved through the woods. The cool shade was a welcome respite from the heat.

"I spoke to Reverend Brown this morning," David said.

"Did he tell you anything interesting about your father?"

The way David looked at her made her stop in her tracks. Then he smiled, as if to reassure her, but it was a strained expression.

"He did," David said. He seemed about to say something else, then appeared to change his mind.

"What's wrong?"

"It's nothing," he said.

He wasn't being open with her. She could tell that he was

deeply worried about something. But she wouldn't push him. She'd let him reveal his thoughts at his own pace.

"Have you ever heard of a woman in town named Pearl?" David said. "She's supposed to be psychic, from what I hear."

"Has Pearl called you?"

"Huh? No."

"Good," Nia said. "I've heard of Pearl. I've talked to her. She called *me*."

"When? Why?"

"She called me a couple of years ago," she said. "I was living in Houston at the time, but I was home for the holidays. She called me and warned me to be careful dealing with my colleagues."

This time, it was David who stopped walking. "Are you for real?"

"Oh, yeah. She was right, you know—Mr. Morgan, the stalker, proves it. My problem was that he was the last one I would've worried about."

"That's amazing. So this Pearl is the real deal, then."

"Let me put it like this: if she were to call me, I would listen to her. I think lots of people in town would agree. Some folks thinks she's a phony, but that's probably because she's never called *them*."

The trail came to a short wooden bridge that spanned a creek. They stopped near the middle of the bridge and leaned against the sturdy railing.

David peered into the brownish water below. "That's how Pearl does her thing then, by calling people?"

"Sometimes. She runs a palm reading and tarot card business out of her house, too, so people usually visit her. She doesn't come into town very often." She looked at him. "Why all these questions about Pearl?"

"I think my dad talked to her, so I wanted to know more about her. I might talk to her about him."

"This stuff about your father," Nia said. "It's really bothering you, isn't it?"

He did not respond immediately. He draped his arm across her shoulder, brought her closer, and kissed her on the lips.

She massaged his broad back with the palm of her hand. He was such a lean, firm man. She loved the feel of him. She felt safe at his side, protected against the world.

"You're right, it's bothering me, Nia," he finally said. She detected that his worries went deeper than she could possibly understand, and that there was much about his father he had not told her. She wanted him to tell her everything, if it would help to lighten his burden, but she would not pressure him. In time, he would open up to her. She had the feeling that they would get to share a lot of time together. Whether Mama liked it or not.

Pearl was afraid.

She had burst out of sleep last night, snatched out of slumber by a threat that she sensed but could not see, and she had been unable to find peace since.

She lived in a small clapboard house located on the bluffs at the edge of town, just her and three cats, and though the home was modest, a vast, grassy field lay adjacent to her property.

Late in the golden afternoon, she walked barefoot through the meadow, her short arms spread, her delicate fingers streaming through the soft weeds and wildflowers.

She was a pixie of a woman, five feet tall, and she weighed only a hundred pounds. She was twenty-four years old.

At times like this, when powerful feelings overcame her, she wished for a bigger body, to better contain all of the energy. She wished she were older and wiser, too.

Great evil stirred in Dark Corner. A malevolent force that

had been asleep for years was about to awaken. Life in the town would never be the same.

She liked to stroll through the field, because it usually relaxed her. She had been born with the gift of clairvoyance. Her mother had possessed the gift, too, as had her grandmother—indeed, the talent spanned several generations. Her elders had taught her that just as it was important to use your gift for the benefit of others, so was it important to learn how to contain your power, to keep it from overwhelming you and driving you mad. She had developed myriad ways to cope: meditation, prayer, soothing herbal teas, gardening, and long walks outdoors.

A breeze rustled the grass. Sunlight bathed her body. Closing her eyes, she stretched her arms above her and tilted her face to the sky, luxuriating in the refreshing warmth.

Suddenly, the earth began to quake.

Her eyes snapped open.

The ground beneath her shook, flowers swaying.

A vision, she thought. *It's only a vision. There are no earthquakes here.*

Nevertheless, she stepped backward.

About ten feet in front of her, a chasm exploded open. Bits of dirt and rocks flew out of the gash, as if a subterranean creature were down there, spitting out debris. Then, it fell silent.

Although dread clutched her heart, she did not run. Running would not solve anything. The haunting images would only follow her. This vision was intended to teach her something.

But what?

Slowly, she walked forward.

It was a pit, drawn in an almost perfect circle, perhaps five feet in diameter. Perfect darkness yawned in the hole, and waves of chilly air rolled out of its depths.

Strange, she thought, hugging herself against the coldness. What did this mean?

She heard movement below. Something dark and enormous

surged to the surface, with a rumbling sound that steadily grew louder.

Involuntarily, she backpedaled.

A geyser of blood erupted out of the pit. Blood sprayed into the air, like lava from a monstrous volcano.

She screamed. She dashed back toward her house.

As she ran, blood rained to the earth, coating her skin and drenching the meadow in crimson.

She slammed into the house. She grabbed a towel off the kitchen counter and frantically scrubbed her skin.

But her skin was dry. There was not a drop of blood on her.

"Dear God," she whispered. She exhaled deeply.

Warily, she pulled away the curtain above the window and looked outside.

The field was quiet, and green. No geyser of gore.

Still shaking, she shooed one of the cats off the counter and set about brewing a pot of tea, to soothe her tangled nerves.

While water heated in the teakettle, she slumped at the small dinette table. She cradled her head in her hands.

It was the most lucid and disturbing vision she'd ever received. It left little need for interpretation.

Violence and bloodshed were imminent.

Could anyone stop it? Visions such as this were warnings, and she never received warnings without eventually discovering a way to prevent harmful incidents from occurring.

She had to learn how the evil could be stopped. She could not stop it herself; she was only a guide. She needed to find the special persons who could combat this evil, and offer them direction.

She prayed that she'd find them before it was too late.

Early in the evening, David left Nia's house. But he did not go home. He drove to Jubilee.

He went to the Mason residence in the hope that he would find some evidence about what had really happened to his dad. His father had taken a photograph at the house, and that could be a clue. Or it could be coincidence. Nevertheless, if there was a connection between his dad and Jubilee—he could not imagine what it might be—David had to find out.

The Pathfinder labored up the steep, bumpy road that climbed toward the estate. Trees crowded the way, casting ink-black shadows.

Cold sweat coated David's palms. Jubilee had given him a chill from the moment he'd seen it, and the stories he'd heard only added to the mansion's fearsome aura. He could hardly believe that he was visiting this place. He was either dedicated to finding the truth—or a little crazy.

He wished that he'd brought King with him. But it was too late to go back home to get his dog.

At the crest of the hill, the lane curved to the left. The gate to the property was around the bend, on the right.

He did not park in front of the gate. He parked along the dusty shoulder of the road, under the boughs of an elm tree.

He sat there for a minute or two, drawing breaths to compose himself.

"Okay, man," he mumbled to himself. "You're here. Now get out and do it."

Climbing out of the truck was like moving through cold water.

Viewed at close range, the estate was more forbidding than ever. Tall, gnarled trees populated the immense yard, dense shadows gathered beneath their branches. A lonely dirt path led to the house. Tentacles of kudzu coiled around the mansion's thick columns. The front windows, reflecting the orange-crimson rays of the setting sun, were arranged in such a way as to resemble a face.

A silver Lexus SUV was parked beside the house.

Who in their right mind would live in this place? David thought.

He approached the gate. He wished he had brought with him the photograph of his father, but he thought he could pick the spot on the veranda where his father had posed for the picture.

Nia's tale about her terrifying childhood adventure replayed through his mind. Had his father seen ghosts, too?

He touched the gate. The iron bars were cold.

"May I help you?"

David spun at the sound of the voice behind him.

A tall, slender black man, clad in black clothes, wearing aviator shades and a black hat, stood on the side of the road. He cocked his head questioningly, long arms clasped behind his back.

David had not heard him approach. He had been so absorbed in the house that he had temporarily forgotten the outside world.

But where had the guy come from? Had the man been taking a walk? That had to be the answer.

David cleared his throat. "Do you live here?"

"I believe that I put forward the first question," the man said casually. David caught an unplaceable accent. "Do you have business at this residence?"

"I was only looking around," David said. "Is this your place?"

"You are persistent." The man smiled briefly. David got a glimpse of his perfect white teeth. "It is my home, for the time. Are you from the town?"

"I moved here a few days ago."

"I see, and doubtless, you've heard stories of haunted Jubilee. Decided that you would muster your nerve and lay your eyes upon the house? Determine whether you sensed any negative vibrations?"

"Something like that, I guess." David edged away from

the fence. There was something unusual about this guy, but he could not determine exactly what it was.

The man whisked past David and pushed open the gate. David noticed that he wore black leather gloves, too.

Weird. It was much too warm outdoors to wear gloves.

The man turned. "You impress me as an intelligent, rational young man. I'd advise you to pay no mind to superstitions and tall tales. The truth is never so . . . entertaining." His lips curved in a smile, then he whirled around and strode across the path.

In seconds, the man had vanished inside the mansion. He moved with fluid, sinuous speed, like a snake.

Now what was that all about? David thought.

It hit him what seemed so unusual about the guy. Although, from what little David had seen of his face, the guy appeared to be young, perhaps in his thirties, he had the manner of an old, wise man.

Strange. But it figured. It would take an unusual person to call this dreadful house a home.

Still, superficial explanations didn't satisfy David. Why had the man, who was clearly a foreigner, moved into the Mason place? Did it have anything to do with his dad?

David looked at the house. Jubilee seemed like a huge ancient tomb, full of secrets. Something mysterious was going on in there. David felt it just like he felt the cool breeze on his face.

He was grasping at straws, but until he learned otherwise, he would assume that everything was connected, somehow. A puzzle had been presented to him, pieces scattered randomly. He would not rest until he had put it together.

Deep in thought, he got in his truck.

Standing near the window, Kyle watched the inquisitive young man depart.

Ordinarily, Kyle would have dispatched Mamu to handle visitors. Since last night, however, Kyle had been restless—and he was feeling protective, as well. He did not dare to allow anyone to disrupt what he had begun.

He had used his ability to travel with extreme speed to appear behind the man. The man, if he had glimpsed Kyle coming across the yard at all, would have seen only a flicker of a shadow. Kyle had leapt over the fence as though it were no taller than a footstool.

Although the human claimed to be innocently looking around, Kyle detected a definite purpose to his visit. The man had almost certainly lied to him.

He wondered if the two laborers who had worked for him yesterday had begun telling others what they had seen. If so, that would be an unpleasant development. He did not relish the prospect of nosy townsfolk poking around the property, seeking a mass grave or some such thing.

Upon arriving in Mason's Corner, Kyle had assumed that he would have several weeks to locate his father, awaken him, and aid his adjustment to contemporary life. He had been mistaken: the people in town would begin to meddle. The visit by the young man was only the beginning. Mother had trained him how to identify patterns in human behavior.

He did not have much time remaining to work in relative peace. Perhaps a week. Certainly not much longer.

He walked to the basement.

White candles were arranged around the perimeter of the chamber. They cast warm, golden light.

Kyle approached the bed.

His father continued to sleep, silently. The undulation of his chest was barely perceptible.

Since they had recovered him, he had not awakened once.

Kyle and Mamu had stripped the ragged clothes off his father's body, bathed him with soft sponges, and dressed him in bedclothes of fine silk. He was like a wooden dummy in their hands, heavy and limp. His muscles appeared to have atrophied, and his ebony skin had an unhealthy, washed-out look.

Mamu had inserted an IV in a vein on the back of Diallo's hand. The IV pumped a special mixture of blood and nutrients into his bloodstream. The fluid would help to rebuild his muscles, revitalize his skin, and strengthen his heart.

Kyle lay his hand against Diallo's broad forehead. His skin was warm, an encouraging sign. When they discovered him, his flesh had been cool.

Gazing upon his father was like looking into a pool of still water. They were so obviously father and son. He slid his fingers along the firm jawbone, across the proud chin, full lips, and strong brow. It was the countenance of a warrior.

Kyle touched his own face. He traced his features, marveling at the similarities between his face and his father's.

To be able to savor this connection with his father was well worth one hundred sixty-eight years of waiting and whatever he faced hereafter.

He put his hand in his father's, squeezed slightly.

He hungered to see his father open his eyes. But there was no known method of awakening a vampire who had succumbed to the depths of a Deep Sleep. Mother claimed that she did not know how it could be done, either. The vampire alone would have to choose to Awaken.

The longest recorded Deep Sleep in history was one hundred eleven years, achieved by a vampire in Brazil. If Diallo awakened, he would have surpassed the record by almost sixty years.

It was believed that a Sleeping vampire maintained a low degree of sensory awareness, no matter how profound the slumber. Kyle was counting on the truth of the belief. He had been visiting his father each hour and speaking to him in a whisper.

Holding his father's hand, he leaned closer.

"Please hear me, my father," Kyle said. "I am your son. You are safe. Awaken. Open your eyes and look upon me."

Kyle repeated the words again and again, in a soft, fervent chant.

He suddenly noticed a change: his father's eyes, rotating back and forth underneath his leathery eyelids.

Diallo was dreaming.

Diallo dreamed of a world drenched in blood.

The sun was a blood blister. The sky was a raw membrane. The mountains on the horizon were giant hunks of bleeding flesh, the trees had been dipped in gore, and the grass did not crunch underfoot; it oozed, as though he tread across a vast carpet woven from threads of dripping skin.

He had created this place. He was at peace, at long last. All of the men who had once overrun the land had perished at his hands, and he had fashioned this world from their steaming corpses.

He walked through a gleaming red meadow, the sun warm on his dark skin. Ahead, there was a huge lake of bright, cool blood. It lapped at the sandy red banks.

He strolled to the shore, bent, and cupped blood in his large hands. He drank, deeply.

It was so sweet, so invigorating.

He was about to turn, to pluck a juicy, blood-filled fruit from a nearby tree, when he saw something shimmering on the lake's surface.

They were visions of his prior life, before he had conquered the world. The images had a clarity reminiscent of how his face had once looked when regarded in a pool of silver water.

He watched the memories, as a spectator views a sport . . .

He was a young man, the village prince, highly esteemed by his peers and family. Always, he had been bigger, taller, and stronger than others. And more cunning, too. For his natural gifts, he had been richly rewarded.

He took several wives but loved none of them, enjoying only the feel of their bodies and their subservience to his will.

He grew into a feared warrior. Rival villages fell. One of the villages, to ward off an attack and ensure peace, offered him their loveliest woman as a wife: Mariama.

Oh, Mariama.

He fell in love with her, cherished her as he had never cherished a woman before. Their souls bonded, and they became as one. She smoothed the edges of his hard heart, and calmed his desire to dominate. Unknowingly, by coaxing him to become a gentle man, she caused the erosion of his skills in battle, too.

An upstart village attacked them, and both he and Mariama were captured. They were sold to the pale men, the European slave traders.

He and Mariama were separated, savagely. As if they were only cattle.

He was shattered. He vowed that, one day, he would see her again, no matter how long it took to find her.

He survived an overseas voyage on a stinking, rat-infested ship, packed so tightly with other slaves that even another man's wastes would seep down his legs and back. As he lay in the cramped space, his body sore and filthy, his stomach aching with hunger, he made another vow: he would not live his life as anyone's slave, and they would not kill him, either. He would kill them first. It was not his destiny to serve as a slave. It was his destiny to be served by slaves.

When the ship arrived at its port, he was sold to a wealthy planter in the state of Virginia. It was a strange new world. No one knew who he was. No one knew his greatness, his prowess in battle. They did not fear him, as they should. They treated him as if he were a common mule.

He did not see Mariama at his new home.

He submitted to the harsh life of a slave, biding his time.

Many times, his rage overwhelmed him, and he lashed out against the overseers. Always, they beat him with merciless glee.

Sometimes, his fellow slaves spoke in hushed tones about escaping. Usually, when they tried, they were captured and brought back to the plantation—or they were killed. He understood that there would be a better way for him. He was a great man, with a destiny to fulfill. Running fearfully through the night was not his path.

Freedom came once he finally killed.

He saw an overseer whipping a young female slave. He seized the man and broke him over his knee, like a plank of wood.

The act demanded that he be put to death, immediately. But he was saved, by the destiny for which he'd awaited: Lisha.

The mysterious black female, feared even by the white men, arrived on the plantation, and intervened to purchase him at a high price. She took him away.

She said that she had been watching him. She offered him a life free from death, a life of timeless power. The life of a vampire.

He accepted without hesitation, recognizing that the power of which she spoke was his destiny. He became Lisha's companion.

They moved to the colorful, vibrant city of New Orleans. There, they lived in a mansion, with servants eager to fulfill their every whim. At night, they left the confines of the estate to satisfy their bloodthirst on the humans.

On one of their hunts, he found Mariama.

He had known that he would find her again. She was as beautiful as he had remembered, in spite of the hardships she'd endured since their separation.

She was a slave for a rich white man. He'd invaded the house, to feed on the inhabitants, and found her asleep. Stunned, he promised to take her away from the place, so she could live with him. Although Lisha had saved him, he would have freely left Lisha to be with Mariama again.

But Mariama barely recognized him. She thought he was a demon. As he tried to convince her that he was indeed her husband, men broke inside, bearing rifles. They fired. He avoided the gunfire. Mariama did not.

Believing that she was dead and lost to him forever, he fled, weeping, to Lisha.

She comforted him, though he wept for a woman. She understood that he loved Mariama more than he could ever love her. She did not seem to care. She only wanted his companionship.

But he wanted more.

He wanted to destroy these men who had caused such pain and torment. He wanted to destroy those who submissively accepted pain. He wanted to wipe all of them clean from the earth. He wanted to drench the world in their blood.

He did not join Lisha on the next night's hunt. He left her.

He began to build his army, to help him fulfill his mission, his true destiny.

With a horde of vampire warriors behind him, he went on a bloody rampage across the land. Plantations fell, much like the rival villages had in his days as a man. He squashed them under his heels and washed himself in their blood.

And incredibly, he found Mariama again.

She walked with a limp, from the gunshot wound, but she was no less beautiful to him. She had been placed on another plantation, and worked inside the master's house.

She recognized him with the same glimmer of fear in her eyes. She said he was not a man. He said she was correct. He was better than a man. And he was going to make her better than a woman, too.

He destroyed the plantation and took her with him. He planned to make her a vampire, once he had the opportunity to complete the secret rituals that Lisha had taught him.

But the very next day, tragedy struck.

This time, Mariama did not survive . . .

Roaring, Diallo punched the lake's shimmering red surface. The blood splashed, and the haunting memories rippled away.

He ran away from the banks, into the crimson forest. He ran and ran.

Then, the woods thinned. He ventured out of the shadows, and into a gleaming red meadow.

He looked up. The sun was a blood blister. The sky was a raw membrane. The mountains on the horizon were giant hunks of bleeding flesh, the trees had been dipped in gore, and the grass did not crunch underfoot; it oozed, as though he tread across a vast carpet woven from threads of dripping skin.

He had created this place . . .

Chapter 7

Tuesday afternoon, David visited one of his father's lesser-known properties: a log cabin located in the forested hills on the edge of the town. Earvin Williams, his dad's estate attorney, had told him about the place. "Your father used to go there when he wanted complete privacy," Earvin had said, then added with a smile, "By the way, it now belongs to you, too."

He hoped he would learn more about his father by visiting the cabin. Since Sunday's revelations, he had not discovered anything noteworthy. His father kept thousands of books, hundreds of photos, and boxes full of papers dispersed throughout the house, in no discernible order. It would take time and energy to dig through everything and piece together the puzzle of Richard Hunter's life.

He followed the directions the lawyer had given him to reach the hideaway. He drove on a quiet, tree-shaded road, away from the residential areas. Ahead, the route hit a dead end, but there was a driveway on the right, between a row of shrubs. He turned onto the winding lane, and into the forest.

King perched on the passenger seat, looking curiously at the dense woods.

"You won't ever roam out there, pal," David said, stroking the dog's neck. "You'd never find your way home."

The dog chuffed, as if he disagreed.

The cabin stood in a clearing, perhaps a quarter of a mile down the road. King, always eager to explore new places, beat him to the door.

Inside, the air was warm and stale. It was a spacious, one-room house with a high ceiling. A kitchenette occupied one side, a bedroom area, the other, and the living space was in front. The bathroom was barely larger than a closet. A desk stood along the far wall. It held a lamp, a jar of pencils, and an old typewriter.

As King sniffed his way through the cabin, David looked around, too. After fifteen minutes of searching, and finding nothing whatsoever of interest, he was ready to leave.

His cell phone chirped. It was his mother.

"How are things in Mississippi?" Mom asked. "I haven't heard from you lately, boy. You've moved there and forgotten about me."

"Hey, Mom. I've been fine, still getting settled, mainly."

Although he normally shared almost everything with his mother, he decided to keep quiet about his investigation. Mom didn't want him there to begin with, and the last thing he wanted to do was upset her with the few discoveries and theories he'd learned so far. She would only insist on him coming back to Atlanta.

Instead, he told her about Nia. He gushed about Nia, actually. He hadn't told anyone in his family about her yet, and the praises flooded out of him. Mom, of course, was glad to hear about her. David knew that she privately nursed a wish that he would settle down soon and start a family. "You'll be thirty next year," she'd begun saying lately. "I don't want to rush you into anything, but you want to have your own kids while you're young enough to enjoy them. You don't want to be a sixty-year-old man out there getting winded trying to play ball with your teenage son." Whenever David countered by telling her that meeting the right woman was hardly a simple task, she accused him of being a workaholic who didn't socialize enough. He could never win.

"Well, it's so nice to hear that you've finally met a nice young lady," Mom said, and he could hear the smile in her voice. "Treat that girl right. A good woman's hard to find."

"You know I'll treat her right, Mom. I had a good teacher in you, didn't I?"

"You sure did." Mom laughed. "I love you."

"Love you, too. Bye."

Hands on his waist, David looked around the cabin one last time. He hadn't found anything useful, but at least he could come there if he wanted some privacy. In fact, it might make a nice weekend getaway with Nia, he thought with a smile.

Outside, he found a gigantic black bird standing atop the Pathfinder's hood. It looked like a crow, though an unusually large one.

"Shoo, birdie," he said. He waved his hand.

The bird did not move. It stared at him with beady, ink-black eyes. It looked directly at him without faltering.

It was not a crow, he realized; it was much too big for that. It was a raven.

"Hey, fly away now," he said.

Behind David, King growled deep in his throat.

The raven ignored the dog. Still watching David, it ruffled its wings.

David took a step backward. Crazily, memories of that Alfred Hitchcock flick, *The Birds,* came to mind.

The bird cawed. It launched itself into the air, swooping right above David—he felt a wave of cool wind as it flapped its broad wings. The creature soared away into the blue sky.

David frowned. Weird. He'd never seen a bird behave so boldly.

King watched the raven vanish into the sky, and then looked at David.

David shrugged. "Nope, pal. I don't know what that was all about, either."

Wednesday night, David slept fitfully. He was plagued by a nightmare of his father.

In the dream, he stood over his father's grave, paying his respects. The ground began to tremble and heave, like the deck of a boat caught in a sea storm. Then the grave burst open, spewing raw earth in pungent clumps, and his father climbed out of the ragged hole. He wore a dark suit and did not appear to have decomposed at all. He looked robust and healthy. He sprang to his feet and seized David by his shirt, and said, "Death is invigorating, son. You should try it some-time . . ."

David jumped awake with a scream trapped in his throat.

"Only a dream," David muttered. He was panting. "It's over."

Silent darkness draped the master bedroom. The digital clock on the nightstand read 3:06. He had climbed in bed only three hours ago, after talking on the phone with Nia. They were going to see each other again on Friday. He had invited her to dinner at his house.

He wished she were with him tonight.

He was too shaken up to immediately go back to sleep. He swung his legs over the side of the bed, and his feet brushed across King's flank. The dog snored softly. King was a deep sleeper.

"Lot of good you are, mutt," David said. "Someone could've been choking me and you'd be snoring."

He stepped around the canine, grabbed his house robe from the hook on the door, and shuffled out of the bedroom.

He decided to surf the Web until he became too exhausted to keep his eyes open. But first, he went downstairs to the kitchen to get a drink. His mouth was as dry as if he had been chewing cotton balls.

Standing beside the counter, he gulped an entire bottle of cold water. Better.

He was walking across the hallway, back toward the staircase, when he heard a creaking sound coming from the living room, just ahead.

He thought of dismissing it as one of those ordinary settling noises that old houses tended to make. But this noise did not fade away. It continued, rhythmically.

It sounded like someone was sitting in the rocking chair.

Cool sweat beaded on the nape of his neck. The darkness in the hallway, relieved only by the dim range light in the kitchen at the end of the hall, pressed in on him like thick walls.

He sucked in a deep breath.

Although he didn't want to go near the living room, he had to look. He had to pass by the room to reach the staircase, anyway.

But most important, he had to see who was in the rocking chair.

What if it was his father?

In the blackness of night, the thought did not seem far-fetched at all.

Lifting his feet to walk required a herculean effort; it was as though he wore lead weights strapped to each foot. He trudged to the living room doorway. He looked inside.

Moonbeams coming through the window cast a pale glow across the room, and in that milky luminescence, David saw a man sitting in the rocking chair. An older man. The man wore a crisp white shirt, bow tie, suspenders, and dark slacks. Wire-rim glasses gleamed on his face, and David made out a pipe nestled between the man's lips.

It looked exactly like his grandfather, John Hunter, or "Big Daddy" as everyone called him.

But Big Daddy had been dead for twenty years.

Big Daddy rocked, rocked, and rocked in the chair. He faced David.

David felt the weight of his dead grandfather's gaze on him, like a slight pressure on his forehead.

The apparition removed the pipe from his lips and spoke, the mellow voice unmistakeably clear.

"The time is coming, son."

"What?" David broke his paralysis and stepped into the room. Fear had been replaced by intense curiosity. "What do you mean, Granddad?"

"You've got to fulfill your responsibility to the family. The Hunters' legacy."

"I . . . I don't understand," David said. "What responsibility?"

"Stay strong, son . . . stay stong . . ."

The apparition began to fade.

"Wait!" David rushed forward. "Don't go!"

Big Daddy vanished. David's hands grasped empty air.

With a cry of frustration, he collapsed into the chair. He pounded the armrest with his fist.

Big Daddy had been telling him something important, something absolutely critical, and he could not figure out what he meant. The time was coming for him to fulfill his responsibility to his family? The Hunters' legacy? None of it meant anything to him.

But it meant everything to his grandfather.

He had no doubt that he had seen a genuine ghost. A few days ago, when Nia had related her own story of spirits she'd seen at the Mason place, he had been skeptical. Not anymore.

Indeed, the rocking chair itself was cold; touching the wood sent a chill through his fingers.

David believed, fully. There was nothing like seeing a specter with your own eyes, and feeling the remnants of its presence with your own hands, to erase every figment of disbelief.

A floorboard creaked in the hallway. David's head snapped up.

King's familiar canine figure regarded him from the doorway. The dog chuffed, tentatively.

"Come here, boy," David said. The dog trotted inside and pressed against him. David stroked King's furry neck, and the dog licked his fingers. Ordinarily David hated for King to lick his hands, but he didn't rebuke the dog this time. King's presence reassured him.

David looked out the window, at the crescent moon in the deep night sky.

Something major was about to happen in his life. Only a fool would choose to ignore the obvious signs.

But what was going to happen, and what was he supposed to do about it?

He would have to discover answers. Soon. He had the feeling that his life depended on it.

Thursday, Nia was on the floor of her bedroom, working through her last set of abdominal crunches, when the telephone rang.

She squeezed out another rep, then hopped to her feet and answered the phone.

"Hello?" she said, breathing hard, trying to catch her breath.

Flat silence came from the earpiece.

"Hello?" she said again.

More silence . . . then, husky breathing. Like a man who was sexually aroused.

A blade of ice lanced Nia's spine.

The beguiling, handsome face of Colin Morgan, the teacher

who had stalked her in Houston, flashed like a red siren in her mind. She didn't know for sure whether he had called; the Caller ID display said "Unavailable." But her bone-deep intuition told her that he was the culprit.

Had he been paroled from prison already? If so, how had he gotten her phone number?

"Who is this?" she said, one final time.

The caller responded with heavy breathing.

Nia slammed down the phone. She stared at the telephone, as though willing it not to ring again.

But it rang. Again, the Caller ID display stated, "Unavailable."

She picked it up. "Hello?"

Quick, excited panting. Like a hungry wolf on the prowl.

She smashed the handset into the cradle with enough force to rock the table.

Hugging herself to ward off the numbing chill that had seeped into her body, she glared at the phone.

It did not ring again.

But her relief was short-lived. What if the caller really had been Mr. Morgan? What if he had been released from jail?

What if he was coming to get her?

"Don't get carried away," she cautioned herself.

She ordered herself to put it out of mind. The caller was surely some harmless loser with nothing better to do than randomly dial numbers and hope that a woman answered. It wasn't worth worrying about. She should relax.

But she suddenly had so much nervous energy that she worked through an extra two hundred reps of crunches.

David spent Friday at home, determined to learn more about his family.

His encounter with the ghost and the growing mystery of his father's death convinced him that vital clues lay within the house. The challenge was to sort through everything, separate the items that seemed important, and figure out how they fit into the overall puzzle.

Nevertheless, he felt that he was slowly being drawn into something that went deeper than anything he had seen so far. He had only traced the surface. Intuition told him that more awaited him.

He only had to be patient. And alert.

While he was in the living room, flipping through the magazines spread across the coffee table, the doorbell rang.

It was Franklin Bennett. David had spoken with Franklin a couple of times in passing since they'd met last week, but he hadn't gotten the opportunity to sit down and have a prolonged discussion with the man.

"You look quite busy," Franklin said. "I'm sorry to have disturbed you."

"I can chat for a few," David said. "Want to have a seat on the porch, there? I can bring you some ice water, or a soda. Which would you like?"

"Water would be fine, thank you." Franklin settled into a lawn chair.

David was glad that Franklin had visited. Perhaps the re-tired professor could share some insights that would help him figure out some things about his family.

David got tall glasses of ice water for both of them. When he came back to the veranda, he found King pressed against Franklin's legs, demanding attention. Franklin stroked the dog's back, but King was eager for more.

"Chill out, King," David said. "Let Mr. Bennett relax, will you?"

King appeared to stick out his tongue at David. Franklin chuckled.

"Sorry, the mutt has no manners," David said. He sat next to Franklin and put the water on the table between them.

"How are you adjusting to life in our fine town?" Franklin said.

"To be honest, I like it," David said. "It's a lot slower than Atlanta, but I like the change of pace. The people I've met have been nice, too."

"I'm pleased to hear that, David. Your father was private, but highly esteemed. In a town like Dark Corner your family's reputation precedes you."

"No kidding. Dad knew everyone."

"How is the Richard Hunter exploration going, if you don't mind me asking?" Franklin casually took a sip of water, but his eyes were keen.

David rubbed his hands together. "So far, I have more questions than answers. But I've just gotten started. I'm not giving up anytime soon, not until I'm satisfied."

Franklin frowned. "Can I be frank for a moment, David?"

"Sure."

"You seem to be a stable, successful young man. You've built a business on your own, you're well-spoken, and intelligent. I'm certain that your family is very proud of you. However, I sense that you aren't completely happy with the life you've built for yourself."

"I don't know, maybe," David said. He looked into the depths of his glass. "I feel kind of . . . incomplete. Like there's this emptiness in me that I have to fill."

"Because you grew up without your father?"

David nodded. "Maybe, yeah. I tried not to think about it too much when I was a kid. But you know, the older I got, I really started paying attention to some of my buddies who were close to their dads, and they had something special. Don't get me wrong, I love my mother and she raised me well, gave me just about everything I could ask for. Still . . . something was missing. That father-son connection."

"It's important," Franklin agreed. "I'm close to my son, and I was close to my father as well. Both relationships have deeply enriched my life."

"You know what I mean, then," David said. "For example, a few days before I moved here, I went to the barbershop. I was sitting in the chair, getting my hair trimmed, and in walks this guy and his son, the kid's maybe five years old. You see this all the time at the barbershop, a father and son going together. But that day, it hit me: my father had never taken me to get a haircut. My mother always took me.

"I almost broke down and cried, right there in the chair. It was a small thing . . . but I missed it. All that father-son stuff. I never had it, and I guess I never will, now. But it eats at me. I feel like half a man or something."

"Half a man? Come now, you shouldn't feel that way, David. Don't be so hard on yourself. You did the best you can given your circumstances. You've been blessed."

"I know, you're right," David said. "I tell myself the same things all the time. But it doesn't change how I feel."

Almost savagely, David tipped the glass and downed most of the water in a few gulps, the rush of iciness punishing his throat. Then he set the glass back on the table so loudly that King jumped.

"Let's change the subject," David said.

"Of course," Franklin said. "I shouldn't have pried. I apologize."

"No, it's no problem," David said. His hands were clammy. He blotted his palms on his shorts. "But I have a question for you. I'm hoping you can help me out since you have a background in history."

"Proceed."

"Okay, if I want to learn more about my family's history, what should I look for?"

Franklin's eyes brightened. "I'm pleased that you've asked. I suggest beginning with photographs. Find as many as you can, gather them together, and review them, to piece together the family story."

"Okay, pictures. Got it."

"But that is only a start. Every family has heirlooms and items that have been passed down from one generation to the next. Jewelry, artwork, antiques, journals, letters, legal documents. And books, yes, including Bibles."

"Bibles?"

"Indeed," Franklin said. "Bibles were sometimes used to record information about the family. They may include genealogical data, and in some cases, accounts of which relative married, died, did this or that and when, that sort of thing."

"Okay, you're right. I think I've heard of that before."

"Researching your family history can be enlightening, but it can also be a challenge, David. The oral tradition runs quite strong in the African-American community. The best way to learn about your family is to sit at the feet of an elder and absorb his stories. Unfortunately, you don't have that luxury."

"Yeah," David said. "There were my grandparents on my father's side, but my grandmother died before I was born, and my granddad . . . well, I saw him only twice, and the last time was over twenty years ago."

David didn't mention that he'd seen his granddad's ghost. Franklin would think he was crazy.

"And Richard did not have any siblings," Franklin said.

"He's always had a small family," David said. "I don't have a lot of resources to draw on for this stuff."

"You'll do fine," Franklin said. He patted David's hand. "Please don't hesitate to ask for my assistance, at any time. The study of history is my passion."

"I'll remember that," David said. "Thanks."

"We'll have to make good on our plans for dinner, sometime soon. My wife is concerned that you're getting by on sardines and crackers."

David laughed. "Definitely, let's do dinner soon."

"How about tomorrow evening?"

"That works for me. Can I bring a guest?"

"Ah, the beautiful young lady, Miss James." Franklin

winked. "Word travels quickly in a small town, son. Of course, she's welcome to come."

David blushed. "I've got to get used to this place."

"See you tomorrow, then," Franklin said.

As David watched Franklin return to his home, he thought about the professor's suggestions. Photographs. Jewelry. Artwork. Antiques. Journals. Letters. Books. Legal documents. Bibles.

He put his hands on his waist, looking around the living room. It was full of stuff, just like all of the rooms in the house. He had no idea where to begin his search.

Start at the top, then, he thought.

In the second-floor hallway, a square panel in the ceiling granted access to the attic.

Standing on a stepladder that he found in the garage, King lying on the carpet and watching him curiously, David slid away the panel. Dust plumed out of the opening. He coughed. The dog sneezed.

After the dust had dissipated, he climbed into the attic.

He switched on a flashlight, panned it around. Cardboard boxes were scattered across the floor. Heaps of clothes. Stacks of moldering books.

Obviously, no one had been up there in years.

But he started looking. Ten minutes later, he made his first noteworthy discovery in a sagging box packed with old science-fiction paperbacks.

A large, leather-bound Bible.

At the kitchen table, David examined the Bible. It was old, there was no doubt about that. The red leather was worn, the gold letters on the cover were faded, and the pages were stiff and yellow. He handled the book carefully, afraid it would crumble into dust.

He wasn't sure what he was looking for. A sheaf of photos stuffed between the Old and New Testaments? Notes scribbled in the margins?

He opened the book. He found an ink sketch on the inside front cover. A family tree?

Actually, it wasn't much of a tree. It was a line drawn in the center of the page; rectangular boxes were spaced at various points along the line, and names were written inside each box.

David recognized the names from the snatches of conversation that he remembered from years ago. At the top of the line, "William Hunter" was scribbled. Then "Robert Hunter," followed by "James Hunter," then "John Hunter," followed by "Richard Hunter."

The box at the bottom read, "David Hunter."

An electric current seemed to snap through David's body.

Who had written his name in this book, and when? Had his father done it?

He rubbed his chin, continuing to stare at the bloodline— that was the only thing he could think to call it.

There was only one child born in each generation, he noted. The child was always a male.

It was weird, especially considering that in the old days of the South, families tended to be large, so the children could help work in the cotton fields.

He couldn't make sense of it. He began to turn more pages.

Various passages throughout the scriptures had been underlined. He read a few verses. They meant nothing to him that he might apply to his family.

He continued to search.

It was an illustrated Bible, evidently. Interspersed between books, he found skillfully drawn black-and-white sketches. He assumed they were depictions of Biblical stories. Interesting.

Leaving the book open, he poured a glass of apple juice.

King padded up to him and dramatically lowered his snout to indicate the empty water bowl sitting on the floor. David laughed and gave the dog some fresh water.

Sipping juice, David leaned against the counter, letting his mind chew over what he'd seen.

His gaze happened upon an oil painting done by James Hunter, his great-grandfather. The piece hung on the opposite wall, beside the doorway. It colorfully portrayed black sharecroppers picking cotton, under the glare of a red sun.

David frowned. He'd never paid much attention to the painting before, but now, he stepped closer to it.

His great-granddad's distinctive looping signature was scrawled in the bottom right-hand corner of the canvas.

"Oh, shit," David said.

The glass of juice dropped out of his fingers and crashed against the floor.

King, lapping water from the bowl, yelped in alarm.

David rushed past the shattered glass, and hunched over the Bible. He flipped to an illustration. It was a sketch of a broad-shouldered black man, dressed in overalls, leaving a hovel that resembled slave quarters on a plantation. The man gripped a long knife. Behind him, a woman took refuge inside the shack.

The name "James Hunter" was scribbled in the lower right-hand corner of the drawing.

Hands trembling, David turned to another sketch.

The male character from the previous drawing stood at the head of a crew of similarly dressed men, leading a charge against a mob of people who were swathed in shadows. James Hunter had created this sketch as well.

Years of Sunday school had familiarized David with the Bible. These were not scenes from any Biblical tales that he'd ever read.

In another sketch, the same male figure, along with two other black men, and two white men, approached what looked like an Indian encampment. The men were bedraggled and empty-handed, as if seeking help.

Yet another drawing showed the broad-shouldered character leading a posse of men toward a cave that was guarded by a slavering pack of huge dogs. The seven-member team—an assortment of blacks, whites, and Indians—were armed with rifles, handguns, and bows and arrows.

If these illustrations had nothing to do with Biblical text, then what did they represent, and why had his great-grandfather created them?

The telephone rang.

Annoyed at being interrupted as he teetered on the edge of a breakthrough, David snatched the telephone handset off the wall.

"Hello?" he said.

A soft, feminine voice said in a whisper, "David Hunter . . . you are."

God help him, it sounded like another ghost.

He stood as rigid as a rod. "Who is this?"

"You are . . . *responsible*," the woman said in her unearthly voice. "You must prepare."

"Responsible for what? Prepare for what?"

"It is being revealed to you . . . you must believe . . . and be strong."

"Who are you?"

The phone clicked.

The caller had hung up.

"Dammit!" David said. He had neither Caller ID nor Star 69 included on the phone service. His father had no use for such modern technology.

Was it a call from the Beyond? Or was there a more ordinary source?

He remembered the psychic who lived on the outskirts of town, whom his father had visited: Pearl.

Nia, too, had told him a story about her experience with the psychic. The woman had phoned Nia to warn her about dating her colleagues—and not long afterward, Nia had been stalked by a fellow teacher.

It is being revealed to you . . . you must believe . . . and be strong.

A raw chill seeped into his bones.

If Pearl was the one who had called him, why had she done it? What was she talking about?

He looked at the old Bible.

You are responsible . . .

Was he living in a bad dream, or what? What the hell was going on?

He paged to another drawing.

In this one, a Goliath with blazing eyes and massive hands curved like claws loomed over the ever-present black man, and the man, whoever he was, appeared to be afraid for his life.

Although Kyle had learned patience in his long life, he wondered how much longer he could stand waiting for his father to awaken from his Sleep.

Diallo had not opened his eyes once. He had not stirred. His breathing was regular, his skin was warm, and his eye movements indicated intense dreaming, all of which were encouraging signs. But he had not awakened.

Kyle paced the mansion, roaming from one candle-lit room to another. Each day, he grew more restless.

He was eager to leave, but he had to wait until his father awakened. It was not safe to move Diallo. He was certain that his father was slowly arising from his Sleep, and to disrupt the process might plunge Diallo back into the most profound depths of his slumber. They had to wait.

Mamu relaxed in the living room, a chess game arranged on the table in front of him. His agent was characteristically calm, but he had every reason to be. Mamu's father was not the one at risk.

A faint sound reached Kyle's sensitive ears. It came from the basement.

He snapped his fingers, capturing Mamu's attention. "The cellar."

Mamu got up so abruptly he knocked over his chair. But he was not nearly as swift as Kyle. Within a human's blink of an eye, Kyle had raced across the corridor and down the basement staircase.

The sound reached him again. A low groan.

Kyle approached the bed.

Diallo's head whipped back and forth across the thick pillow. A moan grumbled from his chapped lips.

"He is awaking!" Kyle shouted. He clutched the bed railing.

Mamu watched from the opposite side of the bed. His eyes were bright. "Yes, *monsieur.* It is happening."

Diallo screamed.

His mouth contorted into a rictus of agony, saliva running from his fangs in thick strands. Veins stood out on his neck like steel cables. His strong hands, clenched in fists, ripped the bedsheets into shreds.

Hearing his father's cry almost caused Kyle to collapse to the floor. He gripped the railing, desperately, to remain standing. Mamu's eyes were enormous with fear.

Diallo's shriek lifted to an octave that made the windows tremble, and then his scream pitched into a thunderous growl that came from deep in his massive chest.

Finally, he fell silent.

And his eyes opened.

Chapter 8

"You don't look good," Nia said to David when he opened the door. "Are you okay?"

"I'm okay." He smiled weakly.

He'd made a dinner date with Nia earlier in the week, before the surreal incidents had thrown his life into a tailspin. After he discovered the Bible earlier in the afternoon, a sickening dread overcame him, and he'd spent the rest of the day napping, as if he could escape his fear by burrowing into sleep. But bad dreams followed him. There was no sanctuary, not even in slumber.

He'd considered canceling his date with Nia, but he hated to be a flake. At the sight of her, he was grateful that she had come. She was a balm for his troubles.

"Are you running a fever? Let me check." She pressed her palm against his forehead, her brow furrowed with concern.

"Really, I'm fine," he said. "I can prove it: I cooked dinner."

"I thought I smelled something burning."

"Ha, ha, very funny." He kissed her lightly on the lips. "Do you mind if we eat now? I'm starving." He had prepared a simple but tasty meal: chicken parmesan, pasta, broccoli, and Texas toast. He opened a bottle of chardonnay and filled glasses for both of them. They dug into the food with gusto.

"I'm so impressed," Nia said, slicing a piece of chicken. "I've found a man who can cook. I bet you can clean, too."

"My mama raised me well," he said. He sipped the rest of his wine, then refreshed his glass.

"Thirsty?" she said.

"I want to sleep like a log tonight."

"What's bothering you? And don't tell me it's nothing. It was obvious something was wrong the second you opened the door."

He pressed his lips together. He decided that he would tell her what was happening. He would share a few things, but maybe not everything. Keeping all of his emotions and thoughts bottled up was threatening to make him implode. Getting drunk would provide only a temporary solace.

"Let's finish dinner, first," he said. "I have to eat, and if I start telling you before I finish, I'll lose my appetite."

A short while later, they had left the kitchen for the living-room sofa. He'd brought the wine with him. Across the room, King settled near the doorway like a sentry.

Perhaps the chardonnay had lubricated David's tongue, because he told Nia everything: the theory that his father had faked his own death (leaving out the fact that Reverend Brown had told him so, as he'd promised the pastor that he would keep his identity private). The photograph his dad had taken at the Mason house. The visitation from his grandfather's ghost. The illustrated Bible. The disturbing phone call.

Nia listened silently throughout his telling, her hand resting on his thigh. Her touch comforted him. He wished he had confided in her earlier. Sometimes, he was tortured by his own self-reliance.

"You've been dealing with so much," she said, once he finished. "I knew something was wrong, but I had no idea that it was anything like that."

"What do you think?" He faced her. "Honestly."

"I believe everything you told me, first of all," she said. "We've only known each other for a little while, but I think you're a rational guy. I don't think you've been hallucinating any of this stuff."

"Thanks." He smiled. "I needed to hear that."

"About your father . . . I'm not sure how him maybe faking his death is connected to the other things that've happened. I think he could've done it. But I'm not sure what it has to do with everything else. Has to be a connection, though."

"I think so, too. I get the feeling that my dad is tied into everything, somehow, and I only have to find the link."

"And the ghost, and the Bible, and the phone call . . . well, it sounds like someone has plans for you, David."

"That's what worries me. I have some kind of responsibility to fulfill, and it's related to my family. But I can't figure out what I'm supposed to do."

"According to the caller, it's going to be revealed to you," Nia said. "I betcha Pearl was the one who called you, too. It sounds like her."

"I thought it was her. I'm going to see her tomorrow, so I can talk to her face-to-face."

"Why don't you? Sounds like a good idea."

"I'll be right back, I want to show you something." He went into the master bedroom, where he'd left the Bible. He brought it into the living room and placed it on the coffee table. "Check it out."

He pointed out the simple family tree on the inside cover, that began with William Hunter and ended with his own name. He showed her the illustrations, too.

Her eyes were thoughtful. "This is really something. And you're right—these definitely aren't scenes from Bible stories."

"But it looks like each scene is part of a story. They seem to be arranged chronologically."

"I think so, too," she said. "First, you've got this muscular man, looks like he was a slave, leaving his shack, armed with this knife. Then he's fighting some wild-looking people. After that, he and some other guys are going to an Indian camp, like they want help . . ." She flipped pages. "Here, we've got seven dudes, three blacks, two whites, and two Indians— a rainbow coalition of fighters, really—about to make a move on a cave that looks like it's guarded by some vicious dogs. Next, they're actually in the cave, with the main guy holding a torch and leading them, and there are only four men left . . . hmm, maybe something happened to the other three guys. Then, the guys are fighting these savages from before, who look like they'd been caught sleeping. Now, in this last one, the hero is about to fight this giant, and it seems like they're deep in the cave."

"There's one more at the back," David said.

Nia found it. "Okay, they *are* in a cave. The walls are crumbling down, trapping the giant inside. The hero is running away."

"Whoever he was," David said. "Unfortunately, my great-granddad didn't write name tags on these characters."

"It's like a fairy tale," she said. She tapped the book. "This giant, along with the crazy-looking folks that the men were fighting . . . they look kinda like monsters, don't you think?"

"Yeah. It's the men against the monsters."

"Right, and we both know that monsters aren't real. So maybe it's all fiction."

"A tall tale," he said. He sighed. "Maybe you're right."

"Make-believe, sweetie." She closed the Bible. She smiled. "Don't worry yourself about this. Focus on the other things—which I'm going to help you figure out, by the way."

"Thanks for giving me some perspective," he said. "I'll stop worrying about it."

Still . . . why did he have the nagging feeling that he *should* be worried?

* * *

As Kyle stared at his father's eyes, he gasped.

Diallo had the deepest, blackest irises he had ever seen in a vampire. Like bottomless pits.

Mamu, too, emitted a sound of surprise. He clutched the bed rail.

Diallo slowly blinked. His face crinkled into a grimace of confusion.

"You are safe, Diallo," Kyle said. He wanted to touch his father, to reassure him, but instinct warned him to keep his distance.

"Safe, *monsieur,*" Mamu said.

Before Kyle could stop him, Mamu reached forward and rested his hand on Diallo's arm.

What happened next was the most incredible act of savagery Kyle had ever witnessed.

Moving with startling speed, Diallo sprang upright, simultaneously seizing Mamu's arm. With a wrenching jerk, he ripped Mamu's arm out of its socket as easily as a hungry man tearing a drumstick out of a roasted chicken.

Warm blood spattered Kyle's face. He cried out and stumbled backward.

Mamu collapsed against the floor. He murmured a silent mantra of agony, blood gushing from the ragged stump of his arm.

Diallo tossed aside the man's bloody limb. He leapt out of the bed, the IV tube attached to his hand tearing out of his flesh. The IV rack clattered to the floor.

Without slowing, Diallo pounced on Mamu.

He was so fast. Faster than Kyle had ever moved. His father's movement was a blur to even Kyle's vampire vision.

Kyle retreated to the far wall. Fear tightened like a garrote around his throat.

He had never foreseen that his father's awakening would happen like this.

Knelt over Mamu, Diallo had fastened his mouth against the man's neck. He sucked the blood greedily, moaning in animalistic pleasure.

Revulsion roiled through Kyle, quickly replaced by sorrow. Mamu was lost to him. He had been an honorable man, an excellent agent, a true friend. Kyle regretted that Mamu had been the unfortunate victim of his father's raging hunger.

But death was eventually inevitable for a man. His father was greater than a man, his life worth far more to Kyle than a dozen Mamus.

Satiated on the human's blood, Diallo whirled around. He immediately spotted Kyle.

"You do not wish to attack me," Kyle said, shakily.

Blood dripped down Diallo's chin, covered the front of his silken bedclothes. His onyx-black eyes blazed.

He appeared to be every bit of the murderous monster that Mother said he was.

But he is not a monster, Kyle thought. *I will not believe it.*

Diallo roared. He charged across the room.

Kyle moved, narrowly avoiding getting crushed in Diallo's arms. He darted to the other side of the basement with all the speed he could manage.

"You do not move like a man," Diallo said. His voice was deep yet ragged from disuse. He drew up to his full height, his head only inches beneath the ceiling. He coughed. The spasm rocked his body.

Kyle had to get his father in the bed again. In spite of Diallo's explosive burst of violence, he was weak and vulnerable. He had not fully recovered from his hibernation.

But he didn't dare to approach Diallo yet.

"You do not move like a man," Diallo said again, as if considering the thought. "Are you a vampire?"

"I am your son!" Kyle cried.

Diallo blinked. He appeared to be confused.

"I do not have a son."

"Lisha is my mother," Kyle said. "You must remember her."

"Lisha!" Emotion contorted Diallo's face. Closing his eyes and shaking his head, he dropped to his knees.

Slowly, Kyle walked closer to him.

"She was pregnant with me when you last saw her," he said. "You never knew. She didn't tell you."

Diallo raised his face. Tears streamed down his cheeks.

"Lisha . . . you," Diallo said, weakly. "I feel Lisha . . . in you."

Kyle could not hold back his emotion any longer.

He embraced his father, and wept.

Diallo held him close for a long time.

Kyle wanted his father to return to bed, but Diallo refused.

"I must walk and use my legs again," Diallo said. He draped his arm across Kyle's shoulders. They shuffled in a circle around the candle-lit basement. Kyle held his father around the waist to keep him balanced.

"Speak to me, my son. We are in a strange place. How long have I been asleep?"

Kyle hesitated. Then he answered: "One hundred sixty-eight years."

"No!" Diallo said. "So long. But I had feared that I would sleep for an eternity."

"What do you remember of your life?"

Diallo sighed heavily. "I remember all of it. As I slept, I relived my life in dreams. Are we in Mississippi?"

"Yes, we are close to the cave in which you were sleeping."

"I have lost so many years, so much living." Diallo stifled a sob.

Sorrow clutched Kyle's heart. He could not fathom the

disorientation that his father experienced. It had been said that for a vampire to recover emotionally and mentally from prolonged Sleep was more difficult than the physical rehabilitation process.

"Tell me everything that has happened," Diallo said. "Spare nothing."

"To explain everything that has occurred in the world would require weeks, Father. I will give you the highlights."

Kyle described how he and his mother, Lisha, left America when Civil War broke out, to seek refuge in the African country of Liberia, a haven for many blacks who fled America. They spent decades in Liberia and other African nations, and eventually immigrated to Paris, where Lisha lived to this day.

Diallo began to weep again.

"Lisha must despise me for what I have done," he said. "She did not come with you."

Kyle did not know what to say. He could not repeat his mother's cautions about awakening his father.

"I owe Lisha my life," Diallo said. "She saved me from a life of slavery. She taught me so much. She made me a vampire."

"Mother loved you," Kyle said.

Diallo's body trembled. Gently pushing Kyle away, Diallo stood on his own. His liquid-black eyes captured Kyle's gaze.

"But Lisha never understood," Diallo said. "I am a warrior."

"Father, the slave trade ended over a century ago. You could not imagine the weapons that humans possess in this age! The power that they wield."

Diallo laughed. "Power? When I am well, I will teach you power."

"Father . . ." Kyle was again unable to speak. How could he explain that there was nothing to fight for? That the injustices for which his father believed he was fighting had been remedied? And that, most of all, as vampires, the business of humans was none of their concern?

Diallo was trapped in his mortal memories. Persuading him to relinquish his old passions would be perhaps Kyle's most daunting challenge.

Diallo wobbled and slumped against Kyle. He breathed heavily.

"Help me lie down," Diallo said. "I must rest, then feed again."

Kyle helped Diallo onto the bed. His father reclined against the pillows.

A small cooler sitting nearby held several packets of blood. Kyle retrieved one and pierced the top. He handed it to his father.

"Drink this, Father. It will nourish you."

"What is it?" Diallo frowned.

"Blood," Kyle said. "Human blood. In this age, we live on blood that has been packaged like this."

Diallo looked doubtful. Kyle demonstrated how to squeeze the packet and draw the fluid between the lips.

Diallo frowned, tried to mimic him.

He vomited explosively.

"I cannot feed on this!" Diallo flung the packet across the room. "The blood tastes foul."

"But you must adapt to it," Kyle said. "It is a safe way for us to nourish ourselves. We cannot hunt and kill prey, Father."

Diallo dropped against the pillows. Sweat had broken out on his face.

Kyle again attempted to feed him the packaged blood. Diallo gagged.

"I need live prey," Diallo said. "Bring me a human."

"You don't understand what you're asking me!"

"I need a live human." Diallo coughed. "Or I fear I will die."

Kyle paced. His father demanded the impossible. He had

not hunted a human in decades, and found the idea inimical—offensive, even—to his nature. He was not a predator. He counted humans as his friends and confidants. How could he prey on them? Mamu had been like a brother to him.

His gaze flicked over Mamu's corpse.

Father needed to feed on him. Now, he needs another. Mamu's death caused me sorrow, but I shall go on, for it was for a great purpose, my father's survival. What would it hurt me to kill a stranger to keep him alive?

The coldness of Kyle's thoughts frightened him. He considered himself a civilized vampire, a lover of culture and art, with refined tastes and habits. Yet he was thinking of regressing into the kind of vampire that he despised: the ruthless predator.

He went to Diallo. Hunger twisted his father's face. A face so much like his own.

Diallo's hand found his, squeezed tightly.

"Hunt for me, my son," Diallo whispered. "Save me."

He had waited almost one hundred seventy years to find his father. Was a human's life worth that much? A human would never live to such an advanced age.

He could not deny his father.

He would not.

He would do anything to keep Diallo alive.

Kyle covered his father's hand with his own.

"I'll return soon," he said.

Kyle drove the Lexus sport utility into town.

Briefly when he had climbed in the vehicle, he'd thought about Mamu and how he typically drove Kyle everywhere that he needed to travel. Then he cleared memories of his friend out of his thoughts. He could not afford to think of any humans in kind, familiar terms, not while he was engaged on this mission. Nothing could distract him from his purpose.

He was a good but cautious driver. Mother had warned him about the pitfalls of automobiles. *Humans are reckless,* she had taught. *It is far too easy for you to be ensnared in a collision; think of the furor you would cause if the humans witnessed you walking away from a head-on wreck, unscathed. Or what if you were to lose consciousness and they took you to one of their hospitals and discovered your unusual blood . . .* Kyle could not quiet her somber voice of wise advice.

As he motored down the steep road, the town unfolded before him, lights twinkling. It was fifteen minutes past eleven.

He hoped that most of the residents had taken to bed. He could not risk being seen.

He turned onto a residential street. Porch lights glimmered on many of the ranch-style homes.

He remembered the last time he had hunted. He had been one hundred and twenty-seven years old, living in Paris. He and his mother had gone to the theater one evening, and after the performance, they followed a young couple along the city streets. Mother led the hunt. She swept toward the couple and forced them into a dark alley with the power of an unstoppable gale. She fell upon the man; Kyle took the woman. He would always remember the terror that had shone in the woman's eyes as his hands grasped her shoulders in an iron grip . . . the sigh of pleasure that escaped her when he sank his fangs into her warm, tender neck . . . and the cloying scent of her perfume mingled with the coppery odor of fresh blood.

A delicious shiver coursed along his spine and rattled through his arms, making his hands tremble on the steering wheel. But nausea followed soon after. The thought of touching his lips to germ-ridden human flesh seemed so repulsive, so primitive.

But he could never forget the rapture of sucking blood directly from an artery and into his mouth.

He reached an intersection. He turned onto a road that appeared to be darker, with fewer homes.

He parked in front of an unlit house. A nearby elm tree concealed the Lexus in additional covers of darkness.

Still, the luxury sport utility was glaringly conspicuous in the humble town. He regretted that he had allowed Mamu to acquire the vehicle. However, he reminded himself that hunting amongst the townspeople had never been part of his original intent.

He climbed out of the truck. The thump of the closing door echoed down the desolate street.

He drew his leather gloves more tightly across his hands. Perspiration coated his palms.

He had never hunted alone. Mother had always accompanied him.

But her teachings returned to him: *You are a prince of the night. Use darkness to your advantage, revel and cloak yourself in it. At night, the world belongs to us.*

A breeze swirled around him, carrying the scent of flowers and the singing of crickets and other creatures.

The world belongs to us . . .

His eyes slid shut.

Like a man submerging a net in a river in search of a fish, Kyle cast his mind into the atmosphere. He sought the warm pulse of a human life. Someone young, but not a child. An adolescent, yes, with ripe blood that would nourish his father.

Within seconds, he had found one.

His prey was a few blocks away. Not too far to travel by foot. A distance he could cover rapidly.

He stretched forward, and to a human eye, he would have appeared to vanish, like a flickering shadow. But he was moving, not relying on sight for direction, but trusting solely in the psychic signal that throbbed in his mind.

He arrived in the backyard of a small house. A wooden fence encircled the yard.

Crumbling concrete steps led to a white door. He tried to open the door. Locked.

He waved his hand across the lock, and it disengaged with a soft click.

In addition to tremendous strength and speed, each vampire possessed special gifts. He had the power of telekinesis: the talent to move physical objects by employing psychic force. He could lift an object that weighed several hundred pounds without exerting any physical effort. The ability came in handy. No door was ever closed to him.

He waited outside the doorway. Silence. No one shouted in alarm or came running. But he sensed a human in the room beyond the door, the individual he desired.

He paused.

Once he went inside the house, he could not turn back. His carefully cultivated image of himself as a sensitive, sophisticated creature would be ruined. He would become a predator.

Hunt for me, my son. Save me.

He had waited a lifetime for an opportunity to see his father. How could he turn away from doing what was needed to ensure his father's survival? If he had to become a predator . . . so be it.

Quietly, he pushed through the door.

He was in a cramped, brightly lit kitchen. Chipped paint on the walls. Pieces of tile missing from the floor. A wobbly set of chairs surrounded a wooden table heaped with papers and cups.

A young black woman was at the counter, her back turned to him. She poured a bright red fluid from a pitcher into a glass.

For an absurd moment, Kyle thought he had wandered into the household of a vampire who was about to feed.

But it wasn't blood, of course. It was some sort of punch drink.

Beyond the doorway, Kyle heard children chattering excitedly.

He only wanted the girl.

She turned with the container in her hand, to return it to the refrigerator, and that was when she saw him. Her mouth spread into a startled "O." The pitcher fell out of her fingers and crashed against the floor, punch spreading like a bloodstain across the tile.

He struck her temple with the edge of his hand, knocking her unconscious. He caught her in his arms.

She was so vibrantly alive. Her head lolled to the side, exposing her smooth neck. Without touching her flesh, he felt her pulse throbbing; it was like a drumbeat echoing in his mind.

He covered her with his jacket. She was not for him. She was for his father.

He carried her out of the house and into the night.

Jahlil and the fellas cruised through town.

T-Bone drove, Poke rode shotgun, and Jahlil was sprawled in the backseat. Hip-hop banged from the speakers, loud enough to give an old man a heart attack.

The past week, no longer burdened by a stupid job, Jahlil spent his days and nights hanging with the crew. He usually rolled out of the bed at noon, played video games for a few hours, and then T-Bone would pick him up and they'd hit the basketball courts, or even better, the car wash, where they talked to all the females who came through. Come nightfall, they'd begin cruising the streets, stopping whenever they saw people they knew, or just driving and bumping music.

Dad hadn't said anything to him about getting a job—yet. Jahlil could tell his old man had another plan brewing. School—another pain in the ass—started next week, too. He was going to enjoy his freedom while it lasted.

They were driving aimlessly down a dark street, nodding to the slamming beat, when Jahlil caught a swift movement on the periphery of his vision. Like a large, passing shadow.

He looked through the rear windshield.

A tall man dressed in black was putting a large, covered package in the rear cargo area of a sport utility vehicle. Except the package had a pair of dangling legs.

"Stop the car!" Jahlil said. He lunged forward and grabbed a fistful of T-Bone's jersey. "Man, someone's putting a dead body in that truck!"

"What?" T-Bone lowered the volume of the music. "What the hell you talking 'bout?"

"The Lexus we just passed, man." Jahlil had both knees on the seat cushions and stared out the window. The man had put the body—Jahlil was sure it was a body—inside the truck and strolled to the driver's side door. "A dude was putting a body in the trunk!"

"You high as hell and hallucinatin' shit," Poke said. "You ain't seen nothing."

The taillights of the Lexus flared. The vehicle moved forward, away from them.

"He's getting away!" Jahlil said. "I'm not lying and I'm not seeing things. I saw him put something in the trunk that had legs like a person."

"Like a female's legs?" T-Bone said. "All nice and smooth?"

"Yeah, I think so," Jahlil said, amazed that T-Bone had seen it, too.

"Did she have long, silky hair?" T-Bone said. "Make you wanna run your fingers through it?"

"I don't know. I didn't see her hair."

"Did she have a face like Halle Berry?" T-Bone said.

Jahlil frowned. "Fellas, I'm serious."

T-Bone and Poke broke into wild laughter.

"That's the weed working on you, J," Poke said. "Chill out and enjoy the ride, man."

"Whatever," Jahlil said. The Lexus had rolled out of

sight. He began to wonder if his boys were right. Maybe he
hadn't seen a man putting a body in the trunk. Maybe he had
been hallucinating. He was, after all, as high as a space satel-
lite.

But if it was only an illusion, why was he so afraid?

Kyle presented the unconscious young woman to his father, like a gift.

Diallo sat up in the bed. He smiled. "Ah, my son. I am
proud of you. You have saved me. As I lay here, I had felt my
life slipping away."

"I will never let you go hungry." Kyle placed the woman
on his father's lap. "Hurry, before she wakes."

Diallo savagely twisted the woman's head, lifted her neck
to his mouth, and plunged his fangs into her jugular vein.
Blood spurted. The woman sighed, a sensual sound. The
coppery odor of fresh blood permeated the air.

A pleasant chill passed through Kyle as he watched his
father feed. He marveled that he could enjoy watching a
vampire feast on a human. The mere thought used to revolt
him.

Something was happening to him, he realized. A profound change was occurring deep in his psyche, like tectonic
plates shifting under the earth's surface.

He was certain that finding his father, finally, had trig-
gered the transformation. He was metamorphosing into a
mature vampire. More daring. More confident.

More in touch with his natural desires.

As he watched his father suck the human's blood, he
licked his lips.

Suddenly, he was hungry. Famished. Although he had fed
only a couple of hours ago on a packet of blood.

Perhaps his father would share the woman with him.

But Diallo did not offer. He drained the human's body,
then carelessly flung the corpse off the bed.

Kyle's hunger vanished. He wasn't genuinely hungry. What was wrong with him?

He had to maintain control of himself. Hunting prey for his father was essential, but only until his father had adapted to packaged blood. He could not join his father in feeding on live prey. If he did, they would regress into predatory savages. The idea was madness.

But only yesterday, I had thought that murdering a human was madness, too, hadn't I?

"You are in turmoil, my son," Diallo said. He rested his hand on Kyle's shoulder. "Sit with me."

Kyle sat on the edge of the bed.

"What troubles you?" Diallo said.

"Mother has taught me a different way of life for a vampire," Kyle said. "A way that she feels is more civilized."

Diallo smiled. "Lisha is wise. But she is a female. You are a male. And I am your father. Only I can show you how a powerful male vampire ought to conduct himself."

His father's eyes were dark, absorbing.

"I needed you to save me," Diallo said. "You need me to guide you. We need each other, my son."

"Yes, Father," Kyle said. Intense emotion swelled his lungs, making it hard to breathe.

He had never experienced such a heartfelt connection with anyone, vampire or human.

"We need a daylight watcher," Diallo said. "I understand that the man you had befriended served in such a capacity. But he is no more. I will show you a watcher that is better than a man."

"What do you mean?"

"Help me walk. Let us go outdoors."

Kyle assisted his father in getting off the bed. Across the basement, a short flight of steps ended at a solid set of storm doors. The doors were unlocked; Kyle had brought the woman into the cellar through this doorway.

They ascended the stairs and walked into the night.

It was cool and quiet. The sky was clear, sprinkled with stars and a pale half moon.

Diallo drew in a deep, deep breath. He laughed, like a giddy child.

"The night!" Diallo said. "I have missed the freedom of darkness. At night, all things are possible for us. Always remember that truth."

"All things?" Kyle said.

Instead of answering, Diallo dropped to his knees in the grass.

Alarmed, Kyle went to him, but Diallo waved him away.

His father ripped away the sleeves of his silk shirt, exposing his muscular arms. He spread his arms to their full length. He closed his eyes and raised his face heavenward. Moonlight seemed to shimmer around his head, like a halo.

What is he doing? Kyle wondered. His father's behavior did not follow anything Mother had taught him. What was this talk of finding a watcher that was better than a man?

Tension thickened the air as his father meditated, his body like an onyx statue.

The silence endured for several minutes . . . and then Kyle heard, faintly, the gallop of approaching animals.

It sounded like dogs.

David and Nia were in the living room when the dog went berserk.

They had temporarily given up discussing the Bible, the ghost, and the other strange things that David had experienced lately. They just didn't have any solutions. Tomorrow, David would visit the psychic woman, Pearl, to get some answers.

They were watching a sappy romantic comedy movie that Nia had insisted he would like, when King went nuts. The dog had been lying on the floor, viewing the television as if engaged in the story. Abruptly, King jumped up and began to bark.

"What's wrong, boy?" David said. "What're you barking at?"

King ran out of the living room. He continued to bark.

Confused, David looked at Nia.

"He could be hungry," she said. "Or want to go outside."

"He doesn't normally act like that."

He found the dog in the hallway. King stood on his hind legs, scratching the front door, barking.

David looked outside the window. There was no one in sight.

King quit barking, and whined.

"What is it, boy?" David said.

The dog looked at him with yearning, as though frustrated by their inability to communicate directly.

"What's wrong?" David said.

King ran to a window. He scratched the glass. He whined.

"Do you want to go outside?" David said. "Wanna go outside?"

Whenever David made the suggestion in the past, if King wanted to take him up on it he wagged his tail. King's tail did not wag this time.

David grasped the doorknob. King growled.

The dog only growled at him when they were play-fighting, and there was nothing playful about what was happening now.

Cold anxiety touched David's spine. He was not afraid of his dog. He was afraid of what his dog evidently sensed, a threat that he could not see on his own.

He went to a window and looked outdoors once more. He saw only the night—silent, deep.

Stories that his father had faked his death. Ghostly visitations. Anonymous phone calls. Mysterious family Bibles. So much bizarre stuff. Add a freaked-out German shepherd to the list.

"Is everything okay in there?" Nia said.

"Why don't you answer her?" David said to King. "You seem to be the one here with the sixth sense."

King trotted past David and into the living room. The dog settled on the carpet beside the coffee table. He was his ordinary, lazy self again.

"One of these days," David said, "you're going to learn how to talk, or write, or something, and you're going to tell me what that show was all about, Mr. King."

King yawned.

Puzzled, but deciding to leave it alone, David returned to the living room.

Kyle watched his father as the approach of the dogs grew louder.

Diallo remained kneeling, arms spread, eyes closed, face tilted skyward. Like a worshipper of the moon.

A pack of a half-dozen dogs swept around the corner of the mansion. They looked like mutts that had been left to fend on their own and find their meals in garbage cans and handouts. None of the animals wore a collar. All of them were full-grown, and none of them weighed less than thirty pounds.

The hounds passed Kyle as though he did not exist. They gathered around Diallo.

Oddly, though the dogs were excited and panting, they did not bark. They were quiet, expectant.

Kyle had never witnessed a vampire using a canine for any purposes whatsoever, other than ordinary security. His father, he believed, was going to do something with these beasts that Kyle had never seen before.

Diallo uttered a soft cry. With his nails, which had grown into sharp claws, he slit a gash in each of his wrists. Thick blood streamed across his skin.

Kyle winced.

Diallo offered his bleeding wrists to the dogs.

The dogs padded closer to him. They lapped the blood, three of the hounds on each of his arms.

Comprehension came to Kyle. Diallo was going to make these hounds his servants.

He viewed the rest of the spectacle with amazement.

Almost as one, after the canines fed on Diallo's blood, they dropped to the grass. They squirmed and squealed. Saliva bubbled from their lips.

Diallo motioned for Kyle to come forward. He grabbed Kyle's hand and got to his feet.

Diallo's self-inflicted wounds had closed.

"I have always used dogs as watchers," Diallo said. "They are a man's best friend. Why not a vampire's?" He laughed.

The dogs wailed in pain.

"Their pain will pass soon," Diallo said. "They are experiencing the death of their mortal bodies."

As Kyle watched, the hounds ceased their cries and seizures. They began to recover.

"These hounds will remain active both day and night," Diallo said. "They will possess extraordinary intelligence. They are obedient to my will. They are peerless guardians and hunters."

"I never knew dogs could be used like this," Kyle said.

"Lisha knows," Diallo said. "She taught me."

Kyle felt betrayed by Mother. She claimed to have taught him all of a vampire's abilities. What else had she kept secret from him?

"When the dogs bite another canine, or a human," Diallo continued, "the bitten one will fall under my influence and will serve as either a servant hound if a canine, or a valduwe if he is a human."

"A valduwe?" Kyle said. He had not heard the word in many years.

"Valduwe have the hunger for blood, but do not possess

all of our talents. They are excellent warriors." Diallo's lips twisted into an enigmatic smile.

"Mother teaches that the valduwe are an abomination," Kyle said. "She forbids their creation."

"When will you put away childish things?" Diallo said. "And claim your birthright as a vampire?"

Kyle did not know how to respond. Diallo smiled. He snapped his fingers.

The dogs arranged themselves in a tight line, like trained soldiers.

Diallo placed his hand on Kyle's shoulder.

"This is my son, Kyle," he said. "Look upon him."

The canines' attention shifted to Kyle. Unlike normal dogs, they did not turn away when he met their gaze. They stared at him, without fear. Unnatural awareness gleamed in their eyes.

"You will obey Kyle as you obey me," Diallo said. "He sits on my right hand. You are my warriors."

Father speaks as though he is preparing for battle, Kyle thought.

In unison, the dogs howled.

Part Two

DARKNESS GATHERS

*I pointed out to you the stars, and all you saw was
the tip of my finger.*
—Tanzanian proverb

If the tiger sits, do not think it is out of respect.
—Nilotic proverb

Chapter 9

Chief Van Jackson got the call Saturday morning: someone had turned up missing.

Tawanda Gary, nineteen years old, had vanished from the home at which she was baby-sitting last night. The woman of the house had come home from work late last night and discovered that her two children were alone, and when her worthless, pothead man came in at dawn, he was clueless, too. A call to Tawanda's grandmother, whom she lived with, didn't turn up any leads, either. Her grandmother hadn't seen Tawanda since she had left to baby-sit.

Tawanda's vehicle, an old Ford Escort, remained parked under the carport of the house at which she'd been working.

Kidnapping and abduction were extremely rare crimes in Dark Corner. Jackson had handled an abduction case only once, and that had been over ten years ago. Murder was equally rare. The only murder in recent memory was when a man had killed his wife in the midst of a domestic dispute, and the murderer had actually called Jackson, personally, to give himself up.

Intuition warned Jackson that this case wasn't going to be

so easy. He began the investigation the best way he knew how: by talking to folks.

Saturday morning, Jackson spent a while talking to the family who'd hired Tawanda to baby-sit. The woman was forthright and trustworthy, a hardworking lady who held down two jobs to make ends meet. He knew her folks, too. They were good people.

But he wasn't impressed by her live-in man, Andre.

In his early thirties, Andre was a known drug user and had never worked a stable job in his life. He hung out at the basketball courts and the car wash with his buddies, smoking weed and drinking beer. If laziness were a felony, Andre would have been serving a double life sentence.

Every time Jackson saw the man, he thought of Jahlil, and what could happen to his boy if he didn't get his life on track. If Jahlil's attitude did not change, Jahlil was Andre in a few years.

Jackson hated the pathetic example that Andre set for the younger boys in town. But his main problem with Andre on this day was that he was sure the guy was hiding something related to the girl's disappearance.

"Come outside with me for a minute, will you?" Jackson said to Andre while they were in the small living room. "Want to chat with you."

"I'm really tired." Andre yawned dramatically. "I was out all night."

"Ain't gonna take but a minute," Jackson said.

Reluctantly, Andre followed him outdoors. Jackson leaned against the patrol car. Andre watched him, his hands buried in the pockets of his baggy jeans, restlessly jingling coins.

Andre didn't look tired. He looked scared.

"First off," Jackson said. "I don't care about your reputation for smoking weed. We ain't here to talk about that."

"But I don't smoke—"

"Don't start lying to me, all right?" Jackson said. "Don't wanna hear it. It ain't the issue."

Andre drew in a shaky breath. "I don't know what happened to Tawanda, Chief. I really don't."

Jackson removed his hat and began to straighten the brim. "I'm the kind of man, I listen to my intuition. You know what it tells me? Tells me that you're telling the truth—part of it."

"I ain't lying, Chief!" Andre said. "I rolled out as soon as she got here to watch the boys, and when I got back to the crib my woman was already here and said Tawanda was gone. I don't know nothing."

Jackson finished flattening the edge of the hat. He set it back on his head. "What're you scared of, Andre? You're shaking like a leaf."

Andre lowered his head. "I ain't scared."

"You got fear stamped all over you, buddy."

Andre dragged his hand down his face. "Look, I can't talk about it."

"Can't talk about what? You can't hide information that could help solve a crime. That's obstruction of justice, buddy. You serve time for that."

Andre raised his head. His eyes were wet-looking, as though he were about to cry.

"You need to check out the crib up there," Andre said. He quickly motioned toward the horizon, then dropped his arm as if he'd gotten an electric shock. "Any wicked shit going down here, you better look there first."

Jackson had followed the man's finger. The only house "up there" was the Mason place.

A coldness wrapped around Jackson, like a mantle of ice.

"All right now," Jackson said. "You got to explain what you mean. What's Jubilee got to do with the girl?"

"Hell, naw," Andre said. "I done already told you too much. I ain't getting any deeper into this shit."

Andre fled inside the house. He slammed the door in Jackson's face.

Jackson knocked. "Open up, buddy. We ain't done chattin'."

No one answered.

Jackson knocked again, then rang the doorbell, and still they ignored him. It surprised him. He had never faced resistance like this from folks in his own town.

But one thing was clear: Andre was scared out of his mind.

He briefly considered using some official force to make Andre speak to him, but he decided against the idea. The guy was flat-out too scared to talk, and he had directed Jackson toward a source that might bear fruit. Jackson didn't like to push folks too hard. It wasn't his style—a good thing, really, because in a small town like this, he'd never needed to be that tough to get the job done.

He only hoped that this case would not push him over the edge.

Sighing, he walked back to the cruiser. He glanced at the Mason house, sitting way up there on the hill.

All week, he had procrastinated visiting the house's mysterious new resident: the bald-headed, sharply dressed black man he had seen driving around town in the Lexus SUV. He told himself that he was too busy fighting crime to squander energy on small-town pleasantries. But if he were being honest with himself, he had to admit that the house made him uneasy. Like most residents his age who had lived in Dark Corner their entire lives, he had grown up hearing frightening tales about Edward Mason's mansion. It was not easy to dislodge images, stories, and rhymes that had been planted in your head when you were a kid.

He got inside the car.

Snippets of childhood rhymes about the house came to mind:

Fast Eddie's always ready, gonna tear out your heart like it's confetti . . .

One, two, buckle your shoe, or something in the Mason place'll come get you . . .

Jackson grasped the steering wheel in an iron grip.

I don't want to go up there, he thought. *Lord help me, I don't want to set foot near that place.*

As he drove away, it seemed that a gravitational force prevented him from driving toward Jubilee. He drove, instead, to pick up some doughnuts and coffee. Feeling like a coward every block of the way.

Malcolm, the mutt that Franklin had taken a liking to in the past year, did not show up for his morning meal. Like one of Pavlov's hounds, the canine usually came running to the house within minutes of Franklin filling the bowl with Purina dog food at nine o'clock.

Franklin whistled. "Malcolm! It's time to eat, my friend!"

The dog always entered the yard from the alley, squeezing between the garage and the Dumpster. But the dog did not appear.

Franklin frowned. He waited outdoors a few more minutes, and when Malcolm did not appear, he went inside.

Ruby sat at the kitchen table, sipping coffee and reading the newspaper. He settled into a chair beside her.

"My dog is gone," he said.

"He'll probably turn up in a little bit," Ruby said. "Don't worry, honey. Malcolm isn't wearing a watch, you know."

"Of course," he said, not sure he agreed at all with his wife's opinion. He had a feeling that something terrible had happened to the dog. Perhaps it had been struck by a vehicle, or injured in a fight with another animal, or had eaten something that made it ill . . .

Or perhaps something worse.

He did not understand the cold finger of dread that traced along his back. It resisted rational explanation. It was a presentiment of doom, like smelling the sour odor of an imminent thunderstorm.

Malcolm's disappearance was a bad sign of . . . something. But what?

* * *

Jahlil's father required that he go to the police station at nine o'clock on Saturday morning, to clean. Jahlil arrived on his bicycle a few minutes before ten o'clock. Almost an hour later than Dad had asked him to be there.

Thankfully, his father was not there to jump on his case about being late. The deputy, Ray Dudu, was the only person in the office. He was a nice guy, if a little weird.

"You need to start reading the *real* news, Jahlil," Dudu said, as Jahlil swept the floor. Dudu raised the latest tabloid he'd been reading. It had a lurid headline: "Lazarus in Arizona! Man Rises from the Dead." "The Chief won't like me showing these to you, but I have a responsibility to share the truth."

"Sure," Jahlil said. Man, what a nut. Where had Dad found this guy?

As Jahlil pondered how to respond to the loony deputy, his father's patrol car pulled up. Dudu hurriedly put away the tabloids.

"Morning, fellas," Dad said. He tossed his hat on the desk. "I ain't made no progress, really, on the missing girl. Nobody knows much of nothin'."

"What missing girl?" Jahlil asked. It was the first he'd heard of it.

Dad sat in his desk chair and leaned back, crossing his fingers across his stomach. "Tawanda Gray, lives over on Boone Drive with her grandma. She was baby-sitting last night and has turned up missing."

An image flashed with startling vividness in Jahlil's mind: a man putting a large, covered object inside the back of a Lexus SUV. A package that had a pair of dangling legs.

At the time he had seen it, he been convinced that he was not imagining things. But the fellas had talked him out of it, saying the weed was making him hallucinate. But what if it had really happened, just like he'd seen? What if he was the only witness to the crime?

"You got a funny look on your face, son," Dad said. "You know something about this?"

Jahlil chewed his lip.

He told his father everything.

"Shit," Dad said. Jahlil rarely heard Dad curse. But Dad continued, "Shit, shit, shit."

"What's wrong?" the deputy said.

"That Lexus truck." Dad grabbed his hat and rose. "Belongs to the fella who moved into the Mason place."

For the first time in years, the last time being the day the doctor had announced that his mother had cancer, Jahlil thought his father looked afraid.

Jubilee was the last house in the world that Van Jackson wanted to visit. But he couldn't procrastinate any longer. If what his boy had said was true—and he had no reason to suspect that Jahlil had lied—the fella who had moved into this place was the prime suspect in the girl's disappearance. It was Jackson's duty to question the guy, and arrest him, if need be.

Jackson parked in front of the tall iron gates.

Clouds passed over the morning sun, cloaking the world in grayish shadows.

It had been many years since he had last visited the Mason place. He'd last been there to investigate a vagrant who was squatting in the house. The guy had gotten inside through a window. When Jackson discovered the man, he was not prepared for what he had seen. The guy feasted on dead animals and insects: a stinking heap of crows, squirrels, beetles, flies, and spiders were spread at his feet, like a hellish buffet.

Pull up a chair and have a bite, the man had said in a raspy voice. *There's plenty of food to go around.* He bit off the brittle head of a beetle and chewed with pleasure.

Jackson had gagged, then arrested the man. It turned out the guy had escaped from a psychiatric hospital in Memphis.

But those were the kind of incidents that happened at Jubilee. Nothing but bad, bizarre things.

Jackson got out of the car.

It was strangely quiet up there. The Mason place might have been located atop a mountain, far away from human habitation.

Jackson felt his heart whamming like a bass drum.

The Lexus sport utility was parked at the end of the long driveway. The resident was home. Public enemy number one.

Jackson walked to the gate. It wasn't locked. He pressed a lever, and the gate opened with a soft squeak.

He went inside. He rested his hand on the butt of his .357 Magnum.

Pushed by a stiff breeze, the gate clanged shut behind him.

As if summoned by the noise, a group of dogs bolted out of the deep shadows beneath the trees. Big ones. Four of them. They barked, snapped, growled.

Shit. Talk about a mess.

He didn't have time to make it outside before they caught him. They were moving fast—faster than he had ever seen hounds run. What the hell were these mutts raised on?

He snatched his .357 out of the holster. He backed up against the fence, aiming the gun in front of him.

The dogs surrounded him in a loose semicircle. They were a ragtag pack of mutts. They growled, thick saliva dripping from their mouths, their eyes wild and red. But they did not attack. He figured they must have been trained to capture, and only attack if their quarry tried to get away.

He didn't dare try to run. He would never make it. In fact, though he had the gun, he didn't feel confident about his chances if he took a crack at the mutts. He could take down one of the hounds with a bullet, but if they decided to attack him, as one, he was finished.

His mouth was dry.

The dogs glared at him, as if challenging him to make a move. Damned if they didn't look him right in the eyes. They held no fear of him.

I ain't never seen no dogs act like this.

A man dressed in black emerged from the house. He strolled across the driveway. He wore a long, heavy jacket, a hat, aviator shades, boots, and, oddly, gloves. The temperature outdoors was in the low nineties. Wasn't this guy burning up in all those clothes?

But the most noticeable thing was that this was not the man Jackson had seen driving the Lexus around town. That guy had been shorter, and stout. He had never seen this guy before.

As the man approached, he raised his hand—a gesture the dogs could not have possibly seen—and the canines backed away, as if he controlled them with puppet strings.

Jackson cleared his throat. Something damn strange was going on here.

He lowered the gun, but he did not put it away.

"I'm Chief Jackson," he said. "I'm here on police business.

"Greetings, Chief," the man said. "How may I help you?"

The fella had an odd, untraceable accent. French, kinda, but not exactly. Jackson couldn't pin it down.

"Nice dogs," Jackson said. The canines had retreated into the shadows. He finally holstered the gun. "Think they wanted to take a plug out of me."

"They might have, if I had not been present," the man said. "You've ventured onto private property, may I remind you."

"I ain't here to snoop around. Got some police business to discuss with you."

The man folded his arms across his chest. "I'm all ears."

Jackson took his handkerchief out of his pocket and mopped sweat off his forehead. "Say, ain't you hot with all those dark, heavy clothes on? Last time I checked it was ninety-some degrees out here."

"I'm comfortable," the guy said, in a tone that invited no discussion about his choice of clothing. "You were saying about the purpose of your visit?"

"We've had a girl in town turn up missing. Black female, nineteen years old. We've got a reliable witness who says that late last night, a tall fella wearing black—kinda like you—was seen putting what looked like a body in the back of a silver Lexus SUV. Just like the one parked up there by the house."

Jackson watched the man's reaction closely, looking for a facial tick that indicated discomfort or guilt. But the man's poker face did not change, though Jackson could not see his eyes because of the dark shades he wore.

"If I understand this correctly," the man said, "you suspect that I was involved in the disappearance of this young lady."

"Suspicion is kinda pointing toward you having something to do with it," Jackson said. "Where's the bald-headed man who lives here? Kinda stocky? I saw him driving through town a couple times."

"He is away. But he is not the man you want, Chief. I am the one. I am guilty."

Jackson was not often taken by surprise. But his mouth slipped open.

"You're telling me you're guilty?" Jackson said. "You're confessing?"

"I abducted the young lady," the man said. He smoothly removed his glasses.

Jackson gasped. This guy's eyes . . . dear God. They were like twin black holes that sucked Jackson right into them. Jackson could not look away. A force as powerful as gravity compelled him to stand rigid and gaze, deeply, into the man's inhuman eyes.

Fella's done something to my mind, Jackson thought dimly. *Reached in and taken control of it, like in those* Star Wars *movies, he's working a Jedi mind trick on me, so help me, God.*

As Jackson stood, entranced, the world receded as if swept away by a strong tide. The only reality was the man's eyes. Jackson no longer felt the oppressive heat and humidity. He no longer felt the ground under his feet and the sweat-drenched clothes that clung to his body. He no longer tasted the traces of the coffee he had sipped only minutes ago. No longer heard the soft wind that drifted across the yard.

The man's eyes were his world, his universe. They were everything.

When the man spoke again, his resonant voice was inside Jackson's head.

"Chief Jackson . . . you are an honorable man and desire to serve your people, but now you will bend to a power greater than yourself. I required the young woman for purposes that you could not fathom in your mortal imagination. You will not arrest me. You will not question me further. You will not harbor any suspicion of those who currently dwell on this property. When you leave this place and continue your investigation into the woman's disappearance, you will direct your attention elsewhere. When you leave this place, you will not remember seeing me or the dogs. When you leave this place, the idea of ever visiting this residence again will fill you with paralyzing fear. You will not remember me issuing these commands to you. You will act upon them as though they spring from your own consciousness.

"Do you understand?"

"Yes," Jackson said, numbly, not feeling his own lips move.

There was a popping sound, like fingers snapping.

Jackson blinked.

He stood in front of Jubilee's gates, alone.

Such sudden terror overcame him that he nearly collapsed. It was a wild, senseless fright, like a child's fear of the darkness. But he could not rationalize it away, could not argue it into submission. He was convinced that if he stood for another second on this property, the earth would buckle and erupt open like a hungry, gaping mouth. And swallow. Him. Whole.

"Jesus, Jesus, Jesus." Babbling, he ran to his patrol car. He hustled behind the wheel and roared away, spinning up gravel.

He did not look back.

Concealed in the shadows under a maple tree, the dogs flanking him, Kyle watched the police chief flee in his vehicle.

Mother frowned upon controlling the minds of men. She believed in finding peaceful ways to co-exist with humans and manipulating them through subtle, indirect means. Mind control was only to be used in the most extreme situations.

Kyle doubted that Mother would approve of what he had done to the chief, but so be it. His father approved. Father had encouraged him to confront the police officer and command him to do his bidding.

Kyle loved his growing confidence in exercising his talents. Being in his father's presence was transforming him, *freeing* him. He could feel the shackles of Mother's stringent rules falling away from his spirit, liberating him to become the powerful vampire that he had the right to be. A vampire like his father.

You must claim your birthright, my son, Diallo had said. *I am a king, and you are my prince. Put away childish things and be my prince.*

Kyle knelt in the grass. The hounds pressed close to him, competing for his attention. They were eager to fulfill his will. The will of a prince.

Tonight, he would hunt again for his father, and he would take the dogs.

*   *   *

Late Saturday morning, David went to visit Pearl, the reputed psychic whom he suspected had called him yesterday. He wanted to find out why she had warned him and what she could tell him about his father and the bizarre events that were going on lately.

Nia had given him directions to the woman's house. Pearl lived on the northern edge of town, in a small, one-story home that sat at the end of a long, dusty path ranked with oak and maple trees.

David parked at the end of the drive, beside a white Jeep Cherokee.

A screened-in porch fronted the house. David climbed the short flight of steps, to ring the doorbell. He found a note taped to the door handle.

The message, written in neat cursive handwriting, read: "I'm waiting for you in the back, David."

His breath caught in his throat. How did she know that he was coming there?

A cool breeze whispered around him, tinkling the wind chimes inside the veranda.

Feeling slightly light-headed, he walked around the side of the house.

He wandered into the rambling backyard, and it was like walking into a botanical garden. Bright flowers and lush plants grew everywhere. He saw a small figure moving amongst a flourishing rose garden, in the far corner of the yard. That was where he headed.

He was unprepared to see what Pearl looked like. She appeared to be in her early twenties. She was short, perhaps five feet tall, and petite. Her lustrous black hair was woven into thin braids that hung to the middle of her back. She had large, almond-shaped brown eyes. Her smooth skin was the color of mocha. She wore a green tank top, denim shorts, and sandals.

She's like a black china doll, David thought. However, her beauty was not the sort that brought to mind swimsuit models or voluptuous women in hip-hop videos. Hers was the beauty of delicate features that were sculpted in perfect balance.

She looked at him, holding a yellow rose between her slender fingers. A large monarch butterfly crept along the petals.

"I'm David Hunter," he said. "You called me yesterday."

She smiled. Her voice was soft and musical.

"Greetings, David Hunter. You arrived just when I thought you would."

"How did you know I was coming?"

"How did I know the sun would rise this morning? It was meant to happen."

He frowned. Was this what talking to her would be like? Sentences full of New Age babble?

Pearl cocked her head and smiled.

She knows what I'm thinking, he thought. *She knows that I'm a skeptic.*

"Why did you call me?" he asked.

"Your name was given to me. I had not known that you had moved into the town, and I dialed the number not knowing whether anyone would answer. But of course, you did."

"What do you mean my name was given to you? By who?"

"I am a only receiver, David. I receive messages, and it is my responsibility to pass them to the intended party."

"So you get psychic radio waves or something."

She shrugged. "That's a crude analogy, but yes." She sat gracefully on the ground, Indian style, a colorful wall of flowers behind her. "Sit with me, and rest."

He hesitated for a beat, then he sat, too. The scent of roses enveloped him.

Pearl twirled the yellow rose in her fingers. The butterfly leapt from the petals and onto her knee, like a trained pet. She gently stroked its wings.

"You definitely like flowers and plants," he said. "It's like Calloway Gardens back here."

"It brings me peace," she said. "In life, we have to hold fast to that which comforts us. What comforts you, David Hunter?"

"Learning the truth."

"What if the truth is painful?" she said.

"Then I can deal with that. For me, not knowing hurts more than anything."

"It is your nature to seek the truth, at all costs. It is an admirable quality, but you will suffer much heartache because of it. Some truths are best left uncovered—like serpents sleeping beneath rocks."

"Such as?"

She only shook her head. The butterfly crawled into her palm. She lifted her hand, and the insect fluttered away.

He wanted to get back to a focused line of questioning. This talk of the agony of learning the truth was not helping him.

He leaned forward. "On the phone, you said I was responsible, that I have to prepare. What did you mean, exactly?"

"It means what it means. The message is simple, David."

"But what am I responsible for?"

"It is being revealed to you. I cannot reveal it. Because I don't know."

"I thought you were supposed to be psychic?"

She smiled, but a thread of sadness ran through her expression. "Again, I am only a receiver. Sometimes the messages are quite detailed. At other times, they are vague. The communication is uniquely tailored for each recipient, based on what they need to hear."

"Well, mine was *very* vague. I feel like I've stumbled into an episode of *The Twilight Zone*."

"That is actually an apt example," she said. "You will be

challenged to believe in that which may appear so impossible you will think you have entered another reality."

"Okay, you've got to explain what you mean by that," he said. "Please."

"Oh, David." She sighed heavily. "Do you believe that your moving to Mason's Corner was a coincidence? You came here seeking to learn about your father. Please do not ask me how I know your purpose, for to know such things is my gift. But what if everything that you have learned about your father since you have come to this town was woven into a deeper truth that you would be inclined to dismiss as impossible?"

"You've just confused me more," he said. "Listen. I've seen a ghost of my granddad that basically told me to fulfill the family legacy. I've found an old Bible with weird drawings. I've talked to people who've told me that my father faked his death. I've seen a photo my dad took at that supposedly haunted mansion. Then you call me talking about how I'm responsible for something. Maybe I'm dense, but I don't see how any of those things are connected at all."

"I'm sorry that is it confusing," she said. "But I cannot grant you any more insight on the matter. You will have to discover the meaning on your own."

He blew out a chestful of air. He felt as if he were back in his college calculus class, in which the professor would have the answer to the problem but refused to share it no matter how frustrated the students grew.

"Did my father really fake his death?" he said. "Can you answer that?"

"I haven't received an answer to that question, David. I don't know."

"Great," he said. "Then I've pretty much wasted my time coming to visit you."

"No, I have something I'd like to share with you."

"Another puzzle that will give me a migraine?" He laughed bitterly. "Do I really want to hear this?"

Her expression was somber. "I was the last person in town to see your father before he disappeared. He visited me, seeking to learn the outcome of his fishing trip. He claimed to have a bad feeling about it and wondered whether he should cancel it."

"What did you tell him?"

"I told him that if he went on his trip, and followed through on whatever secret mission he was embarking on— as it was clear to me that he had an ulterior motive—he would pass a terrible responsibility on to you. You would be called to do something for which you had not been properly prepared."

"Are you serious?"

"Do you know what Richard's response was? 'I've spent my life preparing David for what he might need to do one day.' "

"What?" David said. "That's the craziest thing I've ever heard. Spent his life preparing me? He was never there for me!" He had not intended to shout, but the emotion exploded out of him.

Sadness framed Pearl's face.

"That, I think, is how he believes he prepared you," she said.

Saturday was the biggest lawn-cutting day of the week for Junior. He'd begun early in the morning and steadily worked down his list of customers.

So far, he'd cut five lawns and earned sixty dollars. He loved the feeling of the knot of bills bulging in his pocket. He couldn't wait to get home and sock the money away in his secret hiding place.

Maybe he should open an account at the bank. But Mama had warned him about trusting banks. She said they took her money, and when she would go to check on it, there was less in there than she had given them. But that was a long time ago. Maybe banks were different these days.

Next on Junior's lawn-mowing list was Doc Bennett. Junior liked the old guy. He was real sharp and full of good stories.

Junior pushed his mower into the driveway, and knocked on the front door. Doc Bennett came outside.

"Morning, Junior," he said. "Sure is hot to be cutting grass."

"It don't bother me," Junior said. "I'm used to it."

"I've said it many times and must repeat it again: you're the hardest working man in Mississippi. John Henry wouldn't have anything on you."

"Who's John Henry?"

"John Henry was a legendary African-American railroad worker, renowned for his strength. He once competed in a contest to see whether he could lay track faster than a new-fangled machine, and though he won, he died soon afterward."

"Ain't that something?" Junior said. "Man died racing a machine. You know they say computers is gonna rule the world one day."

"So I've heard. Say, you get about town quite a bit. Have you seen my dog, Malcolm?"

"The mutt that comes around here? No, sir. Ain't seen him."

Doc Bennett looked sad. "Malcolm hasn't come around today. I don't know what's become of him. Please let me know if you see him."

"Sure will, Doc," Junior said. He turned to start up the lawn mower, but then he looked back at Doc Bennett. The guy had a thoughtful look on his face and stared at the sky.

I'm gonna tell him what happened at the cave, Junior thought suddenly. Doc Bennett was the smartest man in town and would be able to make some sense of what Junior had seen. Junior could not get his own thoughts around what he had seen that night while digging with Andre, and Andre was too scared to talk about it.

The scary guy in black had warned them not to tell any-one what they had seen, but Junior had to tell someone. It was eating him up inside. He'd never been good at keeping secrets.

"Say, Doc," Junior said. "I wanna tell you somethin'."

"Certainly." Doc Bennett stuck his hands in the pockets of his khakis. "Go ahead, my friend."

"It might take a little bit."

Doc Bennett pursed his lips. He opened the front door.

"Then I suggest that you come inside."

Franklin had heard some amazing tales, but nothing com-pared to the story that Junior Hodges told him.

A nighttime job offered to Junior and his cousin by the bald black Frenchman who had moved into Jubilee. Junior and his cousin digging into a cave located on the property—an earthen tomb filled with skeletons. A mysterious man dressed in black who, when he discovered Junior and Andre peeping into the cavern, flung them against the wall with an invisible force . . .

Franklin did not want to believe it. Junior was a nice young man, but he was, unfortunately, a bit slow. Franklin did not believe that Junior was lying, but he suspected that Junior had unknowingly embellished a few elements. Even the most intellectually sound individuals found it difficult to recall incidents in flawless detail.

Or perhaps, Franklin thought, *I am afraid to believe every-thing this young man has told me. His story goes against the grain of my beliefs. It is easier to discount his tale than to ac-cept it completely.*

"That's all of it, Doc," Junior said, his big, callused hands wrapped around a glass of water. They were in the living room, Junior sitting on the edge of the sofa, while Franklin sat in the recliner, turning his pipe in his hands. "Do you . . . do you believe me?"

Franklin chose his words carefully. "Junior, that is a rather astounding story."

"You ain't lying." Junior laughed, uncomfortably. "Can't hardly believe it myself."

"I believe that you encountered something bizarre and unsettling. But I will have to reserve judgment until I have more information."

"I'm telling the truth." His eyes were pleading. "Please, you gotta believe me, Doc."

"I believe enough to begin an investigation. I confess that I've been curious about the motives of the persons who have moved into Jubilee. Although your story is decidedly unusual, it is far too compelling for me to dismiss out of hand. I thank you for sharing it with me."

"All right." Junior appeared to be satisfied. He put the half-full glass of water on the end table. "I better finish cutting that grass. I gotta keep to my schedule."

"Of course. Anytime you need to talk, Junior, I am willing to listen."

"Well . . . thank you, Doc," Junior said. He seemed to be debating whether to speak again. "Hey, what you think of banks?"

"Banks? I'm not sure I follow you."

"Would you put your money in a bank, for saving?"

"I certainly would, and have done so for decades. We have a fine bank here in town. Are you thinking of opening an account?"

"I kinda am, I guess. Mama didn't trust banks, but if you say I can trust 'em . . ." He looked nervous.

Franklin was saddened. Junior was in his early thirties, and no one had taken the time to educate him on basic finances. It worried Franklin to think of what the kid had been doing with his money.

"I strongly encourage you to open an account, Junior," Franklin said. "You're a hardworking young man and need to protect your earnings. Give it a try."

Junior grinned broadly. "Thanks, Doc. I'm gonna take your advice. I'm going next week."

"Always happy to help." Franklin saw him out. Junior started up the lawn mower with a mighty pull, then began to cut the grass.

Franklin returned to his chair. He tamped his pipe, lit it with a match.

He considered Junior's fantastic tale. How much of it was true? Any of it? All of it?

He went to the study. A large map of Mason's Corner was pinned to the wall. He had drawn the map to aid his historical research.

He located Jubilee on the map, and marked it with a red pencil.

When Junior finished mowing the lawn, Franklin would call him inside again. To determine the location of the cavern.

Before he visited the cave, he needed to know where he could find it.

On Saturday, Nia slept in. Last night, she had stayed at David's place until three o'clock in the morning, and by the time she arrived home, she thought she'd sleep until noon the next day.

The phone rang, jarring her out of her slumber.

Groggy, she reached toward the nightstand, grabbed the phone.

"Hello?" she said.

"Still sleep, huh, baby?" It was a man's deep voice. Immediately familiar.

Nia sprang up like a jack-in-the-box.

"Who is this?" she said, knowing in her heart the answer to the question.

He chuckled. "You know who I am. Were you dreaming about me?"

It was Colin Morgan, the teacher who had stalked her in Houston.

The telephone handset was like a block of ice in her hand.

"I've been dreaming about you every night, Nia. I can't wait to touch your pretty skin again."

Although his words were not threatening and could even be considered romantic, in the context of the situation, she could not have been more revolted and terrified if he had screamed perverse, violent curses at her. Her stomach twisted.

"Don't you ever call here again," she said. "Leave me alone."

"I can't help myself, Nia. *I've gotta have you.* You're mine—"

She slammed down the phone.

It rang again.

She didn't pick up. She hugged herself against a chill. The Caller ID did not reveal Morgan's number or location. He was smart enough to conceal such details. Smart enough to find out her unpublished phone number.

Smart enough to find out where she lived?

After ringing five times, the phone fell silent. Voice mail picked up after several rings.

The red message indicator light began to blink.

She punched in the code to access her messages.

It was Mr. Morgan. He spoke only one sentence, in a whisper.

"I know where you live."

Chapter 10

David picked up Nia early in the evening, to join him for dinner at Franklin Bennett's house.

He had not discussed his visit to Pearl's with anyone. But when Nia got into the Pathfinder, looking fresh and lovely in shorts and a red blouse, the words burst out of him.

"I saw Pearl today."

Nia smiled hesitantly. "What did she say?"

David told her everything. It felt good to share the experience with her. Allowing the words to flow out of him cleansed him, clarified his thoughts.

"That's deep," Nia said when he had finished. "I can't believe your father felt that by neglecting you all of your life, he prepared you for whatever's going to happen."

"It's twisted," he said. "His self-centered excuse to justify himself. Although, in a way, he might be right."

"How so?"

"Growing up without my dad forced me to learn a lot when I was a kid. I had to learn how to fend for myself, think through things, set goals, take risks. My mom was supportive, but she couldn't teach me everything, especially about how to be a man. I had to learn a lot on my own. It's made me self-reliant, and maybe I'll need that in order to do . . . well, whatever I'm supposed to do."

"I see your point," she said. "But think of how much stronger you might be if your father had been there for you."

"Honestly, I think my dad knew he wouldn't make a good father. He was too self-centered to take care of a family. It's better to have no dad around than to have a dad in the house who makes your life a living hell."

"Good point." She nodded. "But what I want to know is, what are you supposed to prepare for? What's going to happen?"

"Pearl just wouldn't say, claimed she didn't know." He patted the illustrated Bible that lay beside him on the seat. "I'm hoping that when we see Franklin tonight, he can help me piece together some things. He's a big history buff, you know."

"Too bad he won't be able to help me, too."

"What's wrong?"

"Remember the guy who stalked me in Houston? Mr. Morgan? I think he's out of jail. He's called me twice."

"You're kidding."

Her eyes were haunted. "He said that he knows where I live."

"Damn," David said. "You think he really does? Maybe he was only trying to scare you."

"He found out my phone number, which is unlisted. Why not my address?"

"Have you called the police?"

"What could I tell them? I can't prove that he's the one who called me. I don't have any solid proof of anything, not yet."

"There has to be something we can do." He guided the SUV across the road. The Bennetts' house was ahead. Since they lived across the street from him, he parked in his own driveway.

"I could stay with you, let you protect me." She smiled. "Okay, that was a joke."

"Good to see that you're keeping your sense of humor."

"If I didn't, I'd scream. Seriously, I don't know what I'm going to do, David. This guy scares the shit out of me."

He took her hand in his. "I won't let anything happen to you."

"I'm not the only one dealing with drama here. What if something happens to *you*?"

She had him on that one. His own situation was as bad as hers—perhaps more so, because it was deeply strange and disturbing.

He couldn't bear to think about it any longer. He kissed her quickly on the lips.

"Come on, Nia, let's go eat."

At Franklin's house, they had a dinner of tossed salad, grilled rib eye steaks, baked potatoes, and corn on the cob. They took their meal outdoors on the wooden deck, sitting on wicker patio furniture.

The evening saw a welcome decrease in the temperature and humidity that had tormented them all day. A refreshing breeze carried the robust scent of freshly mown grass mingled with the aroma of Ruby's flower garden. A couple of torches designed to repel insects burned on the patio railing.

Although Franklin and Ruby were nearly forty years older than David and Nia, David didn't perceive any of the awkwardness that sometimes stifled discussions between members of different generations. Their conversation flowed, touching myriad subjects: current events, politics, sports, music, movies, travel, and more. The Bennetts had not settled quietly into their golden years and allowed themselves to be cut off from the outside world. They were active and well-read, frequent travelers, and full of fascinating insights.

After dinner, Ruby served red velvet cake and smooth Jamaican coffee. Both were delicious.

David sipped the pungent java, then said, "Franklin, when I first moved here, you promised to teach me about the town's colorful history. I've been waiting for my lesson."

"Oh, you've done it, David." Ruby made a mock grimace. "Don't get Professor Bennett started."

"The young man desires instruction," Franklin said. "Do not rebuke the curious mind."

"I'm curious, too." Nia placed her fork on her plate. "I've lived here my whole life, but everything I know about the town's come from hearsay and gossip."

"Which, interestingly enough, often contains kernels of truth," Franklin said. He cleared his throat. "Any discussion about this town must begin with its founder, Edward Mason."

"You've told me a little about him before," David said. "He started a plantation here."

"Correct," Franklin said. "Edward Mason moved here from Virginia, in eighteen forty-one. His vision was to establish the grandest, most prosperous plantation in Mississippi. A cotton kingdom, if you will. He had his stately mansion built on a hill that overlooked the thousand acres under his dominion. He owned three hundred slaves, to work the land from dawn till dusk.

"Mason was a strict, cruel master. He had slaves beaten severely for minor infractions: resting a minute too long, arriving late to work, tarrying too long when drinking water or eating. A slave was killed if he violated Mason's code one too many times. Mason believed that disobedience was inimical to his mission to maintain a plantation that functioned with machinelike efficiency.

"In the beginning, his punishments were fairly standard, as such things were on plantations—lashes with a whip. In time, however, he grew more sadistic and imaginative in his tortures. He once had a disobedient slave tied to the hindquarters of a horse and dragged throughout the countryside. On another occasion, he doused a man in kerosene and set him aflame. Then he had a woman hung from a tree by her ankles, and left there for days. Another time, a teenage slave had fresh meat hung around his neck and waist, and was forced into a pen of dogs.

"In eighteen sixty-one, the Civil War broke out. Edward Mason had no intention of surrendering to Union troops or perishing at their hands. He quickly made special preparations. He'd already had a mausoleum built at a cemetery, especially for his family. Well, now he had a concealed passage built into the crypt. The passage led to a deep shaft that gave access to an underground hideaway. His plan was to seek refuge there whenever Union soldiers approached.

"Alas, Mason never had the opportunity to use his hideout. His slaves, emboldened at the idea of a war that would end slavery, and hearing accounts of slaves escaping bondage to fight for the Union, launched an insurrection. They set the plantation on fire, and they hung Edward Mason from a tree that still stands to this day in the front yard of Jubilee. Many of the slaves were killed in the uprising, but a few of them escaped and crossed the lines to fight for the Union. My great-grandfather was one of them."

"Amazing." David shook his head, and Nia looked equally astonished. "Is that how you know so much about the history of Edward Mason?"

"My great-grandfather was a member of the inner circle of slaves who worked in the Mason household," Franklin said. "His name was Samuel Bennett. Sam was a 'house nigger,' reviled by the slaves who worked in the fields, for they assumed that his lot was better than theirs, his burden easier to bear. In truth, Mason treated the house slaves worse than he treated anyone else, and subjected them to brutalities that I cannot even tell you. When the insurrection hit, Sam was the one who wound the noose around Mason's neck."

"Jesus," Nia said.

"Sam told the story to his son, who in turn told his son, and so it was passed down, eventually falling to me," Franklin said. "I've verified virtually every detail of which my ancestor spoke. For instance, the mausoleum that Mason had constructed stands in Hillside Cemetery, just off Main Street. I have not, however, ventured inside to find the subterranean hideaway. Edward Mason's corpse, ravaged as it was, was interred in his tomb, and his family lies with him.

"In addition, many of the survivors of the slaves who worked on the Mason plantation presently live in Dark Corner. Our chief, Van Jackson, is the descendent of a slave who escaped with my great-grandfather. Nia, your late father, Thomas James, was another descendant."

"I remember Daddy telling me," Nia said, wonder in her eyes.

Franklin nodded. "David, you too have an ancestor who played a role as well: William Hunter."

"I remember hearing stories about him, as a kid," David said. "He was some kind of freedom fighter, right?"

"Yes," Franklin said. "William Hunter was a free man who roamed throughout the South. He frequently assisted slaves in fleeing North on the Underground Railroad. Although he was free himself, he helped to plan the insurrection at the Mason plantation. According to Sam, my great-grandfather, William Hunter was the bravest—and most cunning—man he had ever seen. Sam believed that Hunter had witnessed something, as a younger man, that gave him the fortitude of ten men. But Hunter was secretive about his past."

"I don't know much about him, either," David said. "I never learned much about my father's side of my family. Mostly everything you've said is new to me."

"Doubtless, the ghost stories would be, as well," Franklin said.

David's heart skipped a beat. Nia shifted in her chair. Ruby watched her husband thoughtfully.

"Ah, your reactions tell me that you're more than passingly aware of the ghost stories connected to Jubilee," Franklin said. "Since the slave revolt, people have reported stories of hauntings at the estate. Some claim to see apparitions of slaves huddled under the trees that surround the house. Others said they have seen the ghost of Edward Mason himself, floating through the rooms in a dark suit, his face blue and eyes bulging, presumably from his death due to hanging."

David reached under the table and found Nia's hand. She squeezed his, gratefully.

"The house has been vacant for most of the hundred forty-odd years that Edward Mason has been dead. On rare occasion, someone will move in and attempt to refurbish the estate. I recall an ambitious couple who wanted to restore the mansion's period detail and turn it into a tourist attraction. They lived there for only a month and left in haste, the restoration project abandoned.

"Jubilee has been perhaps the one constant in Dark Corner. Throughout world wars, Jim Crow, the booms and busts of the economy, the Civil Rights Movement, and so on, up to the present day, the mansion has stood, inviolate, an unchanging landmark. Townsfolk despise what the house represents, and they fear the ghost stories, but in spite of that, we've let it stand—a bit like a scar that serves as a reminder of a fight that we've won. You can only understand how far you've come when you understand that from which you came."

"Someone's living in Jubilee now," David said, thinking of the tall man dressed in black whom he had seen a few days ago. "I visited the house."

Franklin put his coffee mug on the table. "May I ask why?"

"I need to tell you about this." David looked around the table at his friends. They watched him expectantly. "I saw a ghost a few days ago. It was my grandfather."

"Lord, have mercy," Ruby said.

"There's much more," David said.

He told them everything.

* * *

"It requires a leap of imagination to believe that your father's death was a hoax," Franklin said. He stared thoughtfully into his mug. "Possible, I suppose."

"It would be terrible, if it's true," Ruby said. "All the pain he's caused so many folks, especially you." She touched David's arm.

"Well, it's only a theory," David said. "I don't have any solid proof. But I do have some evidence of the other stuff I mentioned."

He unzipped the backpack that had been lying beside him on the deck. He pulled out the old Bible and handed it to Franklin.

"Ah, yes, this is an artifact." Franklin carefully opened the Bible.

"The illustrations were done by my great-grandfather, James Hunter," David said. "He was an artist, but you probably already knew that."

"But I never realized he did work like this." Franklin pushed up his glasses on his nose, leaned closer to the book. "My God."

"What is it?" Nia said.

Franklin put the Bible in the center of the table. It was open to one of the drawings David had seen before: a pack of dogs guarding the mouth of a cave, and a group of men nearby, crouched amidst some trees.

Franklin's eyes were bright. "The young man who cuts my grass, Junior. He was recently asked to do some work at a cave in this very town, by the man who moved into Jubilee. Digging. Junior and his cousin did the work late at night, about a week ago. They saw the stout, bald-headed man who'd requested their assistance, and a tall man dressed in black."

"The guy who wears black is the same man I saw when I visited the Mason place!" David said. "There was something strange about him, too. He seemed a lot older than he looked."

Franklin nodded. "After Junior and his cousin finished the work of breaking a passage into the cave, they were dismissed. However, being curious, they peeked inside. Junior claims that he saw a heap of skeletons, with rags clinging to their bones. And the man in black saw Junior and his cousin and . . . well, used a supernatural force to throw them against the wall."

"Okay," Nia said. "Now you're creeping me out."

"Me, too," Ruby said.

David, too, felt a cool dampness at the nape of his neck.

"That is what Junior told me," Franklin said. "He's a simple man, without guile. I wasn't completely convinced of his story, of course, but David, you've confirmed the existence of the mysterious character in black. Also, these depictions of the cave are highly suggestive. It must be the same one. Only fools believe in coincidence."

"But those drawings must've been done decades ago," David said.

"Indeed." Franklin paged to another illustration. This one showed men inside a cavern, facing a legion of savages.

"What does it all mean?" Nia said. "Can you figure it out, Franklin?"

Franklin contemplated the Bible, silent.

Around the table, David, Nia, and Ruby anxiously awaited his response.

Franklin's head snapped up. He pointed at David.

"You are being summoned to perform a task, David. A task that deals with this." He tapped his finger against the sketch. "This is *your* family history here, lucidly portrayed."

"How do you know it's my family's history? What if it's just a bunch of drawings of some fable, some tall tale—"

"No, no, no!" Franklin hammered his fist against the table. "This is history here, I can feel it in my old bones. Your great-grandfather was almost certainly telling a visual story of an episode from Hunter family lore."

"But what am I supposed to do?" David said. "That's what I can't figure out."

"Whatever is required of you, which will become clear in

time, as Pearl advised," Franklin said. He looked at each of them, somber. "Let's not lie to ourselves. We are facing something unearthly."

"Stop it, Franklin," Ruby said. "You don't know that yet."

"I know what I feel, and I have an inkling of what David is feeling. He is seeing ghosts; psychics are relaying messages to him. I doubt that he is being prompted to perform a task as mundane as replacing the plumbing in the Hunter residence. His mission is obviously as strange as the signs that he has received thus far. It only makes sense."

David had a chunk of red velvet cake remaining on his plate, and the coffee was still warm, but his appetite was gone. Franklin, as he had hoped—and feared—had confirmed, in no uncertain terms, that a grave responsibility awaited him. And he had made their next step clear, too.

Nevertheless, David asked, "What should we do?"

"I believe you know the answer to your question," Franklin said. "My friends, we are going to embark on a field trip tomorrow. To the cave."

Shenice Stevens loved the night.

As a child, she'd loved to sit on the porch with her mother and gaze at the stars that were scattered like diamonds across the sky. "The stars are God's eyes, sugar," her mother would say. "He's always watching you to make sure you're safe."

When she grew older, her love of nightfall and silvery moons stayed with her. She especially loved night in Mississippi. There, the darkness seemed purer, deeper. Without the harsh lights of a big city—like Memphis, where she attended college—washing out the gloom, she could soak up the blackness as though it were water and she were a sponge, letting it fill her up with tranquillity.

Probably the only thing more comforting than the night was her boyfriend, Trey. His presence soothed her, no matter the time of day.

They were at a park, sitting on the cool hood of Trey's car. They sipped a chilled, peach-flavored wine from plastic glasses, the half-full bottle propped between them.

She was a junior at the University of Memphis, and had come home to Mason's Corner for the summer; Trey, a grad student at the same school, drove from the city every weekend to visit her. They spent many nights like this, sitting outdoors talking, sometimes sipping a sweet wine, and listening to soulful music. They had been dating for almost a year and Shenice was sure that they would marry after she graduated. Trey was the kind of man who was all about business and knew what he wanted out of life. She was a free spirit, a good balance for him. They complemented each other.

On the car stereo, a sensual Maxwell ballad came on, "Lifetime."

"Oh, I love this song," Shenice said. She leaned into Trey. He drew her closer, kissed her cheek.

"That brother Maxwell can sing," Trey said. "He can represent for brothers like me, 'cause you know I can't sing a lick."

"Why don't you try?" she said. "Sing a verse for me, sweetie."

"Girl, please."

"It's only the two of us out here. Sing for me, please?" She batted her eyelashes, which always made him melt like chocolate in her hands.

He opened his mouth and was about to sing a note. Then he paused.

"Look over there." He pointed.

Swaying to the music, she turned.

A large dog stood in the corner of the parking lot, revealed in the dim, yellow-orange light cast by a nearby street lamp. The oddly quiet canine watched them with glimmering eyes.

"I think it's a pit bull." Trey's voice held a trace of anxiety.

"Yeah, it does look like a pit," she said. "Why is it staring at us like that?"

Pit bulls terrified her—those dogs were murder machines. When she was in high school, her neighbor had owned a pit bull, and once, the dog had gotten loose and locked its teeth onto the leg of the postman, Mr. Jones. They had to literally crack the dog's skull in order to get it to release its grip on the poor guy. Mr. Jones required fifty stitches and had walked with a limp ever since.

The flesh of her neck tightened as if squeezed with pincers.

"Look over there," Trey said. "There's another one. Looks like a rottweiler."

On the other side of the parking lot, another massive hound had stepped out of the shadows and into the light. This one watched them in eerie silence, too.

"That looks like my cousin's dog," she said. "He has a rottie, named Kilo. He's sweet."

"He doesn't look so sweet to me. Where did these mutts come from? They don't have collars, see?"

She saw. She didn't like it at all. Her cousin's dog would never be running loose and collarless. She didn't know who these hounds belonged to.

She screwed the cap on the wine bottle. "We better get in the car, Trey."

"I was about to say that. Move slowly. We don't want to agitate them."

They cautiously slid off the hood of the car.

As though acting under the command of a single malevolent mind, the hounds stepped forward. Low growls rumbled from their chests.

The dogs were about twenty feet away. It would take only seconds for the canines to close the gap.

Shenice grabbed the neck of the bottle and held it like a club, wine sloshing around inside.

"Move slowly," Trey said. He sidled alongside the car, to the door. "Keep your eye on them. They'll think you're afraid if you look away."

Shenice wanted to tell him that she doubted it would matter whether she met the dogs' gazes or not. She was terrified and was sure the dogs could smell her fear, like sour sweat.

She touched the door handle.

The dogs snarled and charged.

Shenice screamed and ripped open the door, taking her eyes off the hound behind her, but able to hear its feet scrambling across the pavement at a furious rate. Coming fast. God. She had to move. Get in the car, fast, fast, fast.

Trey screamed.

She was halfway in the car, and Trey had gotten the driver's side door open, but the canine, the pit bull, had clamped its teeth on his leg. It was dragging him away, pulling him across the parking lot, his glasses falling off his face, his hands scrabbling for a hold but finding nothing but smooth concrete.

"Go, Shenice, go!" Trey shouted between garbled screams.

A thunderous roar, behind her. She whirled, and the rottweiler tackled her, knocked her out of the car and to the ground.

She shrieked. The dog's sharp teeth tore into her shoulder. Her vision blurred with tears, she remembered the bottle in her hand. She swung it at the dog's head and connected with a *crack!* Glass exploded, wine spraying everywhere, but the hound squealed and staggered away.

Weeping, she crawled into the car. She shut both doors, locked them.

Thank God, the key was in the ignition.

A cold pain burned in her wounded shoulder. Her blouse was wet with blood, and she tasted blood on her lips, too. She had bitten her tongue.

"Oh, Trey," she said, thickly. The pit bull had dragged Trey to the corner of the parking lot. The dog stood on his chest, deadly jaws only inches away from his face.

A man draped in dark clothing stepped into the light. Looming above Trey, he rested his hand on the canine's head.

What the hell, had this guy commanded the dogs to attack them? What was going on?

The man looked in her direction.

The pit bull leaped off Trey and bounded toward her. The rottweiler, having recovered from the blow with the bottle, charged the car, too.

Shenice gunned the engine. The car started with a throaty growl. She slammed into reverse, tires wailing.

The dogs jumped onto the hood. Snapping and barking, they mashed their snouts against the windshield as though to tear inside.

Screaming, Shenice wrestled the steering wheel sideways, to aim the car toward the road. She mashed the accelerator. The vehicle sprang forward with a jolt that rattled her vertebrae.

The dogs bounded off the hood.

She bounced across the curb and veered onto the road.

Hot tears blinded her. The numbing pain that had begun in her shoulder spread like a ravenous cancer throughout her body. Rabies. The damn dog probably had rabies. Or some other terrible disease. She had to get to the hospital.

Oh, Trey, I'm so sorry, sweetie. I'm sorry I couldn't save you. I hope nothing bad happens to you. I hope you get away.

She had left her cell phone at home and would have to call the police when she reached the hospital. But a sickening sense of foreboding made her worry that calling the cops would be useless. Trey would be gone, she feared. As if swallowed by the very night that she used to love.

In the candle-lit basement, Kyle placed the young man's unconscious body at the foot of his father's bed.

"You've done well," Diallo said. He sat up eagerly. "Did you enjoy the hunt?"

"A woman escaped," Kyle said. "She saw me. She will tell others."

"It does not matter. You've planted a command in the chief's mind to ignore us, and he will obey, for a while yet. It is good that one of our hounds bit the woman."

"How did you know a dog attacked her? I didn't tell you."

"I see through their eyes," Diallo said. "As the infection spreads through the woman, she will become one of the valduwe. It will not take long." He clapped Kyle's arm. "You've made me proud, my prince."

"I assumed I was incompetent," Kyle said. "But if I pleased you, that will be sufficient."

"You are my flesh. Could I be displeased with my own flesh? I would be insane."

Kyle smiled awkwardly. It was strange and wonderful to receive his father's praise. His father never tired of complimenting him, coaching him, *fathering* him. Mother had been so terribly wrong about Diallo.

His father plunged his teeth into the human's carotid artery.

Kyle's tongue tickled. He hoped that his father would invite him to share the blood.

But he did not. Father drained the human's blood and threw the corpse to the floor.

I should not be selfish, Kyle thought. *My father needs to feed far more urgently than I do. If I want to feed on a human, I should capture one for myself.*

The alien thought visited his mind, uninvited. He examined the idea. Rather than being revolted, he found the prospect quite pleasing.

Why not hunt his own prey? Who would stop him? His father surely would not. Father would encourage him to hunt.

Mother's teachings came to mind: *Only barbaric vampires hunt human prey. Such vampires do not know any better; they do not understand that we are the most civilized race on earth. We are not animals, we are a sophisticated, complex species who must learn to peacefully coexist with mankind. . . .*

But he had hunted for his father, violating Mother's vampire code, and he had enjoyed it, intensely. He had not felt like a degenerate. He'd felt like a conqueror.

What harm was there in hunting for himself?

As Kyle pondered his course of action, Diallo climbed off the bed. He extended his long arms to the low ceiling.

"My strength is returning," he said. "Soon, I will be healthy and ready to begin our mission."

But Kyle did not absorb Diallo's words. He was consumed by his own thoughts.

"Father," Kyle said, "I think I am going out again."

"Are you?" Diallo said. "But I have already fed. I will not need to feed again until tomorrow."

"This isn't for you," Kyle said, in an unsteady voice, and then he added, more firmly, "This is for me."

He spun and left the basement.

Watching him leave, Diallo smiled.

In the cramped living room of a trailer home, Kyle stood over his prey: a woman he had found outdoors sitting on the trailer's steps, smoking a cigarette.

A sharp blow to her temple had knocked her unconscious.

Wearing a green house robe, the woman was middle-aged, slightly overweight, and lived alone.

Kyle had laid her body across the sagging couch. He knelt before her.

Her skin and clothes reeked of cigarette smoke. But the warm flesh of her neck was smooth, and her pulse throbbed in a hypnotic rhythm.

He parted the robe, fully exposing her throat. His hands shook.

Across the room, a breeze stirred the flimsy curtains. An enormous dark-feathered bird had perched on the window ledge. A raven.

The bird glared at Kyle with disdainful eyes.

"I know who you are," he said. "Hello, Mother."

The raven cawed.

One of Mother's talents was her ability to utilize avian creatures as watchers. He should have anticipated that she would be spying on him. How long had she been monitoring him and his father?

Only barbaric vampires hunt human prey . . .

"You can't stop me," he said. "You've stopped me my whole life. But not anymore, Mother."

He turned away and sank his fangs deep into the woman's jugular vein.

Hot blood spurted into his mouth. He closed his eyes, his body quaking. A moan escaped him; the moan spiraled into a croon of ecstasy.

The raven watched for a while, then flew away into the night.

Sunday morning, Chief Jackson went to the hospital to check on Shenice Stevens. He wanted to question her about last night, if she was awake.

The head nurse on duty was Ruby Bennett, Doc Bennett's wife. She came around the nurse's station to speak to him before he entered the girl's room.

"There's been no change in her condition, Chief," Ruby said. "She's sleeping."

Jackson sighed heavily. "I'll just look in on her for a hot minute, then."

"Five minutes," Ruby said.

Jackson hated hospitals. They reminded him, painfully, of his late wife. She had spent the last few months of her life suffering in a Memphis hospital. He had visited her daily, powerless to do anything to help her, forced to watch her waste away into the grave.

As he removed his hat and entered the room, his mouth grew dry.

Shenice Stevens lay on the bed, swaddled within sheets.

Her mother sat in a bedside chair, her eyes red and puffy. Jackson had seen the mother several hours ago, when he was first summoned to the hospital, and the woman still wore the same clothes. Damn shame. There was nothing worse in the world than watching your child suffer.

"Hello, Mrs. Stevens." Jackson settled into another chair. "How's the girl doing?"

Mrs. Stevens was a slim, attractive lady, a savvy businesswoman who sold real estate and never had a hair out of place. But today, her hair was like a wild plant, and when she looked at Jackson she blinked, confused.

"I'm the chief," Jackson said, helpfully.

Her eyes sharpened. "Chief, have you found out who's responsible for this? The dog that mauled my baby should be decapitated, and the owner should be jailed. What are you going to do about it?"

"I'm working on the case, ma'am." Jackson's lips tightened into a firm line. It was frustrating. The young lady had driven to the hospital last night, bleeding profusely from a dog bite. By the time the staff rushed her to the emergency room, she was unconscious. She had awakened for only brief periods since.

As far as Jackson knew, the diagnosis was rabies, or something like it. He'd called Chester County's animal services, but they hadn't been able to locate the dog that had attacked her, which kept the vet from running rabies tests. The girl had said a rottweiler had bitten her, and a number of folks in town owned that breed—and not all of them had bothered to register their pets with the city. It was like finding the proverbial needle in a haystack.

Mrs. Stevens confirmed that the girl and her boyfriend had been out last night. They had not found the boy. He had vanished.

Shenice had driven her boyfriend's car to the hospital. That fact chipped away at Jackson's initial suspicion of foul play.

Intuition told Jackson that the woman had been running from something, something from which she had barely escaped with her life, and that her boyfriend had not been so lucky.

But who was responsible? A dog? It seemed ridiculous that one dog could maul two adults, though there had probably been similar cases of such things. Jackson had never seen such an incident in his time as a cop.

He had no leads. He hoped the girl woke up so she could give him a clue.

The girl's face was like a wax mask, her lips pale and chapped. She was caramel-skinned and quite pretty; Jackson recalled that she had won a recent town beauty pageant. But she was only a distant echo of her healthy self.

The girl's eyes fluttered open. She blinked. Her lips parted.

Mrs. Stevens shot out of her chair.

"Mama's here, baby." She tenderly touched her daughter's face. "You're gonna be okay."

Jackson pressed the button to summon the nurse. Within seconds, Ruby hurried into the room.

"Girl's waking up," Jackson said.

Shenice mumbled something inaudible.

"What she say?" Jackson said.

Mrs. Stevens shook her head. "I . . . I don't know."

"The dogs," Shenice whispered.

Something about how the girl spoke the words, as if she hinted at a deeper meaning, rendered Jackson speechless. An icy chill fell over him.

What's wrong with me? he thought. *She didn't say anything that should scare me.*

"The man . . . the dogs," she said.

Perspiration rolled into Jackson's eyes. He snapped out his handkerchief and blotted the sweat.

"What is she talking about?" Mrs. Stevens said.

The man . . . the dogs . . .

"Girl's babbling, gotta be delirious," Jackson said. His voice trembled.

"You might be right, Chief," Ruby said. "Please leave now. She's not in a condition to handle any questions. I'm calling the doctor."

Jackson didn't argue with her. He did not want to hear another word out of the girl's mouth. Her words terrified him, and he could not put his finger on why.

He hurried out of the hospital. In the parking lot, he jumped into his cruiser.

"I don't know a damn thing about what she said," he said, aloud. "Don't know nothing about it at all."

But why did he feel that he was lying to himself?

Franklin knocked on David's door.

"Are you ready for our cave expedition, my friend?" Franklin said.

It was noon. Franklin was dressed like a man going on an African safari. He wore tall leather boots with thick soles, khakis, a matching shirt, and a wide-brimmed hat. He carried a brown leather bag over his shoulder.

"You look a lot more prepared than I do." David looked down at his Timberlands, jeans, and T-shirt.

"You'll do," Franklin said.

"We only need to pick up Nia, then we can go," David said. He grabbed his duffel bag.

It was a typical, sweltering Mississippi summer day, with the temperature in the mid-nineties. David was glad that he had thought to pack a few bottles of cold water.

"I must tell you," Franklin said, getting in the Pathfinder, "there have been further, possibly related, developments since last night."

David put the SUV in gear, switched on the air conditioner, and rolled down the street. "What happened?"

"Ruby works at the local hospital a couple days a week. She's the head nurse. She called me this morning about a young lady who had been mauled by a rottweiler."

"Damn. That's terrible."

"Quite. The woman drove herself to the hospital late last night. Evidently she had been with her boyfriend—who has vanished, by the way. She drove to the medical center in his car and collapsed shortly after the staff took her inside.

"The young lady was unconscious until this morning, when Chief Jackson visited to question her. Ruby was bedside when the woman awoke and muttered about seeing a man, and dogs. Ruby suspects the chief has some knowledge of what she said, because he was visibly disturbed. Unfortunately, the girl has lapsed into sleep again and cannot be roused."

"A man, and dogs?" David said. "I don't get it."

"I called the police station and spoke to Jackson," Franklin said. "He denied that the woman said anything of importance. He was agitated and abrupt with me. I must say, such behavior is out of character for Jackson. He's ordinarily a cool customer."

"I remember thinking the same thing when he visited me after I moved here. Seemed to be a laid-back guy."

"Anything that upsets the chief is worth investigating," Franklin said. "Being an indefatigable researcher, I made some calls to various resources. I learned that a young woman was reported missing, two days ago. She was baby-sitting for a family when she disappeared. No trace of her has been found."

"Two disappearances, in two days," David said. "The woman's boyfriend, and the baby-sitter. In a town this small, that has to be pretty damn rare."

"It's unprecedented here," Franklin said. "Include Junior's unearthly experience at the cave, and the strange happenings that you've seen—"

"Everything has to be connected," David said.

"Precisely."

"But how?"

"That, my friend," Franklin said, "is why we are going to the cave. To discover answers to our questions."

Chapter 11

Franklin, Nia, and David approached the dark mouth of the cave.

Using Franklin's map, they had navigated a route to the forest that formed the southern fringe of the Mason property. They'd parked on the shoulder of a quiet road that outlined the edge of the woods. A steep hill led from the roadway to the forest wall. They had hiked through the woods for about a quarter of a mile before they reached a clearing—and the cave.

David was drenched in sweat by the time they stopped walking. He withdrew a water bottle from his bag.

"Only take a few sips, David," Nia said. She wore Bermuda shorts, a tank top, and Nike running shoes, and she didn't appear to be half as wrung out as he was. Light perspiration gleamed on her skin, like polish.

"Still haven't gotten used to this heat," David said. He put his hand against a tree to support himself while he drank.

He looked at the cave. A jagged black maw, perhaps seven feet high and five feet wide, gave access to the cavern. Mounds of rocks and dirt covered the ground outside the passageway.

The area was preternaturally still and silent.

Franklin's camera hung around his neck. He took a photo of the entrance.

"David, take out the Bible, please," he said.

David did as he asked. Franklin stood beside him and turned the pages, stopping at one of the illustrations: the drawing of the large dogs gathered outside the cave's doorway, and a group of men crouched in the woods, watching as if waiting to attack.

"The men huddled back there," Franklin said. He indicated the wall of trees and shrubbery behind them.

"You're right," Nia said, peering over David's shoulder at the illustration.

"It's a good thing these dogs aren't here," David said.

"Not yet," Franklin said in a low voice. He looked around warily. Due to the trees, cool shadows dwelled around them.

"I know what you're thinking," David said. "The girl in the hospital was mauled by a dog, and mentioned something about a man who used dogs to do . . . something. Attack, maybe."

"You and I are on the same wavelength," Franklin said.

"We better hurry up, guys," Nia said. "Let's get inside there and do what we came to do."

"One moment," Franklin said. He raised his camera and snapped another shot of the cave entrance.

"Now, let's proceed," Franklin said.

The first and only time David had ventured into a cave, he had been eleven years old. They had been taking a family trip to Chicago to visit relatives, and on the way they had stopped in Cave City, Kentucky, to do some sight-seeing. On their way down into the cavern depths, he'd seen a spider on the wall as big as his face. The memory had stayed with him ever since.

This cave was much smaller than the one in Kentucky, but it was no less forbidding. When they stepped inside the passageway, cool air swirled around them, like disturbed spirits. The sound of their breathing was amplified, as if they were shut inside a tomb.

David swept a flashlight across the limestone walls. Thank God, he didn't see any giant spiders clinging to the rocks.

As they moved deeper within, a foul smell assaulted his nostrils.

Nia wrinkled her nose, too. "What's that awful smell? It can't just be old dirt."

"Death." Franklin came up behind them. "When I was in graduate school, I worked part-time in a crematory. This is the malodor of incinerated corpses."

David didn't need to ask why the stench of death polluted the air. The guy who'd told Franklin about this place claimed to have seen a heap of skeletons.

"Can we please hurry up and do what we have to do?" Nia said. "I don't like the feeling this place gives me."

"Give me light, please," Franklin said. "I will commence with my photographs."

They crept farther inside. As David and Nia shone the flashlights around the area, Franklin snapped photos.

Ahead, a bend in the cavern awaited.

"This looks like the illustration in the Bible," David said. He fumbled out the book. He found the representation of the four remaining men, armed with weapons, walking deeper into an earthen tunnel.

"Unlike those valiant men, we didn't have the foresight to arm ourselves," Franklin said. "Let us hope that it won't be necessary."

They walked around the corner. Nia gagged. David covered his mouth with the edge of his shirt.

"We've discovered the source of the stench," Franklin said. He took a picture.

A brownish-gray mixture of dirt and ashes covered the cavern floor. Walking through it was like stepping through a sandbox.

"Junior said he saw bodies back here," Nia said. She coughed. "Someone must have burned them."

"To hide evidence," David said.

"But whose bodies were here?" Nia said. "God, I'm going to have nightmares for a week after this."

David turned to another drawing in the Bible. It depicted a swarm of savage-looking people, dressed in rags, crowded inside the cave.

"Maybe it was these people," he said.

"I'm sure it is the vicious mob illustrated there," Franklin said. He had walked forward through the ashes, and begun to study the wall. "Both of you please, come. I'd like a light here." He pointed.

David and Nia went behind Franklin and directed the light at the area he indicated.

Large symbols were engraved in the stone. It was a language that David did not understand.

Franklin clicked a couple of photographs. "This is a west African tongue. Malinke, I believe, a Manding language from the Niger-Congo family."

"Really?" Nia said. "Can you read it?"

Franklin squinted. "It has been many years since I have encountered this." He traced his hand across the carved symbols.

David glanced at Nia. She shrugged.

Franklin abruptly looked at the ground. He tested it with his foot. His boot found a depression and sank in deep enough to swallow his ankle.

Mumbling under his breath, Franklin took the Bible from David. He paged to another drawing.

"Okay, what are you thinking, Franklin?" David said. "Have you figured this out?"

"Look." Franklin tapped the page. This illustration portrayed the Goliath of a man who was trapped behind a crumbling rock wall.

"This character in the drawing," Franklin said, "he was buried here, I think."

"Buried?" Nia said. "But the others, according to Junior's story, were piled on the ground."

"Not this one." Franklin's eyes gleamed. "No, he was special." He pointed to the engraved symbols. "Translated from Malinke, this says, roughly, 'I shall rise again to slay my enemies.' Diallo signed his name to this vow. Have you ever heard of him?"

"Never," Nia and David said together.

Franklin looked excited. "Diallo was a prince in eighteenth century Mali. A prince and a warrior, in fact. After losing a battle, he was captured, sold to European slave traders, and shipped to America, at which point, as it was with so many of our ancestors, we lost track of him and his lineage."

"How do you know that the same Diallo wrote this stuff on the wall?" Nia said. "Thousands of slaves came from that area of Africa, from what I remember from my history classes."

"I'm taking an intuitive leap," Franklin said. "In the absence of complete data, historians must often use their imagination to connect the dots, if you will. It feels genuinely correct to me."

"Let's say you're right," David said. "How did he come to be buried here? And why is he featured in drawings in this Bible?"

"Valid questions," Franklin said. "But our most urgent question is: where is he now? As you can see, his body is gone."

"The man in black," Nia said. "Junior said that the man in black, and another guy, were in here. What if they dug up his body and took it somewhere?"

"Why would they do that?" David asked.

"I don't know," Nia said. "But it makes sense, doesn't it?"

"I must consider these questions." Franklin pressed his hands to his temples and closed his eyes. "I must consider them carefully before I reach a conclusion."

"My conclusion is that we get the heck out of here," Nia said. "We've seen everything we need to see, and I can't stand any more of this place."

An alarming sound suddenly reached them: the echo of barking dogs.

This is unreal, David thought. *It's like something out of one of these Bible illustrations.*

"Grab some stones," David said. He reached down and scooped a couple of rocks in his hands, each stone roughly the size and heft of a softball. Franklin jammed his camera into his bag, and set about retrieving rocks. Nia did the same.

The dogs' barking grew louder. Closer.

"They're right outside," David said. "We can't stay in here, or we'll be trapped. We have to go outside. Follow me."

He led them around the bend in the cavern, toward the entrance. The dogs' snarling and snapping rang off the walls in staccato bursts. He was unable to figure out how many hounds were out there, but there were at least two, for sure.

He was wrong. There were four.

He crept through the passageway and into the daylight. Four large, muscular canines surrounded the cavern mouth. They were spaced equidistant from one another, like soldiers in formation.

Running to escape was out of the question.

The dogs had trapped them. There was nowhere to run.

Although David held heavy rocks in his hands, he thought that throwing them would be a bad idea. These canines looked wild, vicious—downright strange, actually. Their eyes were rimmed with red. Mucus crusted their nostrils. Thick strands of saliva hung from their lips.

And their teeth—especially their canines—were longer and sharper than usual.

What was going on with these animals? Were they genetically engineered attack dogs or something?

The dogs had ceased barking, but their muscles were tense, ready to pounce. They glared at David with baleful, intelligent eyes, as if challenging him to flee or fight.

"It's Malcolm!" Franklin said. He pointed at the dog on the far left. "That's my dog. Hey, boy! Hey, Malcolm!" Franklin whistled.

The dog, a mixed breed, growled.

"He must not remember you, Doc," Nia said.

"That's impossible," Franklin said. "I fed him for a year, spent time with him daily, until he ran away a few days ago . . ." His voice trailed off. He frowned.

"These mutts aren't going to let us get away without a hell of a fight," David said. His hands were clammy; one of the stones almost slipped out of his grasp. "I'm not liking our odds too much, guys."

"If we go back inside the cave, maybe we can find another way out," Nia said.

"Unlikely," Franklin said.

A wind whisked across the forest. The dogs' ears pricked, as though in response to a call only they could hear. The animals retreated into the woods, in the direction opposite from where David and the others had come, heading north, toward Jubilee.

"What was that all about?" Nia said.

"The hounds are trained to detain," a man said. He emerged from the shadows of the trees. "They do not attack unless commanded."

David drew in a sharp breath. This was the same guy he had

seen several days ago, when he had first visited the Mason place. Still clothed in black, he wore dark sunglasses, gloves, and a hat. The man cut a striking figure as he entered the clearing and stopped in front of them.

"Explain your business on this property," the man said. "Or perhaps I will summon my friends again."

Franklin stepped forward and cleared his throat. "I'm a history professor. These two are my students. They're taking a graduate-level history course, and one of the lessons calls for a field trip."

"Is that so?" the man said. He appeared to be amused. He inclined his head toward David. "I've seen you before. What is your name?"

David paused.

"Each of you will give me your name," the man said, "or my hounds—"

David and the others quickly told him their names.

"David Hunter, were you doing fieldwork for your history course when you last visited my residence?"

"Uh, you could say that," David said.

"Is that your purpose, as well, Nia James?" the man said. "Course work?"

"Yes." Nia stood rigid.

The man laughed. It was a hearty, good-natured sound.

David noticed that the guy's teeth were a brilliant, perfect white.

"Indulge me, if you will," the man said. "What did you find of historical value inside the cavern?"

Franklin flashed a glance at David and Nia, as if to signal them to remain silent.

"We found ashes covering the floor," Franklin said. "It is my opinion that bodies—human, perhaps—had been burned therein."

"Fascinating," the man said. "Go on."

"I found an inscription on the wall," Franklin said. "It was written in the Malinke tongue."

"Malinke? Excellent. What did it say?"

" 'I shall rise again to slay my enemies,' " Franklin said. "It was signed by a Diallo."

"Is that so? You've taught me a lesson. I had been unable to decipher the words on my own. Thank you for that piece of valuable information." He smiled. " 'I shall rise again to slay my enemies.' " He spoke the words with evident delight.

"Let's cease the nonsense," Franklin said. "Who are you, and what are you doing in this town?"

"My name is Kyle Coiraut. I came here to find my ancestor's body. He had come to an unfortunate end and had been entombed in this godforsaken cavern for over a century and a half. I've spent years searching for his remains. I wished to give him a burial appropriate for a prince."

"Diallo, is he the one?" David said. "The prince from Mali who was brought to America as a slave?"

"Yes," Kyle said. "You undoubtedly discovered his grave inside. We recovered his body. We will be leaving soon and will trouble your humble town no longer."

"Trouble is all our town has seen since you've arrived," Franklin said. He shook his head grimly. "You are giving us some of the truth, I suspect, but you are lying to us about your true motives."

"Touché," Kyle said. "You may in fact be a professor, but these are not your students, and you are not here on an academic outing."

Anxiety clenched David's stomach. He put his hand on Nia's shoulder, and tapped Franklin's arm. "Hey, we better get going."

"Wise young man," Kyle said. "Especially as I am sensing that my dogs are in the mood for a chase."

"But—" Franklin started.

"Let's go!" David said. He grabbed Franklin's arm. Nia hooked her arm through Franklin's, and both of them literally carried him out of the meadow. They stumbled into the forest and broke into a run.

Running, David risked a glance behind them.

The man who called himself Kyle had vanished, as if he had been no more than an illusion.

No ordinary man could move that quickly. Impossible.

But David stopped thinking about it. They had to get away. He heard, distantly, the barking of the wild dogs.

"Run, run, run!" David said. He clutched Franklin's hand in his, and Nia did the same. They could not allow Franklin to fall behind.

Hands interlocked, their bags thudding against their bodies, they raced through the underbrush. David's breath roared in his ears. Cold sweat poured out of him, and he worried that he might collapse from heat exhaustion before they made it out of the woods.

Far behind, but growing closer, David heard the snapping-crackling of weeds and bushes as the dogs charged into the forest.

Franklin wheezed, his glasses askew on his face.

"We're almost there!" Nia shouted, her hair plastered across her cheeks.

David's thighs burned. His lungs ached. The humid air was like steaming stew.

They exploded out of the woods and onto the steep hillside that dropped down to the road where David had parked the Pathfinder. The sudden dip in the land threw David off balance. His ankle twisted viciously, he cried out in pain, and he slammed to the ground and rolled down the bumpy hill, the strap of his duffel bag sliding off his arm, the bag getting snagged on a snarled root. He kept tumbling down the hill, grass and dirt smearing his face and clouding his vision.

He finally whammed against the gravel shoulder of the road, and the impact sent another bolt of agony through him.

Through his haze of pain, he heard the pursuing dogs roaring.

They're gonna tear me to pieces, he thought.

But strong hands hooked under his armpits and pulled him upright. Nia.

"I've got you, baby," she said. "Where are your keys?"

"Right pocket," he said in a thin voice.

Dragging him toward the vehicle, she dug into his pocket, retrieved the key chain, and pressed the button to deactivate the locks. Franklin, looking weary and disheveled, swung open the rear passenger door. They helped David inside.

He lay across the seat cushions, but not before he saw the dogs navigating down the hill. One of the canines plucked his duffel bag off the ground and trotted away as if it had found a prize bone.

"Hurry up," David said, in what he thought was a shout, but his words only came out as a hoarse whisper.

He heard the dogs, closer. Then doors opening and slamming. The engine rumbling. Spinning tires ripping through gravel.

"We made it!" Nia laughed deliriously.

It was the last thing David heard before he blacked out.

"We've got to get David home," Nia said. She drove, and Franklin rode in the passenger seat. "I think he sprained his ankle pretty badly, and he might have heat exhaustion, too."

"All of us are fortunate that we escaped with our lives." Franklin dried his face with a handkerchief. "Those fearsome dogs . . . I do not understand how my own dog could turn against me so. He seemed not to recognize me at all."

"I don't know," she said. "This field trip of ours just raised more questions."

"Why was this Kyle character dressed in heavy, dark clothing on a hot day?" Franklin said. "Virtually none of his skin was exposed, did you notice?"

"He could be allergic to sunlight," Nia said. "Really, I have no idea."

"The control that he exerted over the animals. It was uncanny."

She wiped perspiration from her brow, steering with her other hand. She did not want to puzzle over the questions that Franklin raised, but she could not help herself. They had stumbled into something of unprecedented weirdness.

"Doubtless, Kyle and his hounds are responsible for the young woman who was mauled last night," Franklin said. "I would wager that he is guilty of the disappearances of the two people as well."

"We need to call the police," Nia said.

Franklin laughed bitterly. "Nia, we have no compelling evidence to support our theory. Although the dogs chased us, we were trespassing on private property, remember. Frankly, I'm not certain that Chief Jackson would be willing to listen to me speak on any topic. He practically hung up on me this morning. He has been behaving strangely."

"I don't know what we should do," she said. "All I want to do right now is take care of David. He's my priority."

Franklin peered in the rear seat, shook his head sadly. "Very well, you attend to David. We need him to be healthy for what we have ahead of us. In the meantime, I'm going to visit the young lady in the hospital. I want to know what she saw last night."

The dogs returned to where Kyle waited on the veranda of Jubilee.

Sitting in a cane rocking chair, he smiled. He had not expected the animals to capture the humans; he only wanted to frighten them to keep them away. They were meddlers, and too clever for their own good.

The laborers Mamu had employed must have informed others about the cave. It was only a matter of time before word reached humans who possessed expert knowledge, such as the professor.

Destroying the three humans would have raised a dangerous alarm in the town. He could not handle them in the manner that he had manipulated the police chief, either; he was talented, but unable to hypnotize more than one individual at a time. Allowing them to escape was the only safe course of action.

However, he would have to remain vigilant against the encroaching humans. He wished he and his father could leave this place, but he had to await Diallo's recovery.

As he thought of his father, his father's vow reverberated in his thoughts.

I shall rise again to slay my enemies.

He was grateful that the professor had translated the cave inscription. He knew the translation was correct. The hunger for vengeance burned in his father's heart.

The dogs flocked around Kyle. One of them carried a duffel bag between its teeth. The dog dropped the parcel at Kyle's feet.

Kyle remembered that David Hunter had been carrying this bag.

"Good work," he said to the hound.

Inside the bag, he found a flashlight, a bottle of water, a notebook with empty pages, pens, and a large, thick book with a worn cover. A Bible? Why would the man have brought this with him?

He placed the text on his lap. He slid his fingers across the front cover, which was emblazoned with a faded gold cross.

Contrary to myth, vampires did not fear the cross, or any

religious symbols whatsoever. He had entered churches and temples on many occasions, seeking sanctuary and enlightenment. Being an immortal in an imperfect world could be a wrenching burden, and Mother could not answer every question to his satisfaction. He often sought Divine guidance.

Kyle had read the entire Bible several times. He longed to discover a reference to a vampire, but he had found nothing. The reason, according to Mother, was that vampires were predatory beasts, akin to lions and bears. Clearly, not all such animals were catalogued in the Bible.

It is our fate, our joy and our burden, to feed on mankind, Mother taught. *Heaven, salvation, nirvana—these things are for man, not for us. Our souls are the souls of predators. Would you expect a wolf to be granted eternal life in the house of God?*

When Kyle challenged Mother by asking her what became of the souls of humans who metamorphosed into vampires, Mother could not answer him. She was frustratingly ambiguous on matters of spirituality, and when she grew tired of his questioning, she advised him to put the troublesome thoughts out of mind. He would only aggravate himself, she said.

Although Mother was satisfied to avoid seeking answers to difficult questions, Kyle questioned the point of a cold, soulless existence. He yearned for more.

Maybe Mother was right about him. Maybe he was too human.

He opened the Bible, but it was only the same series of familiar books. Genesis, Exodus, Leviticus, Numbers . . .

He stopped, flipped back a page.

An expertly rendered black-and-white drawing filled the paper: a battle between a group of men, and a mob of manlike creatures that bore a resemblance to vampires. One of the creatures towered above all.

He searched for more illustrations. He found others, randomly placed.

"Impossible," he whispered.

These were drawings of the climactic battle between men and the legion of vampires led by Diallo.

Even his father's entrapment in the cave was illustrated.

When Mother finally confessed that his father was not dead, but was Asleep, she had told him the story of how his father had come to be imprisoned. Her tale was brought to vivid life in the pictures, with such accuracy that her words might have personally guided the artist.

The artist, indicated by the corner inscription, was James Hunter.

The name meant nothing to Kyle. The identities of the humans in the pictures were mysteries, too.

One man, in particular, appeared in nearly all of the drawings. He was depicted as a leader, a hero. The man who had entombed his father.

The man who had taken his father away from him for one hundred sixty-eight years . . .

He clenched his hands into fists.

The dogs, sensing his change in mood, leapt off the veranda and fled across the yard.

It was irrelevant that the man responsible for imprisoning his father in the cave would certainly be dead. The man would have ancestors, and by virtue of their lineage, they bore responsibility for what he had done.

He would learn the identity of the human who had taken away his father.

He would begin with the young man who had possessed the Bible: David Hunter.

David awoke to warm kisses on his cheek.

"Hi, Nia," he said, groggy, and reached out and touched an unexpectedly furry head. He blinked. "King!" He wiped the dog's saliva from his face with the heel of his hand.

The German shepherd breathed in David's face, grinning.

"You wild and crazy mutt." David laughed. His laugh was cut short by a sliver of rawness in his throat. He had never been so thirsty.

He lay on the bed in the master bedroom of the house, a thin blanket tucked over his body, the ceiling fan spinning slowly. Gray daylight slanted through the curtains. The bedside clock read 3:24.

The day was far from over, but he'd had enough adventure for a week. It hurt his head to think about everything that had happened. None of it made any kind of rational sense.

Nia walked into the room. She had changed into a pink blouse and shorts, and had wound her hair into a ponytail.

"You're a sight for sore eyes," he said.

"I'm glad you're awake," she said. Carrying a tall glass of water, she smiled and sat beside him on the bed. Gently, she touched his head. "You're in bad shape, Mr. Hunter. You twisted your ankle, then passed out from heat exhaustion. Here, have a sip." She brought the water toward him.

He raised into a sitting position, and she helped him drink. Water had never tasted so good.

"I lost my bag," he said. "The Bible was in there."

"Sorry, we weren't able to go back to get it. If we had tried . . ."

"I know." He sighed. "Where's Franklin?"

"He's home. He plans to go see the girl in the hospital whenever she wakes up again. He wants to question her about what she saw last night."

"Did he reach any conclusions about what we saw at the cave?"

"Not really. We only have more questions. Like, why that guy, Kyle, was dressed all in black in hot weather, covering up his whole body, practically."

"I thought about that the first time I met him. Weird."

"How did he control the dogs the way he did? We don't know the answer to that, either. Franklin's own dog acted like he didn't recognize him, remember?"

"I sure do." David pointed at King. "You ever act like you don't know me, King, and I'll disown you."

King licked his fingers.

"What I wonder is how my father has anything to do with what's happening," he said. "Pearl hinted that he was connected, somehow, but she couldn't give any details. It's a mystery."

"I don't have a clue, either. But Franklin is convinced that this Kyle guy is responsible for the disappearances in town. He and his killer dogs."

"I'd sure like to go with Franklin when he visits the girl in the hospital."

"Negative, Mr. Hunter. You're staying right here until you heal. You're in no shape to be running around playing the intrepid investigator."

He shifted his leg to test his condition, and a vise of pain tightened around his ankle. He grimaced.

"Okay, you're right." He leaned back against the pillow. "Talk about bad timing. This has to be the worst possible time for me to get hurt."

"While you were sleeping, I went to my house and picked up a pair of crutches. I suffered my share of injuries in my track running days, you know." She motioned behind her, indicating the aluminum crutches that leaned against the armoire.

He took her hand in his. "Thank you for taking care of me, Nia. I don't know what I'd do without you."

"You're welcome." She smiled. She leaned down and kissed him softly on the lips.

"Hmm. Your lips taste like orange and spice," he said.

"It's the tea I was drinking. I found a stash in the kitchen cabinet. I hope you don't mind."

"Mi casa es su casa, senorita. A few more of those kisses, and I won't be the only one lying across the bed."

"You can't handle any vigorous physical activity in your condition," she said, but she kissed him again.

He slid his arms around her waist. His hand roved under her shirt, traced circles across her back.

She peeled aside the bedsheet and carefully moved on top of him, straddling his body.

"Oooh." She reached down and felt his erection. "One muscle sure isn't sprained." She squeezed, teasingly.

He unbuttoned her blouse, slid it off her shoulders. He smoothly unhooked her bra. Her full, firm breasts tumbled out.

Her nipples, rigid with her arousal, were like chocolate drops. He kissed them, tasting their sweetness, and began to flick his tongue across them. She moaned.

"You are so lovely," he whispered. "No matter what happens to me while I'm here, coming was worth it so that I could meet you."

She placed her lips against his neck and slowly moved downward, kissing each inch of him, until she reached his navel. Her kisses left a trail of pleasurable sensations tingling on his skin.

He ran his fingers through her hair, moved his hands down and cupped her breasts, massaged them with his thumbs.

She rolled down his boxer shorts. She took his erection in her hand, slowly stroked him up and down. Ripples of pleasure spread through him.

"You sure you want to do this?" he said.

"Yes, I want to do this. I want to do you."

He reached out, grasped the drawer handle of the nightstand, and yanked so hard the drawer flew off the runners and crashed against the floor.

A laugh burst from Nia. "Has it been *that* long, sweetie?"

He chuckled, too. "It's been long enough."

"Hold on, I'll get them." She began to move from on top of him.

Summoned by the crash, King came back in the room, ears raised. Before Nia could reach the unopened box of Trojan condoms, the dog plunged his snout into the items that spilled out of the drawer, and came up with the condoms snared in his teeth.

"King!" David said. "Get back here!"

"Be a honey, King, and give those to me," Nia said.

The dog, perhaps overwhelmed by the attention and thinking it was time to play, darted out of the room, tail wagging.

Nia rolled her eyes. "Your dog is something else. I'll be back right back—after I give him a Mississippi beat-down." She pulled on her blouse and hurried out of the room.

I feel like I'm living in a movie, David thought. *And whoever is directing can't decide whether he wants a horror flick, or a comedy.*

His gaze happened across the drawerless slot in the nightstand. A manilla, business-size envelope lay within. A letter?

He plucked it out of the gap.

"All right, baby," Nia said. She came into the room and held up a couple of wrapped condoms. "I salvaged two before your mutt tore up the box. If you ask me, I think he's jealous."

"Bring your dog next time to keep him company," David said, absently. The mail was addressed to his father; it had his Mason's Corner address in black, typed characters. It bore a London return address and was postmarked in London, England, six years ago.

Nia sat beside him. "Where'd you get that?"

"It was in there." He pointed to the empty space. "It must've been hidden underneath the drawer."

"Hidden? That's strange."

He touched her leg. "As much as I hate to say this, I think we'll have to postpone getting our love thang on, right now. I've gotta check this out. It might be important."

"I was going to suggest the same thing, though my body's gonna need a minute to cool down. You had a sista ready."

"Not as ready as I was." He kissed her quickly. "Don't worry, I'm a fast reader."

"Hmph. Something tells me you won't be able to rush through reading it. You'd better take your time."

His palms oiled with sweat, he carefully opened the envelope.

At home, as he waited for Ruby to call and inform him that the young woman in the hospital had awakened, Franklin settled into his study and continued to research their findings at the cave.

This was, by far, the most intriguing historical research he'd ever done. He felt that he walked along the brink of a discovery that would shatter everything he thought he knew about Dark Corner. It was both exciting and a bit frightening, too. But he was compelled to continue.

The study was his favorite room in the house. Several maple bookcases lined the walls, containing over a thousand volumes on topics such as history, politics, philosophy, and culture. He had read most of the titles on the shelves, but in recent years, he had turned increasingly to the Internet for his reading material.

His huge maple desk was the centerpiece of the study. A late-model, laptop computer sat on the desktop. It was connected to a cable modem, ensuring a speedy Web connection.

A glass of iced tea close at hand, Franklin sat in a leather chair and tapped away on the laptop. He had uploaded the digital photographs he had taken at the cave into his computer; the pictures filled the display. He examined each of them, and stopped at the image of the engraving on the wall. He enlarged the photo.

I shall rise again to slay my enemies.

He possessed only a general knowledge of Diallo. He had found more information about the man on an African history Web site. A Morehouse College student had written his master's thesis on high-ranking persons in west Africa who found themselves victims of the American slave trade, and the havoc it wreaked on their psyches.

Diallo was born in Mali in seventeen sixty-seven. For twenty-eight years, he lived as a village prince and became a feared warrior. In seventeen ninety-five, Diallo was defeated in a battle, and sold to European slave traders. He was shipped from Africa to Virginia, where he was purchased by a planter named John Foster.

Diallo was a troublesome slave. Standing seven feet tall and weighing three hundred pounds, he was prone to violent rages, and struck terror in his masters. After he had been enslaved for only three years, he killed an overseer for beating a female slave—an act that required he be put to death. Before his punishment could be dispensed, however, John Foster took the unusual step of agreeing to sell Diallo to an anonymous buyer.

Nothing is known of what became of Prince Diallo afterward . . .

Franklin could not find any resources that provided further information on what happened to Diallo after he was sold to the mysterious buyer. The man dropped off the history storyboard completely.

That is, until he turned up in the Hunter's family Bible, in which he was portrayed as a murderous giant.

Immured in a cave, buried in a grave he may have dug himself, his corpse retrieved over a century and a half later by a man who claimed to be Diallo's descendant, a man who called himself Kyle Coiraut.

Kyle Coiraut, who shielded his skin from the sun and displayed a supernatural ability to manipulate canines. Kyle

Coiraut, who seemed to be responsible for the disappearances of two people in town.

What did any of it have to do with a dead African prince?

The key to unlocking the mystery was Kyle Coiraut. Why was he there? Who was he—really?

Or perhaps the proper question was: *what* was he?

Franklin clicked on another Web browser window. He'd done a search on the phrase "allergic to sunlight." Two subjects appeared frequently in search results: xeroderma pigmentosum, a rare genetic disorder that put one at extreme risk of developing skin cancer due to exposure to ultraviolet light. And vampires.

Vampires.

Franklin was an educated man. But the more he learned about the world, the more he understood that humanity's grasp of reality was tenuous. The world was full of mysteries that defied rational explanation. It was easy for one who lived in a technological society to dismiss many things as primitive superstition.

But vampires? Not Hollywood characters, fictional creatures, or deranged people who sucked blood and dressed in black. But real vampires?

It was madness.

But Franklin could not dismiss it. So many bizarre incidents were occurring that he could not afford to dismiss anything.

Set aside my doubts and imagine it could be true, Franklin thought. *What if Kyle Coiraut is a vampire? He travels to Mason's Corner to retrieve Diallo's body from its earthen grave. Why?*

What if Diallo is a vampire, too? What if he had been trapped in the cave, hibernating like a monstrous bear, until Kyle Coiraut found him?

The phone rang, and its shrill ring nearly tore a scream out of him.

It was his wife. "Frank, the girl's starting to wake up. If

you want to see her, hurry and get here before she falls asleep again."

"I'll be there shortly, dear."

Vampires in Dark Corner.

Franklin hoped his suspicions were wrong. Dear God, he prayed that he was wrong.

Chapter 12

Sunday, Jackson took a vacation from being chief. He changed into ordinary clothes—a button-down shirt and jeans—and got in his off-duty vehicle, a Ford pickup. The truck did not have a police radio, and he left behind his cell phone, too.

He did, however, store his .357 Magnum in the glove compartment.

He drove by Belinda Moss's home and picked her up. He had asked her to prepare a picnic lunch for them. He had beer and soda in a cooler in the back.

Belinda Moss did not fit the narrow image of beauty that was promoted on music videos, trendy TV shows, and magazine covers. She was a dark-skinned, full-figured woman with wide hips, and she stood barely over five feet tall. But to Jackson, she was gorgeous. He found her full lips erotic (and she was a heck of a kisser), and gazing into her dreamy brown eyes made him lose track of time.

They had been dating for five months. Like him, Belinda had lost her spouse, though she did not have any children.

They had known each other for their entire lives, both of them having grown up in Mason's Corner, and with her being the town librarian and involved in various affairs in the town, their paths had crossed often. In spite of how well they knew each other, Jackson often felt strange dating her, as though he were living the life of someone else. After Paulette died, he'd never thought he'd enjoy a meaningful relationship with another woman.

But the loneliness of the widower's life had been too much for him to bear. Even as he admitted that he yearned for the companionship of a good woman, he kept his relationship with Belinda low-key, especially around Jahlil. Jahlil knew he and Belinda were involved, but he was not aware of the seriousness of the relationship. Jackson did not know how to tell him, either. Jahlil would interpret Jackson's relationship with Belinda as a betrayal of his mother.

Chalk it up as one more problem he had with his son. He was taking a day off partly so he could get a break from Jahlil, too. The boy could handle being home alone for one night.

"You haven't told me where we're going, Van," Belinda said.

"Away from this town," he said. "Somewhere quiet."

Belinda found a jazz station on the radio. The soothing sounds of saxophones, trumpets, and pianos filled the cabin.

The day was humid, but gray. Earlier, the sun had disappeared behind the clouds and had not returned.

He took I-55 south, to Enid Lake. There were other lakes closer to town, but he wanted to go outside the immediate area, where no one would recognize him. He'd booked a night at a modest hotel, too. He didn't plan to go back home until tomorrow.

As he drove, he and Belinda didn't talk much. He didn't like to run his mouth all day anyway, and she respected his tendency toward contemplative silence. She was a fine woman.

At Enid Lake, they found a picnic table in a quiet, shaded area of the park, and unpacked the food and drinks. Belinda had brought her portable boom box; a Barry White song drifted from the speaker.

Jackson turned down the radio volume. Belinda looked at him curiously.

"Want to tell you why I had to take this trip," Jackson said. He put down his turkey and cheese sandwich. "I ain't been myself lately. Had to get away for the day and figure out what's gotten into me."

Belinda's eyes were kind.

"Van, you've had a lot to deal with lately, with all the crime going on in town. You're stressed. Everyone needs to take a break sometimes."

"Yeah, but that ain't it. Doc Bennett called this morning, asked me about the young lady in the hospital that got bit by the dog. I laid into Doc like I ain't laid into anyone in years. It ain't my style to talk to folks like that."

"It really does sound like stress, honey. Don't be so hard on yourself."

"Naw, naw. You know what it is?"

"What is it?"

He sipped his beer, looked away into the trees. "I'm scared."

Belinda took his hand in hers.

"Doc Bennett's digging into something that's gonna explain why things ain't been right in the town," he said. "I can feel it, right here in my gut. Don't know what he's gonna find, but it scares the hell outta me to think about it."

"Doc Bennett's a sharp man," Belinda said. "And you're a *brave* man. You can handle anything."

"But I was too scared to talk to him," Jackson said. He shook his head. "Whatever's going on, I don't wanna know about it. It . . . it ain't my problem."

He couldn't believe what he had said. It was as though

someone was working his mouth like a ventriloquist's dummy. He did not feel as if he were in control of his own thoughts.

Lord, what was wrong with him?

"You only need some time to relax, honey," Belinda said. She rubbed his hand. "Let's not talk about Mason's Corner anymore."

He nodded and picked up his beer. He downed the rest of the can in a few gulps. Then he popped the tab on another.

Belinda watched, her face creased with concern.

"I'm gonna get drunk, sweetheart," he said. "Just this once. Can't stand to know what's going on in my head, gotta shut it down. Gotta shut it down and get some damn peace."

Silently, Belinda reached across the table, plucked the truck's keys from where they lay beside his arm, and dropped them into her purse.

Shenice Stevens had awakened, but to Franklin, she looked ill. Her skin had an unhealthy pallor, redness marred her eyes, and her voice was raspy.

Including Shenice, there were five people in the hospital room: Franklin, Ruby, the girl's mother, and her physician, Dr. Dejean, a middle-aged Haitian man who had practiced medicine in the town for many years.

Franklin explained his presence by telling them that he was there to pick up his wife—a true statement, and enough for them to leave him alone to observe. The physician and mother were too focused on Shenice to worry much about him.

"Can somebody close those blinds?" Shenice asked. "The sunlight makes me itch." She squirmed under the covers.

Franklin pursed his lips, made a mental note to himself. Ruby lowered the venetian blinds on both windows.

While Dr. Dejean checked the girl's heart rate, Shenice complained of being hungry.

"I'm starving, Mama," she said. "When are y'all gonna bring me something to eat?"

"In a moment, darling," Dr. Dejean said. He squinted. "This can't be correct."

"What is it?" Mrs. Stevens said.

"Her heart rate. It's thirty-one beats per minute. That's the heart rate of a patient who is virtually comatose. Obviously, she is awake and alert."

Franklin frowned. He didn't like this at all.

"Please, bring me something to eat," Shenice said.

"Ruby," Dr. Dejean said with a sharp nod. Ruby hurried out of the room.

Franklin moved to the foot of the bed. The doctor fussed over the heart rate, taking it again, while Mrs. Stevens fussed over the doctor.

Franklin focused on the girl. It was heartbreaking to look at her. She was only a shell of the vivacious, pretty young lady that he remembered seeing around town.

She has an aversion to sunlight, he thought. *Unnaturally low heart rate, red eyes, pale skin.*

The data was persuasive. He decided to take a risk and test his theory.

"Tell me about the man and the dogs," Franklin said to her.

The doctor and Mrs. Stevens gaped at him as though he had wandered out of a mental institution. But Shenice raised her head, and her eyes shone with a strange glee.

"The man is the master's son," Shenice said. She spoke in a monotone, as if repeating words she'd learned from rote memorization. "The dogs are the master's servants."

Jesus Christ, Franklin thought. *It's true.*

Acceptance of the impossible washed over him, like cold water.

Mrs. Stevens looked terrified. "Baby, what are you talking about?"

Shenice blinked. Her eyes became clouded and confused again. "Umm, Mama, when can I eat?"

What is happening here? Franklin thought. *She appears to be vacillating between various states of consciousness, like someone in a trance.*

Dr. Dejean was looking at the girl oddly, too.

But Mrs. Stevens only cooed and patted her daughter's hand. "Ruby's going to bring you something to eat, sweetheart. Just hold tight."

Ruby entered the room, carrying a plastic tray laden with food and water.

"I couldn't find an orderly, so I brought her something to eat myself," Ruby said.

Shenice's eyes blazed when she saw Ruby, but the girl did not appear to notice the food. She began to sit up.

Gripped by a premonition of doom, Franklin snagged his wife's arm before she approached the bed.

"Stay away from the girl, Ruby," he said. "All of you, get away from her!"

They stared at Franklin as if debating whether to get away from *him,* instead.

Shenice hissed.

Suddenly, her gaze was feral and deadly.

She drew back her lips from her teeth. Her fangs glistened like razor shards.

"Why are you fucking up my flow, Doc?" she said. "Who sent you here?"

Franklin took a step backward. Shenice tore away the bedsheet and sprang up. She stood on the mattress, her gown billowing around her legs.

Shock had paralyzed the doctor, Mrs. Stevens, and Ruby. But Franklin grabbed a knife off the food tray Ruby held.

"Stay right there, Shenice." He brandished the blade. "Ruby, go get help. We've got to subdue the girl. Go now!"

Ruby dropped the tray and fled out of the room.

Shenice cackled. The sound made Franklin's blood run cold.

"Can you inject her with something, Doctor?" Franklin said in a shaky voice. "An anesthetic, anything?"

Dr. Dejean stuttered. "Uh . . . let . . . let me see." He moved away from the bed, patting his pockets.

Mrs. Stevens reached for her daughter, hesitantly. Tears rolled down her cheeks.

"No, get away from her!" Franklin said.

"My baby . . ." Mrs. Stevens cried.

Serpent-quick, the girl seized her mother by the neck and lifted the woman in the air with one arm. The woman gagged, her legs kicked. Shenice tossed her mother across the room as if she weighed no more than a Barbie doll. Screaming, the woman hurtled through the air and crashed against the wall. She struck her head and blacked out.

She has superhuman strength, Franklin thought. With only a knife to protect himself, he didn't stand a chance against this fiend.

Dr. Dejean had finally pulled out a syringe. His voice quavered. "Stay still, young lady. I only want to help you."

"You aren't pumping any more drugs into me," Shenice said. She leapt off the bed. Dr. Dejean lunged at her, driving the syringe forward like a lance, and she snared the doctor's wrist. She squeezed. Bones cracked with a brittle snap, and the doctor howled. The girl yanked the syringe out of his hand, raised it high, and plunged the needle into the man's eye. Wailing, he collapsed to the floor, the syringe protruding from his eyeball.

Sickened and terrified, Franklin looked to the door. What was taking Ruby so long to get back with help? Even as he raised the question, he answered it in his head: it was a Sunday afternoon, and they were in a small hospital. There were few people on duty at that hour. Perhaps not enough people to subdue this vampire. She possessed the strength of several men.

That decided him. He took off toward the doorway.

But she was as fast as she was strong. Before he could get out, she seized his arm and threw him. He slammed against the wall, pain rattling through his shoulder, the knife spinning out of his fingers. He slid to the floor. But he did not lose consciousness. He almost wished he had.

The vampire whammed the door shut and angled a chair underneath the knob, effectively barricading the door against easy entry.

Although it hurt to move, Franklin crawled to the knife, grasped it once again.

"Please, don't hurt us anymore," he said. Was there a trace of humanity left in her? Or had she succumbed completely to the inhuman urges?

"So hungry," she said. She hugged herself, digging her nails into her flesh. Her body shook, as if she were experiencing a mild seizure. "Hungry . . . didn't want to . . . hurt anyone . . . so hungry."

Shouting voices, outside. Fists pounded against the door. The knob twisted back and forth.

"We'll get help for you, Shenice," Franklin said. "Please, lie on the bed. We'll feed you."

"Can't, can't, can't." Her head whipped back and forth, her hair swinging in her eyes. "Must feed . . . must feed . . . need *blood*. Oh, God."

She began to sob.

Franklin carefully got to his feet. He was not far away from the door.

He could not allow her to bite him. That was his greatest fear. He would rather let her kill him than allow her to bite him.

Tears ran down the girl's face. She clenched her hair in her fists and shrieked.

He ran to the door. He kicked away the chair, and it spun away, turning end over end.

He wrenched the knob and flung open the door.

Behind him, Shenice screeched.

Eyes wide and frightened, Ruby and two male orderlies retreated from the doorway.

Franklin dove outside the room, but Shenice's hands hooked over his shoulders, like claws. He hit the floor on his stomach, the girl attached to his back.

"Get her off me, get her off me, get her off me!"

Her breath hot against his cheek, her teeth plunged into the side of his neck, like a double pinprick.

He howled.

The men wrestled the girl off him. But she dipped her head and bit into the forearm of one of the men. The guy shouted in pain, and both of the men lost their grip on her.

Weeping, blood dripping from her chin, Shenice raced down the hallway. The men chased after her, but she soon vanished.

Franklin's puncture wound throbbed. Coldness pulsated in his neck and inched through his bloodstream, as if ice water had been injected into him.

Ruby knelt and cradled Franklin's head in her lap. She was crying.

He grasped his wife's hand, held it tight.

"I can already feel it, the numbness spreading through me," he said. "Give me an antibiotic, something that may slow the infection. And phone David! I must speak to him— before I am not myself anymore."

David and Nia had moved to the kitchen. He sat at the dinette table, the crutches propped against a chair, while Nia prepared dinner. King lay near the refrigerator and watched Nia with great interest, alert for a morsel that might drop to the floor.

David reviewed the letter for perhaps the tenth time.

Dear Mr. Hunter,

I have followed your career with great interest since the publication of your first novel. Your formidable talent has been evident from the beginning. The world of letters has been enriched tenfold by your work, and will continue to reap the benefits of your genius long after you have departed.

Now that I have generously stroked your lion's ego and engaged your attention, shall I commence my purpose for this correspondence?

My name is Elizabeth. I have been informed by my associates that you seek an audience with me. I find this discovery rather serendipitous, as for some time, I have considered holding an audience with you as well.

The reason for my interest? I am intrigued by the recurring themes that I see in your literature. Need I restate them? You know your obsessions.

There are answers, Richard. You will uncover them, in due time. But you will require assistance.

One does not thwart Death alone.

At a later date, you will receive instructions on how to communicate directly with me. Do not respond to the London return address printed on the envelope. I use a remailing service to maintain my privacy.

Until then, be comforted by my assurance that your search will soon draw to a close.

> *Regards,*
> *Elizabeth*

It was the most puzzling letter David had ever read. Who was Elizabeth? He'd read every article and interview he could find about his father's personal life, and no one named Elizabeth had ever been mentioned. And what did she mean by "one does not thwart Death alone"?

It seemed to support the theory that his father's death was a hoax. Maybe Elizabeth had helped him pull off the ruse.

But why? Where was his father now? How was any of it connected to what was happening in Mason's Corner?

He was back to the same frustrating questions.

In between his consecutive readings of the letter, he'd called Franklin's home. No one had answered, which probably meant that Franklin was visiting the girl at the hospital. David wished he could've gone, too. But he was confident in Franklin's ability to dig up the truth on his own.

"Dinner is served," Nia said. She set a plate in front of David. "Hamburger Helper a la Nia."

"Looks delicious."

"Thank you." She put her own plate down at a spot beside him. "There wasn't much else here I could use to make a meal."

He smiled. "What can I say, it's the bachelor's lifestyle. All we normally have in the fridge is leftover pizza and beer."

She clucked her tongue.

Halfway through their meal, the telephone rang. Nia handed the phone to David.

It was Ruby. Her voice was troubled.

"David, Franklin's here at the hospital. He wants you and Nia to come immediately."

"Mrs. Bennett, you don't sound good. Is everything okay?"

"Please, come right away, there isn't much time. He's in room 104. He's been admitted as a patient."

"Admitted?" David's stomach plummeted.

"Come right away," Ruby said. She hung up.

David stared at the telephone, numb.

"Is something wrong with Franklin?" Nia said.

"He wants us to come see him at the hospital. He's been admitted."

"Oh, no! Why?"

"Ruby wouldn't tell me." He stuffed the letter in the envelope. "But we need to hurry."

Nia drove them to the hospital. A police cruiser was parked in front of the building.

David's heart clenched.

"This doesn't look good," he said. "I wonder if that's the chief."

Inside, a police officer—a lanky black man—stood outside Franklin's door, talking to an orderly.

"That's Deputy Dudu," Nia said. "I wonder what's happening."

"Is that really his name? Sounds like a comic book character."

"In some ways, he *is* a comic book character. But he tries to be a good cop. Tries too hard, in fact." When they attempted to walk into the room, the deputy stuck out his long arm in front of them, like a traffic guard.

"Hold on a minute, folks," he said. "I know who you are, Miss James, but who is this fella?"

"I'm David Hunter. I live across the street from Franklin Bennett. We're friends."

The deputy blinked, lowered his arm. "Oh, you're Mr. Hunter's son. Chief Jackson told me you'd moved into town. What happened to your foot?"

"I twisted my ankle when I was running," David said. He flexed his fingers on the handles of the crutches. He saw no purpose to lying.

"Why are you here, Deputy?" Nia said. "What's going on?"

"A young lady who was a patient here went into a frenzy, attacked her mother, Dr. Dejean, and Doc Bennett, too. She bit Doc Bennett."

Nia put her hand to her mouth, shocked.

"She *bit* him?" David said.

"Sure did. She's on the loose, somewhere." The deputy looked around warily, his hand on the butt of his revolver, as though he might find her lurking in the shadows of the corridor. "Orderlies couldn't contain her; she's escaped the hospital and is at large. Extremely dangerous, I'd say, judging by the damage she caused here. You be careful and be sure to alert law enforcement authorities if you happen to see her."

"We will," David said.

Ruby came to the doorway. "I'm so glad you're here. Hurry, come in."

As David walked away from the deputy, he thought he heard the cop mumble something about aliens invading the town. Odd. The guy was probably talking about a TV show.

Franklin looked older than usual. He lay in bed, the sheets pulled up to his frizzy gray beard, his thin arms resting atop the covers. His face was drawn, and his lips were pale. He appeared to be asleep.

Ruby went to her husband and tapped his shoulder. "Sugar, they're here."

David and Nia settled in chairs beside the bed.

Franklin's eyes fluttered open. He was not wearing his glasses, and he squinted at them. Ruby slid his glasses over his face, and Franklin scooted up a few inches, exposing the bandage across the side of his neck.

What in the hell?

"I see the consternation on your faces," Franklin said. He coughed. "I come here to visit a young lady and I wind up as a patient myself."

"Tell us what happened," David said. "Tell us everything."

Franklin cleared his throat. Ruby helped him sip water through a straw.

Then he started talking.

"That is what happened," Franklin said, concluding his tale. "Now I will ask you: do you believe me?"

David and Nia looked at each other. She was frightened, he could see, just as he was, too. But he could also tell that she believed. And so did he.

Vampires, for God's sake.

"Yes, we believe you," David said. "There's too much evidence to deny. We don't have time to waste running around like skeptical fools in horror movies who always get killed by the monster they won't believe in. We believe enough to take action."

"Exactly," Nia said. "Until it's been proven otherwise, it's smart, and safe, for us to believe that vampires really exist."

"Good," Franklin said. "My friends, if anyone had told me that a time would come when I would accept the existence of vampires, well, let me say that I would have given that individual a sound tongue lashing."

"This guy we saw earlier, Kyle, is a vampire, but not the head vampire," David said. The words sounded strange coming out of his mouth, but he continued. "Diallo, the one who was buried in the cave, he's the big dog."

"Indeed," Franklin said. "We have not encountered him, yet, and I believe that we've been fortunate. He has a history of bloodshed."

"And Kyle, the kid, wants to set him loose," David said. "He came here, probably from France, to find his father, a monster."

The meaning of what he'd said struck him. Kyle had come to this town seeking his father. Hadn't he, in essence, done the same thing? He came to Mason's Corner to learn more about Richard Hunter, to demystify the enigma, to discover the connections that he and his father shared. In a way, he and Kyle were alike.

"I didn't know vampires could have children," Nia said.

"And if there's a father," David said, "there might be a mother, too."

"What do we know, definitively, about these creatures?" Franklin asked. "All of our beliefs are based on novels, films, and myth. Fiction, in other words—not fact. All of our assumptions could be incorrect. These creatures could possess talents that we cannot imagine."

They were quiet as the truth of his words sank in. David happened to glance outside the window, at the setting sun. Night was coming soon. The day had ushered in frightening revelations. He was afraid to think of what this night would bring.

"I see what you mean," Nia said. "The dogs are a good example."

"Precisely," Franklin said. "The young lady told me, 'the dogs are the master's servants.' The manipulation of canines is not commonly associated with vampires."

"You know what scares me?" David said. "The girl who you said was a vampire, she was bitten by a dog. Not a vampire."

Nia said, "Which means a person can be turned, I guess you could call it, by being bitten by one of those mutts that serves the vampires. Like the dogs we saw outside the cave."

Franklin nodded somberly. "If a number of hounds fall under Diallo's influence, these vampires could spread through town like a brushfire. Dogs tend to travel in packs and could rapidly overwhelm the townsfolk. Infection likely spreads via saliva. Similar to the rabies virus."

"Do we know how long it took for her to change, after she was bitten?" David said. He looked to Ruby.

"Shenice was admitted to the hospital last night, shortly after midnight," Ruby said. "She turned into that damnable thing earlier this afternoon, I'd say around four o'clock, as close as I can place it."

"About sixteen hours for the metamorphosis to complete," Franklin said. "By that estimate, I have only until late tomorrow morning before I am no longer myself."

"Dammit, Frank, don't say that," Ruby said. "You're going to be okay, do you hear me?"

"Ah, I feel the infection spreading like an icy river through my blood." Franklin closed his eyes and drew in a deep breath. He shivered, then looked at them. "I fear that medicine cannot stop its progression. My physician, Dr. Hess Green, prescribed a vaccination of human rabies immune globulin, but my symptoms have continued unabated—they have worsened, in fact. Therefore, I am not optimistic—"

"Excuse me." Ruby quickly left the room, dabbing at her eyes with a handkerchief.

Franklin watched her leave, an expression of deep sadness on his face.

David held Nia's hand tightly.

"We can't lose you, Franklin," David said. "We'd be lost."

Franklin's eyes were fierce. "Listen, you are going to fight this, with or without me—probably without me. I won't tolerate any talk of giving up, of wallowing in sorrow. This is no time for weakness and self-doubt." He pointed his long finger at David. His voice was like iron. "David, this is the challenge, the responsibility, for which you have been brought here." He shifted his finger to Nia. "You must partner with David. He needs you."

"David couldn't stop me from helping him if he wanted to," Nia said.

"But Franklin . . ." David could not finish his sentence. The rightness of Franklin's stern words was undeniable. From the beginning, signs had pointed toward a task that he would be obligated to complete. His grandfather's ghost had warned him; Pearl, the psychic, had warned him. His role was clear.

But he hesitated to accept the job. This wasn't his hometown. He was only a temporary resident. He planned to eventually leave and return to Atlanta. Why were the goings-on in an obscure Mississippi town that barely merited a dot on a road map his problem?

Franklin's eyes drilled into his brain.

"It *is* your responsibility, David," he said. "If you don't believe it yet, you will soon. You have been brought here for a purpose. You cannot run from Destiny."

"Yeah," David said. He sighed heavily. "I know, deep down, that you're right. But what in the hell am I supposed to do?"

"That's my question, too," Nia said. "Are we supposed to start collecting garlic and holy water? Sharpening wooden stakes? Wearing crucifixes?"

"I do not know whether any of the traditional, fictional weaponry will have an adverse affect on them," Franklin said. "But I have a handgun, a Smith & Wesson .38, at my house. It is in the study, in the bottom left drawer of my desk. It is loaded, and additional ammunition is in the drawer as well. Have either of you ever fired a revolver?"

"I haven't, but she has." David hooked his thumb toward Nia.

"I have my own piece," Nia said. "David can use your gun."

"Excellent," Franklin said.

"In the movies, guns never hurt vampires," David said. "I guess we'll find out what's fiction and what's real."

"Shenice bit another man, before she escaped," Franklin said. "A staff member. He refused to be hospitalized and left to go home. What will become of him, I do not know. He may live with others, and attack them, too. Thus, their numbers will multiply." He sighed. "We need Chief Jackson's assistance, to prepare and protect the town."

"I thought you said earlier that he wouldn't talk to you," Nia said.

"I think he is afraid," Franklin said. "But I know that man's heart. He will rise to the occasion. First, you must convince him."

"We'll do our best," David said. "We'll call him tonight."

"I doubt you will reach him," Franklin said. "I asked Ruby to contact him, after she called you to come here. She could not reach him. He has gone into hiding and his own deputy cannot locate him."

"I hope he hasn't left town," Nia said.

"We'll keep trying until we get ahold of him," David said.

"There is a key to my home." Franklin indicated a set of keys on the nightstand. "Retrieve the revolver, let yourselves in and out as you wish. But I warn you, keep your grubby hands off my Crown Royal." He laughed, and they joined in. They laughed harder than his small joke deserved, and David believed it was because they were so absurdly stressed out. Anything to break the tension was welcome.

"I am exhausted, and must sleep," Franklin said. "When you leave, please ask Ruby to return."

"Do you need us to do anything for you, Franklin?" David said. "Anything at all?"

"Yes, in fact, I do."

"Name it," Nia said.

"I want you to pray for me."

David and Nia drove away from the hospital, Nia behind the wheel again. David was tired of being a handicapped passenger, but his only choice was to lean on Nia. Franklin was right. He did need her.

"Thank you for helping me, with everything," he said.

"Like I said a few minutes ago, you couldn't stop me from helping you, David. I'm in this until the end. This is my hometown."

David leaned back against the seat. "Life is so crazy. A little over a week ago, I come here, and the only thing I'm thinking about is hanging out in my old man's crib and learning about him. Now look: I'm a vampire slayer."

"You aren't lying," Nia said. "I don't want to believe that any of it is real. I feel like we're in a nightmare, and if we just hang on and stay alive, we'll wake up and everything will be okay."

"I know," David said. He gazed out the window.

Twilight was upon them. A silver moon glowed in the sky, like a giant coin.

The town, previously so ordinary, had acquired an aura of mystery and menace. As they drove, David watched the houses they passed, and he wondered what was happening within them. Was there another person like Franklin in one of those homes, bitten by a vampire, bedridden as the monstrous transformation took place? How about the Labrador that he'd spotted ambling across a yard—could it be a minion for the vampire?

He felt an acute need to get inside his house and lock the doors.

"Franklin covered a lot of ground, but there are still some things we need to figure out," David said. "Let's talk about them as soon as we get to my place, after we get Franklin's gun."

"Okay."

They arrived at David's home. Nia parked in the driveway.

As was his habit when a vehicle parked nearby, King came to the front window. The dog parted the curtains with his snout. He seemed to be grinning. David was eager to hang out with the silly mutt.

"Do you want to get the gun?" David said. "Don't know if it makes sense for me to do it, seeing as I have these crutches."

"Sure, I'll go."

"I'll wait over here."

They got out of the Pathfinder, David manuevering awkwardly on the crutches. He shut the door, leaned against it.

Nia came around the SUV and stood beside him. "It's quiet out here."

"You're right," he said. "I don't hear a thing. No dogs barking, no crickets. Nothing."

The deep silence had an ominous quality, like the silence before a storm, he thought.

"It's like the silence before a storm," Nia said.

"Nia, you're reading my mind."

A cool wind drifted across them, like a final, gasping breath.

"We're creeping ourselves out," she said. "Let's get this over with. I'll be back in a minute."

"I'll be waiting right here."

He watched her stride through the yard and cross the street.

It's funny, he thought. *I meet the woman of my dreams, at a time when I've fallen into a nightmare.* Wasn't life bizarre?

Nia opened the front door of the Bennetts' residence and slipped inside.

When Nia stepped into the Bennetts' dark, tomb-silent home, a distinct feeling of unreality gripped her.

I'm inside the home of a couple that I hardly know, looking for a gun that we'll use to defend ourselves against vampires. She wanted to laugh. Or cry. It was crazy. She believed the threat was real, but it was crazy nonetheless. Nothing ever happened in sleepy, dull Mason's Corner. Now they were battling the armies of darkness.

She giggled, involuntarily, and the sound was so strange in the preternaturally quiet house that she quickly shut up.

She clicked on a lamp in the living room. Framed photographs of the Bennetts were everywhere. They were a happy, golden pair; they had the kind of fabled, old-school marriage that she'd love to have one day.

But first, she would have to survive.

She switched on the light in the study. As Franklin had instructed, she located the Smith & Wesson revolver in the drawer. It glimmered like a dark jewel.

Although the gun surely only weighed a few pounds, for Nia, it was like lifting a forty-pound dumbbell. The weapon was heavy with its power to spit out death.

Carefully, she put the revolver and the box of ammunition in her purse. As she returned to the door, she cut off the lights. The darkness seemed to chase her to the doorway, and she hurried to step outside and lock up behind her.

Across the street, David rested against the truck. He waved at her.

She smiled tightly. God, she wanted so badly to hold him and close her eyes and forget that any of this was happening. Someone could wake her when it was all over.

Franklin's words came to her thoughts: *You must partner with David. He needs you.*

How could she disobey the words of a man who might be, quite literally, on his deathbed? Abandon David? Desert her hometown?

She couldn't do it, not ever.

She began to stride across the walkway, to the street. She glimpsed quick movement in the corner of her eye—a large shape. Then she heard the low, threatening growl.

She stopped, her heart clutching.

A red Doberman trotted along the curb. There was another dog, a bullmastiff, posted on the opposite curb. The canine on her side of the street rested on its haunches and watched her. The other hound faced David.

These were not the same animals that they had seen outside the cave. How many of these supernatural attack dogs were out there?

Her own words, spoken in Franklin's hospital room, came to her.

"*. . . a person can be turned, I guess you could call it, by being bitten by one of those mutts that serves the vampires . . .*"

She reached her hand into the purse to get the revolver. The Doberman grumbled, its eyes narrowing.

She slid her hand out of the purse. The dog quieted.

"What do you want?" she said, in a whisper. "What the hell are you here for?"

Inside David's house, King barked furiously, pawing at the window, the curtains swaying.

Like a rapidly moving shadow, a blot of blackness flashed along the middle of the road. And stopped.

It was Kyle Coiraut. The vampire.

Chapter 13

If David had harbored any remaining doubts about the existence of vampires, they were squashed when Kyle Coiraut appeared in the street with the speed of a cold wind.

The vampire wore fewer garments than he had been wearing when David had seen him earlier in the day. He was clad in a long-sleeved black shirt, black pants, black boots. The sunglasses, gloves, jacket, and hat were gone.

A drooling hound stood guard behind Kyle. David saw a Doberman on the other side of the road, blocking Nia's path.

Kyle looked at Nia. Seeming to dismiss her, he faced David.

David noticed that Kyle held a book. It was the Bible, which David had lost when running out of the woods.

Shit, David thought. *What does this guy want from me?*

Behind David, King snapped relentlessly. David wished the dog were at his side, though King might not be able to protect him against the two monster hounds and the vampire. Standing on the crutches, with no weapon whatsoever, he was defenseless and vulnerable.

A large black bird swooped out of the night sky and landed

on the Pathfinder's roof. David thought nothing of the bird, but Kyle glared at the creature, then turned to David.

"You must explain how you came to possess this," Kyle said. He tapped the cover of the Bible.

"Why do you need to know?" David said.

The dogs growled. The Doberman moved to flank Kyle.

"Do not waste my time with needless debating!" Kyle shouted. "Do you know the man who took my father away from me? Are you his ancestor? Speak, human, or I will tear the words out of your throat!"

David's hands were clammy on the handles of the crutches. In the corner of his eye, he glimpsed the front door of the house. There was no way he could make it inside before the vampire or the dogs caught him.

Answering the creature's questions was an almost equally dangerous course. The puzzle pieces were shifting into place. Someone in David's family—he'd have to contemplate the family tree to discover who—had been responsible for imprisoning Diallo, the head vampire, in the cave, just as the drawings in the Bible depicted. Kyle blamed David's ancestor—and, by extension, him—for doing so.

David could not tell him the truth, and telling a lie would not help, either.

"You will reveal the truth." Kyle began to march forward, and his dogs kept pace with him. "Or else, my hounds will rend you to pieces."

David retreated. Hands shaky on the crutches. Praying that he did not stumble.

King was in a frenzy of barking.

Atop the Pathfinder, the bird squawked, ruffled its dark wings. It was not a crow, as David had first thought. It was a raven. Ravens were bigger than crows.

Hadn't he seen one just like this a few days ago, when he'd visited his father's cabin?

Kyle glared at the raven. "You will not stop me. Not anymore."

David stopped in his clumsy retreat, confused.

The raven and the vampire were locked in a staring match.

What is going on? David thought.

"You will not stop me!" Kyle said. He waved his hand.

The hounds launched forward.

Jesus, I can't get away from them. They'll pull me down before I get anywhere near the door.

He turned to flee. One of the crutches slipped out of his grasp and clattered against the ground. Robbed of his balance, he fell and slammed against the grass.

Through his haze of pain, he saw a dark mass wheeling in the sky. Birds?

The dogs, maybe only a dozen feet away from David, squealed. Their ears flattened against their heads.

The winged creatures screeched.

No, not birds. Bats.

The bats swarmed to the ground in a black funnel, leathery wings battering the air.

David covered his head, but they did not attack him. The bats attached themselves to the dogs, and enveloped Kyle, too. The vampire shielded his head with his arms and shouted curses.

Wailing, the dogs fled. Kyle zigzagged blindly across the yard, trying to shake off the horde of bats, flailing his hands in an attempt to knock them away. He finally broke away from them and vanished down the street in a black blur.

As suddenly as it had arrived, the swarm spiraled into the sky, and out of sight.

Breathing hard, David looked at the raven perched atop his truck.

It watched him for several heartbeats. Then it flew away into the night.

*   *   *

Nia ran across the street and helped David stand.

"Oh, my God," she said. "Are you okay?"

"I'm all right, a little shaken up," he said. "But I think my mind is blown."

King was still barking, though less vehemently.

"Can you please let him out?" he said. "He's going nuts in there."

Nia opened the door. King bounded outside and leapt onto David so enthusiastically that David almost fell down.

"Easy, boy." He stroked the dog's head. "I'm okay."

"We have to talk about what happened," Nia said. "That was unbelievable."

"Yeah, and it gives us a bunch more questions, too."

David reached down to rub King's neck, but the dog wandered away from David's side and roved across the grass, sniffing.

"Don't run off, King," David said.

The dog poked his snout into the grass and retrieved an object. Holding it between his teeth, he brought it to David.

It was the Bible.

In the house, David and Nia locked every door. They shut and locked every window, too.

If a vampire or a canine minion was going to get them, it would have to break in, David thought.

He was rattled by the vampire's thwarted assault, but he was determined to hold up. They had too much work ahead of them for him to lose his nerve.

They kept Franklin's gun on the dinette table. King sat near the kitchen doorway, his dark eyes unusually vigilant.

After Nia brewed a pot of strong coffee, they sat at the table and pieced together their ideas about the vampires in Mason's Corner.

"I think William Hunter is the man who's in these drawings," David said. He had revisited the lineage of Hunter men traced on the inside cover of the Bible, then begun to page through the illustrations. "William lived through the early and mid-eighteen hundreds, around the time that Diallo apparently attacked a plantation that William lived on." He put his finger on the drawing that showed William and some other men battling a horde of savages—vampires, presumably—on the plantation.

"Yes." Nia cupped her coffee mug, as if for warmth.

David flipped to another page. "But William and a few of these guys somehow escaped, met up with some Indians, and tracked the vampires to the cave, where they were probably asleep during the day. The vampires' monster dogs guarded the cave. The guys had to kill those suckers before they could get inside."

"And I bet it wasn't easy," Nia said. "That might explain why the number of good guys drops from seven to four. Three of them either didn't survive fighting the mutts, or ran away, I guess."

"I think you're right. Then, inside the cave, our heroes attacked the vampires with guns, arrows, and fire," David said. "It doesn't look like they stopped the big guy, Diallo. He still came after them."

"Until someone probably set off some dynamite and brought down the walls," Nia said. "Sealed up that joker in there."

"And that was the end of it," David said. "But my ancestor, William, was never the same after that. He became this fearless freedom fighter. I remember hearing the stories about him roaming throughout the South, helping slaves escape to the North. Then, like Franklin told us, he had a hand in the insurrection at Edward Mason's plantation."

"Yep," Nia said. "Right alongside with my relative, and the ancestors of a good number of people who live in town today."

David closed the Bible. He sipped the coffee, his stomach

fluttering with excitement. Everything was beginning to fall into place.

"Now," he said. "Vampires are supposed to be immortal. Diallo scribbled a message on the wall about rising again to slay his enemies, then he dug himself a grave, and went to sleep. In the movies, vampires can sleep for a long time—for years, really."

"So Diallo slept until his son, Kyle, came to town and dug him up," Nia said. She suddenly put down her mug. "Damn. I know why people have been disappearing."

"Why?" he said. He sensed that he knew the reason, too.

"Diallo has been asleep for, what, a hundred and fifty plus years?" Nia said. "He needs to be revitalized, to have his strength restored. He's been drinking the blood of the people who have dropped out of sight."

"You've got to be right. Kyle is hunting people—food—for Diallo. Kyle and those demon dogs."

"I'm afraid to think about how many people he's taken." Nia lowered her head. "I really doubt they're alive."

"Unfortunately, you're probably right. But I'm willing to bet that Kyle took the victims to the Mason place. Diallo has to be there."

"Where else?" She laughed bitterly. "But as bad as things have been, we haven't seen the worst of this yet. When Diallo is healthy and starts walking around, all hell is going to break loose. I can feel it. Those drawings are like a warning of what we've got ahead of us."

"True." David tapped his lip. "But there's an x-factor in the mix."

"The big black bird we saw outside," she said. "The bats."

"Someone is protecting us. Kyle shouted at the raven, 'You can't stop me.' Then the bats attacked him and the dogs. Someone wants to keep us alive. But who, and why? I've got no idea."

"Whoever it is, they can't really be a bird," Nia said. "You think?"

"Nia, at this point, nothing would surprise me. Shoot, I wouldn't be surprised if King opened his mouth and started singing like James Brown."

The dog turned in their direction, ears perked.

"I'm grateful to whomever helped us," David said, "but I'm afraid to trust that they'll bail us out again. We don't know this person's agenda. For all we know, they might only be keeping us from harm until Diallo finds us."

"He's going to be so pissed when he finds out who you are," Nia said. "The ancestor of the man who penned him up in the cave. That scares me, David."

David reached across the table and grasped her hands in his.

"It scares me, too," he said. "But we've got to stay strong, figure out how we can win this thing once and for all. My ancestor's legacy has fallen to me, Nia. But, God knows, I have no idea what to do. I'm flying by the seat of my pants."

"Let's call Chief Jackson, for starters," she said. She went to the wall phone and punched in the number that was scrawled on the phone's console. "Hello, this is Nia James. May I speak to Chief Jackson, please? He's not available? Can you page him? It's urgent."

Nia shook her head sadly. She hung up.

"He's not around," she said, "and he can't be reached."

"Then we'll try him first thing tomorrow morning."

"What do we do tonight?" she asked.

"Stay inside, then go on-line and research vampires, I guess. And most important of all: stay alive."

Diallo was in the basement, watching television, when Kyle returned.

His father sat upright in bed, pillows plumped behind his back, viewing a history documentary. As part of Kyle's plan to aid Diallo's adjustment to modern life, he had provided an extensive library of films, books, and audio tapes for his father to study. By candlelight, Diallo would watch videos, read, and listen to cassettes from dusk until sunrise, breaking only to feed. Diallo pursued his studies with the same single-minded focus with which he fed on live prey.

He learned rapidly, too. In little more than a week, he displayed a knowledge of contemporary society, politics, and culture that astonished Kyle. His father had frequently engaged him in challenging, thought-provoking conversations.

This will be one of the more challenging discussions, Kyle thought, as he went to the bed.

Diallo lifted the remote control and muted the television volume. "What happened, my son?"

In a low, halting voice, Kyle explained the debacle that had occurred when he encountered the young man, David Hunter.

"Lisha is protecting this man," Diallo said. "Do not be ashamed. There was nothing you could have done. Her power is too great."

"But why would she care about a human? She attacked me to protect a man!"

Diallo folded his hands behind his head. Kyle had expected his father to be enraged, but he appeared amused—pleased, even.

"This incident proves our suspicious are true, my son. David Hunter is a direct descendent of the man who imprisoned me. Lisha is wise. She understands how the hand of Destiny loves to repeat its moves. She knows that to fulfill her wishes, she should work with Destiny, not against it."

"I don't understand."

"Your mother wants to destroy me," Diallo said in a flat voice. "My existence is a threat to her. She worries, as she always has, that my acts of vengeance will call attention to our kind and risk shattering the safe shell of anonymity in which she lives. She cares only about self-preservation."

"But why keep this man safe? What makes him so valuable?"

"Do you still not understand? It is the man's lineage that makes him so crucial to the success of her mission to rid the earth of me. Lisha believes that he will respond to the call of duty, to attempt to destroy me—as his forefather attempted. Ordinary men can be stirred to great courage when their family's legacy is at stake. I know, for I was once such a man myself."

Kyle absorbed his father's words, reluctantly admitting that he was right. It was painful to think that Mother could be so selfish in preserving her own safety. She had said that she loved both him and Diallo, but how could you love someone and then participate in bringing about their demise? It was mad.

"Lisha is a masterful strategist," Diallo said. "But she is not omnipotent. My strength is building, and I will attain more power than she realizes. Enough to defeat her attempts to intervene with *my* destiny." Diallo's eyes burned. The candle flames in the chamber danced, as if blown by a wind.

Kyle clenched his hands into fists.

"Tell me what to do, Father," he said.

In response, Diallo raised his hand.

Across the basement, the storm doors flew open with a crash.

Outdoors, the dogs had gathered around the doorway. A young woman stood in their midst—the same human Kyle had let escape the other night. But she was no longer an ordinary woman. She wore a ragged hospital gown stained with mud and blood. Stringy hair was matted against her face, and dried blood stained her chin. Her eyes were full of hunger, inhuman need.

"She is one of the valduwe," Diallo said softly. "The first one we've created. I summoned her to us."

Her bare feet frosted with dirt, the woman floated down the stone steps and into the cellar. She approached Kyle.

Kyle had seen a valduwe only once, decades ago, and he marveled at his father's creation.

"I'm hungry," the female said in a raspy voice. She watched Kyle expectantly.

Kyle looked at his father, confused.

"She will obey you, as she obeys me," Diallo said. "Take her and the dogs. Invade the town and multiply our numbers. It is time to build our army."

David and Nia spent the rest of the evening in the office, surfing the Internet for information about vampires: specifically, how to kill them.

The house was silent. The only noises were the hum of the air conditioner, and the occasional snuffling of the wind at the windows. David had relaxed a little, but he kept the gun at his side.

As they researched, he questioned the value of their findings. Every resource they found explained how vampires were destroyed—in fiction. They found nothing that described how a bonafide bloodsucker could be defeated. And why would they? No one really believed the monsters were real.

"There's nothing new here," he finally told Nia, after they'd spent over two hours at the computer. She sat beside him near the desk, a notepad and pen in her lap.

"Protect yourself with a crucifix, garlic, and holy water," Nia said, running down her list. "Drive a wooden stake into their hearts, chop off their heads, burn their bodies to ashes. Drag them into the sunlight—"

"Sunlight doesn't kill them," David said. "Kyle's been walking around during the day, though he covers his skin."

"Right," she said. "He sure as hell didn't burst into flames, the way the vampires in the movies do." She closed her notebook. "You're right, there's nothing new. We might as well watch reruns of *Buffy*. It would be more fun."

"I doubt religious symbols will hurt them, either." David picked up the old Bible. "Kyle was carrying this, remember?

According to folklore, holding something like a Bible should've scorched his hands."

"Oh, I forgot about that. You're right."

"So we're back to square one. Guns. Fire, too, I think. Fire would have to hurt them."

"I agree," she said. "We have to talk to the chief first thing tomorrow morning. We need to get him on our side so we can let everyone in town know what's happening, get people to be careful and protect themselves."

"I only hope he believes us." David yawned. His watch read twelve-thirty. He was wiped out.

"Someone's getting sleepy." Nia stretched her arms above her head. "I could turn in myself."

"Are you staying here? I don't want you going outdoors and driving home tonight."

"I'm staying, I only need to call Mama to check on her."

He propped himself up on the crutches and moved away from the computer to prepare for bed. Brushing his teeth while leaning on one leg was a challenge. Changing into boxer shorts and a T-shirt was another trying task.

How am I going to do anything with a twisted ankle? he thought. *I'm useless.*

Nia dressed in one of David's Atlanta Falcons T-shirts, the bottom of the shirt ending just above her knees.

"Mama's fine," she said. "Princess is there to keep her company, so I think she'll be okay. She doesn't like me staying over here, though."

"Laying up with that no-good Hunter boy," he said.

"If only she knew. I wouldn't dare tell her what's really happening, yet. She'd commit me."

They switched off the lights and slid underneath the bedsheets. King settled near the bed, a shadowy shape in the dark room.

They held each other, and there was nothing sexual about their touching. Both of them needed the reassuring embrace and warmth of a companion's body.

David tried to avoid dwelling on what tomorrow would bring, but he couldn't help it. Would they find Chief Jackson and win his support? What about Franklin? Would he really metamorphose into . . .

He pushed the troubling thought out of his mind. He sank into sleep.

He dreamed that he lay on the bed, on top of the sheets, alone. A whispery breeze stirred the curtains; the window was open. A large black bird was perched on the windowsill, watching him. A raven.

The bird hopped off the ledge and fluttered to the floor. It strutted toward him . . . and suddenly transformed into a slim, tall, dark-skinned woman, exquisitely beautiful, dressed in a flowing midnight-blue gown.

Who are you? he said.

The woman only smiled. She came to the bed. She placed her hands on his ankle. Her touch was warm. He did not want to do anything to disturb her comforting touch.

A soft, bluish glow came from her hands, the strange energy flowing like electric current into his limb. His ankle tingled.

I don't know what she's doing to me, but it feels wonderful.

After several seconds, the woman removed her hands and stepped away from the bed.

Get up and walk, David Hunter, she said. Her clear, resonant voice was like the call of a goddess. She smiled. She floated toward the window . . . and metamorphosed into the raven. The bird leapt onto the window ledge, turned to look at him, and then soared into the night.

Get up and walk . . .

David snapped out of the dream with a start.

Nia was asleep. King slumbered as well.

Blackness filled the bedroom. The window was not open, as it had been in the dream. It was sealed shut, and the curtains were still.

The glowing red digits on the bedside clock read 1:47.

He sighed. He had never had such a vivid dream in his life. He remembered every detail of the woman: her beauty, her cool composure . . . her command.

He wriggled his toes. He felt a faint tingling sensation in his ankle, but no pain.

Heart pounding, he swung his legs to the side of the bed.

The crutches leaned against the wall, but he did not reach for them. Not yet.

Holding his breath, he slowly pushed himself off the mattress, to a standing position.

He felt no pain or weakness in his ankle.

Slowly, cold sweat slicking his face, he walked across the room. His ankle supported him as it normally would.

He had been healed.

Half dizzy with wonder, he went to the window, peeled back the curtain.

The raven stood on the branch of the maple tree near the house. The bird regarded him cooly.

Like the woman from the dream.

"Who are you?" he said. "Why are you helping me?"

He would not have been surprised if the bird opened its mouth and spoke, but it said nothing.

"Thank you," he said. "Whoever you are, thank you."

The raven uttered a soft caw, spread its wings, and flew away into the night.

It was two o'clock in the morning, and Jahlil was still hanging with the crew. They were at his house, chilling on the porch, guzzling beer and nodding to a Jacktown song.

There was something really cool about hanging out at his house, the big chief's crib, and drinking brews like they didn't give a damn who saw them. He didn't worry that his father would catch them. Dad had been gone all day—he'd gone somewhere with that woman of his—and wasn't due back until the next morning. Dad gave him the woman's cell phone number, but said to call only if it was an emergency involving Jahlil personally. The phone in the house had rung a million times with people asking where his dad had gone, and Jahlil told them he didn't know, which was the truth. After maybe the tenth such call, Jahlil stopped answering the phone. He wasn't a secretary.

Jahlil had left the door open so they could nod to the hip-hop that throbbed from the stereo in the living room. T-Bone and Poke slumped in the lawn chairs, each of them clutching a can of beer, debating whether the movie they'd watched in the den—a vampire flick with some ass-kicking action—had realistic black characters.

"Look," T-Bone said, raising his beer. "Ain't no niggas gonna stay around the second it comes out that vampires is killing folks. That's why I say that movie was bullshit. Our asses would've been out the door when the first dead body turned up."

Poke was shaking his head. "I hear you, T. But man, what if those motherfuckers had sucked ya mama's blood? You'd still break?"

"Hell, yeah," T-Bone said. "Shit, I'd take her stash of cash and her car and be out."

"You've already got her car," Jahlil said.

Poke laughed. T-Bone cracked a grin. "Kiss my ass, J."

"But for real, what would y'all do if some vampire mother-fuckers was here?" Poke said. He spread his hands, his puffy afro a dark nimbus. "You know, we out here in the middle of nowhere, in this little, sleepy ass town, hardly no police. What would you do?"

"I told you man, I'd be out," T-Bone said. He burped. "You think the white man would be sending the National Guard up in here? Hell, naw, ain't nothing but a bunch of niggas in this joint, don't nobody give a shit about us. I'd be flying like a fuckin' bullet down 55. Y'all fools can lay up in here and get killed."

"I'd leave, too," Jahlil said. "Don't know where I'd go, though."

"You wouldn't be going nowhere, J," Poke said. "Your pops would have you right up here with him battling Dracula." Poke performed an amazingly accurate impression of Jahlil's father. "Hold that bloodsucker down, son. Got to find my stake. Where I put it? Must be back at the station. Keep him there, be back in a sec. Don't mind his teeth."

They laughed. Then T-Bone farted, and they laughed harder, Poke and Jahlil clearing off the porch to get away from the nasty smell. They stood around in the yard. T-Bone came off the veranda and joined them.

The warm night was utterly silent. The surrounding houses were dark, too.

"Sure is quiet out here," Jahlil said.

"For real," Poke said. He swigged his beer. "I don't hear no bugs or nothing."

"Please," T-Bone said. "Y'all motherfuckers done watched that movie and got scared of every damn thing." He flicked his cigarette to the grass, stubbed it out with his foot, and patted his pockets. "I got to get me some more Kools out the car. Be right back."

T-Bone ambled to the curb, where he'd parked the Oldsmobile.

Jahlil had the strangest feeling—a presentiment of dread. It tightened his stomach as if his guts were wrapped in wire.

The booming of his heartbeat might have been the only noise in the still night. The music on the living room stereo seemed to be far away.

"Hurry up, man," Jahlil said. T-Bone had opened the passenger door and was sitting on the seat, digging around inside the car.

Poke must have felt something, too. He slowly retreated to the porch.

"Stop acting like a bitch," T-Bone said. He got out of the

Oldsmobile, a pack of cigarettes in his hand. Leaning lazily against the car, he slid out a Kool, lit it.

"Get back to the crib, man," Poke said, nearly shouting. He stood at the door, his eyes wide and scared.

"Both of y'all trippin'," T-Bone said. He casually took a draw on the cigarette. "If you're gonna act like this every time you see a horror flick, you need to leave that shit alone."

"Just get back up here," Jahlil said. "Something doesn't feel right to me, and Poke feels it, too."

"I don't feel shit out the ordinary, but whatever," T-Bone said. He pushed away from the car, began to shuffle toward the house.

Hurry up! Jahlil wanted to scream at him.

T-Bone walked slowly, pants sagging, cigarette dangling from his lips.

A black Labrador exploded out of the bushes at the edge of the yard. Quick as a panther, it leapt onto T-Bone and knocked him to the ground.

T-Bone screamed, arms and legs flailing.

The dog was on top of him, snarling, flashing teeth tearing into his shoulder.

Jahlil ran forward a few steps, stopped, ran forward—and then stopped for good when another vicious dog ran around T-Bone's car. It was a muscular rottweiler, with red eyes, drooling lips, and teeth like glass shards.

But the woman was the most frightening of all.

When the rottweiler came, she sprang out of the boughs of the elm tree next door, landing on the ground with the agility of a wildcat. She wore a dirty hospital gown, and her face was filthy. But Jahlil knew her. Her name was Shenice, and she had won the town beauty pageant a couple of times.

There was nothing beautiful about her anymore. She looked like a monster.

Hissing, she came after him.

Jahlil scrambled inside the house. He slammed the door, locked it.

His heart pounded so hard he thought he might pass out.

Where the hell had those dogs come from, and why were they so mean? It was like they were rabid or something. And the woman . . . shit. What was wrong with her?

Poke was already inside. He sucked his thumb like a baby.

"We've got to help T-Bone," Jahlil said. "We've got guns in here. I'll find them." He started to run down the hallway.

Poke's eyes glistened. He shook his head back and forth, his thumb stuck in his mouth.

"Get it together, man!" Jahlil said. He grabbed Poke's arms and shook him. "You better not punk out on me!"

"Get off me!" Poke pushed Jahlil away. Poke went to the door and peered out the square window.

"Too late, man," Poke said, in a stifled sob. "We're too late for T-Bone."

"What're you talking about?" Jahlil shoved him aside and looked.

T-Bone's car was parked outside. But the dogs, and the woman, were gone. And so was T-Bone.

Pearl had decided to pursue a dangerous endeavor.

Since she had spoken to David Hunter, she had considered taking this step. Each day, the malevolent force had tightened its stranglehold on Mason's Corner. People had begun to disappear. Domesticated dogs had become like crazed beasts. Her own cats, evidently having a premonition of doom, had run away into the wilderness and had not returned.

And Pearl understood that the worst was yet to come. That was why she had to take this risk. She had to do it for the welfare of the people.

She was going to covertly immerse herself in the source of the evil that threatened the town. To learn its secrets.

Outside in her backyard, under the silvery light of the moon, she sat on the cool grass. The fragrance of fresh roses scented the breeze. Folding her legs underneath her Indian-style, she drew in a deep, invigorating breath.

Her heart hammered. The danger of seeking a doorway into the mind of another, even furtively, was that the entity could detect the invasion, penetrate her consciousness, too, also without her knowledge, and use her thoughts against her. She knew the potentially disastrous consequences. But she was prepared to sacrifice herself if doing so would save lives. To whom much is given, much is expected, her mother had taught her.

She closed her eyes. She opened her hands and rested them on her knees, palms up.

She cast her consciousness into the night as though her mind were a sieve, a vast net intended to capture only one thing . . . something out there cruising the psychic atmosphere like a cold, deadly shark.

After several minutes of intense, silent concentration, she found it.

Her lips parted, and she spoke one word in an anxious whisper:

"Diallo . . ."

That night, their army grew.

Kyle, the female valduwe, and the hounds traveled throughout the city, "recruiting," as Kyle had come to playfully consider their work.

Kyle commanded the dogs and the female to hunt together, apart from him. There was no chance that they would go astray. Diallo's life force ran deep in their souls. They could no more disobey him or his father than they could resist the urge to feed.

Alone, Kyle recruited soldiers. Moving with the stealth of a spirit, he invaded houses, preying upon man and woman

alike. He sucked each person's blood to the point of death—
and then he withdrew, as his father had taught him, confident
that the vampire's bite would perform its powerful magic.

By dawn, he was satiated. But his hunger would return,
soon. Their mission was just beginning.

Chapter 14

The next morning, Monday, David and Nia went to talk to Chief Jackson.

David hadn't gotten much sleep. After the miraculous healing of his ankle, he had awakened Nia, and they had speculated about the identity and motive of the mysterious black woman who had appeared in his dream. Although they reached no conclusions, he was too excited and intrigued to easily sink back into sleep. He lay awake, his thoughts circling ceaselessly, and soon after sleep finally took him, it was time to wake again. They wanted to catch Chief Jackson in his office before he got bogged down in day-to-day issues.

It was Labor Day. Throughout Mason's Corner, David saw people cutting grass and firing up barbecue grills, gearing up for holiday cookouts. It made him edgy. If the residents only knew the trouble that was building, they would be hitting the highway to get the hell out of there. It made him more determined than ever to win Jackson's support.

They parked on Main Street, in front of the police station.

"He's there," Nia said, indicating a man's side profile, visible through the blinds on the front window. "Thank God."

"Let's go sell him," David said.

Inside, Chief Jackson sat behind a small desk on which were piled folders, scattered papers, and an old computer partially covered by files. A teenage boy who bore a strong resemblance to the chief sat beside Jackson's desk. Deputy Dudu, whom they had met at the hospital yesterday, was at his own desk, paging through a file.

None of the three looked happy to see David and Nia. Anxiety lined their faces. They seemed to sense that the visit heralded bad news.

Chief Jackson cleared his throat. "Morning, folks. Guess y'all ain't here paying a social call."

"We've got something critically important to tell you," David said. "I only ask that you let us tell you everything before you interrupt for questions."

The teenager began to chew on his fingernail. The deputy closed his file, leaned forward.

Chief Jackson tipped back in his chair, steepled his thick fingers on his stomach. "All right. Got my attention. Take a seat and start the telling."

David and Nia began to tell the story, beginning with the appearance of the Frenchman, Kyle's assistant, who asked two men to help him dig on the Mason property. David spared only the details of his personal investigation into his father's life, as he was still unsure how his father was connected with what was happening. They spilled everything else to their audience, including their conclusion that they were dealing with vampires. There was no point whatsoever in hiding the truth.

Chief Jackson remained silent throughout their speech. At various points, he idly examined his nails or looked out the window. The teenager and the deputy, however, were captivated.

"That everything?" Jackson said. His face was unreadable.

"Yes, sir," Nia said. "That's what has been going on here.

It explains the disappearances, the attack at the hospital. Everything."

"Got that Bible with you that figures in the tale?" Jackson asked.

"I sure do." David pulled the Bible out of his duffel bag and slid it across the desk.

The chief slowly flipped through pages, humming a song. Then he closed the book. He took a sip of coffee, frowned as if not liking the taste.

"Well?" David said, putting the Bible back into the bag. "Do you believe us?"

"I got a lot of respect for the Hunter family," Jackson said. He nodded at Nia. "The James folks, too. But y'all are way off base on this. I ain't never heard so much foolishness in my life."

"We aren't lying," Nia said. Veins stood out on her neck. "Didn't you hear us tell you what happened at the hospital, how Doc Bennett was bitten by that girl? How she went into a frenzy?"

"Girl was sick." Jackson shrugged. "Folks act up when they get sick."

"Even if it's just a sickness, and it isn't," Nia said, "you should call a town meeting, pass out flyers, get volunteers to go door-to-door, *warn* people. This isn't going to go away, it's only going to get worse."

"Ain't a good idea to get folks all riled up 'cause a girl got sick," Jackson said.

"Doc Bennett can back up everything we've told you," Nia said. "He's in the hospital right now. Call him."

"You said Doc Bennett was sick," Jackson said. "Don't wanna disturb a sick old guy to ask him about some nonsense, he needs his rest."

Nia swore under her breath.

David spread his hands on the desk. "Chief, be straight with us. Do you think we've made up all of this?"

"Ain't say you made up nothing. You might've seen some

stuff happen. But you're interpreting things wrong, buddy. Ain't no such thing as vampires." The chief quickly looked away from them. His fingers drummed the armrests.

"You're scared," Nia said. She looked from the chief to the teenager to the deputy. "All of you are scared out of your damn minds. You *know* something is going on in this town, and you're afraid to do anything about it. Cowards."

The chief glared at her. "Don't forget your place, Miss James."

But Nia kept going. "If you don't get off your butts and start taking action, my place is going to be at the local cemetery—and so will yours."

Chief Jackson pushed away from his desk and rose. "All right, now. Think it's time for you folks to leave."

Nia started to continue the argument, but David put his hand on her arm.

"Forget it, Nia. Let's drop it. Looks like Franklin was wrong about the chief. He said he would rise to the occasion, but I guess not. He's not the man that Franklin hoped he was."

"Will you at least go check out the guy at the Mason place?" Nia said. "Can you please do that much?"

"Got no reason to hassle innocent folk." Jackson nodded in the direction of the doorway. "Door's over there. See ya around."

The teenager and the deputy appeared to be anguished, but David saw no way to get through to them if they allowed Jackson to cow them into silence. Shaking his head, David took Nia's hand, and they left the station.

"Shit, he pissed me off!" Nia said. "He knows something is happening and he's too scared to do anything about it."

"He's going to have to face up to it, soon. Like you said, things are only going to get worse."

They got inside the Pathfinder. Nia folded her arms across her chest.

"I admit, we gave him a lot to swallow," David said. "If I

were him and some people came in and said vampires were the cause of the trouble in town, I'd be doubtful, too. But he could at least check out our story."

"The deputy believed us," Nia said. "I think the chief's son did, too. Maybe they'll be able to talk some sense into the chief."

David checked the dashboard clock. It read 9:21. "I think we should visit Franklin. I want to see if he has any ideas about what we should do, and I'm worried about him, too. It's been almost sixteen hours since he was bitten."

"Good idea," Nia said. "Let's hurry up and get to the hospital."

"Kids done gone crazy," Van Jackson said. He stood at the window, peeping through the blinds as the Hunter boy and the James girl drove away. He turned to face Jahlil and Deputy Dudu. "Vampires! You ever heard some mess like that?" He laughed, a trifle uneasily. He felt a trembling in his knees and hastily sat in his chair.

"They told us about the wild dogs, and Shenice," Jahlil said solemnly, "they took away T-Bone last night, like I told you."

"The same kind of rabid dog initially attacked Shenice Stevens, too," Dudu said. "I've written a report of what happened to that poor girl. After her spree of violence at the hospital, she disappeared—until Jahlil saw her last night."

A bead of cold sweat trickled down Jackson's temple. He wasn't supposed to be feeling like this. He'd taken a vacation yesterday so that he could relax, gain perspective, and wrestle his fear into submission. He thought he had conquered his anxiety, but when he drove back home early this morning, the dread returned, as though it permeated the air in the town like some kind of psychic smog. It maddened him because he could not put his finger on the cause of his fear. It lay heavy in his stomach like an acidic, undigested meal.

His son's eyes pleaded for a solution. A yearning for a bravely delivered command filled the deputy's eyes, too.

"Can't accept vampires," Jackson said. He shook his head firmly. "Can't do it. Too crazy to consider."

"You've got to do something, Dad," Jahlil said.

"I got to think on it a little while," Jackson said. "Got to be a sensible explanation."

"Whatever, man," Jahlil said. He got up. "I'm going by Poke's crib. Later."

Jahlil started out the door. Jackson almost called to his son, to tell him, *Son, I want to help, but I'm afraid and I don't know what to do.* But he said nothing. His kid hopped on his bicycle and pedaled down the street.

Deputy Dudu stood, put on his hat.

"You leaving, too?" Jackson said, not liking the touch of anxiety in his voice. He sounded like a child afraid of being left alone in the dark.

"I'm going to grab some doughnuts," Dudu said. His face was downcast. "I'll be back."

The empty office was the loneliest place on earth. The room was silent and lifeless.

But it was safe.

Jackson admitted to himself that he did not want to step outdoors. There were things happening out there that he'd rather not consider. He would stay inside, man the phones, and dispatch the deputy and perhaps another officer to handle any work that arose.

But first, he would open the blinds, to chase away all the shadows in the office.

Deputy Ray Dudu resolved that it was time for him to take matters into his own hands. The chief was normally a brave, dependable officer. But he wasn't the right man to handle this.

Vampires were not in Mason's Corner. Extraterrestrials were in Mason's Corner.

And Dudu was the only one in town with the insight and courage to lead the human resistance against the invasion. A die-hard skeptic like the chief couldn't do it.

However, it would be good to have a little help. Even the most valiant heroes had sidekicks.

To that end, Dudu cruised the street, searching for the Robin to his Batman. He caught up to Jahlil as the kid was about to cross the intersection of Main and Lumley.

Dudu rolled down his cruiser's passenger window. "Hey, Jahlil! Come here, will you?"

"Yeah?" Jahlil rolled closer to the car, one hand raised to block the glare of the sunlight.

"You and I have something in common, my friend," Dudu said.

"What's that?"

"We're inclined to believe the story that David Hunter and Nia James told us."

A change came over the boy's face that let Dudu know that his instinct was right-on. Caution framed Jahlil's features.

"I don't know. Maybe I believe them, sort of." Jahlil shrugged. "I just want my dad to do something. He's the chief, you know?"

"He's afraid," Dudu said. "I respect your father, but fear is clouding his judgment."

"My dad ain't scared of nothing."

"Normally, I would agree with you. Chief Jackson is a brave man. But today, he's afraid."

Jahlil hung his head slightly.

"Now, I'm not afraid," Dudu said. "This isn't a time to sit idly, paralyzed with fright, needlessly debating whether to call an orange an apple or to admit that it's truly an orange. We have to act! The fate of human civilization is at risk."

"Huh?"

Dudu waved his hand. "Never mind. Jahlil, I am going to investigate the Mason residence, and I want you to come with me."

"Man, you're crazy. I ain't going up there."

"Let's move to the curbside," Dudu said. "We don't want to impede the flow of traffic."

Jahlil rolled his bike onto the sidewalk. Dudu parked in front of a hardware store, then reached across the seat and opened the passenger door.

"Climb in for a moment, my friend."

Jahlil got inside the car. Suspicion tinted his gaze.

Dudu picked his words carefully. "This is a time for the men in this town to be courageous. We have to act in spite of fear. That is what heroes do, act bravely in spite of fear. Do you want to be a hero?"

"I'm not a cop."

"You're the chief's son. Your grandfather was the chief before your father assumed the job. Police duty runs in your blood, and that's good enough for me. You've got the right stuff."

Jahlil watched him closely. Weighing his words.

"Your friend was snatched last night," Dudu said. "You want to know what's happened to him. You want to believe that he's okay and will turn up soon. I want those answers, too. You were there when Hunter and Nia were talking. It's clear that our adversaries are residing in the Mason house."

"But if they're really vampires, man . . ." Jahlil said.

"They will be asleep during daylight hours," Dudu said, punctuating his statement with a snap of his long fingers.

"Oh, yeah, I forgot about that."

Dudu smiled. The boy was finally coming around. Good.

"I'm only going to check around the residence and see what evidence I can uncover," Dudu said. "I want you to accompany me as backup. You will not need to exit the vehicle if you don't wish to do so."

"That's all?" Jahlil said. "Just sit in the car and chill?"

"Yes, sir. It doesn't sound like much, but only you can help me with this. No one else believes and has the courage."

Jahlil was silent for several seconds, chewing his lip.

"All right," Jahlil said. "But if anything goes wrong, I'm calling my dad."

"Fair enough, future chief."

Jahlil smiled briefly. "Let me lock up my bike, over there by the store. I'll be right back."

Jahlil drummed his fingers against his thighs as the deputy drove up the steep road that led to the Mason place.

Although it was a peaceful, sunny morning, Jahlil was on edge. He could not believe that he had agreed to help the deputy.

He watched Dudu out the corner of his eye. Dudu had a firm set to his jaw, and his spiderlike hands clutched the steering wheel in a death grip. The man was afraid, but committed to his duty, and Jahlil admired that about him. He couldn't say as much for his dad. Dad had punked out.

Because Dad was so scared, Jahlil could not help being scared, too. Anything that frightened Dad was worth fearing. But Dudu was right: someone had to act. Someone had to look into what had happened to T-Bone, and the other people who'd disappeared. It was a job for the cops, and Jahlil, whether he liked it or not, would probably become a cop one day. Dudu hit the nail on the head when he said that it was in Jahlil's blood.

Jahlil was on the fence about whether vampires were real. No doubt, some strange shit was going on. But vampires? He wasn't ready to swallow that, yet.

He only hoped that if vampires were in town, they could not really walk around during the day.

They reached the crest of the hill. Jubilee came into view,

swathed in shadows. It was morning, but the place still looked creepy.

Jahlil's hands were clammy. He had never set foot inside the house or on the property, and he had no plans to do so now. He was not going to leave the car. Deputy Dudu could snoop around all he wanted.

The deputy parked across the street from the gate, in the shade of a maple tree.

"Here we are," Dudu said. His voice trembled on the last word.

"Are you sure you wanna do this?" Jahlil said. He half hoped the deputy changed his mind.

"If not us, who?" Dudu said. "If not now, when? Take heart, my friend. The fate of the human race may well be in our hands."

More of that loony talk. Dudu sounded like an actor in an old space adventure flick.

"All right," Jahlil said. "I'll wait in here."

Dudu handed him a walkie-talkie. "Keep it turned on. I'll have mine with me. If I need backup, I'll request your assistance."

"Man, be careful."

"There's one more thing." Dudu reached forward and popped open the glove compartment. A shiny handgun was nestled inside: a Smith & Wesson nine millimeter

"Cool," Jahlil said. "Is that one for me?"

"If you need it," Dudu said. "I'm sure the chief has instructed you in the proper use of firearms."

"Yeah, but I hope I don't have to use it."

"Likewise. I'll return soon." Dudu smiled tightly. He got out of the car and walked to the gate, his small head bobbing.

Jahlil found a good station on the car radio, switched on the walkie-talkie, and waited.

* * *

The gate was unlocked. Dudu pressed the opening mechanism, a small lever, and the entrance creaked open. He warily stepped inside.

The gate clanged shut behind him. Instinctively, he rested his hand on his Glock.

He looked around the rambling yard, paying special attention to the ground. He had to stay alert for alien pods. He had seen photos of such phenomena in the tabloids. They resembled giant eggs and were a surefire indicator of extraterrestrial activity.

He did not spot any pods, yet, but that didn't mean anything. Continuing to sweep his gaze back and forth, he tread forward across the driveway.

Jubilee loomed in front of him, like an alien mother ship. Well, the house didn't look like a spacecraft, really, but he had read stories of extraterrestrials who concealed their ships inside large homes. This mansion was spacious enough to contain a starship. They could blow away the roof when it was time to launch. Of course, if it came to that, it would mean that they were fleeing the planet. Dudu planned to destroy them before they could make an escape.

He could already imagine the headline in his favorite tabloid: "Brave Mississippi Cop Prevents Alien Invasion!" Think of the fame and respect that he'd gain! Instead of working in this sleepy town, he'd earn an appointment to a top secret "X-Files agent" position in the FBI, probably out in Nevada. Books would be written about his exploits. TV shows would be produced. Fan Web sites would sprout like weeds.

He would become a legend: Ray Dudu, Earth's Defender.

His fingers tingled on the gun.

Under the tree boughs, he saw small brown mounds spaced in random patterns. He put the edge of his boot in one of the deposits. It was soft and mushy. Like excrement.

The dogs had done this. Or rather, the aliens masquerading as dogs.

Gosh, it smelled like dog crap, too. Curling his lips, he rubbed his sole against a clean spot in the grass.

He neared the mansion. He did not walk across the veranda and knock on the door—only an amateur would do that. He lurked to a window at the edge of the porch. He peeped through the glass, cupping his hands beside his eyes to reduce the sun's glare.

The window provided a view of the big living room. It had old pieces of furniture, a vast, crumbling fireplace, and half-melted white candles sitting on several surfaces.

The extraterrestrials evidently had a distaste for artificial light. But he did not see anything else of interest. He would continue to circle the property.

He moved slowly, alert for a trap that might snare his foot. At the corner of the house, he turned to slink along the side of the mansion.

Towering maple trees stood guard on this side. They cast cool shadows.

Ahead, there was another window. This one should give him a look at another room.

He peered inside.

A man stood there watching him.

Shouting in surprise, Dudu backed up and tore his Glock out of the holster. Hands shaking, he aimed the gun at the window.

But the man had vanished. Like a wisp of smoke.

Dudu clicked on his radio. He sucked a couple deep breaths, to steady his voice.

"This is Deputy Dudu. I spotted a suspect inside the house. He is tall, dark-skinned, dressed in black—"

A chorus of deep growls captured Dudu's attention. He turned.

Three large dogs stepped out of the shadows: a pit bull, a mixed breed collie, and a Doberman. Redness burned in their eyes, and saliva dripped from their jaws in heavy strands.

Aliens masquerading as murderous canines. Like *Invasion of the Body Snatchers*.

A chill pressed against Dudu's spine, like another layer of clothing.

"Three canines are blocking my path to the front," Dudu said into the walkie-talkie. "I'll try to scare them away, but I need backup, and I need it now!"

No response from Jahlil. Had the kid wet his pants?

Dudu shoved the radio into the case on his hip. He trained the Glock on the hounds.

"Back off, mutts!" he said.

The dogs stared directly into his eyes, challenging him.

He swallowed.

They were far too intelligent and fearless to be ordinary animals.

Another rumbling growl on his right. Two more alien mutts.

Dudu raised the gun skyward, and fired. The bang echoed across the land.

A normal canine would have scrambled at the sound of gunfire. These hounds only grumbled, unfazed. They moved closer.

There were too many for him to take down with the Glock before one of them tackled him and ripped out his throat. It would be suicide.

He did the only thing he could think of: ran.

Jahlil was enjoying a song on the stereo when the walkie-talkie crackled into life and the deputy's terrified voice came over the airwaves.

"This is Deputy Dudu. I spotted a suspect inside the house. He is tall, dark-skinned, dressed in black—"

An Arctic chill wrapped around Jahlil's body. Could it be a vampire, the one he had seen a few nights ago putting a body in a truck?

Dudu's voice crackled from the speaker again: "Three canines are blocking my path to the front. I'll try to scare them away, but I need backup, and I need it now!"

Those vicious vampire dogs. Shit.

The radio sputtered into silence, following soon after by an unmistakable sound: a boom of gunfire that came from somewhere near the house.

Jahlil gnawed his lip.

He could radio for Dad, but it would take several minutes for him to get there, if he came at all. His father was acting so strangely Jahlil was not sure what he would do. The deputy needed backup *right now.*

Jahlil opened the glove compartment. His sweaty hand closed over the gun.

He would notify Dad, quickly, then move out to help Dudu.

He switched on the police CB radio on the dashboard, plucked the handset off the hook.

"Dad, it's Jahlil. Are you there?"

His heart pounded a half dozen times before Dad answered. "What are you doing on the radio?"

"I'm at Jubilee with the deputy—"

"What the hell are you doing up there?"

"Dad, there's no time for that! Some dogs are after Dudu and he needs help. We need you here now. I'm going out there to help him."

"Dammit, boy, you stay in that car, you hear me!"

"Gotta go." Trembling, Jahlil replaced the handset.

"Stay away from that house, boy!" Dad shouted.

"Sorry, Dad, but someone has to help," Jahlil said under his breath.

While his dad commanded him to sit tight, Jahlil climbed out of the patrol car.

He had not heard another gunshot, and he could not see what was happening around the mansion. The trees blocked his view.

Gripping the gun, he crossed the road and approached the gate.

As if they had materialized from the ether, three dogs raced out of the shadows, barking.

He drew back.

Snapping, the dogs ran up the fence. They were big animals, and their eyes were like burning coals. Saliva foamed from their mouths. Their teeth appeared to be sharp enough to snap through iron.

They were just like the dogs that had attacked T-Bone last night. Vampiric mutts.

He was grateful that the fence was at least six feet high. But he would have to find another way onto the property.

As he backed away and looked down the deserted road that twisted in front of Jubilee, he heard a clinking noise.

One of the dogs, a German shepherd mix, stood on its hind legs. With its forepaws, it tapped the lever to open the gate.

Unbelievable.

The gate eeked open.

Jahlil spun and ran.

The hounds chased after him.

After he heard his son's frantic call, Van Jackson did not know how long he stared at the radio. Time had slowed; it crept forward with the sluggishness of syrup on a winter morning, and his thoughts were amplified in that segment of distorted time, looping endlessly through his mind.

He gnawed his fingernail with the feverishness of a trapped raccoon chewing on a snagged paw.

Gotta help my son and the deputy, but I'm scared . . . gotta help my son and the deputy, but I'm scared . . . gotta help my son and the deputy, but I'm scared . . . gotta help my son and the deputy, but I'm scared. . . .

Ink-black eyes floated into his mind's eye. Eyes as deep

as wells. And words, too, delivered with the coolness of a seasoned killer.

When you leave this place, you will not remember seeing me or the dogs. When you leave this place, the idea of ever visiting this residence again will fill you with paralyzing fear. You will not remember me issuing these commands to you. You will act upon them as though they spring from your own consciousness . . .

A revelation broke through Jackson's thoughts, like a cracking rifle shot.

That man at the Mason place has been controlling my mind.

"Shit!" he said.

He looked at his finger. He had bitten past the nail and punctured the skin. Bright blood oozed from the wound, and it throbbed with dull pain.

But he had gotten his mind back.

At last, he remembered visiting Jubilee and speaking to the tall man draped in heavy black clothes. He had been there to question him about the disappearance of a young lady. The man had boldly admitted his guilt—then somehow erased the incident out of Jackson's mind as though his brain were merely a blackboard. He'd injected Jackson with a liberal dose of crippling fear, too. Nothing else explained the irrational dread that had dogged him lately. He had been brainwashed.

But Jackson remembered everything now. The anxiety that coiled around his gut this time was not irrational, but very sensible. They were dealing with something supernatural. Perhaps a vampire, as Hunter and James claimed, or perhaps something else. Whatever it was, he had never dealt with it before.

Now he had to face it. His son and his deputy were up at that godforsaken house. They'd probably gone there because he'd been acting like too much of a coward to fulfill his duty.

He would never forgive himself for this.

He ran out of the station and to his patrol car.

He roared down the street, sirens blaring.

Surrounded on two sides by vicious dogs, Deputy Dudu's only alternative was to run toward the back of the Mason house.

He had never been a fast runner. Although he had long legs, he lacked coordination, always had. His clumsiness made him the butt of jokes in school. Nicknames such as "The Stickman" and "Dudu the Dodo Bird" had followed him all the way through to high school graduation.

He heard the taunts in his thoughts as he sprinted along the side of the house. His hat spun off his head. The alien dogs were on his butt. They were too close for him to dare looking behind him.

He rounded the rear corner. A set of storm doors were ahead. They yawned open, like jaws.

He ran toward the doorway. It was the only place to escape.

A short flight of crumbling stone steps led into a dark chamber. He leapt across the stairs and landed on the concrete below. Pain jolted through his knees. He stumbled, grimacing.

Above him, the doors closed with a boom. Darkness filled the stairwell and the room beyond.

A lock snicked into place.

Had someone been hidden outside, waiting for him to plunge into the cellar so they could trap him?

The dogs had fallen silent. They did not scratch against the door, either.

It was as if the hounds had purposefully driven him to the basement. Their work complete, they were leaving him in the hands of whatever unearthly evil awaited him inside.

Cut it out, he thought. *You don't know that.*

Nevertheless, fear tightened his throat.

He thought of using his radio to call for help again, but he was afraid to make any noise. The kid had already heard him the first time, anyway. It was up to the boy to do the right thing and get him some assistance. Quickly

The sound of his breathing was loud down there, as if he were shut inside a coffin.

He gripped the Glock in one hand. With his other hand, he unclipped his small flashlight from his belt, clicked it on.

He panned the light around. No windows at all. Gray brick walls, ranked with melted candles. An entertainment center that housed a television and other electronics was positioned in front of a large, hospital-style bed. The white sheets covered a large, humanoid shape.

He remembered what the folks had told him earlier about vampires. The master vampire—or alien, as Dudu preferred to think of it—was supposed to be in the house, feeding on blood and building his strength. Dudu would wager that this was the creature's room. The faint, coppery smell of blood flavored the dank air.

Was the vampire lying in the bed, asleep?

His eyes had mostly adjusted to the darkness. He wanted to free his hands, so he balanced the flashlight on the floor. The funnel of light angled upward and provided decent illumination throughout the center of the room.

He moved to the foot of the bed. He grasped the end of the sheet. Aiming the gun at whatever lay on the mattress, he pulled down the blanket.

Three fluffy pillows lay on the bed. There was no one there. No alien, no vampire.

"Crap," Dudu said. He released a pent-up breath. He'd been frightened out of his mind for nothing. There was a threat in his midst, but it was not in here.

You've got to be braver than this, Dudu, if you want to earn the title of Earth's Defender.

He smiled a little.

Something warm dripped onto his arm. Frowning, he looked up.

A giant black man hung suspended against the ceiling like a monstrous spider, lips parted to reveal sharp fangs that dripped with saliva.

Dudu cried out and swung the gun upward. The man's long arm swooped like a scythe through the air. He swatted the revolver out of Dudu's hands. The gun clattered into the darkness.

Frantic, Dudu drew his nightstick out of its loop on his belt.

The man unpeeled his body from the ceiling and fluidly came to stand against the floor. He was huge—a whole head taller than Dudu, who stood six-four. He was as muscular as Dudu was skinny. He wore a ragged black shirt, jeans, boots.

The creature's eyes were black holes.

Blinking, Dudu stumbled backward.

For the first time in his life, he was face-to-face with an extraterrestrial. This wasn't a tabloid photograph. This was real.

He felt a warm gush running down his leg. He had urinated on himself.

"What . . . what world are you from?" Dudu said. He was amazed that he had the presence of mind to ask such a question. "You're not a vampire. You're an alien!"

Grunting, the creature lunged at Dudu. Dudu yelled a battle cry and swung the nightstick with all his strength. The creature seized the baton in midair and snatched it out of Dudu's hands. It snapped the stick in half as though it were a pencil.

Weaponless except for his bare hands, Dudu began to throw a punch, but the creature clapped its hands over Dudu's shoulders and squeezed, pinning his arms to his sides. Dudu struggled, but it was like being trapped in a steel clamp. He couldn't get away.

The creature opened its wide, fang-filled mouth.

Last summer, a raccoon had become trapped in Dudu's chimney, and the stink of the dead animal had contaminated the entire house. The smell that roiled from this beast's maw was equally sickening: it was the stench of death.

The creature lifted Dudu in the air and drew him forward.

Dudu finally realized where this monster had really come from, and it was not Venus, Mars, the Andromeda galaxy, or any other galactic world.

It was from hell.

David knocked on the door of Franklin's hospital room before he and Nia went inside.

Sitting at Franklin's bedside, Ruby looked up. She still wore her nurse's uniform. Her hair was frizzy, and her red-rimmed eyes were puffy from crying.

David's heart ached. Ruby had undoubtedly been at her husband's side all night.

Franklin lay on his back, eyes closed, chest rising and falling slowly.

"How's he doing?" David said.

"He's been sleeping on and off," Ruby said in a scratchy voice. "Dr. Green came in earlier to check on him, and he still can't figure out what's wrong. They think it's a virus of some kind. They're waiting on blood test results."

"Which might not prove anything," David said. "Of course, no one told his doctor anything about vampires."

"Dr. Green would never believe a story like that," Ruby said. "I wouldn't believe it either, if I weren't living it."

"I'm so sorry, Ruby," Nia said. She rubbed the older woman's shoulder.

David stood near Franklin. Franklin looked so sickly, nothing like the man who had kindly greeted him when he moved into his father's house. That day seemed like a lifetime ago.

David held Franklin's hand. The man's fingers were cool.

David was afraid to wonder how close Franklin was to changing.

Franklin opened his eyes, blinked groggily.

"I don't have much time left, do I?" Franklin said, in a weak voice.

"Oh, sugar." Ruby kissed Franklin's cheek. "You have all the time in the world, we're going to make you better, you hear me?"

Franklin smiled, but it was a sad expression. "Where are your crutches, David?"

"A lot has happened since we last saw you," David said.

"Tell me, please," Franklin said. He scooted up a few inches. "I may be in my last hours as a man, but that hasn't diminished my thirst for a good story."

Jahlil jumped into the patrol car and locked the doors.

Although he had a gun, he wasn't quick enough on the draw to drop three super-fast, monster mutts. Trying something like that would be crazy.

The vampiric dogs charged across the road. One of them leapt against the passenger door, angry snout mashed against the glass. Another pounced onto the hood.

The car rocked under the creatures' assault, metal creaking and buckling. The canines' relentless snarls hurt Jahlil's ears.

He grabbed the radio handset. "Dad, where are you? You've gotta get up here now! The dogs have trapped me in the car!"

Dad's voice came over the airwaves, barely audible over the dogs' ferocious barks. "On my way, son. Sit tight. You got the key?"

Jahlil looked at the ignition. The key dangled there. His terror had blinded him to the obvious.

"If you got the key, drive the hell away from there," Dad said.

"Got it," Jahlil said.

"Drive away, but don't go too far. I'll be there in a couple of minutes."

"Okay, Dad."

Shaking, Jahlil twisted the key.

The engine coughed, but did not start.

"Oh, no, no, no!" Jahlil hammered the steering wheel. "Don't do this to me!"

The third dog bounded onto the roof. The ceiling wailed under the animal's weight.

The hounds' ceaseless barks mangled his nerves.

He turned the key again.

The engine caught and turned over.

Thank you, God.

He punched the accelerator. The car rocketed forward, throwing the dogs off balance, and Jahlil realized, too late, that because the deputy had parked the vehicle on the downward slope of a hill, he had angled the tires toward the curb. The burst of acceleration launched the car off the shoulder and directly into a deep, muddy ditch.

Cursing, Jahlil jacked the gear into reverse and pressed the gas.

The tires spun uselessly, spitting up gravel. He was stuck.

The monster hounds roared and attacked the car.

Chapter 15

Chief Jackson had stopped thinking about himself. He focused on one person: his son.

Never in his life had he been so determined to see anyone safe. He would not lose his son, not to those dogs, not to a vampire or whatever it was, not to anyone. His son was all he had left in the world.

The car's engine shrieked as he accelerated up the steep hill leading to Jubilee.

Anger pressed on his heart. Someone should've burned down that goddamn house a long time ago. When this was all over, he just might do the deed himself.

At the crest of the hill, he veered onto Mason Road, tires screaming.

He saw the deputy's cruiser ahead, lodged in a ditch. The spinning tires threw a shower of dirt in the air.

Three big dogs swarmed on the vehicle, like wolves eager to tear apart a lame deer.

Jackson loved animals, but he itched to blast these hounds to hell.

He skidded to a stop in the middle of the road. He grabbed his Remington twelve-gauge shotgun.

Hunched atop the car, the canines glowered at him.

He remembered seeing these hellish things when he'd visited Jubilee earlier. They weren't dogs anymore. He could blow them away with impunity.

He banged open the door and braced his arms in the crevice between the door and the car.

A dog jumped off the cruiser and ran at him.

You might be mad, mutt, but you ain't half as mad as I am.

Jackson always had been a crack shot, having lived around guns all his life. This time was no exception. He pulled the trigger and drilled the dog in the chest. The hound squealed and rolled backward across the asphalt like a tumbleweed blown in the wind.

One down, two to go.

The other two animals were undeterred by their fallen mate. They leapt off the car and raced across the road after Jackson.

Jackson squeezed off two more shots, hitting the animals squarely in the chest. They flopped to the ground, squirming and howling. Their cries of agony touched him for a moment; they sounded so much like ordinary dogs.

But they aren't, and they were gonna rip my kid to shreds, he reminded himself.

The creatures stopped moving, and fell silent.

Jackson lowered the smoking shotgun.

"All clear, son!" he shouted.

The cruiser's door flew open. Jahlil staggered out of the vehicle. He fell to his knees, doubled over, and vomited in the grass.

Jackson rushed to him.

"It's all right." Jackson patted the boy's back. "Those mutts are dead."

"I've never been so scared," Jahlil said, gasping. He wiped his mouth with his shirt. "They scared the shit out of me. Sorry."

"Hell, I'm the one who should be apologizing. I was something less than a man back there at the station, and I'm sorry. My fault you got into this. You were being brave."

Jahlil shrugged. "Someone had to help the deputy." He looked at the mansion. "I don't know where Dudu is. I haven't heard anything else from him."

Jackson spat on the ground. Fear of what awaited them inside the house chewed at him, but he pushed it away. He was not going to be stopped again. "We got to go in there and get him."

"Hell, no," Jahlil said. "Sorry, Dad, but that's nuts. Dudu told me that he saw one of those vampires watching him through the window—he saw the tall guy who's always wearing black. I know vampires are supposed to stay in their coffins during the day, but *he wasn't asleep.*"

"Son, I can't leave my deputy to die, like I couldn't leave you."

"Yeah, but I wasn't in there." Jahlil pointed at the house. "There were more of those vampire dogs running around the yard up there, too. We'd need an army to make a move on that place. You and I couldn't do it."

"Yeah." Jackson spat again. "Makes a lot of sense."

"We should go back to the station and hit up that guy David and the woman, Nia. We need them to help us come up with a plan. They've figured out all of this stuff already. Later, we can round up some people and storm the Mason crib to get Dudu, if he's still alive."

"Smart plan, but I hate to leave my man in there."

"Then try him on the radio," Jahlil said.

Jackson clicked on his walkie-talkie. He called for the deputy. Several attempts yielded only flat static.

"He's gone," Jahlil said. "I hate to say it, Dad, but I can feel it."

Jackson put away the radio. "All right, we're gonna follow your plan. But we're coming back later for my deputy."

Jahlil was about to say something when he looked behind Jackson. His eyes grew as large as golf balls.

Jackson turned.

The dogs were stirring. Their legs trembled, their jaws clenched and unclenched, and their eyes blinked as though they were awakening from a nap.

But the blood was still damp on their gunshot chests.

A numbing coldness came over Jackson.

"That ain't possible," Jackson said. "It ain't. I plugged each one of 'em in the heart with a twelve gauge."

Groaning, one of the dogs drew its legs under its body, preparing to stand.

Jackson and Jahlil ran to his car.

"Look at that," Jahlil said, when they were locked inside the cruiser. "All of them are getting up."

Jackson saw it. And it hit him—really, hit him—that they were dealing with something supernatural. He couldn't dance around the subject and put a nice, acceptable label on it. He had flattened those dogs himself, and now they were on their feet. Resurrected.

How am I gonna protect folks against this? he thought. *They didn't talk about nothing like this at the police academy.*

The hounds gathered together and faced the car. They growled. Fresh saliva drooled from their lips.

"Let's get out of here!" Jahlil said.

The dogs took off toward them.

Jackson hit the gas, and they didn't look back.

"That is quite a story," Franklin said. A spasm of coughs racked his body. It took him a minute to speak again. "I believe you and Miss James have cleverly solved the puzzle of the vampires that have arisen in Dark Corner."

David was pleased to win Franklin's approval. "We took your ideas and ran with them, that's all. We couldn't have done it without you."

"It's too bad Chief Jackson doesn't believe us," Nia said. She sat near Ruby on the other side of the bed, her lips curled in disdain. "What a bull-headed man."

"He'll come around," Franklin said. "He won't have any choice. Events will soon be building to a head."

"What makes you say that?" David said.

Franklin closed his eyes. His voice lowered to a whisper; he seemed to be in a trancelike state. "I am changing. Oh, yes, I am. I sense Diallo's desires, the way a servant intuits the ambitions of his master. Diallo is cultivating a fearsome army that he will unleash on this town, very soon."

David bent forward. "How can we beat him?"

Franklin's eyes snapped open. He blinked. "What did you say?"

"How can we beat the vampires?"

"Pardon me, I don't know what I was saying, must've lost my bearings for a moment." Franklin appeared confused. He sighed. "I suggest that you speak to Pearl. With her talents, perhaps she can discover a way."

Doubt must have colored David's face, because Franklin clutched David's hand.

"You are going to prevail, David. You were brought here to fulfill your family's legacy. It is your destiny to succeed."

"Franklin . . . I don't know. We've pieced together a lot, but at the same time, I feel like we don't have a clue about how we'll beat this thing."

"Let go of your doubt. Everything will become clear, you must have faith." Franklin's eyes drilled into David. His weary voice was only a weak imitation of how it used to be, but the underlying, grave seriousness of his tone could not have been more riveting. "Listen. You originally came to Dark Corner to unravel the mystery of your father, and you have learned little about him that satisfies you. Why? Because you do not need to understand your father in order to be complete. You will not discover any keys in your father's life that will unlock secrets in your own heart. Let go of doubt and worry. Let it go, son. God is lighting your path and will grant you all that you require to fulfill your destiny and lead a life of which you can be proud. You aren't half a man, David, as you once called yourself—you're all the man that you will ever need to be. You *will* prevail."

David bowed his head. Franklin's words sliced like a paring knife into his heart. He'd been given similar pep talks before, from his mother and relatives, intended to make him feel good about his fatherless life. When he was a kid, it was common for him to hear praise such as: *You're a great boy. Don't let your father's absence bother you. It's not your fault. You're going to be a success without him.* Then, as he matured into adulthood, the compliments became: *You're a strong, responsible man who's made your family proud. You did it without your father. Be proud of yourself, because we are.*

And David was proud of what he had become and accomplished. But occasionally, doubts surfaced. What had he missed by growing up without a father? Would he be a better man if his father had been there for him? If he ever had a son of his own, would he know how to be a father to his child?

In spite of the nurturing his family had given him all of his life, those doubts festered like weeds in his soul. It took coming to Dark Corner to delve into his father's life . . . it took being compelled to fulfill a terrifying family duty . . . it took hearing an exhortation from Franklin Bennett, a man he had known for only a brief time, a man who exemplified the virtues that David held dear, a man poised on the edge of a supernatural metamorphosis . . . it took all of those things for David to break down, at last. David wept, and they were tears of purification, tears of release.

Comforting hands rested on his shoulders. Nia. He put his arms around her waist and pulled her to him, his wet face dampening her blouse.

"We're going to do this," she said softly. "You and me, together. Watch us."

David dried his eyes, sniffled. "I'm okay. Really, I am. I needed to hear that. Thank you, Franklin."

Franklin smiled weakly. "I want you to promise me one thing, David."

"Whatever it is, I'll do it," David said.

"Promise me that when I become a vampire, you will destroy me yourself."

"Franklin, I can't—"

"Please." Franklin squeezed David's hand. "Promise me."

"It's not going to come to that," David said. He exhaled a deep breath. "But okay, I promise."

"Thank you." He released David's hand.

As if a button in his brain had been pressed, Franklin immediately fell asleep. Head turned to the side, lips parted, arms slack, he looked, to David, like a corpse in a coffin.

He's gone, David thought. *When he opens his eyes again, he isn't going to be a man anymore. God, I don't want to see him like that.*

Ruby dabbed her eyes with a Kleenex. She knew it, too. Her sense of her husband's passing human life would be sharper than David's. Living with someone for over forty years would have forged a psychic bond.

"Ruby," David said, "do you think it's safe for you to stay here?"

"I won't leave my husband," she said.

"We understand," Nia said.

"This hospital won't be safe by the evening," Ruby said. "Eight patients were admitted this morning who've been bitten."

"Eight?" David said.

"More still are probably in their homes," Ruby said. "Doctor doesn't have a clue as to what's happening to them. He thinks it's a strange kind of virus."

"In a way it is, " Nia said.

"You two better get on getting on," Ruby said. "You're going to have your hands full by tonight."

They hugged Ruby, asked her to call if she needed anything, and left the room.

In the parking lot, David and Nia got into the SUV.

"Where are we going next?" Nia said. "Or do I already know the answer?"

"You do," he said.

"Okay. Pearl's place is only ten minutes away."

On their way back to the station, Jackson drove, and Jahlil used his cell phone to try to call the Hunter boy or the James girl. Jackson had wasted enough time sitting around with his thumb stuck up his butt. It was time to make plans and take action.

"Neither one of them are home, Dad," Jahlil said. "Now what?"

Jackson tapped the steering wheel. "Try the hospital. Have 'em buzz Doc Bennett's room."

Jahlil got Ruby Bennett on the line and handed the phone to Jackson. She didn't sound good at all.

He felt like an ass for doubting the story the kids had told him this morning. While Ruby was suffering at the bedside of her sick husband, he'd been sitting there in the office, denying the obvious.

"David and Nia are on their way to visit Pearl," Ruby said. "They left a short while ago."

"Got to find them right away," Jackson said. "Thank you, Ruby. I'm praying for Doc Bennett."

"So am I, Chief," she said.

Jackson tossed the cell phone into Jahlil's hands. He executed a U-turn in the middle of Main Street.

"Where are we going?" Jahlil said.

"Going to see Pearl."

"That psychic woman?" Jahlil said, eyes wide.

"Yep."

"Why?"

"Hunter and James are gonna be there."

"What're they going to see her for?"

"Guess we'll find out when we get there."

"Do you believe she's a real psychic?"

Jackson glanced at Jahlil.

"Right now, son, I'm ready to believe damn near anything."

"I knew you would be coming again, David Hunter," Pearl said. She invited them inside her house. "I knew Nia would be with you, too."

"Is there anything you don't know?" David said. This woman continued to amaze him.

Pearl's face darkened. "Knowledge can be a frightening thing, sometimes. Ignorance can be bliss, if only for a short while."

"We know what you mean," Nia said. "We've learned more than we wanted to know about what's happening in this town."

Pearl beckoned them into the living room. "Please, make yourselves comfortable. We will have more guests soon."

"We will?" David said.

"I'm preparing a pot of chamomile tea," Pearl said, avoiding his question with a gracious smile. "It will be ready in a moment."

She vanished into the kitchen. David and Nia traded puzzled glances. They settled on the sofa.

It was a small but comfortable living room. Furniture in soothing earth tones, glass tables, brass lamps. African masks adorned the walls, and intricately carved wooden statues stood on the end tables and floor. A faintly sweet incense scented the air.

A clock on the wall ticked away the seconds. It was a

quarter to eleven, only late morning, but David felt as though time were racing. He dreaded the thought of nightfall and what it might bring.

Pearl returned carrying a silver tray on which stood five ceramic mugs and a tea kettle. She placed the tray on the coffee table and began to pour tea.

Outdoors, a car pulled into the driveway. Through the thin curtains, David glimpsed the shape of a patrol car beacon.

"Is that the chief?" Nia said. "I don't believe it."

Pearl smiled mysteriously and went to open the door.

Chief Jackson and his teenage son, Jahlil, came inside. Both of them looked weary, and David instantly knew that they had suffered through something related to the madness in town. He recognized in them the turbulent emotions that he struggled with himself.

The chief removed his hat and looked gravely at Nia and David. "We got to talk, folks."

"That's why all of us have come together here," Pearl said. "Please have a seat, take a cup of tea, and we'll begin."

Jackson and the boy slumped on the overstuffed chairs. Each of them expelled heavy sighs and took the tea Pearl offered. They were so obviously father and son in their mannerisms that David almost laughed.

"Why are y'all here?" Jackson said. "Thought you had pulled everything together. You laid it out pretty nice this morning."

"You believe us now?" David said.

"The deputy and I went up to the Mason place after you guys left the station," Jahlil said. "I stayed in the car, and Dudu went to check out the crib. When he was up there, some dogs came after him."

"Oh, no," Nia said.

"I radioed Dad, and then, when I was gonna go help Dudu, some more dogs came after me," Jahlil said. "I got back in the car and hid out, and Dad came up there and shot the mutts."

"And a few minutes later, those mutts rose up," Jackson said, visibly disturbed. "I hit each of 'em in the chest with a twelve-gauge shotgun, and they got up. After I saw that, well, I knew y'all were right. Apologize for being so stubborn this morning."

"Thank you, Chief," Nia said. She touched his arm. "We need you on our side."

Jackson nodded solemnly. "It's my duty to protect and serve this town. I'm ready to do my job."

"What about the deputy?" David said. "Have you heard anything from him?"

"Not since he went into that house." Jackson glumly stared into his tea. "Couldn't get him on the radio."

"What do you think?" Jahlil asked Pearl. "You're psychic. Is Dudu alive?"

Sitting in her chair, Pearl had folded her legs under her Indian-style. She looked like a life-size porcelain doll.

"I am sorry, Raymond Dudu is dead," she said. "Diallo killed him."

Jackson swore softly.

"How do you know?" David said. "We never told you the vampire's name."

Pearl closed her eyes. "These past several days, I have spent many hours in meditation, seeking direction. Last night, I decided to penetrate the consciousness of the creature who is responsible for the evil rampant in Dark Corner. I secretly immersed myself in his mind."

"That sounds dangerous," Nia said. "Could he find out that you've been probing into his thoughts, or whatever you call it?"

"Possibly, yes," Pearl said. "It is a risk that I was prepared to take, for the welfare of all."

"What else you know 'bout him?" Jackson hunched forward, hands cupped around the mug.

David leaned forward, too, the tea forgotten. His thirst for knowledge surpassed his desire for any drink.

Eyes closed, Pearl swayed slowly as she spoke, as if listening to music that only she could hear. Her soft voice was hypnotic. "Some of this you have already learned. Diallo was a prince in Mali, a mighty warrior with a taste for violence and vengeance. Upon losing a battle, he was captured, sold to slave traders, and shipped to America. He could not tolerate serving as a slave. He fought his masters viciously, and the resistance culminated in his murder of an overseer. Such a crime demanded that he be put to death. But Diallo was saved from his punishment by an ancient vampire."

David thought of the raven, and the ethereally beautiful black woman who had visited him in a dream and healed his ankle.

"The ancient one's name is Lisha," Pearl said. "She is very old—indeed, her age is a mystery. She invited Diallo to be her companion, to become a vampire, and he accepted. They moved to New Orleans and lived there safely for many years, but Diallo, though he was no longer a man, never set aside his mortal memories. He despised white men for enslaving him and his people. He despised his own people for submitting to slavery. He had come to hate all mankind. I believe he is tormented by something else, as well, that fuels his rage, but the answer eluded me. The end result is that Diallo decided to use his powers as a vampire to wage war against man.

"Lisha knew of Diallo's mission, but she was unable to persuade him to set aside his hatred. He left her, while she was with child."

"Kyle," Nia said. "The vampire that we've seen."

"Yes," Pearl said. "While Lisha was pregnant with Kyle, Diallo built an army of vampires. They went on a rampage across the South, attacking plantations and killing Negro slaves, whites, and Indians—no human escaped their wrath. They slaughtered hundreds, and the bloodshed might have continued for years, had not William Hunter, David's ancestor, led a courageous mission to defeat Diallo."

The others in the room looked at David.

"Entombed in a cave, Diallo slept in a grave for over a hundred and fifty years," she said. "Vampires have the ability to hibernate for long periods, but the longer the sleep, the longer the recuperation process. Somehow—perhaps from his mother—Kyle learned of his father's whereabouts, and he came to our town to awaken his father. For several days now, Kyle has been capturing innocents in Dark Corner. He has been feeding them to his father, to revitalize him. Diallo, like all vampires, feeds on blood."

"How many people so far?" Jackson said. "I've gotten reports of five missing."

"There are more," Pearl said. "I do not know the precise number, but some disappearances have gone unreported. Diallo has been feeding nightly, sometimes twice a night."

Jackson's lips puckered sourly.

"Diallo's thirst for violence is unquenchable," Pearl said. "Once he is at full strength, he will launch an attack on the town."

"When?" David said.

"Perhaps tomorrow," Pearl said. "Perhaps tonight. He will wait until dusk, though he, like all true vampires, can walk in daylight by dressing appropriately. But he is more comfortable in darkness. They are nocturnal creatures."

"What's up with these vampires?" Jahlil said. "Are they just like they are in the movies?"

"Not exactly," Pearl said. "As I said, by dressing appropriately, they can walk in sunlight. Ultraviolet light irritates their skin, but it does not kill them. Crucifixes, holy water, and other religious symbols do not harm them. These creatures are not anti-Christian creations spawned by a fallen angel. Consider them as a separate species. First and foremost, they are predators. Humans are their primary source of food. They feed on our blood."

All of them were silent, absorbing Pearl's words. David clasped his hands, listening.

"There are two kinds of vampires," Pearl said. "Diallo and his son, Kyle, are the first kind. They are high-level vampires—purebloods, if you will—and possess extraordinary strength and talents. There are not many such vampires. As I understand it from skimming Diallo's thoughts, the process for a human to become one of these creatures is dangerous, lengthy, and usually fatal. Diallo barely survived the transformation himself.

"The second kind of vampire is more common. They are called valduwe. They possess their critical faculties, and can behave at a functional level, but they are under the influence of the master vampire who created them. They do not have any supernatural talents, but they are physically powerful and can recuperate from injuries that would destroy a normal human. They feed on blood, as well. When Diallo went on his bloody rampage across the South, he had a horde of valduwe with him.

"I must not forget the vampiric dogs. These mutant canines are especially useful to Diallo. They serve as spies and guardians, and they can be active during daylight hours. When they travel in packs, they make vicious adversaries, too.

"These lower-level vampires and dogs are far less dangerous than Diallo, but they pose a threat because their numbers can grow rapidly. The infection can spread via a bite, or blood; the substance carries the life force of the master vampire, ensuring that all who are infected fall under his influence. You can imagine how he could build a powerful army in a short time frame."

"It's already building," David said. "This morning, Ruby told us that there were eight people in the hospital who've been bitten."

"Eight?" Jackson said. "Christ."

"Those are only the cases we know about," Nia said. "Other folks could be at home, in bed, thinking that they've only caught the flu or something. We have no way of knowing how many people are infected."

"Diallo is the source of the disease," Pearl said. "He is like a power generator. The vampires that he creates cannot exist without his life force. Destroy him, and his army, both canine and human alike, will fall."

"Sounds good, but how do we do that?" Nia said. "Chief Jackson said he tagged those dogs with a shotgun, and a few minutes later, they got up." Jackson and Jahlil nodded vigorously.

"Gunfire can halt them, temporarily, but it cannot kill them," Pearl said. Passion infused her voice. "You must burn these creatures. Burn them to ashes. Nothing else will suffice."

"Sounds like we need some flamethrowers," Jackson said. "Shit."

"Fire is all that will work," Pearl said. "I wish it were easier, but it is not."

"But from what you told us," David said, "our best chance is to just kill Diallo. If we can do that, all of the others will be taken care of, too."

"Wait, aren't you all forgetting something?" Jahlil said. "These other vamps are people that we know. Like my boy, T-Bone. He was bitten by a mutt last night and no one's been able to find him since. You're saying that if we kill the head guy, everyone who's been bitten will die, too?"

"If they have been through the complete mutation, yes, they will," Pearl said. "It is unfortunate, and that is why you must do your work quickly, to save others from the same fate."

"That really sucks," Jahlil said. "It ain't fair."

"Jahlil raises an important point," Pearl said. "The most difficult task will prove to be facing those that you know personally who have degenerated into vampires. Your mother, your best friend—these people may become your enemies.

You must realize that they are no longer the ones that you love. They are monsters."

"Any way you look at it, we got to take care of 'em," Jackson said. "We let them alone, they'll be coming after us. Taking out Diallo sounds like the way to get to the heart of things."

"It is," Pearl said. "But Diallo is cunning and powerful. More powerful than you can fathom."

"You make it sound like we don't stand a chance against him," Nia said.

Sadness tinted Pearl's eyes. "Nia, I cannot lie to you. Destroying Diallo will prove to be the most difficult task any of you will undertake in your lives. He is a brutal, merciless creature, with considerable power. For instance, when a human is bitten by one of his valduwe, it takes hours for the victim to mutate into a vampire. But if Diallo delivers the bite, it takes only *minutes*. Remember that."

"We sure will," David said.

"He possesses other talents that I cannot even imagine," Pearl said. "You must prepare yourselves."

"But if we burn his ass up, he's dead," Jahlil said.

"It will not be so simple," Pearl said. "I warn you, don't underestimate him, or his son, either. Kyle is a worthy foe in his own right, and he will fiercely protect his father."

"You're right," David said. "We can't forget about Kyle. If it hadn't been for the raven that sent the bats to chase him away, we'd be dead."

"The raven is a tool of Lisha," Pearl said. "She uses the bird from afar, like one of us might use a puppet. I sense that she is many miles away, perhaps overseas."

"Why did she help us?" David said.

"Lisha wishes to destroy Diallo," Pearl said. "She regards him as a threat, like a renegade who must be squelched. Vampires thrive in anonymity, and their numbers are few. She worries that the attention Diallo will attract by starting a war will endanger their existence."

"Kinda makes sense," Jackson said. "Can't stay secret if one of your fellas is raising Cain."

"Lisha will assist you, again, I believe, but I cannot say when, or what form her aid will take. Do not put your trust in her, I warn you. I feel that she has her own motives that do not necessarily concern your ultimate well-being."

David nodded grimly. The help from the mysterious being *had* seemed too good to be true.

"Is that everything, then?" Jahlil said. "It's eleven-thirty. We need to get busy."

"It is not everything," Pearl said. She focused on David. "David Hunter, be careful. More than anyone else, you are a target for Diallo and his son, for you are the descendent of the man who conquered Diallo. Anyone who keeps company with you will also be at extreme risk." She looked at Nia.

"We'll be careful," David said, and Nia touched his hand.

Jackson finished off his tea and set the mug on the table. "All right, let's head out and get cracking. I'm gonna get some top folks on the horn. The mayor, Reverend Brown, and the county sheriff, for starters. We're gonna put our heads together and come up with a plan to keep people safe, something we can roll out in a town meeting. We got to inform folks, officially, and we got to do it today, holiday or not."

"That would be wise," Pearl said.

"You're gonna tell people that vampires are here, Dad?" Jahlil said. "No one'll believe that."

"Naw, they sure wouldn't, not without some proof. I've been listening to what y'all said about how it's like an infection. Think we can use a medical angle, something about a virus, maybe, to get folks to be careful and watch out for one another."

"Get Franklin's physician involved," David said. "His name's Dr. Hess Green, I think. He's seen the symptoms of what happens when someone's bitten. He could give you some medical backup."

"Know the man, lives over on Olive Road. I'll jot his name on my list." Jackson had taken out a pocket notepad and scribbled on it.

"We want to help, too," Nia said.

"Shoot, I need y'all most of all," Jackson said. "Goes without saying that you're helping."

Pearl smiled. She unfolded her legs, and stood. "I believe that I've played my part. All of you sound as though you're prepared to move forward. There's only one thing left to do." She motioned for them to stand. "Gather in a circle, please. Hold the hand of the person next to you."

They formed a circle around the coffee table, David holding Nia's hand on one side, and Jahlil's on the other. Jahlil held his father's hand; Jackson held Pearl's; Pearl held Nia's.

"I could never send you into the world to face this adversary without a prayer," Pearl said. "I don't care about your religious beliefs, or lack thereof. I request that you set aside your doubts and negative past experiences and allow the loving spirit of the Creator to fill your heart. Brother Hunter, will you please lead us in prayer?" She looked at him with her clear, perceptive eyes, and nodded slightly, as if to say, *Yes, I called on you. It's your time.* Then she closed her eyes and bowed her head.

David swallowed. He'd rarely led prayer for a group, except at dinner for family gatherings. His mind was devoid of a single coherent thought.

Everyone had closed their eyes and lowered their head. The only noise in the room was the sound of five people breathing softly.

David's gaze skipped to the front window. A large monarch butterfly had attached itself to the glass. Sunlight glimmered on its delicate, colorful wings.

He exhaled, and closed his eyes. The words came, without any conscious effort; a passage from the book of Psalms. His mother had taught him to recite the verses when he was a child and would occasionally awaken at night, frightened by bad dreams. Although he had not read the psalm in many years, he remembered it completely.

His voice, threaded with cautious hope, resonated through the air.

"'The Lord is my shepherd, I shall not be in want. He makes me lie down in green pastures, he leads me beside still waters, he restores my soul. He guides me in paths of righteousness for his name's sake. Even though I walk through the valley of the shadow of death, I will fear no evil, for you are with me . . .'"

As everyone left Pearl's house, David hung behind the others and turned to Pearl.

"What are you going to do?" David said. "Are you coming in town later for the meeting?"

"I'm going to stay here," she said. "You will do fine without me. I have faith in you."

"Thank you so much for your help. We couldn't do what we have to do without you."

She smiled. "You should marry her."

"Who?" He chuckled. Nia was in the driveway, climbing into the SUV. "Do you see it in our future?"

Pearl laughed. "I was speaking as a woman, not as a clairvoyant. The two of you are a beautiful couple, inside and out."

"We'll see what happens. I'm not ruling out anything."

"Spoken like a true brother afraid of commitment." Pearl laughed again. She took his hands in her small fingers. "Blessings to you, David Hunter."

He kissed her on the cheek, then walked down the porch steps. The chief's car idled at the mouth of the driveway. They would follow him to police headquarters.

"What were you two gabbing about?" Nia said.

"Oh, nothing, really." David shifted into drive. "I was thanking her for helping us."

"That's all, huh?" Nia said.

"That's all." He rolled down the driveway.

"So why are you grinning like that?"

He winked. "Wouldn't you love to know?"

As they turned off the gravel path and onto the road, a cocker spaniel with a mud-spattered coat dashed across the street and burrowed into the thick bushes that flanked the road.

David's smile slipped away.

"Are you thinking the same thing as I am?" Nia said. Worry clouded her eyes.

"Yeah," he said. "We're being watched."

Back at the police station, his head ready to blow up from everything Pearl had told them, Jackson threw the town's machinery into high gear.

Upon arriving at the office, he'd hoped, in vain, to see Dudu's cruiser in the parking lot, and his deputy inside, lanky legs propped on his desk as he flipped through one of his silly tabloids. But the deputy was not there. Jackson made a mental note to return to the Mason place later to retrieve Dudu's patrol car. He sure wasn't looking forward to that trip.

He settled behind his desk and began to work the phone. As he made calls, David, Nia, and Jahlil sat around a table and brainstormed the design of an informational flyer that they could distribute throughout the town.

Jackson spoke to the mayor, Cleotis Davis; Reverend Brown, pastor of New Life Baptist, the biggest church in town; the Chester County sheriff, Johnny Chaser; and then Dr. Green. He was amazed at how easily he got in touch with everyone. For once, things seemed to be going their way.

"All right, folks," he said to the others. "Everyone'll be here in an hour. Looks like the show's on the road."

"It better be, it's already past noon," Nia said. "I checked the paper. The sun sets around eight-fifteen. We have a lot to do in only eight hours, and time is flying."

"Hey, everyone, check this out," Jahlil said. He watched the small TV that stood on the deputy's desk.

Jackson, David, and Nia came behind Jahlil. It was the local weather program. A severe thunderstorm was gradually rumbling toward the area.

It would reach them by nightfall.

Part Three

FRIGHT NIGHT

When the webs of the spider join, they can trap a lion.
—Ethiopian proverb

The hunter knows his prey.
—Nilotic proverb

No matter how long the night, the day is sure to come.
—Zairean proverb

Chapter 16

The emergency town meeting was scheduled to begin at four o'clock, but people did not begin filing into New Life Baptist Church until twenty minutes after four.

Even in the middle of something like this, folks are on Colored People Time, David thought, and could not repress a rueful smile. He and Nia sat together in a pew near the back of the sanctuary. He remembered when he had visited the church only a week ago. What a difference a few days could make. He had entered a strange new world.

The past few hours had been busy. They'd had a meeting at the police station with the town's leaders, and they had convinced them that they faced a citywide health crisis that demanded immediate action; they accomplished this without stating the word, "vampire." David shared Chief Jackson's sentiment that without proof, no one would believe their far-fetched story of supernatural beasts roaming Mason's Corner. They offered the leaders the more palatable theory of a fast-spreading, rabieslike virus that afflicted canines and humans. Dr. Green, Franklin's physician, supported the idea, which helped his comrades fall into line. Together, they outlined a simple but effective plan that they would roll out to the residents in the town meeting.

To notify everyone of the afternoon's discussion, David, Nia, Jahlil, and his friend, Poke, had traveled throughout town distributing hundreds of flyers that Nia had designed and printed at Kinko's. Due to the Labor Day holiday, most people were home, fortunately, and received the information. The flyers announced the meeting time, location, and topic, which was, "Health Emergency in Mason's Corner: What You Must Do Now." The flyer stressed the critical importance of attending the meeting, but for those who were unable to attend, Jackson had arranged a hot line—a voice message on his cell phone—in which he outlined the basics of the threat and what residents must do to ensure their safety. Again, they avoided mention of the word, "vampire."

David hoped that they were not doing the townspeople a disservice by concealing the true nature of the crisis. He was eager to hear what people would say at the meeting when the floor opened for discussion. Undoubtedly, others had witnessed things that defied explanation. Diallo and his clan had been busy lately.

Their last task had been stockpiling tools and weapons. They had a war ahead of them and could not wade into battle unarmed. They had delved into their collective resources and prepared the best they could. David only hoped it would be enough.

He checked his watch: 4:25. It was about four hours until nightfall, and they still had a great deal to accomplish.

A steady stream of people flowed into the church. David recognized many faces. Several folks greeted him as they filed past.

Reverend Brown had volunteered his church as the meeting location. The sanctuary could seat about three hundred, and could accommodate more if the pews grew full and people had to stand.

David and the others had placed a second flyer on the

seats. This particular flyer outlined the fundamentals of what was going on, and the action plan. Snatches of conversation floated his way. People were reading the document and speculating.

An hour ago, he had called the hospital to check on Franklin. Ruby said he was asleep and had not awakened since they had visited him that morning. David cautioned her to be careful, but he knew she would never leave her husband—even if he attacked her in an inhuman frenzy.

He shivered.

"Why hasn't Mama come yet?" Nia looked around. "I asked her to be here at four. She's never late."

"I'm sure she's on her way," David said.

"I hope so. I'm going to call her if she isn't here in five minutes."

At the front of the church, Chief Jackson, the mayor, the county sheriff, Dr. Green, and Reverend Brown sat in a row of tall chairs in the chancel. Jackson read his watch, glanced at the other leaders, and they nodded.

Jackson approached the pulpit. He cleared his throat, raised the microphone closer to his lips.

"All right, folks. Thanks for coming to this meeting on short notice and on your holiday. I 'spect more folks will be coming in, but we got to get started. We're facing something I ain't never seen in this town, and I've been here in Dark Corner all my life, like a lot of you.

"Let me run down the basics for you . . ."

Junior Hodges sat in a middle pew, fidgeting. He wore his overalls and boots, and he felt out of place coming to church dressed as he was, though no one else was dressed in their Sunday best, either. Mama had taught him that whenever you entered the house of the Lord, you had to wear the best clothes you could afford. Junior owned a navy blue suit that he'd worn for years, but the woman, Nia, who pressed the flyer in his hand while he was cutting grass told him that this wasn't a worship service, it was a town meeting, and he could come dressed as he was. He took her suggestion, but he felt uncomfortable, anyway. Especially with Reverend Brown sitting up there.

Junior read the flyer he'd picked up from the seat. It talked about a "health emergency," a virus, and how dogs and people seemed to be the ones that caught it. You could get infected if a sick dog bit you, or if a person who had the illness bit you, too. The ones who were sick were in so much pain that they might hurt you, the paper said. If you knew someone who seemed to be acting sick lately, who was sleeping all the time and not leaving the house, you were supposed to write their name on a list that would be passed around. Those people would then get "proper medical care," whatever that meant.

Junior knew at least five people who were sick. Vicky Queen was one of them. Earlier, he'd visited her house to offer to trim her hedges, something he did every now and then, and her mama answered the door. Her mama said Vicky was sick and in the bed. Junior cut the hedges anyway, for free. It made him feel better.

What worried Junior most of all was that he had the feeling that this health emergency had something to do with the work he and Andre had done at the Mason place. Nothing had been right in the town since they'd dug open that cave. Maybe they'd let out the virus. The scary man in black seemed like the sort of fella who was up to no good.

The pews were filling up. He didn't see Andre, or his father. The last time Junior had seen Pa, his father was sleeping off a hangover at home, and Andre . . . well, he didn't know where he was. Probably somewhere getting high.

Junior returned his attention to Chief Jackson. The chief was running down the stuff on the flyer.

". . . trying to keep this in layman's terms, see," the chief said. "We've got Doc Green here if you want him to lay it out for you with big medical words. Like I said, we think it's a virus, like rabies. Get it when you get bit. Dogs are running around doing the biting, but people might bite you too, if they've been bit and got infected. They're sick and ain't themselves . . ."

A teenage girl who sat near Junior was frowning.

"It sounds kinda like vampires, doesn't it?" she said.

"Sure does," Junior said, and thought again of the man in black. He felt a chill. "Just like vampires."

Emma Mae Taylor allowed her sister, Lillie, to drag her to the town meeting. Earlier, she'd banged on Emma's door like she'd lost her mind, then shoved a green flyer in her face.

"If you got any sense, you'll go to this," Lillie had said. "You need to come outta that house from up under that man and learn about the evil that's running through this town."

"I got me some gardening to do," Emma said. She'd gotten one of those flyers about the medical whatever happening in town. Some meddling fool had slid it under her door, and Emma had skimmed it, then thrown it away. Emergency? Please, it was all a matter of perspective. She didn't let things get under her skin like most people did. She was cool.

"Emma, you come outta there or I'ma drag you out," Lillie said. Her eyes narrowed. "I'm sick and tired of you not caring what's going on here. You need to learn for your own good and for that man you so crazy 'bout."

"All right, all right, I'll go! Damn, you a pain in the ass. Let me fix my hair." Emma spun away from the door, not bothering to invite Lillie inside. Lillie was a cleaning freak and would start criticizing Emma about cleaning her house, and Emma didn't feel like hearing it.

After she fixed her hair, she checked on Blood. He'd been under the weather all day. She was sure it was because some mutt had bitten him last night when he was leaving the bar. She'd taken him to the emergency room, to get a rabies shot;

afterward, the doctor had wanted Blood to stay there, but Blood hated hospitals and begged Emma to take him home. She couldn't say no to him, so she brought him home against the doctor's protests. Since then, Blood had been running a slight fever and sleeping like a log.

Medical emergency, she thought, with a pang of anxiety. She didn't like leaving him alone in the house.

"We gonna stay at this meeting one hour, and that's it," Emma said to Lillie, coming outside. "I got to get back, I got things to do."

"Where's Blood?" Lillie said. "He needs to come, too."

"Aww, he's got a hangover and he's sleeping it off."

"Hmph, I ain't surprised," Lillie said. Emma let her snide remark pass. Blood's condition was none of her sister's business. Lillie ran her mouth too damn much.

Now she sat beside Lillie in the church (where she hadn't been since Mama had died, eight years ago), as Chief Jackson explained what was happening. A virus, passed by a bite from a dog, or a person. Now that was some upsetting shit. Emma couldn't stop thinking about Blood.

". . . we gonna set up a special area in the hospital, to keep all the folks that's been bit," the chief said. "Kinda like a quarantine. We need to put 'em there so we can keep an eye on them, make sure they're getting the care they need, make sure the infection don't spread, too. So if anybody's in your house who's been bit, we want you to fill out the sheet that we're passing 'round. And if your neighbor or friend's been bit, we wanna know that, too. Doc Green's crew is gonna come pick them up and take them to the hospital . . ."

A paper attached to a clipboard was thrust in front of Emma. At least a half-dozen names were scribbled on the list. They were all people that she knew. Damn.

But Blood didn't want to stay in a hospital, and she wasn't going to make him. Hell, how did she know what was really going on? They might be planning to operate on them folks that got taken into quarantine, or they might pump some kinda drugs into them. It could be the government running biological weapons experiments or some shit. She didn't trust these people. She'd keep Blood at home and take care of him herself.

Pressing her lips together, she passed the clipboard to Lillie.

Nia had not seen her mother enter the church. It was not like Mama to be late, and Mama would never miss something as important as this meeting, if for no other reason than it would give her some fresh gossip to spread to her friends.

"I'm going to go outside and call Mama," she whispered to David. "She still isn't here."

"Are you sure?" he said. "There's a couple hundred people in here, she could've slipped in when you weren't looking."

"I'm positive. I'll be right back."

At the pulpit, Dr. Green had come to stand beside Chief Jackson and was delivering his jargon-filled theory of the "virus." He sounded so convincing and knowledgeable that Nia would have believed him herself if she had not seen the vampires with her own eyes.

In the lobby, Nia used her cell phone to call her house. The phone rang five times, then the answering machine picked up. Nia ended the call, and tried again. Still no answer.

She looked through the lobby's glass doors and at the parking lot, which was full of cars. She did not see her mother's green Chrysler.

Maybe Mama was on her way. But the church was only three minutes away from the house. Mama could've left home and arrived there in the time that Nia had been standing in the lobby. There was never any traffic to speak of in Mason's Corner—unless it was a funeral procession.

Her gut spasmed.

As she debated her next move, David pushed through the wooden sanctuary doors.

"Is everything okay?" he said.

"Mama's not answering the phone. I'm worried."

"You want to swing by the house to check?"

"Yes, but you can't leave, David. Jackson needs you here. Remember our plan."

"Yeah." David bit his lip.

"It's daylight," she said. "I'll be okay. I'll have my cell, and you're wearing yours, too. I'll call you if anything happens."

"Be careful." He handed her the keys to the Pathfinder.

"I'll hurry back, promise."

She kissed him quickly, then rushed outside.

Jahlil and Poke sat in a pew at the back of the church. Jahlil had thought he would be bored by hearing his dad and the other people discuss what was happening, but he was on the tip of his seat, listening.

He had never seen Dad address a group of people this large. Dad spoke with authority, in a no bullshit tone, and people paid attention.

Before today, Jahlil had been quick to downplay his dad's job. He was a police chief in a tiny town where nothing ever happened. So what? Anyone could've done his job. Or so he'd thought. To see Dad up there, leading these people—it made something kick inside Jahlil. A long-forgotten piece of him stirred. It was something like admiration—awe, even— of his dad. He remembered a time, as a young kid, when he used to think Dad was the most amazing man in the world, stronger than any superhero, smarter than any scientist. *Can you lift a car, Dad?* Jahlil had asked him once, and Dad had said, *Reckon I could, son, if doing it meant saving you and your mother.*

Jahlil's eyes grew watery. He quickly rubbed them dry. But Poke didn't notice. The boy was sucking his thumb. He had been sucking his thumb like a lollipop since T-Bone had vanished last night.

"Like Doc Green said," Dad said, "we've been on the line with some top people in Memphis; they're sending a crew of experts our way soon. Meantime, we've got to handle things properly. After we open up for some questions, we're gonna ask for volunteers for our citizen patrol teams. Got to have able-bodied men and women to help us here . . ."

After Chief Jackson finished explaining that they would be soliciting volunteers for the citizen patrol teams—the teams David would command—at the end of the meeting, the mayor, Cleotis Davis, came forward. He spoke briefly about the townspeople pulling together to help one another out, and how "we're all one big family," and tossed in a couple other newsworthy sound bites. The county sheriff, Johnny Chaser, talked a minute about how he'd use the county's resources to help them out. Then Reverend Brown arrived at the pulpit and talked about what God might have planned for Mason's Corner, and how in times of distress, one could reach a profound understanding of God's grace, and so on and so forth.

David tapped his leg. It was already a quarter after five, and they had a lot of work ahead of them. This meeting was supposed to be as focused and brief as possible and last no longer than an hour, but it was nearing the hour-long point and they had not opened the floor for questions yet, which David anticipated would be the lengthiest part of the discussion.

And where was Nia? She had left almost fifteen minutes ago, and had not called him. He hadn't liked letting her leave alone—he felt that they were at risk at all hours of the day, not only at night—but she had been determined. Besides, she was right. The chief needed him there to round up the citizen patrol teams.

He blew out a tight breath. He would wait a few more minutes, then call Nia if she did not contact him.

At the pulpit, the reverend concluded his speech, and Jackson came forward again.

"All right, now," Jackson said. "We're ready to take questions. We've got some microphones at the end of the aisles, all 'round the church, so please step to the mic when you talk so everyone can hear you . . ."

The afternoon sky was gunmetal gray as Nia zoomed down Main Street.

Please, let Mama be all right, she prayed.

She practically stood on the brake as she screeched to a stop in front of her house.

Her mother's Chrysler was parked in its usual place under the carport. But an unfamiliar car was parked behind it: a blue Ford Thunderbird with Texas plates.

Mr. Morgan. Her former teacher colleague. Her stalker.

It couldn't be him.

But he'd called her a couple of days ago, hadn't he? And her number was unlisted.

Somehow, he'd shattered her shell of security.

Don't freak out, it could be someone else, and Mama could've been outdoors and not heard the phone ring. . . .

Nia carried her own gun, a Beretta .32, in her purse. She unzipped her purse, for quick access.

As she walked down the path to the front door, she expected to see her dog, Princess, appear in the window and start barking excitedly. But the curtains remained still. Perhaps the dog was asleep.

Nia inserted her key in the lock of the front door, turned it. She slid her hand inside the bag, curled her fingers around the cool gun handle. With her other hand, she twisted the doorknob and nudged the door. It creaked open.

Mama was in the living room. She was bound to a dining room chair with several lengths of duct tape. Tape covered her mouth, too. A purple-black bruise marked her eye, and her hair was in disarray.

Mr. Morgan reclined on the sofa. He looked much like he had when she had last seen him. Tall, lean, brown-skinned, with intense eyes. The only difference was that he had grown a thick beard.

A large, sharp knife rested beside his leg.

"It's about time that you came home," Mr. Morgan said. "I've been here chatting with my future mother-in-law for a while and wondered when you would decide to show your pretty face, Miss James."

Nia's throat was dry. She could not summon sufficient saliva to speak.

Mama's eyes were wild, and she was trying to talk, but the tape held back her frantic words.

Mr. Morgan smiled. "You're looking mighty fine, Miss James. Sure were worth the drive from Houston." He patted the seat cushion. "Come sit over here, so we can get reacquainted."

Nia did not move. She finally said, "You hurt Mama."

Mr. Morgan picked up the knife. "I told you to come sit over here, Miss James. You know I don't like to repeat myself. Don't act like one of my hard-headed students."

The Nia whom Mr. Morgan had known prior to his incarceration would have lowered her head in defeat, and shuffled to sit beside him while desperately trying to connive a way out of her bind. But that Nia was gone. The events of the past several days had turned her nerves to iron.

She drew the gun and gripped it with both hands, as she had learned.

"Put down the knife, asshole," she said.

Morgan's mouth dropped open like a trap door. The blade slipped out of his hand.

Behind the tape, Mama sounded like she was squealing in shock.

"You won't . . . you won't shoot me," Morgan said, his voice shaky. Then, more confidently: "I know you don't have what it takes to look in my eyes and pull the trigger."

"Don't test me." Nia's finger tightened on the trigger. "You don't know what I've been dealing with lately. I promise you—I *will* shoot you."

Morgan's hand fidgeted near the knife, but he did not pick it up. He appeared uncertain, cocky machismo wavering.

"Get on the floor, on your knees," Nia said. "Put your hands in the air."

Instead of kneeling, as she ordered, he stood, hands raised.

"I'm going to leave, Miss James," he said. "We're going to resume this discussion later. Unless you prefer to kill me in cold blood." He smirked.

She itched to shoot him, she really did. But as Morgan walked past her and toward the door, keeping a distance of several feet between them, she did not fire. She ground her teeth.

Morgan pushed through the door and went outside.

Nia lowered the gun.

Outside, Morgan backed his car out of the driveway and roared down the road.

Nia locked the door, stuffed the gun in her purse, and went to Mama.

"Oh, Mama, I'm so sorry," Nia said. Tears streamed down her cheeks. She gently pulled away the duct tape from her mother's mouth.

"I'm all right." Mama's voice was raspy. "Are you okay, baby?"

Nia hugged Mama tightly.

"I'm going to cut you loose and put something on that

eye," Nia said. She paused. "Did Morgan . . . do anything else to you?"

"No, that asshole was saving his energy for you," Mama said. "Pardon my French. He's an evil man. I wish you'd shot him, God help me."

"The police will get him," Nia said, though she doubted that capturing Morgan would be a priority, in light of everything else going on.

Nia found a knife in the kitchen—she did not want to touch the blade Morgan had handled—and sliced through the tape that bound her mother.

"Mama, where's Princess? I would've expected her to protect you."

"Princess ran off when I let her out to pee. Some mangy-looking mutt walked by, and Princess chased after it. Matter of fact, I was out front calling for her when that evil man pulled up."

"Oh, no." Princess had never run away before. She was an obedient, sweet-tempered dog.

Nia wanted to look for Princess, but time was short. Night was coming. She hoped her dog would turn up, but she had her doubts. The streets weren't safe for dogs anymore. The streets weren't safe for anyone, anymore

Her face must have given away her troubled emotions, because Mama said, "Nia, what's going on in our town?"

"Mama, I want you to stay with Aunt Loretta for a few days," Nia said. Her aunt lived in Southaven, a safe distance from Dark Corner. "I promise I'll tell you what's going on, soon, but you have to leave right away. Will you please do that for me?"

"Okay." Fear brightened Mama's eyes. "Are you coming with me?"

"I have to stay here and help David and some other people. I'll be okay, don't worry."

"David . . . I'm sorry I was mean to that boy. You seem so happy since you've met him."

"He's a good man, Mama, and he has to do something very important. He needs my help."

Mama hugged herself. "I'm scared, baby. I don't know what's going on, but I'm scared."

Nia wrapped her mother in her arms.

"So am I."

Jackson thought they had done a pretty fair job of educating the townsfolk about what was going on in Dark Corner, and what the people should do, without them giving away the frightening truth that surely would have driven the crowd into a panic of disbelief, fear, and superstition. But twenty-plus years of working with the public had taught him that even if you explained something as clear as glass, people would have questions. When he opened up the floor to the audience, he gripped the edges of the pulpit and braced himself for the worst.

Out of the hundreds of people in the church, his cousin, Elmer, was the first to get to a microphone. Hitching up his pants, his sleeves rolled up around his chubby forearms, Elmer hurried to the mic positioned in the middle of the sanctuary. His bald head glistened in the fluorescent light.

Jackson dreaded giving his cousin a chance to speak in public, but he had to be fair. He pointed toward Elmer and said, "Go ahead, Elmer."

Elmer cleared his throat. "I don't know what the other folks in here think, but I think y'all got it all wrong. You say a virus is in our town and you don't know where it came from. I know where it came from—the federal government. They're using our town for experiments—"

Christ, Jackson thought. *Leave it up to Elmer to open up the government conspiracy box.*

Members of the crowd nodded in agreement.

"—we ain't nothing but guinea pigs for them," Elmer

said. "They don't care about the welfare of a town full of black folks. Bet it's some kinda biological weapon they're testing out. Far as they're concerned, we're expendable. A black life ain't never meant shit to Uncle Sam."

"Like Tuskegee, Alabama," a man said. "Remember those syphilis experiments they did on the brothers, back in the day."

"AIDS started off as a government experiment over in Africa," another man said. "They don't care about us."

Murmurs of agreement swept through the group. Elmer cracked a smug grin and folded his arms as if to say, *What you gonna say to that, cuz?*

Jackson clenched his teeth.

"All right," Jackson said. "Say it is an experiment by some government outfit. What you think we should do about it, Elmer?"

Elmer cleared his throat. "Well . . . umm . . . well . . . maybe call up the NAACP."

"And stage a march, huh?" Jackson said. "Meanwhile, folks getting bit and falling down sick."

"The chief got a point," a woman said.

For once, Elmer didn't have a comeback. Jackson hurried to move past him. He pointed to a young woman on the right. "Next question. Your turn, miss."

She stepped to the microphone. She was a cute girl, maybe no older than twenty, and wore a plain blue dress and thick glasses.

"I'll be frank," the girl said. "I'm scared. I've been having nightmares for the past week, and my own dog, Pete, has become like one of these infected dogs that you've mentioned. He isn't a normal dog anymore, and he ran away from home. I don't think it's a virus or a government plot. I think it's evil. Something evil and supernatural is in our town, and I know I can't be the only one in here who's felt it. Be honest with yourselves."

Silence fell over the crowd. Coolness tapped Jackson's spine. Had he underestimated what the people were willing to believe?

Be honest with yourselves.

He felt exposed as a liar. What good was he doing these people by hiding the truth? The young lady was right. Anyone with a pulse could feel that something evil and unnatural had taken root in the town. *Be honest.*

"The devil's walking in Dark Corner!" a man shouted.

"We got to call on the Lord!" a woman cried. "Only He can deliver us!"

An outburst of clapping and shouts of *Amen* followed.

Jackson drummed the pulpit.

What the hell have I got to lose by telling the truth? he thought. *By nightfall, they're gonna see proof themselves.*

He saw Jahlil in the back of the church. His son was nodding. So was David. As if they understood his dilemma and encouraged him to lay the full story on the audience.

To hell with it. I'm gonna unload.

"Okay, gonna be straight with you, folks," he said. "It *is* evil, to the core. I've seen proof myself. What we dealing with is something you might not wanna believe, but I owe it to you to be honest. We've got vampires here in Dark Corner."

Gasps and exclamations of shock erupted from the audience. But surprisingly, a lot of folks nodded, as though pleased that Jackson had put their nameless fear into words.

Jackson checked behind him. The members of the leadership team gaped at him as if he had gone crazy. He might be jeopardizing his job by telling the people about vampires, but so be it. Besides, no one tried to stop him. Maybe, in their secret thoughts, they perceived the chilling truth, too.

He continued to speak.

"Took me some time to swallow the truth," he said. "But

I saw one of 'em myself, and I bet some of you in here seen 'em, too. We don't think too many of our people have turned into the vampires, yet, but a lot of the dogs have. Yep, you heard me right. Some of the hounds are working for the vampires. Understand, they ain't normal dogs. They're smart, vicious, and tough. I shot three of 'em with a twelve-gauge shotgun, and those mutts got up five minutes later and came after me again."

Curses of surprise and frightened looks came from the crowd.

"Break it down, brother," a man said.

"Go 'head, Chief!" a woman urged.

Jackson bent closer to the microphone. "I don't claim to know everything about these monsters, but I know they ain't exactly like what you've seen in the movies. They do feed on blood. But these dogs I told you about—well, if one of them bites you, you can get sick and change into one of the vampires. And it looks like crosses, holy water, and religious stuff doesn't hurt 'em none, either. The strongest ones can walk around during the day. The only way you can kill them, for sure, is with fire. Guns don't work, wooden stakes don't work, knives don't work. You've gotta burn them to ashes."

Throughout the church, people scribbled notes.

A woman sitting in one of the front pews raised her hand. "Is there a master vampire, like in the movies? Someone has to be responsible for starting it in the first place."

Jackson paused. "Yeah, guess there is one. No one's seen him yet, but we know he's out there. We're gonna find him and take care of him, I promise you.

"But look, everything we said about the virus and what we need to do, that ain't changed. We're asking folks to stay in the house, only come outside for an emergency. Keep your doors locked and your windows shut. Stay away from dogs, and keep your own dogs penned up in the house. We still need you to tell us the folks that've been sick lately, 'cause they're the ones who might change. We're gonna quarantine the sick people at the hospital so we can watch over them, and make sure they don't hurt anyone."

"You gonna burn them up?" a man said. "You said that's the only way to kill 'em, was to burn 'em. My wife's been sick all day. You gonna put her in the hospital and burn her?"

Jackson swallowed. "I didn't say we were gonna do that."

"But that's what you're implying, Chief!"

Jackson stammered, "Now, hold on—"

But more questions and angry shouts pelted him.

"You can't be killing our people, man!"

"Where'd the head vampire come from?"

"We need to set the town on fire! Ain't nothing here, no way!"

"I'm leaving town soon as I get outta here!"

"You're full of shit, Chief, you don't know what the hell's going on!"

"What about my little girl who's been sick?"

The chaotic energy boiling in the church made Jackson dizzy. People stood in the aisles and pews, eyes bulging, mouths yapping. Other people grabbed the microphones and shouted into them, their voices jumbled together. Some people were beginning to argue with one another. An older woman smacked a younger lady in the mouth. In another pew, two guys were starting to wrestle, knocking over others in the process. Still more people were on their knees at the altar, praying loudly, tears streaming down their faces.

Jackson turned. Even the mayor, physician, sheriff, and pastor were barking at one another.

Pandemonium was what Jackson had feared.

He shouted for order. He hammered the pulpit with his fist.

No one paid him any mind.

So he unholstered his .357 Magnum, raised it skyward, and fired. The gun boomed like a cannon. Chips of wood rained from the ceiling and showered the crowd.

Everyone froze, as if zapped by a magic spell.

"Listen to me!" Jackson said. "We've gotta stay calm and stick together. We ain't got time for no foolishness—'cause just like in the movies, these vampires *do* come out at night." Now he really had their attention again; he dramatically tapped the face of his watch. "We've got less than three hours till dusk. That ain't a lot a time for us to do what we've gotta do.

"Like I was saying, Doc Green's team is gonna drive around and pick up the folks that're sick and take 'em to the hospital. So you need to put the names of the sick on that list we're passing around. Don't keep it secret, I'm warning you. Might wind up with something on your hands that you ain't prepared to handle.

"Next, David Hunter, please come forward."

David rose from a pew in the rear of the church and walked down the center aisle. Astonished murmurings of "Look, that's Richard Hunter's boy" followed him. Jackson, for his part, was pleased with how David handled himself. The kid looked strong and capable, like a born leader.

In front, David faced the audience, hands on his waist, like a man ready to take care of business.

"Hunter is heading up our citizen patrol teams," Jackson said. "Why? 'Cause he knows more about these vampires than anyone in this building. His family fought them before—long, interesting story that maybe he'll share with you one day. We need at least twenty volunteers for our teams. If you volunteer, you'll be put in a small group, and at night you'll be either patrolling the streets or put at different locations. We'll keep in touch with walkie-talkies. You'll get more information at our patrol team meeting later. Anyone who's interested, stay here after we dismiss this meeting, and you'll be part of the team. We need you.

"If you ain't volunteering, then we need you to show common sense. We've only got each other. Look out for one another. Stay in the house at night. *Run* to and from your car if you gotta go somewhere. Don't go nowhere alone. Now, more than ever, we've gotta be *true* brothers and sisters, hear me? We've only got each other. They ain't sending in no National Guard, or the FBI, and the state and county police probably ain't gonna be much help, either. We've only got each other. But each other's all we need."

Applause broke out. Jackson straightened, a warm feeling spreading through him. David gave him the thumbs-up sign. In the back of the church, Jahlil clapped, too.

If we can keep up this unity, we'll win this, Jackson thought. *Sure as hell we will. Vampires can't stop a people united.*

He felt a hand on his shoulder. It was Reverend Brown. The pastor smiled.

"Well said, Chief," he said.

"Sorry 'bout your ceiling, Reverend," Jackson said sheepishly.

"You'll find the repair bill in the mail tomorrow," Reverend Brown said, and chuckled. He put his arm around Jackson and leaned closer to the microphone.

"For those who are interested, we're having a night of prayer, praise, and fellowship here at New Life Baptist," Reverend Brown said. "We'll be here from eight o'clock this evening until eight tomorrow morning, worshipping our all-powerful God. These vampires, these servants of the Devil, will not breach the house of the Lord. You are invited to come here and be safe."

Another wave of applause, and shouts of *Amen.*

"Anyone who wanna party can come to my place!" a woman cried into a microphone. Jackson recognized her: Emma Mae Taylor. An older woman, she was always throwing wild card parties and playing loud music. A thin, elderly woman tried to snatch the microphone out of Emma's hands, and Emma pushed her away. "Shut your mouth, Lillie, I'm just inviting folks. With all the shit goin' on here we all need a little sunshine. I'm at 2147 Coldwater Lane, we gonna have chicken and ribs and booze and music and be playing cards all night, so come on by, y'all."

Jackson hastened to get to the mic before chaos broke out again. "Okay, everyone, that's it. Volunteers, please stay behind. Everyone else, go on home. Thanks for coming. May the Lord be with us all."

There was a final smattering of applause, then people began to file across the aisles to the exit doors, chatting all the way. Jackson was pleased to see that a couple dozen people remained seated. They would need all the help they could get. With a strong team, they had an honest-to-goodness chance to win. He would not allow himself to think otherwise.

It was ten minutes to six o'clock. Night would fall shortly after eight.

Time was ticking away.

Chapter 17

Twenty-eight people volunteered for the citizen patrol teams, not including Nia, Jahlil, and his friend, Poke. The volunteers' bravery impressed David. If he had been in their shoes, he would've been tempted to leave town before dark, an option that, judging from the comments he'd overheard during the meeting, more than a few people had picked.

Nia had come to the front of the sanctuary, to stand beside him. Before the chief had called David to come forward, Nia had returned to the church and told him what had happened at her house. He hated that Morgan had gotten away, but he was grateful that Nia and her mother were not hurt. It could have been much worse. Nia was sure that Morgan would resurface, later, and he agreed. They would have to stay alert for him.

David directed the group to sit in the pews nearest the altar, so he could speak to them without using a microphone. The people were mostly between the ages of twenty and sixty, but there was a nearly equal number of men and women, a nice balance.

He gave the volunteers more details about the vampires

they were dealing with, explaining the distinction between "pure" vampires such as Kyle and Diallo, and lower-level creatures such as the vampiric dogs and the mutant people, the valduwe.

He told them how guns could temporarily slow the monsters, but only fire could destroy them. He was pleasantly surprised when one of the volunteers, a bald white man named Mac who owned a grocery store, announced that he had a flamethrower in working condition. "Part of my collection," Mac said with a wink. "I'm a retired sergeant, United States Marines." Everyone else, in addition to having a gun or knife, would be given a plastic water gun filled with a flammable mixture, and a book of matches. They would have a supply of Molotov cocktails, too.

David organized the volunteers into seven groups of four members each. They would distribute a two-way, handheld radio to each team.

The assignments followed: one team would patrol the hospital, where the infected people would be quarantined. The second team would patrol the east side of town. The third group would handle the west side; the fourth team, the south side; the fifth group would watch the north side. The sixth group was an emergency response team that would be stationed at police headquarters, and would provide backup as needed. Against Jahlil's wishes, Jackson placed his son and his kid's friend on the backup team.

The seventh and final team would assist David, Nia, and Chief Jackson on a mission to Jubilee; David was sure to include the war vet who owned the flamethrower in this group. Instead of waiting for the vampires to strike, they planned to take the initiative against Diallo and Kyle. "So we're the suicide mission team," a member joked, and no one laughed.

"We'll be checking in with one another every hour," David said. "At seven o'clock tomorrow morning, we'll regroup at the police station. Plan on staying up all night: take some No-Doz, drink some coffee or Mountain Dew, do whatever you have to do to stay awake. *We have to stay alert.* You won't believe how fast these vampires and these dogs can move. None of us can afford to lose our edge.

"But let me tell you what the hardest thing will be," David said. "It's going to be fighting someone—maybe hurting someone—that you know, who has become a vampire. It could be your spouse, your child, your parent, your best friend. If you're put in this situation, you have to remember that the one you love who's now a vampire . . . they don't exist anymore. You're seeing a monster that only *looks* like the person you remember. You must absolutely remember that, and be strong. It won't be easy, but you have to protect yourself."

The volunteers nodded, their faces grim. David looked at Jackson, and the chief gave him the "OK" sign.

"If you're bitten, you must let your team members know," David said. "You'll be taken to the hospital and quarantined, and we'll find someone to take your place."

He was quiet for a moment, checking everyone's faces, to make sure his words sank in.

"Does anyone have any questions?" David said. "If so, fire away—pardon the pun. We don't have much time until nightfall."

"I've got a question," a young man in an oil-stained T-shirt said. "Is killing these bloodsuckers the first option, or the last resort?"

David looked at Jackson, then at the young man. "Unfortunately, I think it's the first option. Once a human has changed into a vampire, they're lost to us. We haven't found a way to turn them back. We have to do what's necessary for the greater good of the town."

"How long does it take for someone to become a vampire, after being bitten?" a woman asked.

"We don't know, exactly," David said. "So far, it seems to take at least sixteen hours. If the bite comes from the master vampire, though, it takes only minutes. That's why *anyone* who gets bitten is dangerous to be around, and that's why we have to get victims into quarantine, ASAP."

A middle-aged black man with an afro and dressed in a dashiki raised his hand. "Why did this happen here, brother? This is a small, peaceful town full of God-fearing folks. Why here?"

"I don't know," David said. "I guess that's how life works sometimes. Ordinary people are called to do extraordinary things. When we beat these monsters, think of all the people we'll save in the long run. It seems to me that if a town is called on to beat back an evil force, that town would need to be full of good, brave folks. So I can turn around your question to ask: Why *not* here?"

Nia smiled at him, and so did many of the volunteers.

After answering a few questions about logistics, they wrapped up the meeting. Jackson led them into a conference room, where they had stored the team supplies in duffel bags on a long table. Jackson distributed one bag to each team: each contained a radio, a loaded handgun, extra ammunition, a knife, a flashlight, a roll of duct tape, four plastic water pistols filled with flammable fluids, four glass bottles full of the same lethal mixture, a box of wooden matches, and a first aid kit.

David and Nia had purchased most of the items from a Wal-Mart in Southaven. Jackson donated the firearms from his personal collection and the police department's arsenal.

"Feel like I'm back in 'Nam," Mac said. He chomped on a cigar. "I knew some weird crap was going on in this town. Could feel it in my blood. I can't wait to fire up old Suzie again."

"Old Suzie?" David said.

"My flamethrower," Mac said. "Saved my ass plenty of times."

David could not resist smiling. "My friend, I'm glad you're on my team tonight. We'll need all the firepower we can get."

Mac grinned around his cigar.

The teams left the church. The members would return to their respective homes to pick up any essential items, and would later rendezvous at their assigned post. David's team agreed to meet in front of the police station in thirty minutes, at seven-fifteen, about an hour before sunset.

Plenty of time to take care of business at Jubilee. He hoped.

"How're you feeling?" David asked Nia, as they left the church and crossed the parking lot to his SUV. They were among the last to leave. Jackson and his son had left in the patrol car. Inside the church, Reverend Brown and his staff prepared for the all-night service.

"Honestly?" Nia said. "I've never been so scared in my life."

"Fear is good. It'll keep us alert. I think we've got a long night ahead of us."

"But if we find Diallo and Kyle at the Mason place, we can end this early."

"I hope we do," he said. "But it would seem almost too easy to find them there. Maybe I'm being a pessimist. Sorry."

"You're only being realistic. We have to be prepared for anything."

He started up the truck and pulled out of the parking lot. He would swing by the house to pick up King, and to get everything he needed for later.

Thick gray-black clouds mantled the sky, giving the false impression that twilight had already arrived. A stiff wind buffeted the vehicle, and the sour odor of an imminent rain permeated the air.

"The thunderstorm is going to hit soon," Nia said. "The timing couldn't be any worse."

"I know," he said. "I wonder how Franklin is doing. I'm afraid to find out."

"I'll call." Nia punched a number into her cell phone.

David's heart pounded. Naïve hope tugged at him. He wanted to believe that vampires did not exist at all, and that it was a curable virus, and all they needed to do was discover an effective treatment. . . .

"Ruby, it's Nia," she said. "How is he doing?"

David clutched the steering wheel.

"Oh, he's sleeping?" Nia said. "He hasn't been awake since this morning? I guess that's good news, considering what we were expecting." Nia chatted with Ruby for a couple more minutes, murmured words of comfort, then ended the call.

"Maybe our theory about how long it takes to change into a vampire was wrong," Nia said. "Franklin was bitten over twenty-four hours ago."

"Maybe," David said. "Or maybe he's waiting."

"Waiting?"

"Remember what Pearl told us? She said Diallo would launch an attack on the town. If that's what he's going to do, it would make sense for him to keep his troops quiet until he's ready to go to war, then suddenly hit us with everything he's got."

"Aren't you just full of optimism? Come on, David. Be encouraged."

He shrugged. "Sorry, I'm only trying to consider this from Diallo's viewpoint. He's not a mindless brute, he's a warrior. He's going to have a strategy. We have to keep that in mind. Pearl warned us not to underestimate him, ever."

Nia was silent. She knew he was right. But he took no pleasure in being correct. He yearned to be an optimist in these circumstances, to believe that it was not going to be as bad as they thought, but to do so would be to ignore the cold dread that twisted his stomach into knots. The dread that they were going to face a horror that was worse than what they imagined. The dread that their well-laid plans were going to prove worthless. The dread that, by sunrise, all of them would be dead.

Junior was a member of the patrol team that was assigned to the hospital. Before he reported to his post, he went home to pick up something he wanted to have with him during his watch.

As he pedaled across the road on his old Roadmaster bicycle, he kept on the lookout for monster dogs and vampires. He didn't see any, but night was coming soon.

He was frightened of what was going on in town, but he felt sort of responsible. He and Andre, after all, had dug open the cave and let those vampires out. They hadn't known any better at the time they'd done the job, but that didn't mean that they weren't responsible. Junior was obligated to volunteer for the patrol team. Andre was, too, but Junior was sure his cousin was somewhere getting high.

Junior didn't find it hard to believe in vampires. He'd seen the man in black, and he didn't seem like a normal man at all. Plus, Chief Jackson said vampires were real, and that was good enough for Junior. The chief was a smart man.

Pa's rusty Ford was parked beside the trailer. Junior set down his bike beside the steps. He noticed a green flyer tucked underneath the door. He picked it up and went inside.

The only light came from the small television. Pa was sprawled in the recliner, head tilted back, mouth open. His snores made the thin walls tremble. Cans of Coors beer stood on an end table—five cans arranged in a pyramid. Pa had a strange habit of stacking up empty cans in weird structures and would pitch a fit if Junior moved them.

'Course, Pa was drunk, as usual.

Junior wondered whether he should wake up his father and tell him what was going on. He decided against it. Pa was impossible to talk to when he had been drinking, and Junior was in a hurry.

He went into his tiny bedroom and dug underneath the bed. He pulled out an old cigar box.

Inside the box, wrapped in velvet, gleamed a silver locket on a necklace. Mama had given it to him before she died. Opening the locket revealed a black-and-white photo of his mother when she was a young woman.

Junior never wore the necklace because he was always working outdoors and didn't want to lose it or get it dirty. If he had a job in a nice, clean office, he'd wear the locket every day.

He slipped the necklace over his head and tucked the pendant under his T-shirt, treasuring the feel of the cool jewelry resting against his heart.

He was ready.

He was about to leave the trailer when he turned and looked at Pa.

Would Pa wake up before morning? What if a vampire came for him while he slept?

It wasn't right to leave his father there, alone, with no information at all.

Junior had put the green flyer on the kitchen counter. The flyer talked about the "Health Emergency in Mason's Corner" and announced the town meeting. It didn't say anything about vampires, but it did have a phone number listed as an emergency hot line. Junior found a pen, underlined the number, and wrote "Call!" beside it in his shaky handwriting. He placed the flyer in a spot where Pa was certain to see it: inside the refrigerator, on top of a six-pack of Coors. It would be the first place Pa would look as soon as he woke.

Junior locked the door, then hopped on his bicycle and left to do his work at the hospital.

The "special mission team," as Chief Jackson had come to think of it, gathered in the parking lot of the police station promptly at seven-fifteen. The sixth team—the backup group, which included Jahlil—was inside headquarters, sitting tight and handling phone calls.

Five minutes ago, Jackson had talked to Dr. Hess Green via cell phone. Although the doctor had every right to be upset with Jackson for how he had initially lied about what was happening in Mason's Corner, Green had put aside his anger and was doing an efficient job of picking up the ill. The doctor and his two assistants had taken six individuals to the hospital, and had three left to transport. Factoring in the nine people who had already been admitted to the medical center, that would bring the total of bitten people to eighteen.

Eighteen potential vampires. Sweet Jesus.

Those are only the ones that we know about, too, he reminded himself. Not everyone in town had attended the meeting, and even among those who attended, he was sure that some of the people had declined to write the name of an ill person on the list. Jackson's confession about vampires notwithstanding, some people in town were suspicious of authority and anything that smacked of government intervention. They would keep their sick at home and care for them in secret, and would not realize their mistake until it was too late.

One of the toughest truths of serving in law enforcement was that no matter how hard he worked, he could not save everyone. Sometimes you showed up at the scene too late to prevent a tragedy; other times, you didn't receive a crucial tip until the damage had been done; often, the victims themselves were participants in their own demise, refusing to call police when they most needed to, or ignoring the helpful advice that you gave them. Accepting that he could not save the world had been a difficult lesson for Jackson to digest, but once he did, his life got much easier. Nevertheless, at a time like this, he wished he could impose martial law for the town's own good.

And wouldn't *that* move win him favor when the time

came for his annual performance review! The county sheriff and the mayor had already reprimanded him for his "ridiculous" speech at the church, and made it clear that if the shit hit the fan, he was going to take the heat. But interestingly, they did not intervene. Jackson understood why: they were scared shitless and wanted him to do the dirty work. He didn't mind. He wanted them to stay out of his way.

He wanted his loved ones out of the way, too. After the meeting, he had asked Belinda Moss to leave town for a few days, for her own safety, and she had agreed to stay with her brother in Memphis. As for Jahlil, he had assigned him to the back-team stationed at police headquarters. He hoped his son stayed put and didn't try to be a hero.

David came up to Jackson. Jackson was more impressed with the kid at every turn. He had handled himself well when pulling together the citizen defense teams, guiding them with calm authority. Jackson had heard from his own father that the Hunters were some tough bastards, and this one here was making good on the family's reputation.

"Looks like everyone is here," David said. He looked at the dimming sky. "Night sure is coming fast."

"I don't like the look of those clouds, either," Jackson said. "Thunderstorm's gonna hit soon."

There were seven of them on the team; Jackson liked to think it would be lucky for them. The team included himself, David, and Nia; old Mac, the grocery store owner and war vet; Tanya Lester, who coached volleyball and taught physical education at the high school; Ben Jones, a thick-bodied construction worker; and Bertha Clark, a square-shouldered, middle-aged lady who worked as a security guard at a casino in Tunica. A nice mix of folks.

The mood was jovial. They milled between the cars, chatting and joking. They might have been a bunch of friends on their way to bowling league night. Jackson had a good idea of why they were so upbeat: they were psyching themselves up for the horrible job that lay ahead of them.

"Time for us to round up," Jackson said to David. He walked to the center of the group. The friendly chatter ceased, everyone's face suddenly serious.

"Folks, it's time for us to do what we came together to do," Jackson said. "Got about an hour of daylight left. Not a lot of time, but enough. Everyone ready?"

"Yes, sir," they said, in unison. Old Mac saluted Jackson.

Mac owned a Dodge Ram pickup truck. Jackson asked him if all of them could pile inside the truck, and Mac was happy to oblige.

"Everyone 'cept me and Hunter climb up in Mac's truck," Jackson said. "Put our equipment in there, too. Hunter and I are gonna lead the way in my patrol car."

The crew loaded the duffel bags and weapons in the cargo area of the pickup and then climbed in, two people inside the cab and the other three sitting on the flatbed. Jackson and Hunter got in the cruiser.

The two-vehicle caravan pulled out of the parking lot and onto Main Street, heading east, toward the Mason place.

"Need to talk to you 'bout something, that's why I wanted you to ride up with me," Jackson said. He was figuring out how to work his way into this discussion. He was about to ask Hunter a favor he had never asked of anyone.

"What's up?" David said.

Jackson spoke carefully. "Got an idea about why you came to our town in the first place. You're looking to learn about your daddy, a reasonable thing for a boy to want to know. Am I right?"

"I don't know where you're going with this, but yeah, you're right. That's why I moved here."

"I got a point to make, hang on. What I'm getting at is, you understand how *important* it is for a father and his boy to have a good relationship. Ain't nothing like a strong bond between a father and son. Even if a boy ain't had the benefit of a decent relationship with his daddy, one day, he'll usually wish he had. Know where I'm coming from?"

"Too well," David said. Pain flickered in his eyes. Jackson had yanked a nerve.

Jackson returned his attention on the road. "My boy and I, we don't get along too well. Cancer took my wife a couple years ago, and things ain't been the same since with us. Can't figure out what I'm doing wrong. He'd rather hang out with his knuckle-head friends than spend a minute with me. Grades been low; he don't wanna work nowhere. I try to talk to him and it don't do any good."

"Lots of teenage boys go through that phase," David said. "He'll grow out of it."

"Maybe he will, if someone's around to catch him when he stumbles every now and then," Jackson said. "But if ain't no one there for him, no telling what can happen. In my line of work, I see what happens to young men who ain't got no guidance."

"I don't get it," David said. "You're here for your son, even though he doesn't appreciate it right now. But you'll be there when he needs you."

"That's what I'm getting to. Listen, I don't know you that well. But I'm a damn good judge of character. You're a good man, Hunter. I might be out of line asking you this, but I ain't got no one else I can ask. My family's scattered around here and there, and we don't really talk much."

"What do you want me to do?" David said.

Jackson's hands tightened on the steering wheel. "If I don't get through the mess that we're trying to do here, I want you to look out for my son. I'm not asking you to be his daddy. Be his friend, a big brother. Check on him sometimes. He's gonna need someone like you around, Hunter. He doesn't know it yet, but he will."

His eyes thoughtful, David gazed out the window. They rode in silence for a minute.

"Okay," David said. "If it comes to that, and I hope to God it doesn't, I'll do it."

"Appreciate it." Jackson's grip relaxed on the steering wheel, and he enjoyed a momentary sense of relief.

The tension returned, but for a different reason, when his car began to climb the steep hill on the eastern edge of town. Ahead, at the crest of the rise, Jubilee loomed.

"Is it only me, or does the house look bigger?" David said.

"It ain't only you. I feel it, too. That's fear talking to us, Hunter. Frightening things look bigger sometimes. Makes you sort of feel like a kid again, doesn't it?"

They turned onto the road that ran in front of the property. When Jackson and Jahlil had left this place, a few hours ago, Dudu's patrol car had been stuck in a ditch.

The car was gone.

A crazy image, disturbingly vivid, flashed through Jackson's mind: Dudu, his face pale and bloodless, dragging himself to the vehicle, getting in, and cruising around town, fangs dripping with saliva, clawed hands flexing on the steering wheel . . .

Cut it out. Pearl said Dudu was dead.

He looked around. Then he saw the deputy's cruiser. It was parked near the mansion.

What the hell? Who had moved the car? Frowning, he parked on the shoulder of the road. Mac parked behind him.

The wind harried the surrounding trees. Distantly, thunder grumbled.

"Be careful getting out," Jackson said. "Remember those dogs I told you about."

"Gotcha."

Jackson checked to ensure that his .357 was loaded, then he climbed out the car.

It was time to roll.

* * *

David's impression that Jubilee looked larger was not a temporary illusion. The mansion genuinely appeared to have grown bigger since he had last seen it, like a magical evil castle in a fairy tale. The rooftops seemed to pierce the underbelly of the stormy sky.

"The house looks huge, doesn't it?" Nia said, when she got out of Mac's truck.

"You know, I really hope you're able to read my mind like this when this is over," he said.

Together, the team unloaded the cargo from the pickup's flatbed. Mac strapped the handheld flamethrower across his shoulders, the fuel-filled cylinder tanks weighted on his back. Back at the station, Mac had taught David how to use the flamethrower. There was always the possibility that Mac would be injured—or worse—during their mission, and David thought it was a good idea for someone else to understand how to wield the powerful weapon.

Each team member carried a handgun; Jackson had made sure that each person on this crew would be armed. They took the water guns, too, holstering them in their pants.

"I feel like I'm in a horror flick," Ben said. He winked at Tanya, the gym teacher. "I've been told that I favor Wesley Snipes, you know."

"Then you woke up," Tanya said. They laughed.

"No more time for jokes," Bertha Clark said. "It's getting dark. I don't want to be in there at night."

"Then let's hurry and hammer out our plan of approach," David said. He was getting antsy, too. It was already a quarter to eight, and the thickening blanket of storm clouds was another ominous sign.

They congregated on the side of the road, opposite the estate's iron gates.

"How do we wanna take down this shit hole?" Mac said. "I'll take the point, 'cause I got old Suzie here and don't none of you wanna get in her way. Everyone else can follow after me."

"How about we send a scout to check out the place?" Ben said.

"Bad idea," Jackson said. "We lost my deputy that way. I ain't letting nobody go up there alone."

"The deputy went inside through a door on the side or the back of the house, according to Jahlil," David said. "He never came out. I vote that we go through the front door. Some of the other doors might lead into traps. Once we get inside, we'll split up, and go floor by floor."

"All right," Jackson said. "Let's move, folks."

Here we go, David thought. *We're moving past the point of no return.*

David pushed open the gate. He motioned for Mac to enter first. Everyone else filed in behind him.

They walked on the gravel lane that twisted toward the house. David and Nia were side by side, Ben and Tanya were paired together, and Jackson and Bertha brought up the rear.

"There's dog shit all over the place." Ben wrinkled his nose. "Sure am glad I wore my work boots. I should've brought a gas mask, though."

Large, stinking clumps of excrement littered the yard and the path. But other than the crap, there was no sign of the vampiric dogs. Dense shadows lurked under the trees, and the area was silent, the only sounds the blowing of the wind, the faraway rumble of thunder, and their footsteps crunching through gravel.

"I'm doing the very thing I said I'd never do again," Nia said, close to David. "Going back to this place." Her hands gripped the gun so tightly it seemed that her veins would burst.

They passed under the boughs of the giant tree from which, according to Franklin's history lesson, Edward Mason had been hung by his slaves and left to swing in the wind.

A chill chugged through David.

A police car was parked at the end of the driveway. Dried mud streaked the fenders, tires, and doors.

"My deputy's car," Jackson said. "Was stuck in the ditch by the road back there earlier today. I don't know who the hell moved it up here." He peered through a window. "Ain't nothing out the ordinary in there. Let's keep on."

David noted that the Lexus SUV was gone. Did that mean anything?

They trudged forward. Mac set his boot on the sagging veranda step.

"We should burn down this place," Nia said. "There's no reason to go inside. Just burn it down."

"I wish we could," David said. "But you know we can't. Not yet."

They ascended the short flight of porch stairs and huddled outside the door.

Dead leaves and branches covered the veranda's hardwood floor. Vines of kudzu twined around the thick white columns.

David picked out the column against which his father had leaned when he took the photograph. In spite of everything he'd learned since he'd found the picture in the living room, he wasn't much closer to understanding his father. He wondered whether it mattered anymore.

The front door of the mansion was like the entrance to a vault.

"Here goes nothing," Mac said. He twisted the doorknob.

The door creaked open, like a parody of every haunted house that had ever existed in a movie. A wall of blackness greeted them.

They turned on their flashlights and stepped inside.

They were at the mouth of a long hallway. A spiral staircase was on the right, the ornate wooden railing dressed in cobwebs. On the left, an arched doorway led into a sitting room full of old upholstered furniture. Melted white candles were spaced throughout the hallway and the rooms.

The stench of rotted wood and mildew clotted the air. Underneath those odors, David detected, faintly, the coppery scent of blood.

His stomach tightened.

"Hey, there's a tape player up here." Mac indicated a device sitting on a wooden table in the hallway. He shone his flashlight over it; it was a small cassette recorder housed in black casing. "There's a note on here. It says, 'Play Me.' "

"Go ahead," David said.

Mac pressed the Play button. David and the others crowded closer.

Static crackled from the speaker. Then came the crisp, slightly accented voice of Kyle, the vampire.

"Good evening, David Hunter and friends! My father and I had foreseen that it would not be long before you and your crew of intrepid adventurers made an expedition to our temporary residence. We had grown tired of the visits by your meddlesome kin, and have therefore found another sanctuary.

"Ah, David Hunter—my dear mother has built a fence around you. But my father grows more powerful with each passing hour, and when he makes himself known to the world, tonight, not even my ancient mother will be able to protect you from my father's fury. Nor my fury, I might add. Your ancestor shut my father away from me for all of my life, and for that, you are responsible and bear the burden of your ancestor's trespass against us. We promise you a fate worse than death.

"And Nia James—how endearing that you are standing by your man. But I've decided to seek a vampire bride, and you would be a fine choice. Consider it carefully, my lady—or follow your doomed man to his demise.

"Chief Van Jackson—finally shaken off the crippling fear, have you? I reached inside your puny brain before and shaped it as a sculptor manipulates clay. To do so again would be simple. But that would be too gentle a punishment for you.

We have something better in mind. Make provisions for your son, we advise.

"To all of you: you *will not* defeat us. My father lived as a mighty warrior in Africa during his time as a man, and since then, his prowess in battle has advanced to greater heights than your mortal minds can fathom. Your wisest course of action would be for you to leave this town, but that would provide only a temporary respite, I must caution. Mason's Corner is only the beginning for us, the launch pad of a bold mission that will carry us around the world.

"By the way, before you leave the premises, please visit the cellar. In our absence, one of your friends would enjoy the pleasure of your company.

"We eagerly anticipate meeting you tonight.

"Until then, *adieu.*"

Trembling, David shut off the cassette recorder. Jackson and Nia looked furious. The faces of the others were taut with resolve.

"To the basement," David said.

Chapter 18

Jahlil hated being cooped up at the police station.

Yeah, Dad wanted to keep him safe and away from the dangerous action that might go down tonight, but Jahlil wasn't some little kid. He wasn't helpless. He knew how to use guns, and he knew what these vampires were all about. He should be out in the streets, not penned up in here with these other people who didn't know what the hell was going on. These people were glad that they were on the team that would only get called in for backup. Cowards.

He had to get away from them. He and Poke were in the tiny room in the back of the station. The room was full of dusty files and papers. Poke was playing a Gameboy. Jahlil was flipping through one of Deputy Dudu's tabloids. Dudu had been a goofy dude, but he'd wanted to do the right thing. Jahlil missed him.

In the main room out front, Jahlil heard the team members talking on the phone and speculating amongst themselves about what might happen that night. Boring, pointless conversation. Jahlil needed to be taking action.

"Hey, man," Jahlil said to Poke. "We should break out of here."

"For what? I kinda like chillin' here. I don't want to be in the middle of no shit, know what I'm saying?"

"I want to be in the streets doing something, not laying up in here like a coward. You know how to use a gun, man. Your dad used to take you hunting."

Poke shrugged. "That was a long time ago. And it don't matter, 'cause I don't wanna get bit by some motherfucking vampire mutt like T-Bone did."

"Don't punk out on me, Poke. I need you to have my back on this. We gotta go out there and do some damage. Get some revenge for what they did to T-Bone."

Poke sighed. "Why you gotta be a hero? T-Bone's one of them now; he might be coming after *us*."

"Then we owe it to him to put him out of his misery," Jahlil said. He stood and threw the magazine on the floor. "I'm rolling out, with or without you."

Poke looked as though he wanted to hurl his Gameboy against the wall. "Dammit, J, you a crazy motherfucker, you know that? You been watching too many movies. You gonna get us both killed."

Jahlil shrugged and walked out of the room.

Behind him, he heard Poke's chair scrape against the floor.

He smiled to himself. Poke could complain all he wanted, but there was no way he would abandon Jahlil. They were like brothers.

Out in the office, the patrol team sat around talking, looking nervous.

Jahlil walked to his father's desk like he owned the place and pulled open a drawer. He fished out a set of keys.

"Hey, where you going, little man?" one of the men said. Jahlil recognized the guy from the ball courts. His name was Bobby. He had a long, dripping Jheri curl, a gold tooth, and always wore faded basketball jerseys.

"Me and my boy got some business to handle." Jahlil walked toward the door, where Poke waited.

"Hold on, the chief said you were supposed to stay here with us," Bobby said. "I'm telling."

"Don't be a punk." Jahlil pushed open the door. "Later, people."

Dad had parked his pickup in the corner of the parking lot. Jahlil unlocked the doors and climbed in, and Poke rode shotgun.

The engine revved up with a roar. Although Jahlil did not have a driver's license, he had learned how to drive when he was twelve years old. He grasped the manual gearshift with confidence.

"Where we going?" Poke said.

"We're gonna drop by my crib to pick up some guns, and make some of those Molotov cocktails," Jahlil said. "Then, we're going vampire hunting."

The door to the basement awaited them.

David could only imagine what they would find down there. Vampires? Corpses? Demon dogs? There was no way to tell. The house was as silent as a morgue.

"Why are we going down there?" Ben whispered. "We know the head vampires are gone, and they're the ones we want. I'm telling you, we're walking into a trap."

"Could be a citizen down there, sick," Jackson said. "We're the law in this town, y'all. We've go to do our duty to protect and serve."

"The guy on the recording said a friend of ours was waiting for us in the cellar," Tanya said. "It has to be someone that we know."

"Speculating isn't gonna do us any good," Mac said. "We've got to charge down there and take control. Act like soldiers." He grasped the doorknob.

"Be careful with old Suzie, Mac," David said. "We don't want to set the house on fire. Not with us in here."

Mac grunted by way of reply. He pulled open the door.

A swamp of darkness lay below. A horrible stench roiled from the room, too. When he was a kid, David had once discovered a dead squirrel that had gotten snared in an attic crevice, and this stink was similar, only stronger. He tried to keep from gagging, but a couple other team members coughed, and Ben cursed softly.

Mac slid his hand across the wall inside the doorway. He flipped a switch, but no light came on.

"Gimme some light, guys," Mac said. "Get those weapons ready, people. It's show time."

They brandished their guns. Ben shone his flashlight over Mac's shoulder, exposing concrete walls festooned with cobwebs, and a narrow flight of wōoden steps.

Mac began to descend the stairs, the tip of the flame-thrower emitting a faint glow. The steps creaked under his weight.

In tight formation, Ben followed Mac; then Tanya, David, Nia, Bertha, and Jackson. David felt Nia's hot breath on the back of his neck, and the sensation was absurdly arousing. This was a hell of a time to be thinking about sex—

"Holy shit," Mac said. He was at the bottom of the staircase. "Chief, you ain't gonna like this."

The rest of them joined Mac below. And saw what he meant.

On the other side of the basement, revealed in the flashlights, Deputy Ray Dudu hung from a ceiling pipe—hung from his ankles. His eyes were closed. His gangly arms were crossed over his chest. He looked like a grotesque human bat.

He still wore his police uniform. The shirt was stained with blood.

I'd rather die than become something like that, David

thought. He felt as if he were viewing a spectacle at a carnival freak show.

Suspended from the pipe, Dudu swung back and forth, slowly, as if rocked by a gentle breeze.

"What wrong with him?" Ben said.

"He's a vampire," Jackson said. He stepped forward. "Pearl said he was dead. I know what she meant now. He ain't human no more. Old Mac, do it."

Mac wiped sweat from his brow. "Chief, he kinda looks like a man. I don't know about this."

Dudu's eyes opened.

Someone screamed.

The creature who had once been Ray Dudu launched forward, flying across the room and into their midst. The team scattered; David grabbed Nia's arm and pulled her away from the melee. Flashlights clattered against the floor, light beams swerving crazily around the room. As David fumbled with his gun, a man screamed, and in a strobe of light he saw the vampire crushing Ben in a bear hug. The vampire savagely bit into the man's neck.

"Mac, hit him with the flamethrower!" David said.

"Damn thing won't light up!" Mac said. David heard a frantic clicking sound.

Come on, come on, come on, David thought. He had pressed himself against the cold wall. He gripped Nia's arm tightly. She was panting, too.

Another shriek—a woman. David raised the flashlight, moved it around, and captured the vampire in the act of tearing into Bertha's jugular vein.

"Someone, shoot him!" David said. He raised his gun.

But Jackson was first. Across the cellar, he fired his .357. The bullet hit the fiend in the chest. The vampire stepped backward, stumbled, but did not fall.

"How could you shoot a fellow officer?" the vampire said. Its voice was raspy. It bared its fangs. "I never liked you, Chief Jackass."

Jackson nailed the vampire with another bullet, this one in the head. It staggered against the wall, but it would not go down. Rage and inhuman hunger blazed in its reddened eyes.

"Ready, get back!" Mac shouted. He aimed the flamethrower at the vampire. A jet of flames spat out of the weapon with a *whoosh!*

The blast of heat sizzled the sweat on David's face.

Engulfed in fire, the creature screeched. It dropped to the floor and rolled, as though to extinguish the flames.

"Hit him again, Mac," Jackson said.

Mac punished the vampire with another stream of fire.

The flames consumed the monster as though it were made of dry rags. Howling, flailing its limbs, the vampire struggled, but could not defeat the ravenous fire.

Finally, the creature lay still and quiet. Rancid gray smoke steamed from the corpse.

David prodded the corpse with his foot. The vampire did not move.

He looked around. Ben and Bertha lay on the floor, having collapsed after being bitten. Jackson, Mac, Tanya, and Nia appeared as if they had crawled through hell and back.

They had only just begun. It was going to get much worse before the night was over.

"Well, team," David said. "We've killed our first vampire."

Junior regretted that he had been assigned to the hospital.

He'd gotten there on time, at seven-fifteen. The patrol team had a desk and a few chairs stationed on the north wing of the medical center, in front of a set of heavy doors. A handwritten sign taped to the doors read, "Quarantine Area: Authorized Personnel Only!" Past the doors, the half-dozen or so rooms were full of sick people. (He could not think of them as people who had been bitten by vampiric creatures;

he preferred to think of them as being sick, it was easier to get his mind around it.)

To get into the quarantine section, you had to be either a member of the patrol team or a medical person—or be sick. Curious, Junior had used his team member status to get inside, to look around for a minute. He peeked inside the dimly lit rooms.

Many of the people that lay on the beds, comatose, were folks that he had done work for in the past. Good people, all of them. It disturbed him. But nothing disturbed him as much as seeing Doc Bennett in a bed, too.

Junior stepped inside Doc's room. Mrs. Bennett sat at his beside. She looked tired.

A woman lay in a bed on the other side of the room, asleep. Junior didn't know who she was.

"Hi, Junior," Mrs. Bennett said, in a weary voice.

"Hi." He stood just inside the doorway; unconsciously, he touched the pendant that lay on his chest, underneath his shirt. "How long's Doc Bennett been sick?"

"Since yesterday."

"Oh." Junior lowered his head. "I hope he gets better real soon."

"We all do." She sighed. "This is a quarantine area, sugar. I can be here because I'm a nurse, but are you supposed to be back here? I wouldn't want anything to happen to you, too."

"I'm on the patrol team, ma'am," he said. "I was just checking on people."

"You're a brave man, Junior. I'm praying for all of you."

Junior nodded. He didn't know what to say. He thought of saying that it was partly his fault that Doc Bennett had gotten sick—he was the one who had told Doc about the cave in the first place—but Mrs. Bennett already looked so sad that he didn't want to say anything that would make her feel worse.

"Well . . . let me know if you need somethin'," Junior said.

"It's going to be night soon," Mrs. Bennett said. She glanced out the window. Darkness was coming. "You be careful, sugar, okay?"

"Yes, ma'am, I sure will."

He shuffled back to his post. He felt kinda sick himself, but his pain was due to heartache. He wished he had been assigned to go somewhere else. Here, misery hung heavy in the air, as powerful as the antiseptic smell that characterized all hospitals.

He sat on a chair next to his team members, and whittled away the time chatting with them. Every now and then, Dr. Green and his assistants would push ill folks toward the doors, on stretchers, and then Junior's team would put the sick individual's name on a list. Within an hour, they had checked in eight people, and Junior knew every one of them. But when the ninth person was brought in, he jumped up so suddenly that his chair crashed against the floor.

It was Vicky Queen.

He knew she had been ill, and he'd figured that she was sick with the same thing as everyone else, but seeing her rolled in on a stretcher—it did something to him. He stood in front of the doors, blocking the medical assistant's route to quarantine.

"Miss Queen?" he said. "That can't be you."

The woman tucked under the white sheet was asleep. It looked like Vicky, but then it didn't. She didn't have any makeup on, but Junior had always thought she was so pretty she didn't need makeup anyway. This woman had Vicky's fine features, but she was drab and limp, like a wax dummy or something. No, not like a wax dummy. Like someone lying in a coffin.

He gripped the edges of the gurney in his big, callused hands.

"Excuse me, please," the medical assistant said. "I need to get this young lady into quarantine."

"Her name's Vicky Queen," Junior said.

"Are you a relative of the patient?"

"Huh?"

The assistant sighed. "Are you related to Vicky Queen?"

"No, umm, I'm just a friend. I've known her my whole life."

"I see. Will you sign her in for me, please?"

"Okay, sure."

The assistant rolled her eyes, like she was annoyed at Junior or something. He didn't get it, but sometimes people did things that baffled him.

"What room is available?" the assistant said. "I have to know where to take her."

Junior stammered. One of his team members stepped forward, put Vicky's name on the list, and said she could go in room 113.

Vicky Queen was swept away through the swinging doors. Junior watched her being taken into a room near the end of the hallway.

He would make sure that he kept an eye on her. She had always been so nice to him. He would hate for something bad to happen to her. He would do whatever it took to protect her.

Darkness embraced the world.

The arrival of night thrilled Kyle. This one would forever hold a valued place in his memory: the night that he and his father stood side-by-side and launched a war against humankind.

The war was long overdue. For too long, vampires such as Mother had lived in secret, preying upon humans as if they were lowly parasites, like minuscule fish clinging to the belly of a great whale. The truth, as his father had forced him to realize, was that vampires were the superior race, and it was time for them to assume their rightful, dominant position in the world's hierarchy of species.

When Kyle had lived with Mother, he had often pondered such ideas, but Mother, predictably, would turn his thoughts away from fantasies of conquest. Mother was too wealthy, too old, and too passive to care about elevating their race. But Diallo hungered for blood and dominion, and he had stoked the same flames in Kyle, too.

The prize of the battle in Mason's Corner was David Hunter. Although Diallo had not shared with Kyle how he planned to punish the man, Diallo's sly smile whenever the topic arose made it quite clear to Kyle that the human would curse his unfortunate lineage for all eternity.

As night sucked away the final threads of daylight, Kyle and Diallo left the sheltering walls of their hideaway and emerged outdoors. Diallo strode purposefully through the grass. Kyle walked in step with him.

He admired his father's appearance in the black silk shirt, jeans, and polished leather boots. Kyle wore the same clothing himself; he had acquired the tailored garments before leaving Paris. Kyle imagined that together, they resembled vengeful angels who had visited Earth to set matters right between their kind and man.

He felt Diallo's strength; it emanated from his body like cold air, demanding that Kyle keep a few feet between himself and his father, lest he grow numb from the aura of power. There was no doubt that his father had recovered. Diallo had said that he'd never felt such energy course through him.

A dome of purple-black clouds covered the world. Thunder grumbled. Lightning stuttered on the horizon and illuminated the vast, weed-dense field through which they walked. Maple trees filled the area, looking like shadowy sentinels.

Kyle did not know where Diallo was headed, and he had no inclination to ask. He would go wherever his father led him.

A hill rose ahead of them. Diallo started to ascend it, and Kyle followed, but Diallo stretched out his arm, stopping him.

"I must do this alone," Diallo said. His eyes gleamed like onyx. "Wait behind, and watch."

"Yes, Father."

Diallo marched to the peak, his shirt fluttering in the wind like wings.

Kyle did not know what his father was about to do, but his hands clenched in anticipation.

Atop the mound, Diallo faced the west. He knelt, spread his long arms, and tilted his face upward.

Kyle recalled that his father had assumed a similar stance when he had summoned the first canines that became his slaves. Was Diallo conjuring more hounds? Already, they had dozens of dogs under their command.

No, this must be something different, Kyle thought. *Father is about to perform something wondrous and awesome.*

The atmosphere hummed, raising the hairs at the nape of Kyle's neck. But he was not afraid. He was giddy, eager.

He felt as though he had lived his entire long life to be ready to vividly experience events like this; the lackluster life of luxury and tranquillity he had lived at his mother's estate had prepared him to feel the proper appreciation for his father's electrifying power.

A jagged rod of lightning lashed across the sky and cast Diallo's profile in stark relief. As motionless as he was, Diallo might have been the ancient obsidian statue of a warrior god.

The breeze soughing through the trees picked up speed, branches swaying, leaves rustling. The wind gusted faster . . .

faster . . . faster, the pitch raising from a low moan to an anguished cry.

The collar of Kyle's shirt flew up. The wind shoved him forward, and he dropped to his knees.

I did not know a vampire could possess such talents, he thought. *Mother had never spoken of influencing the weather.* He had thought that the ability for vampires to do such acts was fiction. Once again, Mother had kept secrets from him.

Squinting his eyes against the cutting wind, Kyle raised his face to watch his father.

On the hill, Diallo remained still, kneeling, arms outspread, though the gusts tore at his clothing and shredded leaves whirled around him.

The sky appeared to be boiling, storm clouds churning, shifting, roiling.

A hundred yards away, a sizzling bolt of lightning struck a tree. Orange sparks flew. The maple, cleaved in half as though hit with a giant axe, slammed against the earth.

Kyle suppressed an urge to seek cover. His father had ordered him to wait. Nevertheless, he drew up his collar to guard his sensitive ears. But the makeshift hood could not quiet the shrieking wind.

Thunder roared, so explosively that Kyle feared the ground might open up and swallow him.

Then, in quick succession, several whips of lightning slashed at the town. Kyle could not determine precisely where they struck, only that they were in the vicinity of the residential area. The sky was ablaze in gas-jet blue light.

My father is indeed a genius. What better way to stir the humans into a frenzy of confusion and fear before we attack, than by turning the elements against them?

The howling wind spat leaves and grit in Kyle's face. He reached inside his shirt pocket, withdrew the aviator glasses, slid them over his eyes. The storm-punished land seemed to be drenched in darkness.

Diallo, resembling a giant shadow, finally rose, and began to descend the hill. The furious winds did not hamper his walk; they seemed to escort him, and for an instant, Kyle thought his father was floating.

Although Kyle worried that the wind might flatten him, he stood to meet his father. Diallo touched his shoulder. His grip was like an iron clamp, and his fingers were so hot that they singed Kyle's skin.

Power.

"Now, our army will arise," Diallo said, "and we will join them."

Jackson was eager to get away from Jubilee. He never wanted to set foot in the house again. He never wanted to see it again.

He fleetingly thought of taking Mac's flamethrower and spitting a stream of fire at the place, to erase it from the town once and for all.

He and the team members carried Bertha and Ben out of the basement. By the time they finally stumbled onto the veranda, night had imprisoned the town.

While they were in the cellar, Jackson had called Dr. Green on his cell phone and asked him to come to the Mason place, pronto, to pick up their fallen members. They needed to be taken to quarantine immediately.

None of them spoke as they waited on the porch for the ambulance to arrive. There was nothing that any of them could say that would make sense of what had happened in the basement. Every time Jackson shut his eyes, he saw Deputy Dudu's blood-crazed face—the face of a monster. The lurid image would stay with him for the rest of his life.

Christ, he wanted to get away from this place. From the anxious looks on the faces of everyone else, they were as ready as he was to get the hell out of there.

The wail of the ambulance—which normally alarmed him—was the most appealing sound he'd heard all day. It meant he could leave soon.

Tanya sprinted across the gravel driveway, to open the gate. The vehicle rolled down the path, lights flashing.

Dr. Green typically would never ride in an ambulance, but he was spending a lot of time in it today. As they had for Jackson, ordinary procedures had been thrown out the window.

Jackson met the doctor as he climbed out of the vehicle. Dr. Green, normally a robust-looking guy, seemed as though he had aged twenty years in only a few hours.

Two assistants hurried to where Ben and Bertha had been placed on the veranda.

"Had a mess up here," Jackson said to the doctor. "Appreciate you coming as fast as you did."

Green dragged his hand down his haggard face. "What went on in there, Chief?"

"We killed a vampire. It used to be my deputy, but he wasn't himself anymore. We torched him with a flamethrower. But he bit those two folks before we could take him down."

"I see," the doctor said. Jackson had steeled himself for a frown, or a disdainful glare, but Green looked thoughtful—and scared. Jackson wondered what the doctor had seen while making his visits throughout town to pick up the ill.

"I don't know if we'll ever be able to explain this phenomenon scientifically," Green said, "or treat their conditions with medicine. But I believe you, Jackson. I've seen enough myself so that I'm left with no choice but to believe you."

"Being right docsn't please me none," Jackson said. "Rather be making all this up."

"All we can do is our best," Green said. He shrugged, as though too exhausted to think of a more profound comment. But he was right. All they could do was give it their best shot.

They loaded Ben and Bertha on gurneys and lifted them into the ambulance. After the vehicle sped away, Jackson turned to the remaining four people on his team. They looked weary—way too weary at such an early stage in the fight. The night was young.

"I think we should go back to the police station to regroup," David said. "We've got to put our heads together and figure out where the head vampires might be hiding. We have to stay focused on Kyle and Diallo."

"Makes sense," Jackson said. "We've gotta touch base with the other teams, too, make sure they're holding up."

The others murmured their agreement. They trudged down the path, to the gate.

A breeze had been blowing for most of the afternoon, but then it suddenly picked up speed. Jackson snared his hat before the wind snatched it off his head and hurled it into the darkness.

Thunder groaned, making the earth tremble. Lightning skipped across the sky.

All of them began to run down the driveway.

The gust rose from a moan into a nerve-racking screech. It took the efforts of Jackson and David to force open the iron gate and hold it so that Nia, Mac, and Tanya could get through. When Jackson and David squeezed through it themselves, the gate boomed shut behind them.

Lightning cracked above Jubilee's rooftops, making the old mansion look like every bit of the haunted house that it was rumored to be.

David, Mac, and Nia scrambled into Mac's pickup, and Tanya got in the patrol car with Jackson. Jackson stabbed the key in the ignition. The wind punched the car, snuffled at the windows like a creature scrabbling to get inside.

"Do you think it's a tornado?" Tanya said.

"Don't know, might be," Jackson said. "Wouldn't be lucky for us, would it?"

Mac had slammed his truck into gear, performed a U-turn, and was roaring away down the road, heading back toward town. Jackson executed a sharp U-turn, too.

Dead leaves and weeds, animated by the gale, danced in the middle of the road. The trees swayed, their boughs shaking violently.

Jackson had seen two tornados in his life—one as a child, one as a man—and these winds were growing closer and closer to reaching that level of destruction.

He mashed the gas pedal. The acceleration threw him back in his seat.

Ahead, a fork of lightning stabbed an oak tree alongside the road with an eardrum-splitting *crack!* Hot branches flew like shrapnel, and the shattered, smoking trunk teetered and began to fall toward the road.

Jackson floored the accelerator.

"Watch out!" Tanya said, in a high-pitched voice. She covered her eyes.

In his peripheral vision, Jackson saw the giant tree falling toward him; it would smash the car to pieces if it struck them. But he could not have stopped if he'd wanted to. Adrenaline propelled him to push the engine to the maximum.

The oak missed the car's rear bumper by only a foot. The tree crashed against the ground with such force that the car bounced a few inches in the air and rattled his teeth.

"Are you crazy?" Tanya said. "You could've killed us!"

"I ain't ready to die yet," Jackson said. "Got too much work to do tonight to have time to die."

Tanya opened her mouth, and he heard the beginnings of a first-class cussout coming his way, but then she clapped her mouth shut, folded her arms across her chest, and slid down in the seat.

"Bet you'll ride with someone else next time," Jackson said. He chuckled. Maybe he was losing his mind. He couldn't really see the humor in the situation, but he couldn't stop the laugh from escaping him. He'd heard the saying that when things got tough, you laughed to keep from crying. Maybe that was what he was doing, laughing to keep from crying. Or laughing to keep from dying.

At home in the den, Jahlil discovered that almost all of his father's firearms were gone. The only ones left in the gun cabinet were Jahlil's own pump-action Mossberg shotgun, which he used for hunting, and a pellet gun that Jahlil had used as a kid to take target practice at soda cans.

A pellet gun, for God's sake.

"Dammit!" Jahlil slammed his fist against the cabinet door. "I betcha Dad gave all our shit to the people on those patrol teams."

"Now what we gonna do, man?" Poke said. His face was greasy with sweat. "I ain't got no guns, my pops took all of 'em when he moved out."

"Figures," Jahlil said. He chewed his lip. *Think!* "Okay, look. We're gonna have to work as a team. I'll use the shotgun—"

"—man, that's bullshit—" Poke said.

"—I'm not finished, all right?" Jahlil said. "Just listen. I'll use the gun, and we'll make some Molotov cocktails. When we see a bloodsucker, I'll plug him, to slow him down, and then you'll light him up with the cocktail. We'll be like a tag team. Get it?"

"Hell, naw," Poke said. "I need me a motherfucking gun. Why you get to carry the shotgun?"

" 'Cause it's mine," Jahlil said. He offered the pistol to Poke. "Use this. It's better than nothing. Carry it for backup. All any of these guns can do is slow down these bloodsuckers anyway, they won't kill them."

"I'm gonna get me a real piece before we're through,"

Poke said. His lips curled in disgust, Poke snatched the pellet gun from Jahlil and holstered it in his waistband. "Gimme some ammo, man."

In the ammunition drawer, the only ammo left was for the pellet gun, and the Mossberg. He scooped up two handfuls of pellets and handed them to Poke, then loaded the shotgun. Once it was loaded, he unzipped his duffel bag and dumped the remaining ammo inside. The bag already held a flashlight, a knife, a first aid kit, and several books of matches. Jahlil wanted to be prepared for anything.

Thunder rumbled. Poke checked outside the window.

"What do you see out there?" Jahlil said. Night had fallen, and someone might attack them at any second. "Someone coming?"

"We got a storm coming," Poke said. No sooner had he spoken the words than a gale of wind skirled around the house. The ceiling light in the den wavered.

"Go to the kitchen and get some candles," Jahlil said. "They're in the drawer by the refrigerator. We can't be without light. We still have to make those cocktails."

"Got it." Poke shuffled to the stairs. Did he have to walk so slowly? Jahlil wanted to put his foot up his ass to get him moving. Well, they'd always called him Poke for a reason. He moved like a slug.

Jahlil was starting to get a headache. It was the same kind of pounding-behind-the-eyes pain that he would get whenever he was taking an exam for which he hadn't studied. It was solely due to stress.

The screaming gust beat a tattoo against the walls. Thunder steamrolled across the night, and Jahlil saw flickers of lightning coming in through the curtains, as though someone were taking photos outside.

"Man, hurry up!" Jahlil said. He didn't like being alone down there, not when he understood what awaited them outdoors.

Poke returned to the den with a single, half-melted candle.

"Only found one in there." Poke shrugged. "Guess your daddy raided the crib of all the useful shit today."

"No shit," Jahlil said. "Well, let's go in the garage to make these cocktail things so we can get out of here."

The door on the far side of the room opened into the two-car garage. Jahlil flipped the light switch beside the door. The light did not turn on.

Behind them, the light in the den winked out.

Jahlil cursed under his breath. Could it get any worse? Nothing was going their way.

"Gimme some light, man, hurry up," Poke said. He was so close that Jahlil could smell the Doritos on his breath.

Jahlil clicked on the flashlight. He struck a match and lit the candle that Poke clutched in both hands as though it were the Holy Grail or something.

Jahlil panned the light beam around the garage, searching for the red-and-yellow can of gasoline. It was in the corner, beside the John Deere lawn mower.

Jahlil picked up the gasoline container.

It really could get worse for them. The can was empty.

Junior could not wait any longer. He had to see Vicky Queen.

Ever since the medical people had pushed Vicky into quarantine and rolled her into the room at the end of the hallway, Junior had been unable to keep his attention away from her door. But it was too far away for him to peek inside. He would have to go back there to get a good look at her.

He just wanted to make sure she was doing okay, that's all. It wasn't as though his team needed him right now. One woman, named Maria, handled checking in all the sick people, and the rest of the group only sat around, talking about stuff going on in town. Things were going slow, but that might change soon. He wanted to see Vicky while he still had the chance.

Ron, one of the team members, winked at Junior.

"You're thinking about that woman, ain't you, Junior?"

"Huh? What woman?" Junior played dumb. He didn't like for people to know his business.

Ron smiled. "You know who I mean. Vicky Queen. The finest piece of ass in this town. Don't be ashamed, I've been thinking about her, too."

"What you mean?" Junior asked cautiously.

"She's sleep like all the rest of these folks, man. How about we sneak back there and get a look at her titties? She got them nice, big, round titties, nipples like Hershey's Kisses. We can suck on 'em a little bit, you take one, I take the other—"

Junior seized Ron by his shirt and drove him backward. The back of Ron's head smacked the wall. The guy yelped, like a panicked puppy.

Junior's nose was only inches away from the man's face. "You stay away from Miss Queen! She ain't no . . . no toy. Hear me?"

Ron's face went tomato red. He spluttered. "Let me go, man. I'm sorry, all right? I was kidding!"

"You stay away from Miss Queen, you pervert." Junior gave the guy a good shake, making his head thump against the wall again. Then Junior released him.

Ron moved away, smoothing his shirt with shaky hands. "You need to relax, man. What's wrong with you? We're supposed to be a team. Ain't nothing wrong with joking around."

Junior ignored him. He was slow, but he wasn't dumb enough to be fooled by this fella. Ron was a pervert—Junior didn't realize how he remembered the word "pervert," but the word felt right when applied to Ron.

He looked down the corridor, at Vicky's door.

I'll go in there for only a minute, he promised himself. *I'll make sure she's okay, then I'll come back.*

He put his hand against the quarantine doors.

Maria, stationed at the desk, raised her head. "Where you going, Junior? Quarantine's a restricted area. Medical staff only."

"I'll be right back," he said. "I gotta check on a friend." He pushed through the doors before the woman could tie him up in a conversation.

Although on his last visit to this section he had peeked inside each room, on this trip he was so focused on Vicky's doorway that he didn't bother to look anywhere else.

He paused at the threshold, wiped his face with a handkerchief. Quietly, he stepped inside.

The room was dimly lit. There were four beds inside, each of them layered with crisp white sheets, but Vicky was the last patient brought to quarantine, and had the room to herself.

She lay on the bed nearest the window. Light glowing from the lamp on the nightstand enveloped her in a soft golden aura.

The blinds were open to the night. Outside, lightning snapped across the sky, and thunder rolled.

Junior cleared his throat. "You awake, Miss Queen?"

No response. She did not stir, either.

Hesitantly, he approached the bed, his boots squeaking across the floor.

Although she was ill, wore no makeup, and had disheveled hair, she was the most beautiful woman in the world to him. Her lovely face was turned to the side, and one of her slender, copper arms lay across the bedsheet. Her skin was drained of its usual, healthy shine, but her full lips were soft and rosy.

It was impossible to believe that this gorgeous woman was going to change into a vampire one day. Junior couldn't believe it.

She looked more lively than she had only a short while ago, when she had first been brought to the hospital. Maybe the medical people had given her a dose of something to heal her.

She shifted, sleepily pulling away the sheet a little, as though she were too warm. Her movement partially exposed her firm, ripe cleavage that swelled underneath the thin hospital gown.

Ron's voice came to Junior's mind.

How about we sneak back there and get a look at her titties? She got them nice, big, round titties, nipples like Hershey's Kisses . . .

Vicky's moist tongue slid out and glided across her lips. She moaned softly.

Cold sweat broke out on Junior's forehead.

"You ain't even gotta be awake to make my heart race, Miss Queen," Junior said. He exhaled.

He gently pulled the cover over her chest, in case someone nasty like Ron came inside to see her.

His hand brushed across her face. He felt her smooth skin. He tenderly stroked one of her lush eyebrows, ran his fingers through her long hair.

He remembered a time when he and Vicky had lived next door to each other, and they were both kids. Junior had been roaring down the sidewalk on his bike and had fallen off and skinned his knee, and Vicky, who had been playing with her dog, came over to him and cleaned his knee with her own saliva, then got him a Band-Aid . . .

A scream snatched him out of his reverie.

He shot upright. Who was hurt?

But it was only the wind. Outside, a gust harassed the trees and screeched around the building. As he looked out the window, a pulse of lightning stung his eyes.

He pulled the cord to lower the blinds. They clattered to the bottom of the windowsill.

"There we go," he said, turning back to the bed. "Now, you can sleep in some peace—"

The words died on his lips.

Vicky Queen was awake, and she was smiling at him.

Chapter 19

Franklin Bennett swam out of slumber, immediately consumed with a raging restlessness and an unstoppable urge to do . . . *something*. Something he could not articulate. Not yet. But the nameless compulsion drove him to action.

He flung away the bedsheets.

He was in a hospital room. His glasses lay on a nightstand. He reached for them, as was his habit upon awakening—and paused.

His vision, without the spectacles, was hawk-sharp. He could clearly discern even a speck of dirt on the far wall.

He pursed his lips, confused.

What is happening? I am a patient here, it seems. How long have I been asleep? Days, weeks? I cannot recall. Most important, why am I here?

I cannot remember.

Perhaps he could remember, if he exerted the mental effort, but it did not seem worth the trouble. He was a prisoner to the urge that he could not elucidate. Satisfying the need was the only endeavor worthy of his attention.

He raised into a sitting position. The overstuffed chair beside the bed was empty, but Ruby had been sitting there only a short while ago. He smelled her lingering feminine scent.

Smelled her? What an odd way to determine his wife's whereabouts.

It doesn't matter. I have to find Ruby. I have to get my hands on her. She has what I need. I do not know what it is, but she has it, in abundance.

He bounded out of the bed, with an agility that he had not known since he had been a teenager. His gown billowed around him. He had to get out of this foolish getup. After he had found Ruby.

Across the room, a young woman arose out of her bed. He did not know who she was, and he did not care. She did not possess anything of interest to him. She seemed equally uninterested in him.

He heard footsteps shuffling along the corridor: slow, tired steps.

As the footsteps neared the room, Ruby's scent grew stronger.

Quick as a bat, he hid behind the door.

He shot his roommate a stern glance, warning her not to interfere, though he sensed that she was enslaved to a need that matched his own.

Ruby trudged inside. She saw his empty bed, and gasped. A mug emitting the pungent aroma of cinnamon-apple tea dropped out of her hands and crashed against the tile.

My wife has what I need, and I must have it now.

Franklin blocked the doorway. Ruby spun around.

"Franklin? Sugar, what's wrong?" Fear and worry flashed in her big eyes. But Franklin was less concerned about her eyes, and fascinated with the tender flesh of her neck.

He heard her pulse throbbing. The rapid pounding thundered in his head, like a bass drum.

"Come to me, love." He gripped her shoulders. Ruby opened her mouth, perhaps to scream, but only a high-pitched whine squeaked out of her.

I'm going to do something awful to my wife, my lover, my lifelong companion, my best friend, but I cannot help it, God help me, I cannot resist, she has what I need and I absolutely MUST have it now.

He pulled his wife into his strong arms, bowed his head, and pierced her neck with his unexpectedly sharp teeth. Ruby batted her hands against him, but as his fangs sank deeper, she sighed and leaned against his chest, willingly, as though she accepted that it was inevitable and appropriate that she should be the first to give him what he needed; the only thing in the universe that would satisfy his intense craving, the substance that flooded his mouth like warm, tangy cider and filled him with orgasmic pleasure.

Blood.

Vicky Queen smiled at Junior. "Hey, sweetie."

Her hair had fallen across her left eye, and she brushed it away with a light motion that, for some reason, made Junior's heart throb. Vicky had always been able to do that to him. She affected him in ways that he didn't understand.

But she wasn't the same old Vicky. Her eyes were red and wild. Something about her smile made him pause, too.

When her grin spread wider, he realized what it was: her teeth were wickedly sharp. With teeth like that, she could snap a drumstick in half with a single bite. Or tear into a man's throat and suck his blood . . .

She's a vampire, you dummy, a voice in the back of his mind warned. *Vampires have fangs. Get out of here.*

"Were you checking on me, Junior?" Vicky said. Her long eyelashes fluttered. "That was sweet of you. You've always been so sweet to me."

"I just wanted to make sure you were all right," he said. He sidestepped away from the bed. "Guess I'll be going now. I'll tell the nurse you're up and about; she can come and get you whatever you need."

Vicky yanked away the sheet, revealing the rest of her body. She wore only the gown, and the thin material ended at her upper thighs; her shapely, smooth legs gleamed in the lamplight like polished bronze.

"I need you, Junior. You need me, too."

"But . . ." Junior stuttered. His hand grasped the locket on his chest.

Mama, please give me some strength.

"Come here, Junior," Vicky said. "Lie on the bed with me. Let me kiss that muscular, chocolate body of yours. Let me bring your fantasies to life."

A vivid image flared in Junior's head, sómething he was surprised that he could think of: him lying on that bed and Vicky Queen sitting on top of him, her firm breasts jiggling, his hands squeezing her fine hips . . .

Vicky's alluring eyes were hypnotic.

He had taken a step toward her bed when his attention was diverted by a scream, outside the room. This time, it was not the wind. It was a human scream; a sound of horror and pain.

Junior snapped to alertness. What was he doing, going to Vicky's bed? She was going to do something bad to him.

Vicky hissed. Her eyes narrowed to red darts.

Junior ran to the door. He didn't dare to look behind him and get caught in Vicky's spell again.

In the hallway, he dashed past rooms. He glanced in Doc Bennett's room and saw something terrifying: Doc Bennett was standing and had cradled Mrs. Bennett in his arms, as if she had passed out in a faint. He turned and looked at Junior, and blood streamed down Doc Bennett's chin. His red lips formed a smile that chilled Junior to the marrow.

Doc Bennett's a vampire; Vicky Queen's a vampire; I bet everyone back here's turned into a vampire.

He was afraid to check on the other people and confirm his idea. He concentrated, instead, on getting out of there.

The exit out of quarantine seemed to be a hundred miles

away. Up there, a female nurse strained to open the doors. She had bright red bite marks on her pale neck. She must've been the one who had screamed.

"I got it, miss," Junior said. He pulled open the double doors, and the woman stumbled through. Junior risked a look over his shoulder.

Patients poured into the hallway, like wild animals released from cages. Inhuman hunger burned in their crimson eyes. They hissed and spat. Their long fangs gleamed like needles.

God, all of them had become vampires.

Outside quarantine, the patrol team members looked frightened and bewildered.

Junior snatched the ring of keys off the desk, to lock the doors.

"Don't just stand there!" Junior shouted. "Let's keep them from getting out!"

Then the lights went dead.

David and the remaining members of their special team arrived at the police station.

There, the storm had knocked out the power. The backup team used candles to illuminate the office. The people sat in a circle, as though they were performing a séance.

King, sitting near the doorway, wagged his tail when he saw David. David was glad to see the mutt was okay.

The team immediately slammed him and Chief Jackson with questions.

"Where's Ben?"

"We've been getting calls that the power's out all over town. What should we do?"

"Where's Bertha?"

"We heard lightning's knocked down a bunch of trees. The roads out of town are blocked with 'em. How can we get out of here?"

"Listen!" David held up his hand. "Please, calm down. We'll get to your questions. First of all, is everyone here? Where are the boys, Jahlil and Poke?"

"Gone, man," a guy wearing a basketball jersey said. "They didn't wanna stay."

"You're kidding me," Jackson said. "You let my boy leave?"

"We couldn't stop them," the guy said.

Jackson cursed and threw his hat against the wall. He stormed around the room, fists bunched on his waist.

David was concerned about the kids, but he had to move on. He told the group a condensed version of what had happened at Jubilee. None of them questioned the reality of what David and his group had seen. They were beyond doubts. The world of nightmares had become real.

"On the way here, we saw the strong winds and lightning," David said. "But we had no idea that trees are blocking the main roads that lead out of here, or that the power has been knocked out everywhere. Somehow, I don't think that's an accident. The vampires are setting us up for an attack."

"Diallo?" Nia said. "Jesus, if he's powerful enough to cause a storm . . ."

"I know, I know," David said. "We've got to find him. We have to assume that he's finally on the prowl, out there." He motioned to the window, and everyone peered fearfully at the glass, as though expecting a monster to bust inside. "Once we find Diallo and put him away for good, this madness will be over."

"I don't even know what this vampire cat looks like," the man in the basketball jersey said. "How are we supposed to take him out?"

"You'll know who he is, if you see him," David said. "He's not like you and me, remember. If you see either Diallo or his son, Kyle, you'll know it. Trust me. I expect them to show up on our radar at any second."

A frantic voice crackled from the team's two-way radio: At the hospital, the patients in quarantine were on the move. And all of them were vampires.

Franklin, David thought. Dread rippled through him. *Please, God, don't let me be the one to do it. Don't let me be the one . . .*

When the lights went out at the hospital, everyone panicked—except Junior. Already holding the key in his hand, he calmly found the keyhole, slipped the key inside, and latched the quarantine doors.

But he didn't think they were safe yet. He probably could have busted down those doors himself if he were angry enough. And there were close to twenty people on the other side who were furious about being penned in quarantine.

No, they ain't people, Junior reminded himself. *Not anymore, they ain't.*

A nurse turned on a flashlight and shone the beam at the door.

The vampires pressed their ghastly faces against the square windows. They bared their sharp teeth, hissing.

People screamed. Fear weakened Junior's knees, too. But he couldn't give up. This was the time for him to be brave.

The creatures beat their fists against the door.

Junior braced his hands against the heavy door. "We got to block it with somethin'!" he said. His arm muscles felt like they were about to rip.

Ron and Maria pushed a table across the hall, and Junior moved aside so they could lever the table against the door. Another man, DeWayne, grabbed a desk, and Junior helped him lift it and stack it on top of the table.

The vampires roared, hammered the doors harder.

"That ain't gonna hold them back long," Junior said. Already, the desk rocked.

"What else can we do?" Ron said, his eyes frantic.

"We gotta get ready to fight 'em," Junior said. "We can't let them get out of here or they're gonna get everyone else in town. Gimme a bomb."

Maria slapped a bottle, which they'd called a Molotov cocktail, into Junior's hand. A dry rag dangled from the tip.

He fished a cigarette lighter out of his pocket.

In front of him, the barricade trembled.

Ron and Maria each gripped a bottle bomb. DeWayne had the gun, cocked and ready. They had retreated far enough from the doorway so that when the barrier crashed, they would be out of harm's way. The nurse who held the flashlight was several feet behind them, her terrified face slick with sweat.

Blood-curdling sounds came from the vampires: cries and moans of hunger and aching need. Junior wanted to clap his hands over his ears. He wanted to run away. He looked behind him. The corridor was as dark as a tunnel; the only light came from the lightning that flashed through the windows.

The makeshift barrier clattered. The desk teetered, tumbled off the table, and crashed to the floor.

"Get ready!" DeWayne said. He aimed the gun.

Beside Junior, Maria recited a prayer.

Junior tightened his hold on the makeshift bomb. His thumb itched on the Bic lighter.

The table finally flipped over.

The quarantine doors exploded open.

The vampires stampeded outside like a herd of enraged bulls. Moving fast, oh man, Junior could not believe how fast they were. As soon as DeWayne squeezed off a booming shot, hitting one of the monsters in the stomach, another vampire jumped through the air and tackled the man, knocking him flat on his back. The vampire plunged its teeth into his neck. DeWayne screamed.

Junior was paralyzed.

We ain't got a chance against them, there're too many, and they're too fast and strong.

Ron and Maria lit their bombs, flung them in the general direction of the vampires, and ran. The bottles shattered on contact with the floor. A wall of flames whooshed in the air. Some of the vampires caught fire, and wailed in agony. The others scuttled away, frightened.

The fire alarm rang into life. The showers came on, spraying cold water everywhere.

No, Junior thought. *It's gonna put out the fire!*

Already, the water was pounding the flames into submission. Watching the dying fire cautiously, the vampires began to come forward.

I better run before they get their nerve back, Junior thought.

He took off.

His boots clapped across the wet floor. He ran past closets and darkened rooms. He wondered what would happen to the other, regular patients at the hospital. He didn't see any of the medical staff. Had all of them run away, too?

Far ahead of him, Maria and Ron were in the lobby.

"Hurry up, Junior!" Maria said. "We're getting out of here!"

"I'm coming!"

Ron and Maria vanished through the exit doors.

Junior heard the vampires behind him. Feet slapping against the wet tile. Hissing. Hungry for his blood.

Don't you dare look behind you, Junior.

He finally came to the lobby. He was about to push through the glass doors when he saw Ron and Maria. They were sprawled on the sidewalk outside. A pack of demon dogs swarmed over their bodies, like lions feeding on felled deer. Those mutts that could turn you into a vampire with a bite.

The dogs had been waiting for someone to run outside. He saw more dogs out there, hunched over people in blue medical uniforms.

Then Junior saw the man in black, the one from the cave. The guy strolled across the parking lot, toward the building. Dogs flanked him, like servants accompanying a king.

No one who ran out there would escape, period.

Drenched with water that continued to pour from the showers, Junior scrambled past the abandoned front desk in the lobby. There was another, shorter hallway behind the desk. At the end of the hall, he saw an Exit sign above a door, the blood-red letters glowing in the gloom.

The vampires' shrieks reverberated in the corridors. They weren't far behind.

He reached the exit, whammed open the door with his shoulder, and found himself in a pitch-black stairwell. He thumbed the Bic lighter and held it high, like a torch. It didn't give him much light, but he saw the door at the bottom of the dozen or so stairs.

Keeping the lighter held high, and clutching the bottle bomb in his other hand, he navigated down the steps. His knees trembled so badly he was certain that he would fall and roll down the stairs, maybe breaking his neck in the tumble. But he made it to the bottom without stumbling.

He pushed the door open.

A duo of slavering pit bulls awaited him in the alley. They rose from their haunches and came after him, snarling, foam spraying from their lips.

Frantic, Junior stepped inside and pulled the door shut.

The dogs scraped against the door, growling.

Junior leaned against the wall. His heart pounded so hard that the hammering seemed to transmit itself to the bricks behind him, making the walls throb in unison with his heart.

He wanted to find another way to escape, but he wondered if it would be worth the try. It was like these vampires had thought of all the ways to get out. Even if he jumped out a window, they would probably be waiting for him on the ground below.

At the top of the stairs, the door swished open.

Junior stood rigid.

Featherlight footsteps came inside the stairwell. Then the door was shut, closing out the chaotic sounds of the besieged hospital.

Junior held his breath. He would have to peek around the corner to see who was up there. But in his heart, he knew who it was.

"I can smell you down there, Junior," Vicky Queen said. "You've got that nice, manly scent that I've always liked."

Her sultry voice somehow managed to frighten and excite him at the same time.

Vicky's bare feet began to tap down the stairs.

"I know you've never been with a woman," she said. "I want to be your first, honey. You've waited so long, been holding out for that special woman. That special woman's me, Junior."

Tears pushed down Junior's cheeks. Sniffling, he flicked on the cigarette lighter again, held it aloft.

Vicky came around the corner, into the light. Her face was both beautiful and terrifying to Junior, both alien and painfully familiar.

"I want to give myself to you, after all these years," she said. "I want you to give yourself to me, too. We'll spend the rest of our lives together. We'll never die. Don't you want that for us, sweetie?"

She stepped closer.

Shaking his head, his face wet with tears, Junior raised the bottle bomb.

Please, Lord, please, Mama, forgive me for doing this.

Rage twisted Vicky's face. "Junior, you put that thing away, you hear me? You put it away right now!"

"I always loved you, Miss Queen," Junior said. "Please forgive me."

He lit the fuse. Vicky screeched. Junior rushed toward her and embraced her. The bomb exploded in a brilliant orb of flames, taking them away together.

Jackson caught Hunter as everyone was rushing out of the station to go to the hospital.

"Hunter, I can't go to the hospital with y'all," he said.

David's eyes were understanding. "It's Jahlil, isn't it?"

"I got to find him." He knotted his hands. "Damn boy, always been so headstrong. I know he thinks he's gonna be out there in the streets hunting these suckers. I can't let him be running around out there alone. I'm the police chief, but I'm a daddy first."

"I understand," David said. "Be careful."

"You do the same. When I find my boy, we're gonna come to support you. That's a promise."

They shook hands. A jarring thought struck Jackson—the idea that he was never going to see David again. Whether it was because David was going to die—or he was going to die—he did not know. He didn't voice his thought, fearful that speaking it would guarantee that it would come true.

David left. Jackson looked around the office. Now, only a single candle glowed, leaving most of the room in shadow, but Jackson had spent so much time there over the years that he didn't need any light at all. This place had become more like his home than his own house. He'd been notified of major events in his life while sitting right over there at his desk. His wife going into labor with their son. Jahlil's first shaky steps. His father's death. His wife contracting cancer . . .

There was a lifetime of memories here, both good and bad.

He blew out the candle. Then he left to find his son.

* * *

Jahlil was not about to go into battle against the bloodsuckers without some kind of bomb. When he and Poke discovered that the gas can in the garage was empty, they returned inside the house and went into the kitchen.

He found plenty of flammable stuff inside the cupboards. While Poke shone the flashlight over him, he filled several beer bottles with the dangerous liquids, packed strips of towels into the bottle necks, as wicks, and secured the fuses with wire trash-bag ties.

Rumbles of thunder clinked the plates in the dish rack. An angry wind swatted the window.

"That storm is kicking ass," Poke said. "Where we going when we leave here?"

"We're gonna cruise around town," Jahlil said. "I know there's gonna be shit popping everywhere. I can feel it. Can't you?"

Poke wiped sweat from his face with his forearm. "Yeah. That's why I'm about to piss on myself. I should've gotten the fuck out of Dodge when I had the chance. Carloads of niggas broke out after that meeting at the church. It was like a caravan going to a big-ass family reunion."

"Cowards," Jahlil said. He packed a towel into the last bottle. "How're you gonna give up your crib and everything you have, just like that? My family's been here forever, man. I ain't giving up my shit without a fight—"

"Hey, you hear that?" Poke whispered.

Jahlil listened. He detected a sound, underneath the groaning thunder. It grew louder with each beat of his heart.

"Music," Jahlil said.

"Not just any music," Poke said. "That's Jacktown. I ain't gotta tell you who's always bumpin' their shit."

No, you sure don't, Jahlil thought. His mouth was dry. He pushed a bottle toward Poke. Poke grasped it as if for dear life.

Jahlil picked up his shotgun off the dinette table.

The music, heavy with bass, made the living room windows pulsate. Car headlights burned on the curtains.

"Follow me," Jahlil said.

He went into the living room, Poke moving close behind him. Their bodies cast huge, jerky shadows on the walls.

At the front door, Jahlil lifted the edge of the drape that covered the small rectangular window.

A blue Oldsmobile Ninety-Eight was parked across the lawn, headlamps angled toward the living room. The car's tinted windows prevented Jahlil from seeing who was inside—as if there were any doubt.

"It's T-Bone's ride," Jahlil said. After T-Bone disappeared the other night, his mother had come by Jahlil's place to pick up the car. Looked like T-Bone had gotten it back.

"Fuck," Poke said softly. "He's coming for us, man. He's coming to make us one of them vampire bastards."

The bass line of T-Bone's favorite Jacktown song, "Foot on Ya Neck," began to boom from the car stereo.

In his mind's eye, Jahlil imagined T-Bone leaning in the driver's seat, a joint dangling from his fang-filled mouth, eyes red and frenzied, nodding his head to the funky rhythm.

Jahlil bit his tongue to hold back an outburst of lunatic laughter.

"What we gonna do, J?" Poke asked.

Jahlil leaned against the wall. Before, he was going to laugh. Now, he felt nauseated.

"We're going to go out there to get him," Jahlil said.

"Fuck that, you crazy nigga—"

"Either we go out there to get him, or he's coming in here to get *us*," Jahlil said. "He'll be expecting us to run and hide. We've gotta make the first move."

"Shit." Poke spat on the floor. Ordinarily, Jahlil would've busted him out for spitting on the carpet, but this was no time for pettiness. "All right, cool. You go first."

"We're going out there together. I'll lead."

"Damn. I'm gonna kick your ass when this is all over. I'm tired of you putting me through all this shit."

"Poke, we get through this, and I'll be glad to let you borrow my cleats so you can kick my ass with them," Jahlil said. "Are you ready? Remember our plan. I'm the shooter, you're the bomber."

"Man, I don't know if I can take out our boy." Poke gripped the beer bottle, but his eyes were wet.

"He's not our boy anymore. He's a monster. He'll rip out our throats if you give him the chance. We have to move on him."

"All right, all right." Poke closed his eyes, as if speaking a quick prayer. Then he nodded. "I'm ready."

Giving pep talks to Poke had the side benefit of quieting Jahlil's own anxiety. If Poke had not been there for him to motivate and direct, he would've had a hell of a time dealing with this stuff. Acting as the brave leader for his boy helped him *feel* kind of fearless.

Although he wasn't completely without fear. Before putting his hand on the doorknob, he murmured a short prayer of his own.

Holding the shotgun in one hand, barrel aimed at the ceiling, he opened the door. He pressed the latch on the screen door.

Cold wind smacked him in the face and snatched open the screen door.

In the car, Jacktown's song played on.

The porch was clear. Jahlil moved across it, stepped down the concrete steps. Poke was close on his heels.

"Let's check out the car," Jahlil said.

"Okay, I'll cover you from back here," Poke said.

Jahlil wanted Poke to stick with him, but it was obvious that just getting Poke to come outside had pushed his friend to the limits of his courage. Jahlil decided to let it ride.

Jahlil crept across the grass, closer to the Oldsmobile.

The music's earthquake-bass pounded in his bones.

Don't vampires have supersensitive ears? Jahlil wondered. *If so, how in the hell can T-Bone stand this music?*

He grasped the handle of the passenger-side door. Pulled.

The door opened with a creak, releasing the mingled odors of marijuana, stale beer, and funk.

The car was empty.

"Is he in there?" Poke said.

Jahlil turned to respond—and that was when he saw the shadowy shape on the roof of the house. The figure crouched, muscles bunched, as though ready to leap.

"Run, Poke!" Jahlil said.

But as the words flew out of his mouth, the creature was already bouncing off the roof, as if catapulted into the air by a trampoline. It swooped to the ground and landed behind Poke, and by the time Poke heard Jahlil's warning and started to dash, the vampire had already twisted its arm around his neck.

Poke let out a strangled scream.

The vampire had used to be T-Bone, but it bore little resemblance to the kid Jahlil remembered. Its braided hair was messy and full of dirt. Dried mud was caked on its face, like war paint. Its eyes were bloodshot. Saliva dribbled from its lips, and glistening snot trailed from its nostrils.

A big, fake platinum cross dangled from the vampire's neck, the same necklace T-Bone wore all the time.

Jahlil's testicles felt as though they'd retracted inside his pelvis.

He had been out of his mind for leaving the police station to hunt these things. This was ten times worse than the vampiric mutts.

"Get it off me, get it off me!" Poke said in a garbled voice.

Jahlil raised the shotgun.

But the vampire and Poke were so close together that he

didn't feel confident about blasting the vamp without hurting Poke.

"Let go of him, T-Bone!" Jahlil warned. "Or I'm going to nail you."

The vampire snorted. It jerked Poke higher in the air, lifting him up by his neck. T-Bone was several inches taller than Poke, and the height advantage allowed him to punish Poke with an excruciating stranglehold.

"Go ahead and shoot, you punk ass nigga," T-Bone said, in a coarse voice that sounded nothing like the kid that Jahlil remembered. "You ain't about shit."

Jahlil's finger tightened on the trigger.

Poke's feet kicked in the air, feebly. He was screaming, but due to the choke hold, it came out as a high-pitched whine. The veins in his neck looked ready to burst.

"Last warning, let him go!" Jahlil said. He steadied his aim on the bloodsucker's head.

I've got to drop him now, he thought. *Pull the trigger, man.*

Glowering at Jahlil defiantly, the vampire opened its mouth. Ropes of saliva coated its fangs, like grotesque taffy.

Shoot him.

Swift as a snake, the vampire buried its teeth into Poke's neck.

Jahlil finally squeezed the trigger, the gun's hard recoil snapping through his arms.

The bullet cleaved across the top of the beast's skull, tearing away a chunk of scalp and hair. The vampire screeched. Its arm loosened from around Poke's throat. Poke slumped to the grass like a bundle of clothes.

But the vampire, though wounded, was not dead. It charged Jahlil, teeth bared, hissing.

Frantic, Jahlil pumped the shotgun for another shot—and it got stuck.

Shit!

He heard his dad's voice in his mind, admonishing him to oil and clean his firearms regularly, to maintain their effectiveness. *Now, son, got to take care of your guns. Take care of your guns, and they'll take care of you.*

The vampire ripped the shotgun out of his hands.

Jahlil spun, and, without thinking, dove into the open passenger side of the Oldsmobile. He slammed the door and mashed down the lock with his fist. Found the automatic lock and hit it, too, engaging the locks on all four doors.

The thunderous music made his teeth rattle.

The bloodsucker hopped onto the hood of the car, the metal creaking under its weight. It planted itself there on its knees, drew back its fist, and punched the windshield.

Jahlil screamed and covered his eyes.

Glass shattered, fragments spraying over his head.

The vampire shoved its long arm through the jagged rupture in the window. It seized the front of Jahlil's shirt.

Jahlil could not help thinking that the monster's dirt-smudged nails looked exactly like T-Bone's after a long day of basketball.

He wrapped his hands around the vampire's wrist, trying to break its grip on him, but it was like trying to loosen a steel vise.

The monster pushed its hand forward and closed its long fingers around Jahlil's throat.

Jahlil gagged. The thing's fingers were so chilly they might have been formed of ice.

I'm dead, this is it. He's gonna yank me out the window and suck me dry.

Like a powerful robotic arm, the vampire began to draw Jahlil forward. His body was too wide to fit through the hole, but he doubted that would stop the creature from forcing him through, scraped and bleeding.

As he was lifted forward, his chest pressed against the

steering wheel, activating the horn. It blared a futile warning to the uncaring night.

Stars swarmed at the edges of Jahlil's vision. He couldn't breathe. He was blacking out . . .

A *whoomp* filled Jahlil's eardrums. Then, a howl of pain. The vampire let go of him.

Jahlil dropped against the seat, dizzy. But he saw the vampire: it was on fire. It snatched its hand out of the window and leapt off the car, screaming, covered in flames.

Jahlil tried to open the door, remembered that it was locked, popped up the lock, and rolled out of the Oldsmobile. Bent over, he sucked in lungfuls of sweet air.

The burning vampire stumbled to the edge of the yard, and collapsed on the ground. The stench of torched flesh poisoned the air.

Jahlil staggered to where Poke sat on the grass, near the porch.

"I got that motherfucker," Poke said. The cigarette lighter lay in his hand. He blinked, sleepily. "You was right, he wasn't nothing like our boy no more. He was a fucking monster, man."

Gently, Jahlil turned Poke's head. A bite wound burned bright red on Poke's neck, like marks seared with a branding iron.

Soon, Poke would be one of them.

Across the yard, the vampire lay still, gray-black smoke twisting from its corpse and rising into the stormy night sky.

Taking in the loss of both his lifelong friends, Jahlil could do only one thing.

He lowered his head, and cried.

Although his fellow patients were in a haste to leave the premises, Franklin had the presence of mind to understand that he did not want to venture outdoors in this ridiculous gown. He opened the closet and found his regular clothes. He was grateful to find his favorite pair of khakis, and a shirt.

He closed the door, shutting out the commotion in the hallway. His female roommate had departed with the rest of the mob.

As he dressed, he admired the still, peaceful body of his wife. He had placed her on the bed after he had satiated himself on her blood.

Yes, *blood*. Finally, he could admit the object of his hunger. He felt no shame about his craving, not anymore. The pleasure that blood provided was too sweet, too nourishing, too fulfilling, to ever engender unwelcome feelings. Easier to despise a thirst for water.

He was aware of what he had become. He had metamorphosed into the blood-crazed monster that David (and himself, in his prior life) feared and conspired to destroy. The vampire!

How easy it was to hate that which one did not understand. Such behavior was typical of the ignorant and those who allowed unfounded fear to dictate their lives.

Now, he knew better.

Comfortably attired in his clothes, he approached the bed.

Ruby, as lovely as ever, floated on the tranquil waves of a perfect sleep. Bite marks blemished her neck. He had taken much of her blood, but had intuitively sensed when to cease drinking, to prevent ending her life. It was his earnest wish that she would join him in this wondrous new existence. Without her, immortality would lack meaning and purpose.

He lifted her warm hand to his lips, kissed her fingers.

He did not know how long it would take for her transformation to complete. Perhaps a day, perhaps sooner. She was safe, here. The master would not allow harm to come to those that obeyed him. And to disobey was as unthinkable as refusing to breathe.

He carefully tucked the bedsheet under his wife's chin. He kissed her cheek.

"Sleep well, my dear. I'll return for you soon."

He left the room, fastening the door behind him.

The dark corridor buzzed with activity. The valduwe (the unfamiliar but somehow fitting name came to his mind, like a memory of a dream) raced around in a frenzy, seeking to feed on any human in the vicinity.

Undisturbed, he proceeded down the hall, to the exit.

Upon pushing through the glass doors, two unexpected surprises greeted him. Number one: a street bicycle in good condition stood in the metal bike stall, unlocked. Number two: his old dog, Malcolm, was among a pack of hounds that had brought down a number of hapless humans.

"Malcolm!" Franklin said. He whistled.

Tail wagging, the dog trotted to him. Franklin scratched behind the canine's ears, something he used to do all the time in his prior life, much to Malcolm's pleasure.

But Malcolm did not allow himself to be stroked for long. He whined, licked Franklin's fingers, then dashed off to re-join his pack.

Franklin rolled the bicycle out of the stall. He mounted the saddle.

He pedaled across the sidewalk that led to the parking lot. He passed Kyle, the master's son. Kyle stood at the end of the path, hands clenched behind his back, viewing the action.

Kyle did not look at him—Franklin understood that Kyle did not need to see him in order to sense he was near—but Franklin gave him a wide berth. Instinct warned him to keep his distance from vampires like Kyle. It was a bit like a child exercising caution in the company of a stern adult.

However, he would obey any commands Kyle issued. The master had granted his son authority over them.

But for the time, the valduwe were allowed to roam.

Franklin pedaled across the parking lot and onto the road

that fronted the medical center. His leg muscles were strong—stronger than they had ever been in his prior life, even in his youth. He felt as though he soared on the wings of the gusting wind.

And oh, the night! Night had never been so beautiful, so deep, so *liberating*.

He did not have a destination in mind, but something would suggest itself, soon. He was growing hungry again.

David, Nia, and King were the only ones in his Pathfinder. The rest of the team members had piled into other vehicles to make the five-minute drive to the hospital, where they hoped to stop the vampires' advance.

David clenched the steering wheel. "I know I'm being overly optimistic, but I'm hoping that Franklin is still asleep there. I don't want to have to do this to him."

Although David did not say what "do this to him" meant, Nia did not ask for an interpretation. Both of them had been present at Jubilee when the team had destroyed the vampiric deputy in the cellar.

"Everything's going to be okay, David," Nia said. In spite of her reassurance, her own voice wavered. David noted that her fingernails, which had been painted and manicured when he had first met her, were bitten down to nubs, the nail polish chipped away.

Even King displayed signs of stress. The dog did not move around the backseat looking out windows as he normally did when riding. He sat ramrod-straight, brown eyes watchful, ears raised.

Wind blasted across the town, pummeling the trees and tossing debris through the air. Several trees, snapped in half like matchsticks, obstructed the roads. The street lamps were dead, and the homes they passed were dark and abandoned-looking.

Thunder clapped. Jagged blades of lightning split the purple-black sky.

Rain had not fallen yet, but when it did, David was certain that it would come in a torrent.

At the next intersection, he turned right, onto Coldwater Lane. The hospital was less than a mile away.

I'm stalling, he realized. *I'm putting along at twenty miles an hour. I never drive this slowly.*

But God, I don't want to see Franklin.

Nevertheless, he had a duty to his team. Poke behind too long and they would have to fight without him. He was supposed to be the leader.

He pressed the gas pedal more firmly.

Ahead, on the left side of the road, a green Taurus was parked in a driveway. David would not have paid it any attention, but the interior light was on, as though a door was open, and no one was visible inside the vehicle.

He slowed to take a closer look.

A low growl rumbled from King.

"What's the matter, boy?" Nia said to the dog, but her attention was riveted on the car.

Feeling as though he had been cast into a slow-motion sequence in a film, David inched past the Ford, and even as he saw the spectacle on the other side of the car he had known that this was what he would discover. A young woman in a blue dress lay on the ground beside the open passenger door, bags of spilled groceries surrounding her body. Franklin Bennett, his balding head gleaming in the light, knelt over the woman, as though giving her mouth-to-mouth resuscitation—except his mouth was attached to her neck. A blue bicycle lay on the front lawn, rear wheel jutting in the air.

David's jaws locked, his teeth grinding together. He had pressed the brake to the floor.

Beside him, Nia had stuffed her hand in her mouth, as if holding back a scream.

Keep on driving, a soft voice whispered in his head. *Pretend you didn't see this. This man is your friend, your elder. You can't hurt him, and you know it. Go on, keep driving. Nia won't mind, either.*

He well might have given in to the temptation to drive away, but King began to bark.

Grasping the woman protectively in his arms, Franklin turned and saw them.

Chapter 20

Jackson had prayed, more passionately than he had ever prayed for anything, that he would find his son alive. His prayer was, thankfully, answered. When he swerved in front of his house at a reckless speed in the patrol car, Jahlil sat on the porch. His shotgun, which Jackson had given to him last Christmas, lay across his lap.

A blue Oldsmobile Ninety-Eight was on the lawn. Jackson recalled that the car belonged to Jahlil's buddy, the kid named T-Bone. The boy who had been attacked by monster mutts last night.

Christ.

Jackson parked in the driveway, jumped out of the car, and ran to his son.

"Are you okay, Jahlil? Where the hell you been? Why'd you leave the station after I told you—"

Jahlil raised his hand with the weariness of an old man and waved it feebly, and that motion alone shut up Jackson. Something had happened, and it wasn't good.

"Hey, Dad," Jahlil said. His voice was hoarse. His eyes

were puffy, too. "I'm all right. Haven't been anywhere, just here at the house."

Jackson caught a whiff of a vile smell. It was the same stench that had steamed from the burned creature that had used to be the deputy.

In the corner of the yard, a large shape lay on the ground. The stink came from over there.

"What happened here?" Jackson said.

Jahlil braced his hands behind his neck. "Poke and I came here to get some weapons before we went out to hunt those bloodsuckers. But the thing that used to be T-Bone drove up here to meet us. We had a fight. T-Bone bit Poke, I shot T-Bone, T-Bone almost got me, then Poke set him on fire."

Shock blew the air out of Jackson's lungs. Weak-kneed, he plopped on the steps next to Jahlil.

He had planned to give his kid a no-holds-barred tongue lashing when he found him; between praying for his boy's safety, he'd rehearsed the mad words in his head as he drove to the house. Now, he couldn't remember what he was going to say, and he didn't give a damn. Cussing out the boy would be a fool's move. His son had lost his two best friends, and it didn't matter that Jackson had long believed that the boys were a bad influence on Jahlil. None of that crap mattered anymore. Not in this terrifying new world they had been thrust into.

"I'm sorry, Jahlil," Jackson said. Awkwardly, he put his arm around the boy's shoulders. He was surprised when Jahlil didn't bristle. Jahlil leaned against him, head lowered, and trembled as he gave in to silent weeping.

Jackson remembered the last time he'd put his arm around his son. It was the night that Paulette passed. He had not touched Jahlil since then, not with an embrace or even a handshake. Something seemed very wrong about that. He liked to blame their communication gap on Jahlil being rebellious and resentful of his authority, but maybe he had not been holding down his duty as a father, either.

Well, I'm from a different generation of men, Jackson told himself. His own father had never hugged him, after Jackson grew past the age of seven. Hell, his daddy hadn't liked to talk that much, either. The things Jackson learned from his dad, he learned mostly from watching him. His father was the epitome of the strong, silent type, like a lot of older men Jackson knew.

Ain't no wonder that I'm just like him, then, Jackson thought. *But my boy needs something more than that.*

Jahlil sniffled, and straightened. "Okay, Dad. I'm fine now. I'm not gonna get all soft on you."

"There's nothing wrong with crying, son. Better to let it out than to keep it bottled up, driving you out your mind."

"Yeah, sure. Just like you cried when Mom died, huh?"

The comment hit Jackson like a blow below the belt. He fumbled for words.

"Son . . . ah . . . I cried over your mama. I did. But not in front of you."

"Why?" Jahlil wiped his nose. "Because real men don't cry in front of people, right? Guess I just proved I'm not a man yet."

"I wanted to stay strong for you. When your mama passed, I knew I was all you had left. Couldn't afford to let you see me weak. So I had my tears in private."

"Maybe you didn't hide the tears for me, Dad. Maybe you hid them for you, 'cause you can't handle anyone thinking you're weak."

Jackson pressed his lips together. "Hmm. Might have a point there. Maybe I did it for me. But that's how I am, son. Doesn't mean I loved your mama any less, and it doesn't mean I love you any less, either."

Slowly, Jahlil nodded. Jackson could hardly read his boy's mind—though he wished sometimes he could—but he believed that he had answered a question that had troubled Jahlil for a long time.

"Well, Dad, that's cool," Jahlil said. "I mean, you're a grown man, almost fifty, right? It would be kinda stupid for me to expect you to change your ways."

"Hey, I'm almost fifty, but I ain't hardly dead," Jackson said. He laughed. Jahlil laughed, too, and for a moment, the vibe was right between them: easygoing and good, the way it had used to be before Paulette had died.

Then the wind blew, pushing the stench of death in their faces, and their laughter dropped off. The gravity of their circumstances pressed on Jackson like a lead weight. It was time to get back into gear.

"Where's your buddy, Poke?" Jackson said.

"I took him inside. He's in the guest room, asleep. We need to take him to the hospital, Dad."

Jackson grunted. "Can't take him there. Those vampires are overrunning the place. We sent the backup team there to help."

Jahlil's eyes grew as large as dinner plates. "How many of them?"

"Well, there were close to twenty folks in quarantine. Sounded like all of them have changed into those monsters."

"That's messed up," Jahlil said. "We've gotta go there to help. We can leave Poke here, he'll be fine."

"Till he changes," Jackson said softly. "Wouldn't be no sense in dropping him off with his family; we'd only be putting them in jeopardy." He sighed. "All right, let him stay here. By morning we should have some idea of what to do."

"What about T-Bone's . . . body?" Jahlil's attention flicked to the edge of the yard, and he quickly looked away. "I can't deal with that right now, Dad. Sorry."

"Come morning, we'll have a plan in place. I think we're gonna have a number of cases like this on our hands, though I hate to consider it. Terrible shame."

"Okay." Jahlil stood, swung his shotgun over his shoulder. His face had hardened with determination.

Intense pride swept through Jackson. His son was a fighter, for God's sake. Suddenly motivated, Jackson rose, too.

But the memory of Paulette's deathbed words came to Jackson: *Take care of our baby, Van. You're all he has left in the world. Raise him to be a good, strong man.*

Briefly, Jackson considered making Jahlil stay home, away from the danger. But he rejected the idea. What could he do, lock the boy in his room? Then what if something happened and his son was attacked again? Nowhere in the town was safe tonight. The safest place for Jahlil was right by his side. He would lay down his life to keep his boy alive.

"All right," Jackson said. "Let's go to the hospital."

Cradling the woman in his arms, Franklin Bennett showed his teeth like an enraged animal.

Although David sat in the idling truck, perhaps twenty feet away, he swore that he could see the needle-sharp points of Franklin's fangs.

In the backseat, King barked, spittle flying from his mouth and spattering the windows.

"I can't do it," David said, still clutching the steering wheel. He was dizzy, as though he had been spinning on a carousel for the past five minutes. "I'm not ready for this. I can't do it."

Calmly, Nia pried his hands off the steering wheel. She placed a Molotov cocktail, fashioned from a beer bottle, into his sweaty palm, and pressed his fingers around the neck.

"You can," she said. She took her gun out of her purse. "You have a cigarette lighter. Get it, and let's go. I'll back you up."

Feeling as though his limbs were attached to invisible

strings manipulated by unseen hands, David got out of the SUV. Inside, King growled and clawed at the windows. Nia came around the front of the truck, gun pointed toward the ground.

"Stay away from me, David," Franklin said. He was not wearing his glasses anymore. He let the woman's body fall to the ground.

Hearing Franklin's voice, which sounded the same as ever, wrenched David's gut. Surely, Franklin was only ill. He could not be a vampire. Vampires didn't exist!

But you saw his fangs, didn't you, David? Look at the blood on his chin!

The bottle in David's hand might as well have been a hundred-pound brick. Lighting the fuse and hurling the homemade bomb at Franklin seemed like an impossible undertaking.

"Please, don't make this any harder than it has to be," David said. "I don't want to do this to you. But I have to."

"You don't understand," Franklin said. "I *want* this new life. I am healthier than I have ever been, full of a vigor that I never experienced as an ordinary man. You have no right to take this away from me. You have no right!"

Cheetah-swift, Franklin broke into a run.

Indecision froze David. But not Nia. She fired a shot as Franklin fled across the yard and leapt over a line of bushes with the speed and agility of a track-and-field athlete.

The bullet knocked the vampire off balance. He fell to the ground, moaning. But he started to rise.

Nia rushed forward. She fired again, plowing a shot into the creature's spine. Wailing, it dropped against the earth . . . but crawled forward, resolute.

Nia prepared to loose another shot.

"Stop it!" David yelled at her. "That's enough!"

She turned on him. She was crying, but her eyes blazed with resolve. "Then you finish him, dammit!"

David was both grateful at Nia for preventing the vampire's escape, and furious at her for forcing his hand. But she was right. It was his responsibility to deal with Franklin. That was how Franklin had wanted it.

His legs feeling as if they might give way underneath him, David ran closer to the vampire.

Franklin *(no, don't call him that, it isn't Franklin anymore)* was on all fours. Blood soaked the back of his shirt. He groaned.

David's fingers dug into his pocket, closed around the plastic lighter.

Sensing David's approach, the vampire looked over his shoulder.

"You need not harm me, David," the vampire said. "Go away, leave me in peace. I am not a man anymore, but I have not forgotten the friendship that we shared. I give you my promise that I will never hurt you or Nia."

David slowly shook his head. "No. When you were a man, you made me promise that I would take your life if you ever became . . . something like this. Remember?"

Franklin's mouth opened, a soft gasp escaping him.

"I remember. I charged you with that responsibility . . . and sealed it with your promise. I remember." He sighed deeply.

For a heartbreaking minute, his were not the eyes of a vampire. They were the eyes of Franklin Bennett again, the kind, intelligent man who had sacrificed his life to help David.

A wave of tears threatened to overcome David, and he blinked them away, savagely.

Franklin lay on the grass and rolled onto his back.

"Hand me the explosive," Franklin said. "Once you've done that, ignite the fuse. Move with haste."

"But—"

"Do it. Please. Before I change my mind."

David offered the bottle to him. Franklin plucked it

out of his grasp and pressed it over his abdomen. The dry rag, hanging from the lip of the bottle, fluttered in the wind.

"The fuse," Franklin said.

It took three attempts for David to produce a flame with the cigarette lighter. The fire tasted the rag, and began to consume it hungrily.

"Now run away from here, son."

David ran.

Seconds later, the explosion came. The blast punched a hole in David's soul. He dropped to his knees. He buckled over and vomited, crap pumping out of him, leaving his throat raw, hot tears dripping from his face and plopping into the vomit he had expelled on the pavement.

Then, a comforting hand rested on his shoulder: Nia. As always, Nia.

Their army had arisen.

Standing at the end of the walkway that led to the hospital entrance, Kyle watched their soldiers, the valduwe, pour out of the building.

They were an odd-looking group: men and women of myriad ages and ethnicities (though most of them were black), some of them clad in blue hospital garments, others wearing street clothing, some of them physically fit, others obese, some of them attractive, some of them ugly. But they had two traits in common: their insatiable hunger for blood, and their obedience to the will of his father.

Upon awakening the army, Diallo had telepathically commanded the valduwe to obey Kyle's orders. Kyle had not yet exercised his authority. He enjoyed watching these low-level vampires—these mongrels of their species—attack and feed on every human in the vicinity. They had no finesse, no finely honed hunting skills, only graceless, savage strength. The humans did not stand a chance against them.

By dawn, we will command hundreds of valduwe, his father had promised. *We will suck this town dry of life, and then we will move onward to the next.*

Diallo had ventured elsewhere in the town, alone, to recruit new soldiers. He had instructed Kyle to take these mutants and use them to subdue the city and multiply their numbers. Before sunrise, he and his father would reconvene in their sanctuary.

Kyle had waited a lifetime for a mission such as this. His father had instilled his life with purpose. What purpose was there in living in isolated luxury, avoiding humans as though they were something to fear? It perplexed him how Mother could tolerate her dismal existence.

But he would not waste time worrying about Mother anymore.

Several vehicles veered into the parking lot. Humans. Armed with weaponry. Members of the civil defense team. Fools.

A casual glance confirmed that David Hunter was not among them. Neither were Nia James or Chief Jackson.

Nevertheless, Kyle summoned his army. The time for battle was near.

Jackson and Jahlil roared across town, siren wailing.

A crackling voice on the walkie-talkie—it sounded like Mac—shouted that something like twenty vampires roamed outside the hospital. "One of the head honchos is with them, too," Mac said. "Tall, dark-skinned fella, wearing black, looks young. You gotta hurry up and get here, Chief." Mac's voice quavered. He sounded truly scared.

"Is Hunter there?" Jackson asked.

"We lost him on the way over," Mac said. "Think he stopped for something."

"Shit," Jackson said. He hoped that David was okay. The last thing they needed was to lose Hunter. "We'll be there in a few, Mac. Hold it down."

"Yes, sir." The radio sputtered into silence.

"I'm kinda scared, Dad," Jahlil said. Holding his shotgun on his lap, he stroked the barrel as if for reassurance. "What if . . . what if we can't win?"

Jackson glanced at his son. He understood the true fear that weighed on Jahlil's mind. But Jahlil was afraid to say it.

What if you die, Dad? was the fear that Jackson realized tormented his son.

"Anything like that happens, you call Hunter," Jackson said. "He'll know what to do."

"But I hardly know that guy, Dad. I mean, he seems cool, but . . ."

"You can trust him. He's a good man. I talked to him earlier about backup plans, guess you'd call them."

"Oh." Jahlil wiped a bead of sweat from his forehead. He laughed, but it was a nervous sound. "Forget this, man, I'm gonna start thinking positive. Didn't you used to always say, 'If you can believe it, you can achieve it'?"

"That was me."

"I'm gonna take your advice. This one time." Jahlil chuckled again, and this time, Jackson laughed, too.

Nothing, Jackson thought, *is as important as keeping up hope.* Hope was like food, nourishing you, making it possible to endure what seemed unbearable. A man without any hope was practically dead inside.

But sometimes, hope didn't save the day. Jackson didn't have the heart to tell his son that he had believed, and hoped, that his wife would conquer her cancer. Didn't want to crush his boy's optimism. Just as it was important to nurture hope on your own, so was it important to allow someone to hold tight to his own hope, even when his efforts might be in vain.

The hospital would be around the next corner.

David slumped against a tree, recovering from the incident with Franklin, while inside the Pathfinder, King bustled around impatiently.

He and Nia had taken the young woman upon whom Franklin had preyed inside her house, and laid her body across the living-room sofa. She remained unconscious as they moved her, purple-red puncture wounds glowing on her neck. Undoubtedly, she was already mutating into a vampire.

The thought sickened and angered David. How many other people in town had been bitten and were quietly undergoing the same terrible transformation? They didn't have much time before they lost everyone to Diallo and his bloodthirsty minions.

"We've got to go," he said. His watch read half-past ten. "We've got to help the team at the hospital."

"I hate to bring this up, but what should we do about Franklin's body?" Nia asked. "Should we come back later?"

"Yeah." He refused to look around and see Franklin's corpse. "We'll take care of it later."

As they shuffled back to the SUV, King flew into a frenzy, barking and pawing the windows.

What's gotten into him? David thought. King had freaked out before they'd discovered Franklin feeding on the woman, too. Did the dog have a keen nose for evil?

David looked around. He didn't see anything out of the ordinary.

King stood in the space between the front seats, growling. David locked gazes with the canine, and it struck him, suddenly, what King was going to attempt. He had lived with the dog long enough to be able to predict its actions.

Nia opened the passenger door.

"Don't let him get out!" David said.

King bolted through the doorway in a gray-black streak, knocking Nia aside as he ran.

"King, get back here!" David scrambled after the dog. "Stop!"

The dog did not heed his call. King galloped across a yard and disappeared in the murky shadows behind the house.

"Come back, King!" David chased him.

But King was not in the backyard. A dark alley ran behind the property, and David went to the edge and looked both ways. He did not see any sign of King. The dog could've run anywhere.

It was a dangerous night for men and dogs alike. David's worst fear was that King would be attacked by one of those hellhounds and become a member of Diallo's murderous hordes.

Nia ran up beside David. "Where is he?"

"The hell if I know." If David's hair were longer, he would've grabbed it in his fists and pulled it out in tufts. "He's never run off like this. I don't know what's the matter with him."

"I'm so sorry, David. I shouldn't have let him get out."

"It's not your fault. I should've left King at home in the first place. Damn." He marched to the truck and got the dog leash.

"I know we're supposed to be helping at the hospital, but I can't leave my dog out there," he said. "No telling what could happen to him."

"I'll go look for him," Nia said. "I've lost one dog today, and I'm not losing another one if I can help it. Give me the leash."

"Are you nuts? I'm not letting you walk around alone out here."

"I'll have my piece with me." She patted the holstered gun on her hip. "You can cruise around the block looking for King, and I'll look for him on foot. It makes more sense, David. I can run faster than you. Former track athlete, remember?"

"You're right, but I have a bad feeling about this." He pressed the leash into her palm. "Okay, whether we find King or not, we meet back here in fifteen minutes."

"We'll find him, I promise," she said. "See you in fifteen."

David watched her leave.

She can protect herself, he reminded himself. *Hell, she can handle a gun better than I can, knows how to fight, and runs like a gazelle. She'll be fine.*

But why did he have such an awful feeling of dread?

When Jackson neared the hospital, his first thought was that a mob had crowded in front of the building. But this mob was mostly dressed in dirty patient gowns.

They were the vampires.

Feral-looking dogs, at least a dozen of them, joined their two-legged counterparts.

The bloodsuckers gathered around the striking, unmistakeable figure of Kyle. Clad in black, he might have been an ancient god who had emerged from a chasm in the earth and brought along his evil servants.

I reached inside your puny brain before and shaped it as a sculptor manipulates clay.

As Jackson remembered how this fiend had screwed up his mind, a spider of anxiety skittered down his back.

A couple hundred yards away, at the edge of the parking lot, the citizen defense teams had used their cars to form a barricade. Five vehicles—a Dodge Ram pickup, a Ford

Explorer, a Chevy, a Honda, and a Mustang—were arranged bumper-to-bumper, serving as a makeshift wall.

"This is crazy," Jahlil mumbled.

Jackson parked the patrol car at the end of the line of vehicles.

"Move fast," he said to Jahlil. Jackson grabbed his shotgun, and Jahlil clutched his, too. "Stay behind the line."

Hurriedly, they got out.

About fifteen people huddled behind the bunker. Every one of them had a firearm, and Molotov cocktails were lined up on the pavement.

The team members were visibly relieved when they saw Jackson. Mac approached him, the flamethrower strapped to his back.

"Sure glad you got here safe, Chief," Mac said. "Those dirtbags haven't moved on us yet. They've been hanging back, like they're waiting on something."

"So what're we waiting for?" Jackson said. "Last thing we wanna do is let them make the first move and put our backs against the wall. We've gotta take the initiative, Mac."

Jahlil grabbed his arm. "They're coming, Dad."

I ain't surprised, Jackson thought. *I'd bet dollars to doughnuts that Kyle was waiting on me to get here.*

The vampires shambled across the parking lot, moving in loose formation, like a demonic army. Kyle marched behind his soldiers.

"What do we do, Chief?" Mac asked in a shaky voice.

Jackson quickly summed up the situation and made a decision.

"This is what we're gonna do," Jackson said. "Mac, you and I are gonna climb on the flatbed of your truck. If you don't mind, my son's gonna drive. We're gonna circle around this parking lot, real fast, and pick off those suckers. I'll hit 'em with my shotgun, and Mac'll blast 'em with some fire."

Mac nodded. Jahlil looked scared, but determined to do the job.

Jackson said, "The rest of y'all, stay behind the lines and use your guns and the bottle bombs to knock 'em down. Keep 'em back! Mac and I will do our best to squash the suckers, but we can't fight 'em alone. Everyone ready?"

"Ready, Chief," the group murmured, in anxious voices. They didn't sound half as gung-ho as he'd hoped. They sounded as if they were on the verge of getting the hell out of there.

He couldn't blame them. This was probably a suicide mission. But he had to do it. It was his duty, and forsaking duty was unthinkable.

"Let's go, Dad!" Jahlil said. "They're getting closer!"

The vampire army was halfway across the parking lot.

Mac's pickup was parked at the front of the wall of cars. Mac and Jackson hopped onto the flatbed, and Jahlil scrambled behind the wheel. The truck started with a throaty roar.

"Go, boy!" Jackson yelled, and thumped the roof of the pickup.

Jahlil poured on the gas. The Dodge peeled out across the pavement. They began to roll toward the vampires.

Jackson positioned himself on the side of the truck, near the front, and Mac took the rear on the same side, so they could work in tandem.

"This beats the hell out of 'Nam," Mac said. Gripping the flamethrower, he shook his head. "Christ, I thought nothing could be worse than that."

"I hear ya, Mac." Jackson held his Remington shotgun tight. His heart throbbed painfully.

Thunder rumbled across the night, sounding like mountains colliding somewhere on the horizon. Cords of lightning punished the swollen sky.

As they came up on the monsters, a clarity of vision overtook Jackson. He sank into what he liked to call the "zone of the hunter," a state in which his eyesight was hawk-sharp, his muscles were pumped and loose, and his concentration was unbreakable.

He raised the shotgun.

"Ready when you are, Mac."

"Let's do it, Chief."

Jahlil, handling the Dodge with expert skill, drove directly toward the vampires, as if he were going to steamroll over them. The creatures shrieked, and scattered like rodents. Jahlil smoothly curved to the edge of the pack.

Jackson took aim at one of the suckers—someone he knew, God help him, when the vampire had been a man—and plugged the beast in the head. The creature flopped to the ground.

Mac hit the fallen vampire with a jet of fire, and the monster went up in flames like a bundle of dry sticks.

"Yeah!" Jahlil honked the horn.

Jackson didn't have any desire to celebrate. He was sickened by this terrible work they had to do. This was police duty, at its worst.

After tonight, he might hang up his badge, forever.

The vampires howled, enraged. They chased after the truck.

Jahlil veered around the lot, keeping a good lead on them. Then they made another pass at the horde.

Jackson lowered into a crouch. He squeezed off two shots: one struck a vampire in the back, the second hit another vampire in the chest. Both of the vamps crumpled. Mac torched them the instant they fell.

"We're kicking their asses!" Jahlil shouted.

The vampires seemed to comprehend that attacking the truck was foolhardy. All of them, including the vampiric mutts, made a beeline for the line of cars at the corner of the parking lot, where the team members huddled.

All of them except Kyle. The guy had disappeared.

Where was he? Had he abandoned his group to make them fend on their own?

"Head for the team!" Mac ordered Jahlil. "We've got to back them up!"

"Wait, son!" Jackson said. "Where's Kyle?"

Jahlil slowed the truck, looking around frantically.

"Kyle?" Mac frowned. "You're right, he's gone. Dammit."

"No, not gone, my friends," a familiar voice said behind them.

Jackson turned.

Kyle stood on top of the pickup's roof.

Jackson shouted, backing up so fast he almost fell out of the truck. He fired the shotgun.

And missed. Kyle moved like lightning. He bounced off the roof and onto the flatbed.

He was too close for Mac to spit fire at him with the flamethrower, without all of them being incinerated. Mac drew his machete out of the sheath on his belt. He swiped at the vampire.

And he missed, too. The vampire sidestepped the blade's arc—then snatched the knife out of Mac's grasp with obscene ease.

Jackson's finger sweated on the shotgun's trigger, but Mac and the vampire were so close he feared he would plug Mac by mistake.

As it turned out, it wouldn't have mattered. Kyle sliced the machete across Mac's neck, and the man fell, blood spouting from the gaping wound.

Jackson's knees weakened.

God in heaven, is this what it's come down to?

Kyle advanced on Jackson. Delight shone in his alien eyes.

Before Jackson could pull the trigger, an invisible force ripped the shotgun out of his hands. The gun spun like a baton across the parking lot.

Jackson went for all he had left, the .357 Magnum.

Then, the unseen power took that away from him, too.

"Nothing left, Chief," Kyle whispered. He raised the machete. The blade glinted.

If this is how I have to go, then so be it. God knows I did my best, and that was all I could do.

In his peripheral vision, he spotted Jahlil. The boy had gotten out of the truck, with his own shotgun, and trained the weapon on the vampire's back.

Maybe there was still hope. Maybe . . .

His son fired a second after Kyle plunged the blade into his chest.

Chapter 21

Andre was at The Spot, drinking. He'd been there since the bar had opened late that afternoon, and he would probably stay until the joint closed sometime in the wee hours of the morning. Didn't have any reason to go home. Yesterday, his woman had taken the kids and split for her mama's crib in Memphis, leaving behind a letter. "I'm tired of your broke ass," her note said. "I'm already taking care of two kids, and I'm not taking care of no grown man. Call me when you're ready to get your shit together!"

Sitting on a patched-up bar stool, Andre hunched over his can of Coors. His girl was crazy as hell. But he wasn't worried about it too much. She'd left him at least three times in the past two years, and she always came back. It seemed to happen every six months or so, and she'd stay away for a couple of weeks. Once he figured out that she was just showing out, like a baby throwing a tantrum, he'd begun to look forward to her going away on her little trips to Mama's. It was like a vacation for him. He didn't have to hear her nagging him about getting a job. He could live in his house and have some peace, sleep all day, do whatever the hell he wanted. He loved his woman, but she could be a pain in the ass.

Tonight, The Spot was full of brothers like him, guys who needed a break from the women in their lives. Some of them shot pool. Others played darts. The rest of the customers were sipping drinks, talking, and nodding their heads to the old-school music bumping from the boom box. Every man in there was a regular. There wasn't an unfamiliar face—or a woman—in the joint.

In spite of the regulars in the house doing their usual stuff, things were different at the bar. The thunderstorm had knocked out the electrical power, so the place was illuminated by candles and kerosene lamps, and the TV, jukebox, and arcade games sat unused, like old furniture. It was Labor Day, and The Spot had never been open on a holiday. And if you looked closely, you'd notice a bulge underneath almost every man's shirt, the telltale shape of a gun.

Tension simmered in the smoky air, too. Today, The Spot wasn't a normal hangout. It was like an army barracks in the midst of a war, and none of the old rules mattered.

Motherfucking vampires, Andre thought. That was what people were saying. Vampires. Of all the things in the world, their town had been invaded by monsters out of a horror movie.

He wouldn't have believed it if he had not been there at the cave with Junior. Ever since that night, he found it easy to believe in all kinds of things that he would've laughed about before. He still had not told anyone what he had seen, and he sure as hell wasn't going to open his mouth now. They might blame him for stirring up the shit in the first place. He was going to sit there on his stool, put away brews, and mind his business.

He didn't have a gun, either. He wasn't going to try to be a hero, or plan to battle a vampire—none of that shit. The only thing he really wanted to do was leave town, but some fellas had said the roads were blocked off with heaps of split trees.

Besides, he didn't have anywhere to go, anyway. He sure as hell wasn't going to stay with his woman and her mama in Memphis. Dracula himself would have been no match for his woman's mama.

The CD player on the boom box started to skip on an Earth, Wind and Fire classic, "Fantasy." Booker T, a guy Andre had known for years, rapped the top of the stereo, shook it hard, and finally the song resumed.

Booker T plopped onto the stool beside Andre.

"Don't be tearing up my goddamn property, Booker T," Mr. Clyde, the owner and bartender, said. He was a stout, thick-armed man with salt-and-pepper hair, and had reputedly served time in the state pen for killing a man, twenty-some years ago. "You wanna shake up a boom box, buy one your goddamn self."

"My apologies, Mr. Clyde," Booker T said. "Can you please give me a cola, sir? With a lemon wedge, of course."

Mr. Clyde mumbled. He slid a can of Coke, and a lemon wedge, in front of Booker T.

Booker T's apologetic tone didn't surprise Andre. Mr. Clyde didn't take any shit in his joint. Andre had seen the old guy throw out many a nigga.

Booker T sipped his drink. He was a short, scrawny guy who wore wire-rim glasses, a white dress shirt, and suspenders. A pocket notebook bulged in his breast pocket. People said he was a lunatic genius, one of those cats who was so smart he couldn't lead a regular life. Andre usually saw the guy walking the streets at all times of the day, muttering to himself and staring at things like trees and rocks and birds for hours, and scribbling endlessly in his tiny notebook. A regular at The Spot, Booker T always played darts and drank cola with a lemon wedge floating inside.

"What do you think of what's going down here, Andre?" Booker T said. "Do you believe the story about vampires?"

Andre shrugged. "All I know is, once the sun goes down, I keep my black ass indoors."

"Then you believe it."

"It don't matter whether I believe it or not. Folk's been disappearing, mad dogs been biting niggas. That's all I need to hear to keep my ass inside till it blows over."

Booker T reached into the bowl of peanuts, popped a couple of nuts into his mouth. "Andre, this is a conspiracy engineered by the government. They're testing a virus on us, a biological weapon. Mason's Corner is the testing ground for a new strain of supervirus."

"You read that in a book somewhere?" Andre said.

Booker T guffawed as if Andre had asked the dumbest question in the world.

"No, I did not reach this conclusion by reading a book. Don't you understand that book publishing in this country is manipulated by the government? I reached this conclusion through my field research." He tapped the notebook in his shirt pocket, and smiled smugly.

Andre wanted to wipe that self-satisfied smile off Booker T's face by telling him what had happened at the cave, but he kept his mouth shut. Let the crazy nigga believe whatever he wanted.

"It ain't no goddamn government conspiracy," Mr. Clyde said. He rested his meaty, tattooed forearms on the counter. "You need to take your goddamn nose out of that notebook, Booker T. This is some supernatural shit happening here. Goddamn demons, man. Only God can save us. You can't do no research on *that*."

Booker T shook his head sadly. "As usual, when under duress, our people turn to the comforting bosom of primitive superstition and childish wish fulfillment."

"Watch your goddamn mouth, boy," Mr. Clyde said. "You won't be spittin out them big words when you're picking up your teeth off the goddamn floor."

Andre laughed. "Better watch it, Booker T."

Booker T waved his hand as if it didn't matter. "Please, indulge my curiosity, Mr. Clyde. If vampires are overrunning our town, how did it begin? Did they fall out of the sky?"

"There's one of them master vampires out there somewhere," Mr. Clyde said. He looked at the windows, which were veiled against the night. Anxiety glimmered in his eyes. "Just like in the movies, an old goddamn vampire's come to town and started shit."

Booker T rolled his eyes, but Andre was quiet.

Mr. Clyde's probably more right than he thinks, Andre thought. He remembered the mysterious man in black he'd seen at the cave, who could move faster than Andre could blink. He shivered.

Quickly, he grabbed his beer and chugged the rest of it.

As Andre was about to ask for another brew, the front door banged open, bringing the howl of the cold wind, a rustling wave of dead leaves, and the biggest man he had ever seen in his life.

The man was at least seven feet tall, with a powerful build, like a giant football linebacker. He wore a black shirt that seemed barely able to contain his wide shoulders, black jeans, and gleaming black boots. His skin was a deep cocoa-brown, his head was bald, and his eyes were utterly black, like pits leading straight to hell.

Silence clutched the room in a vise grip. Every man in the joint froze, mouths agape.

Andre held his breath.

The man's gaze swept throughout the bar, and Andre had the feeling that, in one glance, this guy had sized up all of them, and made a decision.

He stepped across the threshold. Shadows flitted across him, like bats.

"My name is Diallo," he said. His voice was deep, yet he spoke in a low tone that carried clearly throughout the place. "I am seeking soldiers. I could use each of you, but I will kill any that do not submit. Which of you men will avert death, join my army, and taste true freedom?"

A pause. Then, almost as one, the men drew their guns and aimed at the man who called himself Diallo.

He's the big dog vampire, Andre thought, wishing that he had a gun, too. He was willing to bet his life that this was the motherfucker that they were just talking about. The guy oozed evil power.

Booker T flipped out a pocketknife. Andre almost laughed, but he didn't have a weapon at all for himself. He noticed an old billiards stick leaning against the wall near him. He grasped it in his shaky hands. Better than nothing.

"Look here," a guy said. It was Calvin Jones, who worked at the barbershop. "I don't know who you think you are stepping up in here like this, but me and the brothers here don't want no trouble. We don't want no part of nobody's army. So push on."

"Right," another man said. He had a big .44. "Get the fuck out of here and leave us alone."

"And I'm backing up my customers," Mr. Clyde said. He took a sawed-off shotgun from under the counter. "I don't want any trouble here. Get off my goddamn property before I blow a hole in you."

Diallo's face was expressionless. He made another step forward.

The *snick-click* of cocking triggers popped through the air.

"The only way that you will leave alive," Diallo said, "is by joining me. Those who submit, come to me, and kneel. If you do not submit, the price for disobedience is death."

"Out," Mr. Clyde said. Perched behind the bar counter, he took aim with the shotgun.

The vampire thoughtfully regarded the firearms pointed at him. A faint smile played across his face.

Andre squeezed the cue stick so tightly it was a wonder it didn't snap in half. He blinked a drop of sweat out of his eye.

The vampire disappeared. Just like that. He was gone.

The door yawned into the stormy night.

Each man in the room released a chestful of air. Then the door, propelled by an unseen force, slammed shut, and someone cried out, "He's behind us!"

Andre looked. Diallo was behind the pool table, gripping a billiards stick. The man nearest the vampire tried to fire his pistol, but he was too slow. Diallo drove the stick through the guy's chest like a man spearing a fish, the bloody tip poking out between the victim's shoulder blades. The man choked out a garbled scream, his arms flailing uselessly at the wooden pole.

Diallo lifted the man high and flung him across the room. The guy crashed into the pinball machine, leaving a smear of blood across the display.

Andre's stomach convulsed. He tasted warm beer bubbling up his throat.

"Shoot him, goddammit!" Mr. Clyde said.

Andre covered his head, and dropped to the floor.

Mr. Clyde's shotgun boomed. More guns fired as the men attacked the monster. Bullets hammered Diallo, but he did not fall, stumble, or bleed. The bullets seemed to bounce off his body. Crouched, Andre could see the floor around Diallo: rounds rained to the hardwood.

He had to get out of there, that was the only way he could survive.

Across the room, Diallo grasped the edge of the pool table. He flipped it across the floor as though it weighed no more than a dinner plate. It slammed against the wall, billiard balls flying, and the men tried to scatter out of the way, but one of the men got trapped between a wall panel and the pool table, and Andre swore he could hear the sound of the man's chest being crushed under the weight. The guy's scream ripped through the air.

Andre rose higher. He was about to make a run for the door, when a beeline of men got there before him and tried to open it. But it would not open. Somehow, Diallo had sealed the door.

I'll go to the back, Andre thought. The hallway behind him was as dark as a snake's throat.

Three men rushed Diallo at once.

Diallo lifted a chair and brought it down on the first guy's head, busting his skull and shattering the chair, the man going down in a hail of wood shards. Diallo plunged his fist into the second man's solar plexus, drove it all the way into the man's guts, then snatched out his hand with a bloody fistful of intestines, the dead guy collapsing, legs kicking. The third man tried to tackle Diallo, but Diallo clamped his hands on his skull and twisted so fast the man's head came clean off. Diallo hurled the decapitated head across the room, where it smashed into the liquor bottles lined up behind the bar.

Mr. Clyde yelped like a frightened child and took cover beneath the counter.

Andre didn't know whether to piss his pants, or vomit. He was so scared he thought he could do both.

There were only five men left, including Andre. Two men strained in vain to open the door, Booker T hid under a table, and Mr. Clyde had vanished behind the bar.

Diallo strolled to the guys near the door. They began to cry.

One of the men kneeled, arms raised in supplication.

Now's my chance, Andre thought. *I'm not kneeling before that motherfucker. No way.*

Staying low, he bolted into the black hallway. Heart beating so hard he thought he might pass out. He couldn't see a damn thing back here. Where was the door?

He shouldered open a door, went into a small room lit with a candle. It was the washroom. Shit. How could he get out? He saw a square window high up on the wall. But the window was too small for him to squeeze through it.

He had to find another way.

He ran into the hall. A giant hand closed over his throat.

Andre gasped, beat his hands at the body in front of him, but it was like punching a concrete wall.

The vampire lifted him in the air. Andre's feet dangled above the floor.

Just when he thought he would black out, the vampire threw him. He whammed against a table, pain barking in his shoulder, salt-and-pepper shakers knocking against his head.

He was woozy, and in a universe of pain, but he had the presence of mind to look around. Four men, including Mr. Clyde and Booker T, knelt near the bar, like sinners at a confessional. Diallo towered above them, an unholy priest.

"Join us," Diallo said. He extended his hand. His eyes, black as bottomless wells, fixed on Andre.

Andre spat out a mouthful of blood.

He crawled across the floor, straightened up.

And kneeled.

"King!" Nia whistled. "Come on, where are you, boy?"

She was in an alley, between rows of houses and short brick buildings. Thickets of darkness surrounded her on every side. Wind blew scraps of litter around her, the scraping of trash against gravel sounding like a bony finger scratching against a coffin lid.

She hugged herself against the chill breeze and the deeper chill that had sunk into her marrow.

"King, wherever you are, come on out."

No answer. Only the rasping wind.

What had gotten into the dog to make him to run off? He had seemed like such a well-behaved animal, as clever as a person, in some ways. Much like her own lost dog, Princess, she remembered with a pang of sorrow.

She walked along the alley, her running shoes scattering pebbles here and there.

"King, come here, boy. It's Nia."

She might as well have been addressing the wind; it would've given her more of a response.

She checked her watch. Ten minutes until she had to meet David. She didn't want to return without his dog. Although David didn't blame her for King's slipping away, she felt responsible for allowing the canine to scramble out of the truck. King was like a kid brother to David. Losing the dog would crush him.

"King, come on out, boy!"

The wind died. A hush fell over her.

She heard, somewhere ahead, a low growl.

Her fingers tightened around the leather dog leash. She jogged forward, lightly, to minimize the sound of her shoe soles striking the ground.

On her left, there was a brown wooden fence. The big gate, wide enough to admit a truck, gaped open.

She thought the growl had come from that direction, but she wasn't sure. It was worth a look.

She stepped inside the enclosure. A blue Dumpster on her left. Stacks of wooden pallets and milk crates on her right. In front of her, a low, gray brick building.

After performing a quick mental reorientation, she recognized that she was behind Mac's Meat and Foods.

One of the steel double doors at the back of the store hung open, giving her a glimpse of a slice of darkness beyond. It puzzled her. Mac ran a tight ship; everyone in town knew that. He would never have closed the market without fastening those doors.

What was going on?

The soft canine growl reached her again. It was definitely coming from inside the store.

What was King—if it was really King inside—doing in there? What was he growling at?

The dog could have been agitated by anything. Something as small and harmless as a cat. Or something bigger and far more dangerous.

Her hand went to the revolver on her hip holster. She unsnapped the holster's buckle, drew out the gun. She wrapped the dog leash around her wrist to get it out of the way.

She moved to the doorway. She cocked her head, listened.

Silence, taut with tension, as if whoever—or whatever—was inside, was holding its breath. Just like she was.

She dug the mini flashlight out of her fanny pack. She swept the thin blade of light across the darkness inside.

A small chamber, full of crates and boxes. But no one was inside.

In the far corner, there appeared to be another door, half open.

She checked her watch again.

Seven minutes, then I've got to go. I want to find King and I think he's in there, but I promised David that I'd return on time. Promised him that I'd find the dog, too.

She pushed open the door and crept into the darkness beyond.

Jahlil had to get his father to a hospital immediately.

The siren wailing on the patrol car, Jahlil sped along the dark streets. He ran through stop signs without slowing. No one was out driving, and even if they were, he was in a cop car, and they should get the hell out of his way.

In the backseat, Dad groaned.

"I'm gonna get help for you, Daddy," Jahlil said. He glanced fearfully at the rearview mirror. Dad was slumped in the seat, eyes shut, his face greasy with sweat. Jahlil squeezed the steering wheel. "Just hold on, Daddy, hold on, please."

After that fucking vampire, Kyle, had stabbed Dad in the chest (not in the heart, thank God), Jahlil had shot the monster between the shoulder blades. But he hadn't killed the vampire. Screaming in anger, the creature had jumped out of the truck and flown away into the night, like a giant bat. He hadn't attacked Jahlil, which was weird. Maybe the asshole figured that the worst thing he could do to Jahlil was try to take his father away from him. If that's what he'd been thinking, he was right.

The other vampires had chased after the rest of the people on the patrol teams. Those folks cut out so fast it wasn't funny, some of them on foot, some of them in their cars. Within minutes, the parking lot was empty, and Jahlil was left with a dead man in the flatbed, and his father.

Somehow, he'd driven to Dad's police car, gotten a first aid kit out of the trunk, and found some pads he used to staunch the flow of blood from Dad's wound. There was so much blood Jahlil had vomited on himself. But he was still able to keep going, and tape bandages on his father's chest. He'd carried Dad to the car and slid him across the backseat. Before he peeled away, he said a quick prayer over Old Mac's body, then peeled the flamethrower off the man's back and stored it in the trunk.

On the walkie-talkie, he tried reaching the other team members, so they could tell him where he could find Dr. Green. But no one answered him. He wouldn't have been surprised if everyone had split town, the cowards. He was on his own.

He didn't know how he kept going in the face of all this

misery and madness. He felt as though he were in a feverish daze, or in a really bad dream.

He pushed the car hard. It pissed him off that the blood-sucker bastards had taken over the hospital in Dark Corner, but there was nothing he could do about it. Outside of town, the nearest medical center was in Hernando, about fifteen minutes away—when driving at the speed limit, that is. He wanted to get there in half the time.

He swerved onto Main Street, at high speed. The tires squealed, and the car tipped to the side slightly, but he didn't roll over. On the straightaway road, he blasted the gas pedal. The engine cried out like a horse popped with a whip, and the vehicle rocketed forward.

The fastest way to Hernando was to take Main Street to the Interstate 55 North exit, then zoom ten miles down the highway. The I-55 exit was just past the bridge that spanned the Coldwater River. Only a mile or so ahead.

Dad groaned again, softer this time. Weaker.

"Hang on, Daddy!" Jahlil pleaded. Oh, God, he just couldn't think about Dad not making it. Couldn't. Wouldn't.

But Dad had lost so much blood, it was like someone had dumped a bucket of red paint on him . . .

"He's going to make it," Jahlil muttered to himself. That was it, end of story. Period.

Ahead, the metal bridge floated into view.

He rammed the accelerator to the floor. The speedometer ticked to eight-five . . . ninety . . . ninety-five . . . one hundred . . .

Hunched over the trembling wheel, he ground his teeth so hard that his jaws ached.

One hundred and ten . . .

The bridge was a couple hundred feet ahead.

Then he saw something unbelievable.

"Oh, fuck!"

He frantically mashed the brake pedal.

The car screeched, skidding to a delayed stop that carried him a quarter of the way across the bridge.

If he had rolled only twenty feet farther, he would have been dead.

Because the bridge had been torn in half. Beyond his side, the support beams had been scorched and twisted, and the roadway was split, as if karate-chopped by a giant; the mangled road dropped steeply into the river below.

Jahlil hammered the steering wheel. "Shit, shit, shit!"

He knew what had happened. That fucking vampire, Diallo. He had done this. Somehow. He had probably thrown lightning bolts at the bridge, like he was Zeus or something.

Shit!

His eyes getting watery, he slammed into reverse, rolled off the bridge and back onto Main Street. He switched off the siren.

He looked over the seat to check his dad. Dad was unconscious, and he wasn't moaning anymore, but his chest rose and fell slowly, a good sign. It could be worse.

"Just keep hanging on, Dad," Jahlil whispered.

But what was he going to do now? Without access to I-55, he'd have to take a bunch of winding country roads to get to Hernando. And that damn vampire had probably blocked those routes, too. He was a slick bastard.

"Think, man," Jahlil ordered himself.

He remembered that Dad had advised him to call David Hunter if anything bad happened. He didn't know what Hunter could do to help him, or if Hunter was even around, but it was the only decent option he had left.

The cell phone was stashed in the cup holder. Thankfully, Dad had programmed Hunter's cell number in the phone.

I hope he's not gone, too, Jahlil thought, pressing the button to dial the number. It seemed like everyone else was.

For once, Jahlil had a stroke of good luck. David Hunter answered on the first ring.

* * *

Darkness rendered the grocery store—a place where Nia had shopped frequently over at least the past ten years—as unfamiliar and mysterious as a moon cavern. Her miniature flashlight did little to alleviate the feeling that she had wandered into a strange new realm.

She had crossed the storage room without incident and entered the main floor of the market.

She was at the back of the shopping area. On her left, there were six dark aisles; on her right, the produce area, the open-air coolers filled with cantaloupes, lettuce, watermelons, oranges, bananas, tomatoes, and other items.

The store was crypt-silent.

She edged to the first aisle. Swept the flashlight beam across it. Nothing but shelves packed with cereals, pasta, grits, rice, and more—she knew the contents of the shelves like she knew the inside of a cupboard at her own house.

She moved forward, to the next aisle. No one there, either.

At the end of the third grocery aisle, she spotted King. He was at the end of the row, positioned behind a revolving rack full of packets of Kool-Aid. The dog appeared to be hiding from someone.

When her flashlight beam touched King's flank, he looked back at her, big brown eyes shining. But the dog did not move. He turned back to whatever had captured his attention.

What was he doing up there? She had never seen a dog behave so oddly.

But the dog's obvious alertness to danger nearby had made a ball of ice form in her stomach. The iciness spread from her stomach and throughout her limbs, until her entire body was chilled.

She lowered the flashlight. Clutching the revolver, she lightly tread across the aisle, stopping just behind King.

She rested her hand on his furry back. His muscles were bunched up.

"What's wrong, boy?" she whispered. "What's bothering you?"

King peered through the rack, and whined. He licked her fingers. His tongue was like sandpaper.

She peeked between the bars of the rack. It gave her a peephole view of the meat department, which occupied the whole wall on the east side of the store. She didn't see anything of concern. But it was dark and nearly impossible to make out any details.

She inched around the rack. She flicked on the flashlight.

Mr. Morgan walked through the passageway at the end of the meat counter.

She gasped.

This time, Morgan did not have a knife. He had a handgun. It was much bigger than hers, too.

Behind Nia, King growled.

"That mutt's got a nose like a bloodhound," Morgan said. "Followed me all the way in here, just like I've been following *you*, Miss James."

Her hand trembling, she shone the light beam at him. He was not a vampire. He was still human. But he was out of his mind and relentless, and that was as bad as him being a bloodsucking monster.

"There's some weird shit going on in this little hick town," Morgan said. "But I don't care about that. Nothing's going to stop me from having you. We're meant to be together. Stop resisting and give yourself to me."

"Never." She raised the gun.

He raised his revolver, too. He aimed at her head.

It was like looking into the tube of a cannon. She swallowed dryly. But she did not lower her gun.

"Drop it, Miss James," he said. "You don't have the nerve to shoot me. You proved that earlier."

Nia felt King tensed behind her, like a coiled cobra.

She decided to take a big risk.

"Okay." She blew out a breath, and dropped the gun on the floor, and the flashlight, too. "You win."

"I knew you didn't have it in you, bitch," Morgan said. He laughed. "Get your fine ass over here. I'm gonna take you behind the counter so we can get properly reacquainted."

Bowing her head, as if defeated, she shuffled forward.

She counted on Morgan relaxing his grip on the gun, and she counted on the darkness coming to her aid.

Most of all, she counted on King.

When she had taken about three hesitant steps, she suddenly dashed to the right, into another aisle.

"You bitch!" Morgan yelled.

He swung the gun around, trying to regain his aim on her, but in the near-blackness, it would be difficult for him to see.

Then King roared.

"Get him, boy, tear his heart out!" Nia urged.

The dog tackled Morgan. Together, they hit the floor. Morgan's gun spun out of his grasp.

"Get off me, you fuckin' mutt, get off me!"

King was on top of the man, snapping and biting. Then the dog yelped in pain, and scrambled away.

Morgan bellowed triumphantly. A blood-smeared switch-blade glinted in his hand.

Oh, no.

King staggered into the wall. The dog's legs gave way, and he settled heavily against the floor, tongue lolling.

As Morgan got back to his feet, smiling maniacally, Nia charged him.

"Back, bitch." Morgan swiped at her with the blade, making her stop in her tracks to avoid being cut. "Don't make me carve up that pretty face of yours."

Nia drew herself into a fighting stance. Her gun was on the floor, out of easy reach. She had only her bare hands to defend herself.

But she had trained for a moment like this. She clenched her hands into fists.

Morgan circled her, like a swordfighter.

"You're all mine," he whispered. "The more you fight me, the more I love you. Keep fighting me, baby, it's gonna make fucking you that much sweeter."

This man was sick. Insane. But she did not lose her cool. As she'd been taught, she skipped backward, light on her feet, as if she were a fencer. She rolled her hands in a dog-digging motion, to distract him and protect her vital areas.

He feinted a thrust. She hopped back, then fired a sharp kick into his shin.

"Dammit!" His face contorted in agony. He gritted his teeth. Then he swiped at her, wildly.

She ducked out of the knife's looping path, and blasted his shin again, in the same tender spot.

He wailed, his leg crumbling under him.

Nia was about to wade in, to knock him out with a blow to the head. But he lunged at her, and this time, she moved too slowly. The blade sliced across her arm.

Crying out, she fell, her arm burning as if doused with gasoline and set aflame.

With only one good leg, Morgan crawled after her.

She whimpered. Holding her arm, blood seeping between her fingers, she scooted backward across the floor.

"I'm gonna fuck you till you bleed, just like you're bleeding now," he said. "Gonna take my time and give you the sweet love you've been missing."

She could not imagine the horror of allowing Morgan to have his way with her. She'd rather die before that happened.

He crawled forward. Saliva foamed from his lips. The switchblade was drenched in gore.

My gun has to be around here, somewhere.

She glanced over her shoulder. The .32 lay near the flashlight, which speared the darkness with a pale yellow beam.

Biting her tongue against the pain in her wounded arm, she scrambled like a crab after the weapon. Got it, gripped it tight.

"For the last time, you won't shoot me, bitch," Morgan said, mockingly. "You're too weak."

Nia took aim.

Twice, she had declined to shoot this man. But as far as she was concerned, he was hardly a man anymore, and circumstances had pushed her way over the line and made her capable of doing anything to protect herself. There was only one way out of this, and it was not the sadistic rape and torture that Morgan suggested.

"Put it down!" Morgan commanded.

"It's over," Nia said. "Finally."

She squeezed the trigger.

The bullet drilled him between the eyes. His head lolled to the side, and his mouth gaped in a silent howl. He fell backward and struck the floor like a lead weight.

She released a sigh that came from the depths of her soul.

Colin Morgan was finally dead.

She threw away the gun. A choked sob burst out of her. She forced herself to hold back her tears, though doing so made her chest swell painfully.

She went to the dog. Lying against the wall, legs drawn under him, King had watched everything. Blood dampened his breast.

"Oh you sweet, poor thing." She gently brushed the dog's head. King feebly licked her hand. "We're going to take care of you, understand? You're going to be okay."

She got her cell phone out of her fanny pack and called David.

With Jahlil trailing him in the patrol car, David screeched to a stop in front of Mac's Meat and Foods.

I never should have let Nia go off on her own, he thought. When she called him on her cell phone and told him what had happened, such anxiety had struck him that his stomach ached. He could have lost her. She had come within a thread's width of death.

While Jahlil waited in the car with his father, David got out and banged against the store's front entrance. Nia pushed open the door.

"You got here fast," she said.

Her hair was disheveled. Dried blood spattered her face, and she had wrapped a thick bandage around her left arm.

He had never been so glad to see anyone. He pulled her into his arms. She squeezed him, digging her fingers into his back.

"God, I'm so glad you're okay," he said, his face buried in her hair. "How're you feeling?"

"Awful, but glad I'm alive. I found King. He saved my life, David."

They went inside. King lay against the wall. The dog raised his head when David came near, and his tail swished back and forth.

"You crazy mutt," David said. He blinked away a tear and rested his hand on King's back. "Look what you went and got us into, trying to be superdog. We're gonna get you all patched up, boy. You'll be all right."

King licked his fingers.

Nia knelt beside them. "I moved Morgan's body. I dragged it into the meat freezer, behind the counter." She shook her head, sighed. "I killed a man, David."

"It was in self-defense. You had no choice."

Her face was haunted. "I know, but that doesn't make me feel any better. I feel sick, really sick. I wish I hadn't done it . . . but you're right, I didn't have any choice."

"I'm sorry, Nia."

"Mac is going to go nuts when he sees what happened in here," she said.

"He won't be around to complain. Mac is gone."

"Gone? You mean . . . dead?"

He nodded slowly. "Jahlil told me. Kyle and his army of vampires . . . they were too much for them. The patrol teams are gone. Everyone either was overwhelmed in the fight, or said to hell with it and ran away to save themselves. We're on our own."

"Me, you, Jackson, and his son," she said.

"Yeah. But Jackson can't help us. He's in the car with his son. He was stabbed—not bitten—and lost a lot of blood. I want to get him to Pearl's, but I'm afraid she won't be able to do much for him."

"She's worked miracles before, so people say."

"Then I sure hope she can work another one," he said. "But we're going to need more than one miracle to get through this alive, Nia. We're going to need a night full of them."

A golden glow radiated from the windows of Pearl's home, like a lighthouse on a night-veiled sea.

Pearl answered the door before David could knock.

"Thank you so much for letting us come here," David said. "We hate to impose on you like this."

"Nonsense. It's my duty to help," Pearl said. "Come on, I'll help you bring your dog and Chief Jackson inside."

David and Jahlil carried Jackson, who was still unconscious, into the guest bedroom; Nia and Pearl took King to a cleared-out space in the living room.

Candles throughout the house provided warm light. Although Pearl lived on the outskirts of town, she too had lost electrical power due to the storm.

Pearl attended to Jackson, while David worked on King.

Because David had taken a first aid class for dog owners a couple of years ago, and had treated King for minor injuries in the past, he competently administered care to the

dog. Fortunately, he had the foresight to always keep a canine first aid kit in the truck, too. He gave King a small dose
of Benadryl, to help him relax. Then he used scissors to trim
the fur around the knife wound. The blood had clotted, a good
sign, and the cut did not appear deep or to have touched a
major organ. David cleaned the wound, using a mild soap
and warm water, then he applied a Telfa Pad, which he'd
coated with Neosporin. He added two more layers of ban-
daging, securing the final layer with tape.

"There, all better now, Mr. King," David said.

King blinked sleepily. The Benadryl would keep him
drowsy for a while.

David went to check on Jackson.

In the bedroom, Pearl sat at Jackson's bedside, and Nia
and Jahlil sat on chairs that surrounded the bed. David knelt
beside Nia.

"What do you think, Pearl?" David said.

"He is in shock," she said, "due to having lost a tremendous amount of blood. I cleaned and redressed his wound.
However, to have the best opportunity to recover, he needs a
transfusion."

"A blood transfusion?" David asked. "We'd have to take
him to the hospital for that, and you know—"

"—the hospital has been overrun with vampires, and the
blood supply doubtless raided," Pearl said. "I understand that
the circumstances are not in our favor, David. I will do the
best I can."

"What if we take him to another hospital?" Nia said.
"There's one in Hernando. It's only a fifteen minute drive."

"We can't leave town." Jahlil shook his head. "I tried. The
bridge is torn up, and I bet the other roads out of here are
blocked, too. They've thought of everything, man." He sniffled, wiped his nose angrily with his blood-stained shirt.
"My dad . . . he's not gonna make it, is he?"

"I have witnessed many miracles in my life, child," Pearl
said. She held Jahlil's hands. "Please, keep hope."

Pearl resumed her healing treatment, which she called Reiki. Her eyes closed, her face serene yet concentrated, she slowly moved her hands across Jackson's body, keeping her palms balanced above his skin. Reiki, she said, was simply a method of channeling and directing life force energy. In the absence of high-tech medical equipment and a staff of doctors, it was the most powerful technique at her disposal. As David watched, he thought about the irony of Jackson's condition. He needed a blood transfusion in the midst of a vampire attack, for God's sake. If they merely took Jackson into the fray of battle, he was sure the vampires would be willing to share a little blood.

Not funny, he thought.

Rain rapped against the windows; the storm clouds had finally begun to shed their burdens. Occasionally a strong wind buffeted the house, like a punch thrown by a furious spirit.

How long would it be before the vampires located them? Surely, they were searching. The fiends would not rest until they had found them.

He looked away from the window.

Nia rose out of her chair.

"Pearl, can I use your bathroom?" Nia said. "I need to clean myself up."

Pearl turned, her hands hovering over Jackson's chest. "Of course. You will find towels in the cabinet underneath the sink." Her dark eyes went to David. "Make yourselves at home, there is some tea I've already brewed in the kitchen, and food if you are hungry. I will be treating Chief Jackson for quite some time."

"Thank you," David said. "Jahlil, can I get you anything?"

"No," he said quickly. "I'm staying in here."

That kid is tough, but he's held together with thin wire right now, David thought. He wished he could do something, but there was nothing he could do. All he could do was prepare himself to step in and be a friend for Jahlil, like he had promised Jackson that he would.

Jackson's features were slack and peaceful. Gone was the melancholy expression that habitually dragged down the police chief's face, making him look twenty years older. But David found the man's placid visage disturbing.

He looked like a dead man on display in a coffin.

Chapter 22

At Emma Mae's, the party was in high gear.

After Emma's announcement at the town meeting, people had begun showing up at her place around eight o'clock. By eleven-thirty, cars and pickup trucks crowded the street, parked bumper-to-bumper for the entire block. Her house was full of loud, carefree people who knew how to have fun. Playing Bid Whist and poker. Eating ribs, chicken, and corn on the cob. Drinking beer and Hennessy. Telling stories and talking shit.

The thunderstorm had knocked out the electrical power, but Emma was prepared for that; candles and kerosene lamps burned in every room downstairs. She had batteries for the boom box, so she could play hits nonstop by Bobbie Blue Bland, Wilson Pickett, and B.B. King. She'd flung up the garage door and set up the big barbecue grill on the edge of the garage floor, fragrant smoke blowing into the air as she served up a seemingly endless supply of ribs and chicken.

No one was going to stop her from partying. Least of all some vampires. Who believed in those damn things, anyway? She'd believe it when she saw one with her own eyes.

Lillie, of course, believed that nonsense. As Emma stood at the kitchen counter, brushing her special barbecue sauce on another steaming slab of ribs, she looked out the window and saw the glow of Lillie's cigarette as her sister hid behind the curtain at her home next door. Spying on Emma, as usual. Emma sneered. If the old heifer was so curious about what was going on, she should've brought her skinny ass over here.

You better take Blood to the hospital, you old fool, Lillie had said after the town meeting. *I know you lying about him having a hangover; I heard that man got bit by one of them demon dogs . . .*

Emma had told Lillie that she didn't know what the hell she was talking about and she needed to mind her own business. But inwardly, she worried. Blood was *still* asleep. That man had never slept through a party in his life, but she couldn't wake him for anything. He would only groan and shift on the bed. He was running a bit of a fever. She had put a cold towel on his forehead, to try to break the fever, and it didn't seem to help. She was really beginning to worry, but she wasn't going to take him to the hospital so they could pump him full of drugs and do government experiments on him like he was some kinda lab rat. She didn't trust the hospital in town, not after what had been said at the meeting.

If Blood wasn't better by morning, she would take him to a hospital in Southaven. In the meantime, she would continue to check on him every hour. It was, in fact, about time she looked in on him again.

She finished slathering sauce on the ribs, then placed the meat in a foil-lined pan. She took the pan to the serving table in the corner of the kitchen. Elmer Jackson, the police chief's cousin, and Buster Hodges, the daddy of Junior, the kid who cut her grass, hunched over the table, piling food on their plates.

"Where's your boy, Buster?" Emma said. "I ain't seen him here tonight."

"Don't know where that kid at," Buster said. "Probably out working. You know that boy ain't happy 'less he working somewhere."

"Ain't that the truth," Elmer said. "Boy been saving up to buy a truck from me. He came by the lot and told me to save him that black ninety-eight Ford pickup I done had for a few months. Said he was gonna buy it."

"He ain't gonna buy shit," Buster said. "That boy got pipe dreams, like his mama did."

"Aww, let the boy have his dreams," Emma said. She set down the ribs on the table. "He's a sweet kid."

Buster grumbled and stabbed a chicken thigh with his fork. Emma almost told him that his son wasn't the only one who'd had a dream once, but she let it go. Buster hated to be reminded of his pro boxing days. A couple of years ago, at another of her card parties, Elmer—never one to bite his tongue—had told Buster that he'd lost a hundred dollars betting on his sorry ass in a fight, and Buster had launched across the table and knocked Elmer on his tail with his fearsome right hook. Since then, Elmer had avoided coming within ten feet of Buster.

But look at them now, Emma thought. The men were fellowshipping like true brothers, eating together. It proved that when things got too heavy to bear, there was nothing like an old-fashioned house party to set things right. A party was good for the soul.

She went through the house, smiling to herself. All around her, folks were having a good time. On the boom box, Wilson Pickett crooned his signature song, "In the Midnight Hour."

Earl Jones, a card-party regular, jumped up from his seat at the poker game as Emma walked past. Drunk as a skunk, he took her hand and twirled her around in a little dance.

Emma giggled, feeling like a teenager again. That heifer, Lillie, didn't know what she was missing, staying cooped up in her house like the crazy old woman in the fairy tale who lived in a giant shoe. The only difference was that Lillie had that pissy weiner dog, Rex, instead of a bunch of cats.

All the cats are gone outta this town, Lillie had said, earlier. *Did you notice that, you old fool? All the cats are gone— scared off by those demon dogs!*

Lillie and her superstitions. Emma didn't care about some damn alley cats.

Earl stumbled in the middle of his jig, and Emma helped him sit down.

"You better sit your tail down and get back to them cards," she said. "You can't hang with me, baby."

"Don't mean I don't wanna try," Earl said. He flashed a lusty grin that was highlighted by a shiny gold tooth.

"You better not let Blood hear you say that." She smiled. "I'm 'bout to bring him down here."

"About time, wake that gimp-legged nigga up," Earl said. He expertly riffled his cards in his big hands. "I wanna get him at this table and clean out his pockets."

"You hush," Emma said.

Upstairs, the hallway was dark; Emma had not bothered to place a candle around the staircase since no one but her had any business going up there, and she had lived in the house for so long she could walk around blindfolded. But the blackness seemed especially thick and warm, shot through with glints of purple. Just her eyes playing tricks on her, she figured. But Lillie's superstitions rang through her mind.

Those vampires are demons, Lillie had said. *You believe in demons, don't you? If you believe in God, you gotta believe in the Devil, too, sister. Demons are the Devil's minions . . .*

"Ain't no such thing," Emma mumbled under her breath. She opened the door to the master bedroom.

Inside the room, a candle on the nightstand cast flickering light.

Blood sat on the edge of the bed, head lowered. He was bare-chested, and wore only his blue pajama bottoms. Curly gray hairs shone on his thin chest.

"How long you been up, baby?" Emma said. She began to walk toward him, ready to check his temperature. "Let me take a look at you."

When Blood raised his head and looked at her, she halted.

An icy finger slid down her spine.

Something was wrong with Blood. The wrongness was in his dark, red-rimmed eyes. Looking into those eyes of his was like looking at a rattlesnake.

Instinctively, she broke eye contact.

"Come on over here, brown sugar," he said. His voice was raspy, but commanding. "I wanna hold your fine body in my arms."

Blood called her "brown sugar" whenever he wanted to romance her, but there was nothing flirtatious about his manner, not this time. His jaw was tight. His fingers clenched and unclenched. He looked like a man who was ready to rumble, not make love.

What was wrong with him? Had the fever cooked his brain into stew?

Or was Lillie right?

Emma took a step backward, the floorboard creaking beneath her.

"Where you going, woman?" Blood rose. He moved with a silkiness that she had never seen from him, as though his bad leg were a thing of the past. "I want you to come to me."

"What's . . . what's wrong with you?" she said. She had to force out the words, her heart was pounding so hard.

"Ain't a damn thing wrong with me, baby. I ain't never felt so good in my life." He laughed. "I wanna make you feel good like I do."

Emma couldn't be sure because of the quivering light and shadows, but when he had opened his mouth to laugh, she thought she had seen long, sharp teeth. The kind of teeth a dog would have.

Or a vampire.

Lillie's know-it-all voice played in her mind: *I told you the truth, you old fool. Why don't you ever listen to me?*

Blood spread his arms. "Come on over to me, brown sugar. Lemme make you feel good."

Spinning around to run was so hard for Emma, it was like trying to move when submerged in water. The air itself seemed to push against her to keep her from getting out of there. But she broke out of the room and slammed the door behind her.

The darkness in the hallway swallowed her. She was careless for not lighting a candle up here.

On the other side of the door, the floorboards groaned. Blood was coming. There was no way to keep him from getting out. She couldn't lock the door from this side.

But she had a houseful of people who could help her. Big, strong men like Buster. They could help her handle Blood, whatever was wrong with him.

She ran across the hall, bumping into things. She flew down the steps so quickly she nearly tripped over her own feet.

"Girl, what you running for?" Earl said. Cards in one hand, he tipped up his glass full of Hennessy, taking a long gulp. He burped, then chuckled. "You come back looking for a real man to handle you?"

Emma opened her mouth to speak—and then she saw movement outside the living room windows.

The curtains were peeled back, giving a view of the front yard. There was a gang of people out there. Folks with pale, grimy faces. Dressed in hospital gowns with dark stains across the front. They moved like wolves on the prowl, hunched over, muscles tensed and ready to pounce, intent on a single, deadly objective.

Emma could not believe it. But it was right there in front of her face.

Her buzz drained out of her like water slipping away in a tub.

"Lock the doors!" Emma cried. "Everybody, we being attacked!"

People gaped at her, their eyes glazed. Like she had stood up and shouted something in Japanese.

"What the hell you talking 'bout, Emma?" a man said in a slurred voice. "You just drunk, old gal."

To hell with waiting on these drunk fools, she thought. She hustled across the living room to lock the front door.

The door exploded open. Emma stumbled backward. Cold wind and rain swooped inside, and two of those vampirelike things leapt onto the threshold, hissing, their fangs bared.

Emma screamed and ran.

All around the house, windows shattered as if from the force of a tremendous gale, but deep in her heart she knew it was no wind that was responsible. Those monsters had probably surrounded her house, and were breaking inside.

With all the folks lounging around her place, coming here would be like a feast for those creatures.

She itched to get her shotgun. But the one she wanted was in her bedroom closet. She couldn't go up there. Blood would be waiting.

She raced into the kitchen. Windows were busted in there, too, and one of those creatures must have hurled itself through the hole—she saw one that looked as if it used to be a young woman. Hell, it looked kinda like Shenice Stevens, who'd won the town beauty pageant last year. But if it were really her, shit, she looked like a mess.

The female monster had cornered Buster Hodges. Buster held up his massive fists in a boxer's stance, his face resolute. The creature darted toward him. Buster threw his famous right hook—and hit nothing but air. The vampire moved way too fast. It seized Buster's arm and bit into his meaty bicep. Buster cried out, and his legs sagged.

Within seconds, the creature had climbed on top of him like she was sexing him up, but its mouth was attached to Buster's neck, and the greedy, sucking sounds made Emma's stomach turn.

Emma was too frightened to try to help him. She whammed through the door at the back of the kitchen, stumbled into the garage.

The barbecue grill spat and sizzled, pungent smoke pouring through the half-open garage door and into the night air.

Throwing this party was the dumbest thing I've ever done in my life, she thought, more lucidly than she had thought anything all evening. *This town has slid into a corner of hell, and here I am throwing a fucking party. How could I be so dumb? I should've split the minute I walked out of that church.*

But it was too late to get away. Vehicles blocked the driveway, keeping her from backing her Ford out of the garage. She would've even taken someone else's car to get away, but she'd have to go back inside the house to find keys, and she was afraid to go back in there.

Screams of pain and sounds of mayhem came from her house. The cacophony of furniture being overturned. Glass shattering. Guns boomed, too; many of the folks at the party carried pieces.

Emma wondered whether a gun would do any good against these demon fiends. In the movies, guns never killed vampires.

Hadn't they said something at the church about fire being lethal to those monsters?

She looked at the barbecue grill. Small flames danced in the charcoal pit, licking at the burned ribs.

She found a length of wood lying in the corner, left over from one of Blood's woodworking projects. She doused the end of the plank with lighter fluid, and dipped it into the wriggling flames in the grill. The tip of the wood lit up with a *whoosh,* the heat baking the sweat on her face.

"You know better than to play with fire, brown sugar." It was Blood. He entered the garage through the kitchen doorway.

His fangs were fully exposed, rivulets of saliva running down his chin. Hunger gleamed in his eyes.

"You stay away from me, Blood," Emma said. She waved the torch in front of her. "I don't wanna hurt you."

Blood's gaze warily followed the flames. He was clearly afraid of fire. He circled her, slowly, and she turned to keep the torch between them.

Anguish twisted his face. "I got to have you, brown sugar. Can't help it. I *got* to. I can't control it."

"You ain't gotta do nothing but stay away from me."

He growled, feinted at her. Emma thrust the torch toward his chest. He screeched as the flames seared his flesh—a horrible sound she had never heard him make, not even when he had once dropped his cane and tumbled down a flight of stairs. She felt guilty, just for an instant, and pulled back, and it was in her moment of weakness that Blood swung his arm, backhanding her across the face.

She had never been hit so hard in her life. She flew several feet across the garage and smashed into a wheelbarrow.

Roaring, Blood shambled after her. He fell on top of her.

Emma was a strong woman, stronger than many men, probably stronger than Blood when he was an ordinary man, but she was weak compared to this creature. She tried to wrestle from under him, but couldn't move him. She bucked her knee into his groin, and it made no difference. She tore her teeth into his forearm, and he didn't release his hold on her.

He dipped his head down to her neck so eagerly that his skull bumped against her chin, making her bite her tongue at the same instant that his teeth pierced her neck. Warm blood spurted in her mouth.

He drank from her like a child suckling at a mother's breast, moaning.

Hmm . . . this isn't so bad, she thought, and sighed. *It feels good to let him suck from me. I don't think I've ever felt anything so good in my life.*

That old heifer, Lillie, doesn't know what she's missing . . .

Lillie Mae stood at the window, watching the happenings at her sister's place, until the monsters arrived.

When those blood-drinking demons lurked toward Emma's house, Lillie snatched the curtains closed and stepped away from the glass.

"I told that old fool not to throw that party," Lillie muttered. She drew on her cigarette. "Mule-headed girl never wants to listen to me."

Although her words were harsh, she was frightened. The devil was loose in town. She felt sorry for her sister and wished she could help her, but there was nothing she could do, not really. She was just an old woman with bad lungs and a toy dog whose bark was bigger than his bite.

She shuffled across the living room. A single candle glowed in a dish on the nightstand. She usually liked candlelight; it reminded her of when she was a child, at a time when the world was a kinder, more considerate place. But this candlelight only stirred her fear. The shifting patches of shadows in the room seemed to conceal threatening things.

Perched on the arm of the sofa, Rex whined softly. The dog picked up on her anxiety, as if they shared a telepathic bond. He watched her with his big, black eyes, his short tail thumping nervously. He suffered from what she called the "Little-Big Dog" syndrome and tended to bark at everything that wandered into the yard, from squirrels to cats to fallen leaves, but tonight, he stayed on the couch, and he kept quiet.

The dog was no fool. It understood danger was near.

"We gonna be all right, little man," Lillie said. She placed her thin hand on the dog's back, while her other hand picked up the phone off the nightstand. She was going to call the police. She could do something to help Emma and her boozing friends.

There was no dial tone. She put the handset back on the cradle.

She was not surprised. The devil was crafty, he sure was. Clipping the phone lines throughout the town would have been one of his first moves. Cut off the people from civilization and hope.

Sounds of terror reached her from next door. Banging, shouting, breaking, shooting, screaming.

She touched the crucifix that dangled on her necklace. She prayed that God would keep Emma and the other folks safe, but even as she prayed, doubts crept into her spirit. Emma never listened to anyone. This would be one time that her stubborn nature would get her into trouble. Lillie hated to think such thoughts, but she couldn't help it.

"Dear Lord, have mercy," she said, and her words seemed loud in the silent house, so loud that she wondered if someone might hear her. Or *something*.

Rex stopped wagging his tail.

Lillie quietly extinguished her smoke in a tin ashtray.

Noise at the front window. *Tap-tap-tap-tap*. A brittle sound like a skeletal finger clicking against the glass.

She lived in an old house, and sometimes it creaked and made settling sounds, but this noise was nothing like that: it had purpose.

Someone was at the window. Someone with evil in his heart. A tangible malevolence seeped through the glass and into the house, like foul smoke.

Fortunately, heavy curtains covered the window. But she wondered whether the creature outside had the power to see through the fabric, and if it was watching her at that moment standing stock-still beside the couch with one hand on her dog and her other hand closed over her crucifix.

Tap-tap-tap-tap-tap.

She closed her eyes.

Please, Lord, send them away. Put a fence around me. Keep me safe.

Under her hand, Rex trembled. But the little dog kept quiet, though his heart throbbed in a frenzy.

She held her breath, praying fervently.

The wind soughed around the house, and it seemed to carry away the threat. The feeling that she was being watched passed.

She exhaled. She didn't realize that she had been holding her breath.

The commotion continued next door. But she had been spared. Thank the Lord.

She was not going to take any more chances. She gathered Rex in her arms, picked up her Bible off the coffee table, blew out the candle, and went to the basement.

It was a comfortable hideaway; her son had lived down there for a year after he graduated college. There were no windows, the walls were brick, and the door was thick and strong. An old refrigerator held bottled water, apple juice, cheese, bread, and Spam. She had stocked up earlier that afternoon, in preparation for a time like this.

She would remain down there until she received a sign that danger had passed.

She lit another candle, and settled onto the old, sunken couch. Rex hopped onto the cushion beside her and snuggled up against her leg. She cracked open her Bible to the book of Revelations—in her opinion, the most frightening thing ever written, but an appropriate choice for tonight— and began to read, picking up from where she had left off earlier in the evening.

" '*And I saw a beast coming out of the sea. He had ten*

horns and seven heads, with ten crowns on his horns, and on each head was a blasphemous name . . .' "

At Pearl's house, David sat on a rocking chair in the screened-in porch, drinking chamomile tea. He'd needed a reprieve from the anxiety that permeated the air inside the house. Perhaps Pearl had worked miracles before, but all of them worried about Jackson's fate.

Cool air swirled through the screen, touched him with its fingers. Silvery rain pummeled the earth, and lightning occasionally made a jagged crack in the dark clouds. In the porch, a candle on a small table provided the only steady light.

What a night, he thought. *If we can survive until morning, maybe we have a chance.*

The door opened, startling him. But it was only Nia. A white towel hung over her shoulder, and her face looked clean and fresh.

"It's a little chilly out here," she said.

"The tea's keeping me warm. I brought some for you. Come have a seat." He patted the chair beside him, picked up the silver teakettle, and poured tea into an extra mug.

"You're a sweetheart." She settled next to him and took the cup.

For a minute, it seemed to him that they were somewhere else; perhaps at a quaint bed-and-breakfast in a scenic coastal town somewhere, winding down after a pleasantly tiring day of sight-seeing, shopping, and eating in charming restaurants. They would enjoy the serenity of the night and then retire to their bed, make love, and sink into the warm folds of sleep.

He shook his head, as though waking from a daydream.

"What's wrong?" she said.

"I was dreaming that we were somewhere else," he said. "Where we could enjoy each other in peace."

"What a nice thought." She smiled, took a sip of tea. "I

feel like I've been living a nightmare tonight. It's kind of relaxing to imagine being somewhere else."

A companionable silence enveloped them. The only sounds were the faint sputter of the candle, the drumming rain, and the whispering wind.

"When this is over," he said, suddenly, "I want us to be together."

She shifted to face him.

"I want to be with you, too, David. More than I've ever wanted to be with anyone."

He touched her face, ran his fingers through her hair. He softly kissed her lips.

Although he'd said he wanted them to be together, he didn't have a full understanding of what he meant. Did he want to marry her, live with her, or what? He couldn't nail down his feelings and define specifically what being together involved. He knew only that his desire to be with her was as powerful as his need to breathe.

Or do I know more than that about my feelings? he wondered. *I need to be honest. Completely.*

"We haven't known each other very long, but I feel as if I've lived a lifetime with you," he said.

"What are you trying to say, David?" Curiosity danced in her eyes.

He smiled, self-consciously. "Am I beating around the bush, or what?"

She only looked at him, smiling.

He sucked in a breath.

"I love you," he said.

Her grin was like sunshine breaking through an overcast day. "I love you, too, David."

He grasped her hand, kissed it. "I really believe . . . we were meant to be together. Even if none of this other crap was happening, somehow, somewhere, we were destined to meet. Does that sound crazy?"

"I knew you were special from the moment we met," she said. "And it wasn't just because you were so cute."

He laughed. She wrapped her arms around his neck and pulled him forward, so that their noses were nearly touching.

"I want you to promise us something," she said.

"Promise us?"

"Yes. Us. Promise us that you'll get us through this."

"Nia, I haven't been doing this alone. You've been there every step of the way—"

"And I will be. But in the end, sweetheart, it's going to come down to you, and you know it. Make the promise, for both of us, for our future together."

"I promise I'll get us through this."

"Thank you." She kissed him deeply. "Thank you."

He leaned back in the chair, holding her hand. He never wanted the moment to end. But it was inevitable. They had work to do.

"We have to talk about our next move," he said. "I think we should leave soon."

She nodded. "I thought about that. We can't help Jackson ourselves, and we're putting Pearl in danger by staying here."

"Exactly. I want to take Jahlil with us. But I know he won't want to leave behind his dad."

"Let's pray that Pearl can heal the chief," she said. "But if it doesn't happen soon . . ."

There was no need for her to finish the sentence. Their path was clear. With or without Jackson, they would have to leave. Soon, the vampires would be coming.

Van Jackson floated into consciousness, awakening into a gray, blurry, unfamiliar world that was like somewhere in a drug-induced dream.

He couldn't feel his body—his body was numb—but he thought he was lying down. Some alert part of him, deep in his mind, told him that he lay on someone's bed. But he couldn't see the walls of the room; they were fuzzy and black. It was so quiet in there that he might have been lying inside a sealed coffin.

Was he in a hospital? He'd been hurt bad, he remembered. He recalled the pain tearing through his chest, and the blood. So much blood.

Was he dead?

Faintly, he heard a voice.

Dad, are you awake? You blinked; I saw you blink.

His son, somewhere nearby. His boy's voice was threaded with worry and cautious hope.

More than anything in the world, Jackson wanted to sit up and put his arms around his kid. He had never been an affectionate man, but he wanted to squeeze Jahlil in his arms so tightly that he would feel his boy's heart throbbing against his chest. It was his *son,* dammit, a precious human being born of his own flesh and blood. He didn't want to leave this world without holding his child, and experiencing the enduring reality of him, one more time.

But he couldn't feel his own limbs, much less move. His muscles would not obey his commands.

Pearl, my Dad's waking up! Hurry up and come back in here!

So were they at Pearl's house? Made sense. The hospital was gone to hell, after all.

Jackson tried to speak a word of reassurance, to tell his son that he heard him, but his lips would not move. His tongue was like a block of wood.

I didn't die earlier, but I'm dying now.

The thought slipped inside his mind with the terrible ease of a splinter sinking into soft flesh. It lodged in his brain and would not go away. It was true. He was dying.

He was not angry at God for allowing this to happen. He felt only . . . regret. He'd wasted so much time working, dutifully serving the public, and had failed to serve his own family. The bond that he had experienced with Jahlil earlier that night had come far too late to appease his guilt.

He heard more voices hovering around him. Female voices, a man who sounded like David, and his son. But he could not see them, or touch them. He floated in a gray haze.

Wake him up again! Jahlil cried. *I saw him blink. Do something to wake him up!*

Tense, anxious voices followed Jahlil's outburst.

I gotta talk to my boy, Jackson thought. He felt that he was drifting away, as though he lay on a rubber raft bobbing gently across a sea. He struggled to resist the pull. He wasn't ready to pass away, not yet. He had to force open his lips to speak his final words to his child. But it was so hard that his lips might have been sewn together with wire.

But at last he parted his lips, drew in a breath, and formed words.

Sitting on the bed, Jahlil cradled his father in his arms. He would not accept that his dad might be dying. Dad couldn't die. He was too young, he had years and years of living ahead of him, he had to be around to see Jahlil graduate from high school, go to college, start a career, get married, have kids of his own, and be a granddad to Jahlil's children. This was not the way it was supposed to be. This could not be happening. This was not real. He had already lost Mom. He could not lose Dad.

But Dad had blinked, only once, and when his eyes slid closed, again, they did not open. His chest rose and fell with agonizing slowness.

Jahlil, with one arm cradled around his father's shoulders, reached down and squeezed his father's hand. His skin was dry, and frighteningly cool.

"I'm not letting you die, Dad. No way. I'm gonna pull you through."

Pearl, David, and Nia huddled around the bed. They were talking, probably trying to calm him, but their words were a meaningless babble to him. He could not focus on what they were saying. He could only hold his father and concentrate on *willing* him to live, as if his own desire to save his dad could thwart God's plan to take him away.

"I ain't letting you die, Daddy." He pressed his ear against his father's chest, near his heart. It was beating so slow, too slow. He had to make Dad's heart beat faster, or else he would lose him forever.

"I . . . love . . . you." Whispered words, spoken so softly Jahlil could barely hear them.

Jahlil raised his head and stared at his father. Dad's eyes were closed, but his lips formed a melancholy smile.

"No, Dad. No."

Dad's hand squeezed Jahlil's fingers. Then his grip slackened.

"No!" Jahlil pressed his ear against his father's chest.

Dad's heart had stopped beating.

"No!"

Hot tears blinded Jahlil. Comforting hands rested on his shoulders, people trying to take him away from his father. He didn't want them to take him away, he wanted to wrap his dad in his arms and will his heart back to life. But he was too weak to struggle, and so sick that he thought he was going to throw up. He allowed them to peel his arms from around his dad. Someone carried him, and put him in a chair. Then someone embraced him; a woman, Pearl, judging from the scent of her. She hugged him and whispered in his ear, "Your daddy loved you, Jahlil, always remember that, sweetheart. He loved you and he'll always be with you. Always."

Jahlil squeezed her close, and wept.

Our worst nightmares are coming true, David thought. *Jackson, gone. Could it get any worse?*

He felt as though someone had slugged him. He staggered to a chair. Across the room, Jahlil desperately clutched Pearl in his arms, as though being torn away from her would sweep him away into oblivion. He felt sorry for the boy. He had lost both of his parents, and he was only a teenager. It was so terribly unfair.

I'm responsible for him from now on, he thought. *I promised Jackson that I would be there for his son. I've got to keep my word.*

Nia came into the room with a fresh towel. She gently wiped Jahlil's face.

Jahlil is in good hands, David assured himself. *Between myself and Nia, we'll take care of him and make sure he has everything he needs.*

On the bed, Jackson lay still. He was a good, courageous, honest man. There weren't enough men like him in the world. Now, he was gone. His prone body had a strange emptiness to it, like a soulless wax figure. The essence of the spirit that was Van Jackson had vacated its earthly vehicle for another, better place.

Despair gripped David. He was convinced that they were engaged in a fool's game. They couldn't win. Franklin was dead. Jackson was dead, too. There were dozens of vampires on the prowl, and perhaps hundreds more to come in the next day. Why continue this pointless fight? Why not find a way out of town and put it behind them for good?

You can't quit, a nagging voice told him. *William Hunter didn't quit. Neither can you. Besides, do you think running will solve anything? Diallo and Kyle want you, most of all. Wherever you go, they'll find you.*

He wished he could silence the voice of his conscience, but it spoke the truth. They could not run away. There was no escape. The only course of action was to do their duty.

He sighed, heavily. The burden of responsibility weighed upon his shoulders like a heavy barbell. Standing up was like rising out of a three hundred-pound squat.

A noise suddenly reached him that sent a shiver of fear through his bones.

Dogs, outside. Barking.

The vampires had found them.

Chapter 23

At the barking of the hounds, David looked at Nia. He nodded slightly, the only indication necessary to communicate to her that they were no longer safe.

Tension clenched his gut.

"They've found us," Nia said. She looked at Pearl. "How?"

"Diallo," Pearl said. She slipped out of Jahlil's arms. Jahlil, blinking slowly, appeared to realize what was happening, for his gaze sharpened. "Remember when I explained the risks of slipping into Diallo's mind? How it could form a dangerous psychic doorway? That is what happened. Just as I secretly entered his thoughts, so he was able to do the same with me. I'm only surprised that he has taken so long to arrive."

"He and his son have probably been out there painting the town red," David said. "Pardon the pun. They've gotten bored and are ready for us."

"Fuck this." Jahlil angrily wiped his eyes and shot to his feet. "I'm gonna kill all those motherfuckers. Everyone stay out of my way." He stormed across the room to where their bags and firearms lay on the floor.

David stepped in front of Jahlil.

"Hold on, Jahlil. I'm not letting you go out there like Rambo. We can't do it that way."

Jahlil's glare could have melted glass. "Get out of my way, man. I'm for real."

He tried to shove David aside, but David held his ground.

"I know you're angry," David said. "You're furious about what they did to your dad. I understand. But I promised Jackson that I'd look out for you, and I mean to stand by my word. There's no way I'm letting you run out there. That would be suicide."

"I don't need you to look out for me, all right? Will you get the hell out of my way?" His nostrils flaring, he attempted to push David out of his path.

David grabbed the boy's arms, held them tight.

Jahlil trembled. David was about three inches taller than the kid and outweighed him by maybe twenty pounds, but Jahlil was so charged with anger that David was not sure he could hold him back. The skin of his arms was hot to the touch.

"You've got to chill out," David said. "This isn't the time to lose your cool, understand? You're a tough kid, but you aren't crazy. You *know* you don't stand a chance in hell against those monsters."

"All right." Jahlil's eyes were red and fatigued. He shrugged off David's hands. David let him go.

"So you're the big boss man," Jahlil said. "What do you want us to do? Stay in here and wait to be slaughtered?"

David checked outside the rain-smeared window. He could not see the bloodsuckers yet, but the dogs' barks steadily grew louder.

Jahlil, Nia, and Pearl watched him anxiously.

"We have to go on the run," David said. "The vampires own the night, and there are too many of them for us to handle. We have to lie low until daybreak. Then, we can catch them in their lair, wherever that is."

"How do we get away?" Nia said. "It sounds like they're coming from the direction of the road. We can't go that way."

"There's a dirt trail at the back of my property," Pearl said. "It begins near the tool shed. The path leads through the woods, then cuts through a marsh and eventually ends at a road in town. But there is no light to guide you, and the swamp is full of water moccasins. My brother was bitten by one as a child and nearly died."

"Shit," Jahlil said. "I ain't messing with no snakes, man. Forget it."

"We'll take my truck," David said. "We'll stay on the trail and won't have to set foot in the water."

Nia looked out the window. "Then if that's the plan, we better get moving. They're getting closer, guys."

David grabbed his duffel bag. Jahlil and Nia hurriedly picked up their belongings, as well.

Pearl solemnly drew the blanket across Jackson's body.

"I am staying here," she said. Her eyes were tranquil. "I will watch over Chief Jackson."

"Good idea," Jahlil said. He swallowed. "I don't want to . . . leave my dad here, alone, you know?"

"Are you sure, Pearl?" David said. "The bloodsuckers are after us, and me, especially, but what if they break in here? It's not safe for you to stay behind."

"Nowhere is safe for me so long as Diallo is alive," she said. "I have violated the sanctity of his thoughts, an unforgivable trespass to him. If I were to come along with you, it would only fuel his determination to destroy us all. I am staying here."

Her tone indicated that the subject was closed to discussion. David bit his lip, debating whether to continue to attempt to persuade her to leave with them.

"You must hurry," Pearl said.

The barking outdoors grew louder.

On shaky legs, King trudged to the doorway. He whined, eyes searching David's face for reassurance.

"Okay, boy, we're leaving," David said. Nia and Jahlil had gathered their things; Jahlil was making an obvious effort to avoid looking at his father's corpse. The kid's eyes were watery.

David felt a strong, almost paternal urge to spirit Jahlil away from this, and to take him somewhere where he could smile again. But it was going to be an arduous journey to reach such a place. First, they had to escape Pearl's house.

Pearl accompanied them to the door. She quickly kissed each of them on the cheek.

"Thank you for everything," David said, "again."

"Keep them safe, David Hunter," she said. "They're your family now."

He nodded, then turned to face the darkness beyond.

The gravel driveway that led from Pearl's house to the main road was as dark as a subterranean tunnel. But David heard the dogs. They bayed and barked ceaselessly. It sounded as though dozens of the hellhounds were prowling closer.

The vampires would be with them.

Jahlil, Nia, and King had climbed inside the Pathfinder. David opened the rear cargo door, to stash their bags in the storage area.

His hands shook so badly that he dropped one of the bags. He cursed under his breath, grabbed the canvas strap, and flung the parcel into the cargo bay.

Hunter.

The voice, deep and sonorous, came to him like a whisper of air against his ears.

David turned to face the long, lightless driveway.

Diallo strode out of the darkness.

Although David had seen only an artistic rendering of Diallo in the Bible illustrations, one look confirmed that he was witnessing the master vampire, in the flesh. He was Goliath-size, standing a head above Kyle, who kept pace with him on his right. Clothed in black garments, Diallo walked as if he owned the night, head raised high and proud, arms swinging casually, each long stride fluid and commanding. He was accompanied by perhaps a dozen lesser vampires, and vampiric hounds. They marched in a formation that spanned the entire road.

A change seemed to buzz through the atmosphere, as though the night itself were comprised of two puzzle pieces that had finally been fitted together with a *click*—a click that echoed in the depths of David's soul. He was gripped by a certainty that he was meant to be here, fated to meet this centuries-old adversary of his ancestor on this Mississippi ground. Another piece of Destiny had slid into the proper groove.

A dizzying mixture of terror and awe coursed through him.

"Come on, David!"

"Hurry up, man!"

David shook his head, disoriented.

Jahlil and Nia screamed at him to get in the truck.

At last, I have found you, Hunter. The resonant voice came to him again. Even from a considerable distance, Diallo's eyes held David in place, like iron stakes.

The vampire army advanced. The mutant dogs' teeth glinted.

"David!" Nia screamed.

David broke his paralysis. He slammed the rear door and hurried to the driver's side.

The engine was already purring.

"What was wrong with you back there?" Jahlil said from the backseat. "Let's get the hell out of here!"

"Everyone hang tight," David said. He resisted the compulsion to check the rearview mirror, fearing that he would once again be transfixed by the vampire. He switched on the headlamps to the highest setting and shifted into drive. He mashed the accelerator.

The tires bit into the dirt, and the vehicle exploded forward. They mowed across the grass.

"The trail, where's the trail?" David said. He had been in Pearl's backyard before, but that was during daylight hours. At night, the landscape was different and unfamiliar. That he was ready to piss his pants didn't help his sense of direction, either.

"Over there, by the shed!" Nia pointed frantically.

David saw it: near the tool shed, amidst the shrubbery, a path that looked barely wide enough to admit a compact car beckoned. He cut the wheel to the right. The SUV clipped a rosebush, crimson petals fluttering over the windows. A series of bumps throughout the yard jostled David and the others in their seats.

"Man, those bastards are on our ass," Jahlil said.

David risked a glance in the rearview mirror. Revealed in the red taillights, the vampiric hounds raced across the yard. Behind them, the valduwe gave chase. Diallo and Kyle were not among them.

Where were they?

Pearl, he thought, with a pang of anxiety. She had been right about the vampire's intent to confront her.

But he could not expend any energy worrying about something beyond his ability to control. Driving this narrow route without smashing into a tree was going to demand all of his attention.

He bulleted through the gap between the bushes. Branches screeched like claws across the truck's body. The leafy boughs of the trees formed a low-hanging tunnel. The path was twisty, the dirt surface moist and orange-red. It was better suited to accomodating a four-by-four recreational vehicle than a truck designed for city driving.

He grasped the steering wheel in both hands, something he did only when driving in hazardous conditions. Still worried that he would spin off the trail, he cut his speed, too. He was traveling only twenty miles an hour.

"They're gaining on us," Nia said. She turned to stare out the rear window. A vein throbbed in her slender neck.

David took her word for it. The dense woods were alive with the dogs' thunderous barking. In the rear passenger seat, King whined.

They aren't ordinary dogs, either, he reminded himself. The beasts were supernaturally gifted and could run much faster than normal canines.

"We've got to slow them down," he said. "I don't know how, but we've got to do something."

"I'll take care of them," Jahlil said. "One of you, roll back the sunroof."

"What're you doing?" Nia said.

"Just do it, will you?" Jahlil shouted.

"I'm not taking my hands off the steering wheel," David said. Gritting his teeth, he navigated the relentlessly curving path. "Nia, please. Let him do whatever he has in mind."

"Fine." Nia punched the button to open the sunroof.

David did not dare to look away from the trail, but from the corner of his eye, he glimpsed Jahlil holding his shotgun, and he knew what the boy was going to do.

That kid is something else, he thought. *His dad would be proud.*

Pearl waited in the bedroom, sitting in the rocking chair beside the bed where Chief Jackson's body rested. Her eyes were closed, and her hands rested on her lap, palms turned up. She was praying.

Dear God, do with me what you will. But please, keep my friends from harm and give them the strength and courage to fulfill the mission you have decreed for them . . .

She was in such deep prayer that she did not hear the snarling pack of monster canines that rushed past her house. Neither did she hear the front door crack open as though split with an axe. And she did not hear the deliberate footsteps that clocked across the wooden floorboards of the living room, thudded across the hallway, and entered the bedroom.

Open your eyes, Pearl. I am here.

The voice slipped into her mind with unsettling ease, interrupting her prayer. Her eyes snapped open.

Diallo loomed in front of her.

She drew in a startled breath. She knew his mind, but not his body. He was a fearsome, yet majestic creature, intimidating, yet beautiful, terrifying, yet awe-inspiring.

"You are brave," he said. His voice was as deep as a summer night. His gaze touched Jackson's covered corpse on the bed. "And noble."

Her heart hammered. "I am only fulfilling my responsibility."

Slowly, he nodded. His eyes were so compelling that she found it impossible to look away from him.

"You fear me," he said. "But not how others fear me."

"Yes," she said thickly. He did not need to elaborate; they had a mutual understanding. This creature had the power to pierce her mind like a hypodermic needle and suck it dry of all her sanity. She found the prospect of being driven insane far more frightening than anything he could do to her physical body.

"You understand me," he said.

"I understand only what you have allowed me to learn about you, Diallo. You were conscious all the while of my presence. Some doors you kept closed to me"

He smiled, mysteriously. "Some doors must remain closed."

"That may be. But I have never understood why you are causing so much pain to innocent people."

Perhaps it was his unexpected candor and casual manner that made it possible, but Pearl captured a thought from him. It was trapped in her quick mind like a fly caught in a spider's web, and before she checked herself, she spoke her discovery aloud.

"It's her, isn't it?" Pearl said. "A woman whom you loved when you were a man, a woman whom you lost."

Diallo's smile vanished.

Quickly, Pearl said, "But you *will* see her again, Diallo. Have hope. She is not lost to you forever."

Diallo shook his head, almost sadly. "You are talented, Pearl. Your talent is dangerous, to you, and to me."

"But—"

A cold, invisible hand closed over her throat, cutting off her words. With a grip as powerful as a machine, it began to squeeze.

Her hands instinctively scrabbled at her neck, but there was no physical choke hold for her to tear away. She gagged.

Diallo watched her silently.

Choking, she rocked in the chair. Her feet kicked in the air.

Then, she gave up the struggle. She allowed peace to flow through her. Although her lungs ached as they thirsted for oxygen, and gasps came from her mouth, peace cradled her spirit, and as the life drifted out of her body at last, she felt herself soaring, into a vast space, enveloped in a warm tranquillity, completely at peace, for she had fulfilled her life's mission, and because of her, others might live and go on to touch and change lives, and so it would go on, forever . . .

What I'm about to do is crazy, Jahlil thought.

But he didn't see any alternative. Crazy situations called for crazy solutions.

"Holler at me when I need to duck," he said to Nia. "I don't wanna get my head taken off by a tree or something."

"Okay," she said. He could tell by her tone that she didn't like what he was going to do. Well, that was too bad. Someone had to do something.

The German shepherd watched him. Maybe it was his

imagination projecting human feelings onto an animal, but the dog looked worried.

Jahlil patted the dog's head. Then, he braced his legs against the back of the front seats. Gripping his shotgun in his clammy hands, he squeezed through the open sunroof.

He'd gotten the idea to do this from a thriller novel he'd read a few months ago. The book was called thunder something and had been loaned to him by a girl he liked. He'd only read the book to impress her, but it turned out to be a decent read, with lots of action and some cool, scary stuff. Not half as scary as what was going on in this town, though. If the guy who had written that book were in Mason's Corner tonight he'd probably shit in his pants. Just like Jahlil was ready to do.

Sharp wind sliced at his face, drawing tears from his eyes. He blinked a couple of times to clear his vision.

The pack of monster hounds gained on them. Their sleek, muscled bodies filled the dirt trail, and in the backsplash of the truck's taillights, the faces of the closest beasts appeared to be drenched in blood.

Behind the canines, about a dozen vampires gave chase, too. He did not see Kyle, or Diallo, the tough ones, but they could not be far behind.

Jahlil steadied the gun on the cold roof.

It's like target practice on a shooting range, he thought. *Think of it that way.*

The dogs' frenzied barking drove a chill deep into his marrow.

No, scratch that. This is war. This Pathfinder is our assault vehicle. I'm the gunner popping out to knock down the enemy soldiers.

He took aim at the closest vampire mutt, which looked like it had been a pit bull in its former life. Straining to keep the gun steady as the vehicle roared across the bumpy trail, he squeezed the trigger.

The kick of the rifle, combined with the wind and the

rough ride, almost slapped the gun out of his grip, but he held tight. He hit his mark, too. Struck in the breast, the creature yelped and tumbled to the ground.

The beast's vicious companions trampled it thoughtlessly, not slowing their pursuit at all.

He frowned. He'd hoped to discourage them by cutting down one of their pack mates. But that wasn't going to work. He would have to shoot all of them.

"Get down!" Nia warned.

Jahlil dipped into the truck. He looked up. A thick branch zipped past, where his head had been only two seconds ago.

"Oh, man," he said. His mouth was dry. "Thanks."

"I wish you would stay in here," Nia said. "These woods are too thick and dark for us to see anything coming until it's right up on us."

"Hey, I knocked down one of the bloodsucker mutts," he said. "I can get 'em all, just watch."

"Throw a bottle bomb back there at them," she said. "The fire will slow them down, and that's all we need. Like I said, it's not safe for you to stay up there too long, exposed like that."

"She's right, Jahlil," David said, his voice taut. "You're a crack shot, I admit, but this road is twisting like crazy. I don't want you to get hurt."

"You guys aren't my parents," Jahlil said. His chest was tight. "You don't even know me. So why do you care?"

He had to almost choke out the last words. He couldn't cry, not now. He had work to do.

Nia placed her hand on his shoulder. Something about the way she looked at him reminded him, startlingly, of his mother, and he felt a loosening of tension in his chest.

"Please," she said softly.

"Well . . . okay." He placed the shotgun on the seat. Curious, King sniffed the gun's wooden stock.

"Use this." Nia offered him one of those Molotov cocktails. "Need a lighter?"

"I have one." He fished a cigarette lighter out of his pocket.

Positioning his legs against the back of the seats again, he popped through the sunroof.

The hellhounds were close. Less than twenty feet away.

"I'm gonna knock you assholes back," he said. He flicked the lighter.

"Hold on!" Nia said. "We're gonna turn!"

Jahlil lodged himself in the corner of the sunroof, to keep his balance. The truck veered around a curve, dark trees floating past.

The lighter flame winked out. He struck it again.

Something thudded against the back of the SUV.

Jahlil raised his head . . . and saw the grimy hands of a vampire grasping the edge of the roof.

He froze.

The bloodsucker had leapt onto the rear bumper. It began to hoist itself up, like a man doing a pull-up. The vampire was someone he knew. It was Mr. Laymon, the dean at the high school.

Mr. Laymon's face was smeared with dirt and dried blood. His white shirt looked as if it had been washed in a mud puddle.

"Gonna take care of you, boy," Mr. Laymon said in a guttural voice. He pulled himself onto the roof. He crouched like a panther ready to pounce.

Jahlil remembered the Molotov cocktail in his hand. In a swift motion, he lit the cloth fuse, then hurled the bomb at the vampire.

The bottle smacked against the vampire's chest. It blew up with a *whoompf!*

Jahlil raised his arm across his face to protect against the flying glass shards and the flames. A sudden push of heat drove him back inside the truck.

Shrieking, aflame, the vampire tumbled off the roof like a

bundle of straw. It crashed onto the pack of vampiric dogs. Yelping, the creatures scattered.

With the pursuing monsters disoriented by the fire, David began to pull away from them.

"Great job, Jahlil," Nia said.

"Thanks. I just wanted to get those things off our ass."

"Good work, but don't celebrate yet," David said. "We're getting ready to enter the swamp."

Death surrounded Diallo.

The dead female seer was sprawled in the rocking chair. The police officer lay under a blanket. Indirectly, Diallo had been responsible for his death, as well; every vampire that walked in this town acted under his command.

However, the experience of standing amidst human death that he had wrought was curiously hollow.

The seer's words echoed in his mind.

You will see her again, Diallo. She is not lost to you forever.

How could the woman have possibly learned about Mariama? How had he dared to let his emotions swell so close to the surface of his consciousness?

He did not understand, and it disturbed him. Yet, strangely, it excited him, too.

What if the seer's prediction was correct? What if he found Mariama again?

No one had ever confirmed his long-held hope that he would one day be reunited with her. No one—until now.

He did not believe in coincidence. Coincidence was a symptom of man's unwillingness to believe in fate. For him, signs of fate at work were the compass of his existence.

Was it fate that he would see Mariama once more?

He yearned to believe that it was true.

But until the truth was revealed, he would have to pursue his mission.

He cast a final glance over the dead. Then went outside the house, where his son awaited him. It was time to find David Hunter.

As David drove down the narrow route toward the swamp, a dense cloud of fog swallowed them. He tried to raise the brightness of the headlights, but they were already on the highest setting.

"David, be careful." Nia watched the road, warily. "You can slow down, we have a good lead."

"Yeah, but I don't want to drive too slow." He squinted through the windshield at the roiling, silvery waves of mist. He was driving only fifteen miles an hour. The vampires had been distracted by their torched comrade, but they would not give up. He had to press forward at a good pace.

The leather-wrapped wheel stuck to his sweaty hands as if melded to them with glue. A persistent itch above his right eyebrow agitated him, but he didn't dare to take his hand away from the wheel.

Thankfully, at this leg of their journey, the trail was straight, though in the fog it was a challenge to stay on course. Patches of mist floated like aimless spirits, and gnarled trees loomed like giant hags in the murkiness.

Fine condensation coated the windshield. He turned on the wipers to clear the glass. They skidded across the window with a harsh *whonking* noise.

"We're in the clear," Jahlil said. "I don't see those assholes coming after us. All you gotta do is get through this swamp. That's it."

"We'll make it," Nia said. "Hang tight."

David gnawed his lip. Their optimism was encouraging, but he would feel better after he'd reached dry land.

The path dropped out of sight.

Terror leapt in his heart. He twisted the wheel, in a desperate attempt to reconnect with the road.

But it was too late. The Pathfinder plunged into the water with a tremendous splash. A giant tree hulked ahead of them. David pumped the brake, but he was too late for that, too. The truck smashed against the tree, the impact throwing David forward, the seat belt tightening across his chest. Nia and Jahlil shouted in surprise. David rocked back into his seat, and that was when he heard the engine cough, sputter, and die.

Chapter 24

David sat still, and silent, stunned by their predicament. Nia and Jahlil—even King—had fallen quiet, too.

Water gurgled underneath the vehicle. Floating serpents of fog slithered across the windows.

"We are *not* stuck here," David said firmly. "Everyone stay cool."

Nia clutched the armrests. Jahlil muttered under his breath. King whined.

He refused to accept that they were trapped. Only minutes ago, he had felt destiny touch him, like an electric charge. They were not meant to stay in this situation, no way.

In the distance, he heard barking dogs.

He twisted the key in the ignition with nearly enough force to snap the key in half.

The engine stuttered, but did not catch. He pushed the gas pedal.

"Be careful, you don't want to flood the engine," Nia said.

"Don't you think I know that?" he said. But then he eased his foot off the accelerator.

"Sorry, only trying to be helpful."

On the dashboard display, the engine light burned. What could be wrong? This truck had only forty thousand miles on the odometer, and he kept it superbly maintained. And he had only bumped the tree. The damage should be minimal.

He tried to start the truck again. It fluttered, then caught. He urged it into a steady thrumming.

"I told you," he said. "We're not getting stuck here. Sorry I snapped at you, Nia."

"We're all on edge." She smiled nervously.

"Enough talk, let's get out of here," Jahlil said.

David shifted into reverse.

The wheels spun, but the Pathfinder did not budge.

"Oh, no," Jahlil said. "We're stuck in the mud."

"Damn," David said. Tension squeezed his chest, as if steel bands were tightening across his torso.

"We'll have to get out and push it," David said. He looked at Jahlil. "You and I. Nia can get behind the wheel and work the gas pedal."

"Man, you're crazy," Jahlil said. "There're snakes in this swamp, remember what Pearl said? Water moccasins. Those things are deadly."

"Yeah, I remember." David peered out the side window at the dark water. "But we don't have a choice. We've got to do it *now*. They'll be on our ass again, soon."

Even as he spoke, the vampiric dogs' barks grew louder. King whined.

"Take weapons with you," Nia said. "Ones you can strap over your shoulder. Just in case."

Jahlil hefted the bulky flamethrower out of the rear cargo area and offered it to David. David grabbed the weapon's strap, and carefully opened his door.

The swamp water was tar black. The murky surface purled only an inch beneath the truck.

He stepped outside, and it was like plunging his feet into a tub of ice cubes. He sucked his teeth.

Nia scooted behind the steering wheel. David shut the door and strapped the flamethrower on his back, as Mac had instructed him.

"Hit the gas when I give you the signal," he said.

Behind them, the mist prevented him from seeing more than ten feet ahead. However, he heard the hounds getting closer. Their snarls echoed through the night.

"Let's go!" he shouted to Jahlil. On the other side of the truck, Jahlil, his shotgun hanging over his shoulder, sloshed toward the front of the SUV.

David trudged through the water. He knew virtually nothing about water moccasins, but he was alert for any sinuous movements. Driftwood littered the marsh, and green vines floated here and there, like disembodied tentacles.

He came around the front of the truck. Insects fluttered in the headlight beams. The gnarled oak with which the vehicle had collided grew on a muddy wedge of earth. He stepped onto the island, and his feet immediately sank into the muck.

"Put a leg against the tree for leverage," he said to Jahlil. "We'll push on the count of three."

Nodding, Jahlil braced his body against the tree trunk. They put their hands on the hood, above the Pathfinder's headlights. David squinted against the glare.

"One, two, three!" David raised his fist so that Nia could see the signal and punch the gas.

They pushed. The tires squealed. David grunted, his muscles burning. The Pathfinder inched backward, the wheels spitting up mud.

After they had moved the truck about a half foot, they hit another rut.

David gave Nia a sign to hold off for a moment, so they could catch their breath. He sucked in great gasps of air.

The bloodsucker mutts had stopped barking. Odd.

He put his hand on the flamethrower, peered into the layered fog.

A vampire charged out of the mist.

It was Kyle. The fiend appeared to be floating on air. In truth, David realized, he was running on the surface of the water.

Jesus.

"Look out!" David said, to warn Nia and Jahlil. He sloshed away from the Pathfinder, to keep from blowing up the truck when he fired the flamethrower.

Kyle bore down on him. His eyes blazed like the flames of hell. "Hunter!"

This is what it comes down to, David thought. *Finally, the big face-off.*

He swung the weapon toward Kyle and pumped the trigger.

The flamethrower emitted only a puff of harmless air.

Roaring, Kyle backhanded David across the face.

David soared through the air as if slugged by a giant. He hit the water and sank underneath, muck pouring into his nostrils and mouth.

He flailed his arms. Gasped for air. Thought he wouldn't make it, he was going to drown, but then he broke the surface, coughing violently. Blood streamed down his chin, and a numb pain spread from his nose and fanned across his face. Bastard had probably busted his nose.

A gun banged. David wiped mud from his eyes, and saw what was going on. Jahlil had stepped away from the truck and taken a shot at Kyle.

God, don't let that kid die. Please.

The vampire took the hit without slowing. Kyle surged forward and smacked the shotgun out of Jahlil's grasp. Jahlil screamed in rage and threw a fist at the monster. Kyle seized Jahlil like a parent grabbing a petulant infant. He tossed the boy across the swamp. There was a resounding splash, somewhere in the misty darkness.

Gotta kill that bastard, David thought.

But he had lost the flamethrower in his fall. The weapon lay against a nearby oak, half submerged in the water.

Still woozy from the blow he had taken, he started toward the tree.

Then he stopped.

A large black-and-green serpent slithered across the marsh: a water moccasin.

It was coming toward David.

When David shouted his warning, things began to happen so quickly that Nia grew almost faint with fear.

Paralyzed in her seat, she watched David try to fire at Kyle, then fail as the vampire hit him, sending him flying through the air.

Then Jahlil, the brave kid, fired his shotgun at the vampire. But it was in vain. The vampire threw the boy across the marsh.

Nia wanted to grab her gun, leap outside, and drill the monster between the eyes. But her good sense overcame her fury. Shooting this vampire would be a waste of time.

In the backseat, King barked madly. The windows steamed up from both her and the dog's frantic breathing.

Quickly, she rubbed clean a spot on the driver's side window, so she could check the side mirror.

The vampire was partly visible behind the truck. He had his back to her.

From the sudden clamor of thunderous barks, she thought that he was summoning his minions.

Certainly, he would know that she was in the vehicle. Perhaps he believed that he could handle her so easily that he could take his time. He underestimated her.

You go right ahead, she thought. *Write me off, you asshole.*

She gritted her teeth. Then she slammed her foot onto the gas pedal.

Please, please, move for me, please!

The truck roared out of the mud.

Kyle whirled, caught off guard.

The vehicle crashed into him, knocking him backward, into the fog.

The snake slithered across the water.

David froze, hands raised. He held his breath. He attempted to refrain from even blinking.

His heart pounded so hard and painfully that he feared that it would be like a drumbeat calling the snake closer.

The long serpent swam to him.

Holy God, Father in Heaven, save me, Jesus, Jesus, Jesus . . .

The reptile, its venomous fangs an inch away from his pulsing heart, seemed to see through him.

David's lungs ached from holding his breath.

The snake curled around his torso, scales glimmering. He feared it would wrap around him like a python and squeeze him to death. He saw himself sinking into the mud, chest crushed, face purple, eyes bulging.

The water moccasin circled him, once, as if embracing him. Then, it swam away into the soupy darkness.

David exhaled explosively.

Across the swamp, the truck bellowed.

He looked up in time to see Nia ram into Kyle, who had turned around too late to move. The collision blew the vampire into the water.

David seized the opportunity. He rushed forward, to the flamethrower. He grabbed it, and, as Mac had taught him, opened the ignition valve and punched the button to activate the spark plug.

The small flame at the front of the nozzle hissed, ready to burn.

Splashing furiously, Kyle started to rise out of the swamp.

David chopped through the water, closing the distance between him and the vampire.

Wobbling into a standing position, Kyle suddenly saw him. The vampire raised his arms protectively, and his eyes enlarged with fear. "No!"

David had never killed anyone, but he did not hesitate. He pulled the fuel release trigger.

A swooshing stream of flames struck the vampire and swallowed him, like a set of fiery jaws.

The creature screeched. Insane with pain, Kyle rocketed into the air, to the crowns of the trees. The burning vampire leapt blindly from branch to branch. His howls—so human-like, yet so alien—chilled David to the core of his soul.

A splashing sound drew David's attention. Jahlil stumbled out of the darkness. The boy looked a mess, mud streaking his face and slimy vines in his hair, but he was alive.

Nia rolled down the window. "Let's go, guys! Before the rest of them come."

High in the trees, the dying vampire continued its cries of agony.

"You drive," David said. He grabbed the rear passenger door.

Before he climbed inside, he glimpsed myriad shapes in the fog, behind them. But the figures were still. They appeared to be entranced with Kyle's fiery demise.

One shadow in the mist stood taller than the others: Diallo.

He's really going to have it in for me now, David thought. *I killed his son.*

David hustled into the vehicle, beside King. Jahlil got in the front.

Nia blasted forward. They found the trail and followed it through the rest of the swamp.

All of them were silent. The silence was finally broken by a sound that did not come from them. It came from behind, reverberating through the night.

A horrible, wrenching cry of grief.

None of them questioned the source of the cry. They knew: it was Diallo, mourning his son.

* * *

The muddy path that weaved through the marsh changed into a dusty trail that curved between thick shrubbery, and finally ended at a paved road. David was relieved to see dry land.

His dog was relieved, too. King tried to stand in his lap and lick his face, and David had to put the dog back on the other side of the seat.

The thunderstorm had passed. Thin patches of clouds scudded across the sky. Moonlight silvered the lonely road and the dense bushes that grew alongside it.

"I know where we are," Nia said. "We're on the west side of town. This is Rice's Bottoms Road. It'll hit Main Street about a mile ahead."

"Good," David said. "From there, I'll know the way to where we want to go next."

"Where are we going?" Jahlil said.

"To my father's hideaway," David said. "It's a cabin on the north side of town, in the hills. We'll be safe there until morning."

"You hope," Jahlil said.

"Think positively," Nia said.

"Only being realistic," Jahlil said. "I didn't expect any of the shit that we've been through tonight. Neither of you did, either, did you?"

David did not answer his question, and neither did Nia. They rolled along, quietly.

The street lamps were burned out. Broken tree branches covered the pavement, like bones emptied out of a mass grave.

They reached Main Street. David asked Nia to turn left. They drove into the small business district.

"It looks like a ghost town," David said.

"You aren't lying," Jahlil said.

Wind ushered leaves and severed branches across the abandoned sidewalks. Every storefront was dark. There were only a few traffic lights in town, and they gazed at the night with dead, unblinking eyes.

Theirs was the only moving vehicle on the street. A few cars and trucks were parked along the curb, but judging from the film of condensation on their windshields, they had not been driven recently. When they passed the deserted police station, David and the others looked away.

"I wonder where everyone's gone," Nia said.

"I don't wanna know," Jahlil said.

"They're safe in their homes, hopefully," David said. "At the meeting, we gave instructions for people to stay in and lock their doors. I hope they listened to us."

"With those bloodsuckers on the loose, it might not matter," Jahlil said. "They can bust in anyplace they want."

David blotted sweat from his face, leaned back in the seat. Jahlil was right, of course. These vampires didn't follow any silly fictional conventions. In their hunt for blood, the monsters would tear into as many homes as they could to satiate their thirst. And David and the others understood that once someone was bitten, the terrible transformation would begin.

The town might be saturated with gestating vampires that would venture into the open tomorrow evening. The possibility curdled his stomach.

We can't take much longer to finish this, David thought. *Tonight, we nearly died. We'll never survive another night.*

"Hey, look out," Jahlil said.

In the middle of the road, a trio of hulking, vampiric dogs crowded around what appeared to be a large carcass.

"Oh my God, that's a person," Nia said.

David bent forward. "Don't slow down, Nia. Go around them, fast."

The vampiric dogs began to snarl. They moved to block the roadway. Nia swerved around the beasts, tires squealing. A hound leaped at the truck; its blood-smeared snout thumped against the side window, drawing a shout of terror from Jahlil and a bark from King. David gripped Nia's shoulder.

"We're past them," Nia said. David relaxed his grip on her. A glance through the rear windshield confirmed that the fiends had returned their attention to their unfortunate victim.

He wondered who the hellhounds had attacked. He decided that he did not want to know. He had reached his limit of anguish; any more, and he would lose his mind. Better for the victim to remain a nameless stranger.

"Tell me where to go, David," Nia said. "Give me directions. I want to get the hell out of here."

High in the forested hills, Nia parked in the driveway beside the log cabin.

"Well," Jahlil said. "Looks like you were right, David. I don't think anyone will find us here."

"My dad used to come here when he wanted complete privacy," David said. "I checked out the place about a week ago. We'll be safe here for the rest of the night."

David yawned. His watch read 1:02, but he felt as if he had been awake all night and a day. He was eager to get inside and sleep.

They unloaded their bags. David was keenly aware of the stillness of the night. They might have been in a remote area of the Colorado Rockies.

Behind them, the long, tree-shrouded lane that twined through the woods was dark and quiet.

David unlocked the front door of the cabin, pushed it open. He reached inside the doorway and flicked the light switch. No power up here, either.

"We can find some candles inside," David said.

They switched on their flashlights and filed inside. King promptly set about sniffing around the edges of the room. David gave the area a once-over, to make sure nothing nasty awaited them inside, and then he locked the door.

The cabin had been shut for many days. The air, as a result, was stale and heavy. David cracked open a window.

They found a half-dozen candles stored inside the pantry in the kitchen. David and Nia lit each one and distributed them throughout the place, suffusing the cabin with a warm, golden glow. Jahlil lingered in the kitchen.

"Hey, is there any food in here?" Jahlil asked. "I'm starving."

"Check out the cabinets," David said. "I think there's canned foods, ramen noodles, stuff like that. No pizza and beer, unfortunately."

"I don't care, I'll eat anything." Jahlil began to open cabinets.

Nia edged close to David. Lines of fatigue crinkled the flesh underneath her eyes. Death had grazed them too many times tonight. It would be a long while before either of them looked, or felt, normal, again.

"You look so tired," she said. "Like I feel."

"I think we're all wiped out. But I won't be able to sleep a wink until we secure this place."

She sighed. "I knew you'd say that. You're right. But that bed looks so inviting."

"It won't take long," David said.

While Jahlil rummaged for food, David and Nia fortified the cabin. They pushed the heavy oak dresser in front of the door. There were four windows; they locked three of them and left one partly open, to encourage fresh air to circulate.

"It's pretty unlikely that any of these precautions will hold back those bloodsuckers," David said. "If nothing else, the sounds of their breaking in will warn us."

Nia did not look comforted, and honestly, neither was David, but it was the best they could do.

"Food's ready, folks," Jahlil said. "Come and get it."

It was perhaps the strangest meal that David had ever seen assembled on a table: mixed nuts, granola bars, and beef jerky. To drink, they had the bottled water that David had packed in his small portable cooler.

King would dine on a bowl of water and a few sticks of beef jerky.

Nia blessed the food, and they pulled out chairs and sat at the dinette table.

"I'm so hungry, this tastes like prime rib to me." Jahlil bit into a beef jerky.

They spoke little as they ate, each of them consumed with the single-minded focus to feed and replenish their energy. A breeze whisked around the cabin, making the thick logs creak and whistle. David flinched when he first heard the sound, then relaxed when he realized that it was only the wind.

Sipping water, Nia suddenly belched.

"Sorry." She smiled self-consciously.

"How unladylike," David said. "We ought to send you to your room, Miss James. You know better."

"I've got a better idea," Jahlil said. "We make her sleep on the floor with King. There isn't enough room on that bed for the three of us. And if she's gonna burp like that there's no telling what a mess she might make in the bed."

David laughed.

"All right, that's enough boys," Nia said. "Or else I'll make both of you sleep on the floor with King. Isn't that right, King?"

King looked up curiously from his space on the floor, as though wondering why they kept mentioning his name.

They laughed.

It feels so good to laugh, David thought. It had been an awful night. The laughter nourished his spirit just as the food sustained his body.

The wind fluted again, a piercing cry, and the lighthearted moment of camaraderie slipped away.

David looked around the table. "We have to talk about our next move, guys."

"About the only move I can make is to the bed." Nia yawned. "Honey, I'm exhausted."

"Me, too," Jahlil said. "As soon as I'm done grubbing, I'll be out."

"I figured that getting a few hours' rest would be part of the plan," David said. "We're in no shape to do anything else tonight. There wouldn't be much point in trying, either. Like I said earlier, the night belongs to the vampires."

"And the day is ours," Jahlil said.

"You've got it," David said. "I say, we get up early in the morning. We find Diallo's lair. We find it and we do the same thing to him that we did to his son."

"Torch him." Nia shivered at the memory of the gruesome incident.

"Yeah," David said. "We take care of Diallo, and the rest of the vampires will be history. Remember what Pearl told us? All of these vampires, together, are like a monster with a hundred arms, and Diallo is the heart of the beast. Destroy the heart, and the monster dies."

"Okay, but how do we find him?" Jahlil said. "He's not gonna be at the Mason place anymore. He could hide anywhere that's dark and safe for him. We could waste all day looking, and then night will come again . . ." He left the sentence unfinished, and the anxiety that flashed in his eyes communicated what he feared would happen.

David pinched the bridge of his nose. He was so tired that he was beginning to see double images.

"I honestly have no idea where he'll be resting," David said. "We'll have to brainstorm a list of potential places, and then visit each, one by one. That's the only plan that makes sense to me."

"Yeah, me too," Nia said. Chewing on a fingernail, Jahlil nodded tightly.

"Then that's the plan," David said. "Tomorrow morning, we'll get into the specifics."

Their meal and discussion complete, they pushed away from the table. As David cleaned up the remains of their meal, King shuffled to the door. The dog whined.

"You would want to go outside to potty after we've barricaded the door," David said. King wagged his tail.

"I'll take him out," Jahlil said. "But you better be quick, doggie."

"Don't worry, he's a regular minuteman," David said.

They pushed the dresser aside. Jahlil escorted King outdoors.

Through the window, David and Nia watched the boy and the dog walking around the moonlit yard.

"He's a good kid," Nia said. "A little stubborn sometimes, but brave as hell."

"A natural leader, like his father," David said. He sat on the king-size bed. The mattress was firm. He patted the space next to him, and Nia sat there.

He curled his arms around her waist, drawing her closer. He kissed her lips.

"I love you," he said.

She pressed her body into him and energetically reciprocated his kiss. "Love you, too."

Although he was wrung out, and dread of what tomorrow would bring lay heavy on his heart, a powerful libidinous urge surged through him. He ached to make love to Nia, right now.

"I wish we could have one night, alone, with no worries," he said. "Just one."

"We'll have it, soon. We'll have more than one night like that, too. You'll see."

She pulled him down onto the bed. They lay facing each other. He traced his finger along her cheek.

She grasped his hand and took one of his fingers into her moist mouth. She glided her tongue across the tip of his finger, suggestively.

"You are something else," he said. But he was getting aroused. He moved closer to her, slid his hand across her hip.

Jahlil and King came back inside.

"All right, y'all," Jahlil said. "Time to break it up. I'm not into watching folks get their groove on."

Nia smiled, whispered to David, "Later, honey." They got off the bed, put the dresser back in place in front of the door, and David checked again that the three windows were fastened. Cool wind slipped through the gap of the last, partially opened window. He would leave it open while they slept, to allow fresh air inside.

He thought he heard, faintly, the sound of barking dogs. Frowning, he listened closer.

"What is it?" Nia asked.

"Nothing." He shook his head. "Just my imagination."

Sometimes, the memory of terror could be as vivid as the real thing.

He only hoped that he slept without nightmares.

Like a storm cloud, Diallo traveled slowly through the night.

He had left behind his army at the swamp, commanding them to leave him and hunt on their own. For only the third time in his life, he was too anguished to withstand the burden of leadership.

He had discovered his son tangled in the branches of a water oak, high above the marsh. Kyle's flame-ravaged body smouldered like a dying ember. He was little more than a brittle skeleton held together with tenuous strands of charred flesh.

"My son," Diallo had said. He could not say any more.

Carefully, he had extricated his son from the boughs. Holding Kyle in his arms, he glided to the earth. He began to walk.

"I have lost too much," Diallo whispered. "I will not lose you."

As Diallo marched through the darkness, Kyle's limbs swayed like branches in a breeze, clattering softly. The flesh was seared away from his skull, making his once-handsome face utterly unrecognizable. Most critically, fire had swallowed his vampire heart, too. He was, without question, dead.

"I will not lose you," Diallo vowed. "You are my only son. You must live."

The wind rustled through the field in which he walked, tall blades of grass hissing like serpents. The fat moon gazed down on him, as distant and uncaring as ever.

Diallo looked deeply into the dark, eyeless sockets of his son's skull.

"You will live," Diallo said.

The breeze threw a fistful of dead weeds over his head.

Resolute, Diallo journeyed through the darkness to bury his son.

In spite of the terrifying day and night that he had endured, David slumbered deeply and dreamlessly, his exhaustion rewarding him a sound sleep.

He awoke to the pinkish-gray light of dawn slanting through the thin gaps between the blinds. King, ears raised alertly, stood at the half-open window across the room, staring through the glass with a peculiar intensity.

David raised into a sitting position, his tired bones creaking. Beside him, Nia slept quietly; Jahlil was asleep on the far side of the bed, snoring softly.

The makeshift barricade in front of the door was undisturbed. The other windows were shut, too.

"What're you looking at, boy?" David asked the dog. "Is a squirrel out there making fun of you?"

King glanced at David. The dog wagged his tail, once, but did not move away from the window.

Wiping his eyes, David pushed off the mattress and padded across the cool hardwood floor.

He rested his hand on the dog's back and knelt so that he could peer out the blinds at the same eye level as King.

A maple tree grew in the yard outside, its leafy arms extending to within a few feet of the window. A huge black bird had perched on a nearby branch: a raven.

The raven.

David's heartbeat accelerated.

The dream image of Lisha, the beautiful and ancient female vampire, shimmered through his mind's eye.

Feeling as though he were in yet another dream, he reached forward and grasped the pull cord, raising the blinds. They clicked upward.

The bird's liquid black eyes found David's. Its stare was intense, and, David thought, *expectant.*

She's waiting for me, he thought. *Waiting for me to do something.*

The bird ruffled its feathers, impatiently.

She's waiting for me to follow her.

The thought came to him so lucidly that he wondered whether it had originated in his mind at all; perhaps the idea had been implanted in his brain by the mysterious vampire who communicated with him through the raven.

But follow her where? Why did she want to lead them somewhere?

Pearl had said that the vampire who puppeteered the bird might assist them in their mission, yet Pearl had also cautioned them that Lisha had her own ulterior motives, too.

The raven cawed, as if pushing him to reach a conclusion.

David made a decision based solely on gut instinct.

"Okay," he said. "We'll follow you. Wherever you want to take us."

He could have sworn that the bird smiled.

Chapter 25

David awoke Nia and Jahlil.

"Everyone, up and out," he said. "We've got to leave, right now."

"Huh?" Nia stretched, blinking. Her voice was scratchy. "What's going on?"

"We've got a guide to help us," he said. "Remember the raven? She's waiting for us outside."

Understanding flashed in Nia's eyes. She threw off the blanket. Jahlil followed suit.

It took them less than five minutes to dress and grab their bags. They moved the dresser that served as the barricade, and opened the door.

The raven awaited them on the walkway. It watched them, black eyes glinting with a sentience that was downright creepy.

"I'll be damned," Jahlil said. "I remember you guys telling me about this bird, but seeing it . . . that's something else."

The raven cawed and strutted across the yard.

"Let's move," David said.

His watch read six-thirty. Rosy light glowed in the sky. Dew dampened the grass.

Seen in the light of day, the Pathfinder was a mess; it looked as if the vehicle had been competing in a mud race. David made a mental note to get the truck washed, and then almost laughed at himself for thinking about such a thing at a time like this.

As they piled inside the SUV, the bird launched into the air.

"Hey, it's flying away!" Jahlil said. "Don't lose it."

"We won't," David said. He made a U-turn in the driveway.

They rolled across the dirt lane. The raven circled above the cabin, then descended until it was only a few feet above the vehicle, and perhaps ten feet ahead.

The bird guided them along the winding path, through the hilly woods.

"I wonder where it's leading us," Nia said.

"You've asked the million-dollar question," David said. "I have no idea where it's going, but it has to be important."

Shafts of daylight pierced the overhanging trees. Ahead, a squirrel that seemed about to venture into view vanished into the roadside shrubbery when it spotted the raven, as though identifying it as a bird of prey to be avoided.

They followed the bird out of the woods, and onto the shaded country lane that intersected the mouth of the cabin's driveway. The bird soared west, toward the town's residential area. The raven rose higher into the air, but remained in clear view.

"She's taking us to the vampire's lair," Jahlil said from the back. "I betcha a thousand bucks. That's where she's leading us."

David looked at Nia, and she nodded. Jahlil had voiced the thought that had entered David's mind, and he was sure Nia had hoped for the same thing.

"Let's not get our hopes up," David said, probably more to himself than to anyone. "We'll just have to see."

"You *know* that's where she's taking us," Jahlil said. "Can't you feel it? I feel like I used to right before a big football game. Like something huge is about to happen."

"Whatever it is, we've gotta be ready," David said. He flexed his fingers on the steering wheel. Nervous energy sang through his blood.

The raven wheeled through the air like a toy glider. Following, they turned onto Main Street.

In the morning light, the area looked worse than it did last night. Debris was everywhere. Windows were shattered, glass littering the pavement. The traffic lights continued to stare like dead eyes.

But there was no pack of dogs blocking the street, no human carcass lying on the ground. There were no signs of life at all. It might have been a forgotten movie set at a bankrupt Hollywood studio.

"I hardly recognize this place," Nia said. Her voice teetered on a sob. She covered her mouth.

David could not think of anything to say. No words of comfort would reassure her. The worst was yet to come.

They left the business district. The raven began to descend.

A tall, wrought-iron fence that fronted the road indicated their destination, and when David saw the bird swoop inside the enclosure, he realized that he should not have been surprised. Where else could this nightmarish adventure have concluded?

He drove through the open gates of Hillside Cemetery.

The raven alighted on a stone monument just inside the entrance, in the cool shade of a maple tree.

David parked nearby, on the shoulder of the narrow asphalt path that curved through the graveyard.

"This is it?" Nia said. "I don't get it."

"Me, either." David's heart drummed. "But let's check it out."

"You want to bring King with us?" Jahlil said. "Or leave him in here?"

"He's coming," David said. "He's part of the team, too."

They climbed out of the truck. A wind whispered through the cemetery, like a forlorn spirit. Morning mist shrouded the headstones, and the boughs of the large elms and maples drooped, as if burdened with sorrow.

David and the others strapped their bags over their shoulders. Each of them drew a weapon: David and Nia had handguns, and Jahlil carried his shotgun.

Standing atop the monument, the raven regarded them.

David approached the bird.

"Why did you bring us here?" he said.

Staring at him, the raven cawed. But the telepathic moment that he had experienced at the cabin did not repeat itself.

King's ears prickled. The dog growled.

"He senses something," Nia said. "But what?"

King started to trot through the grass.

"Let's follow him," David said. He looked at the raven, but the bird only watched them, impassively.

They jogged in order to keep pace with the dog. They followed King in a twisting route around the headstones and monuments. David read some of the inscriptions on the graves. Most of the people had been buried decades ago.

Farther ahead, deep in the heart of the cemetery, standing atop a slight hill, a dark mausoleum rose out of the fog, like a temple to some ancient god.

King halted. But the dog continued to growl. He glowered at the crypt as though it were his mortal enemy.

"Oh, my God," Nia said. "I get it."

"What is it?" David and Jahlil said simultaneously.

"Edward Mason was buried in there," Nia said. "That's the Mason family mausoleum. Remember what Franklin told us, David?"

David nodded. "I remember. There's a shelter, under the

crypt. Mason had it built so that he could hide there if Union troops ever invaded the area."

"Are you for real?" Jahlil said. "That thing leads underground?"

"For real," Nia said.

"Think about it," David said. "What a perfect hideaway for a vampire. A sanctuary amongst the dead."

"No, not all dead," Nia said. "Look."

Like ghosts, large shapes emerged from the mist around the mausoleum: vampiric hounds.

King was barking. David, Nia, and Jahlil had raised their firearms.

Three bloodsucker hounds gathered in front of the crypt, like modern-day counterparts of Cerebrus, the mythical, vicious guard dog that guarded the gates of Hades.

"I'm sick of these fucking mutts," Jahlil said. "They act like they own the town."

Cold sweat plastered David's shirt to his torso. He was frightened beyond reason, and they had not confronted Diallo yet. He had to buckle down and handle this. He *had* to.

"Listen, we know that guns won't kill those mutts," David said. "At best, they'll knock them down, temporarily. We hit them with enough firepower to paralyze them, then we move on, inside. Let's not waste our energy and resources trying to kill them. Remember: we take care of Diallo, and every creature under his power will die, too."

"All right, sounds like a plan," Nia said. Her fingers tightened on her gun. "Let's do this."

The monster canines broke into a run, scattering in various directions.

"They're gonna try to trap us in a circle!" David shouted. He swung around. The hounds dashed through the cemetery like trained soldiers. Shit, those suckers were smart. "Everyone, spread out and take a different side. I'm out front, Nia, you get the right, Jahlil, grab the left. Go!"

They positioned themselves as he commanded. King remained at David's side, snapping furiously.

A huge, vampiric canine charged straight toward them, its eyes ablaze with supernatural hunger. David fired the .38 and missed terribly, the bullet ricocheting off a headstone.

The beast leapt high and tackled him. He slammed to the grass.

The monster dog's strong paws dug into his chest. Saliva poured from its lips, and a rank stench spewed from its mouth.

I can't let it bite me; if it bites me, I'm through.

The gun had popped out of his grasp when he had fallen. He was defenseless.

Snarling, the vampiric mutt dipped its large head, to tear into his neck.

He would have been finished, had it not been for King. King jumped onto the creature and tore into the back of the hound's neck.

The creature shrieked. It fell off David's chest.

David rolled over. His gun had fallen beside a headstone. The inscription bore his first name.

No death today, dammit, not for me.

He grasped the gun. The vampire dog was trying, unsuccessfully, to throw off King. The German shepherd had locked its jaws onto the creature's neck.

David scrambled forward, took aim, and shot the monster in the head. It dropped to the grass with a whimper, legs kicking spasmodically.

Saliva glistening on his lips, King seemed to grin at David.

"Good boy," David said.

Gunfire rang through the graveyard. David turned to see how the others were doing, and that was when Nia screamed.

She lay on the ground, clutching her leg. A vampiric dog

lay in a heap in the grass nearby, blood leaking from its breast.

"It bit me before I could finish him." Nia gritted her teeth. Blood seeped through the gash in her jeans, high on her thigh. She pounded her fist against the ground. "Dammit, I don't believe this!"

David knelt beside her. Jahlil had just dropped the final vampiric mutt with his shotgun, and he hurried to kneel beside her, too.

David touched her shoulder. Her skin was hot, and she was trembling.

He might be more frightened than she was. He could not bear the thought of losing her. He could handle anything else, but not that.

"How do you feel?" he said.

"David, I'm not going to turn into one of them," she said savagely. "Hell, no. We're going to finish this before that happens."

"But you're gonna start getting weak," Jahlil said. His eyes were wet. "When that vampire poison gets into your blood, it numbs you, knocks you out."

"Then we better finish while I still have the strength," Nia said. She began to push herself to her feet. David tried to assist her, but she brushed off his hand. "Don't baby me, honey. Please. I'm with you on this all the way, I'm not going out like a punk. Let's move while those mutts are down."

"Let me at least put something on your wound," David said. "There's a first aid kit in the truck."

"There's *no time* for that, David," she said. "We've got to keep going."

David had never loved her more. But his fear that he would lose her was just as powerful as the love that poured through him.

"Okay," he said. He looked at each of them, then faced the mausoleum. "Let's go inside."

* * *

The mausoleum had been standing for over one hundred and forty years, and the granite structure had endured the time well. The exterior walls and the two supporting columns were smooth and shiny, as if they had been recently polished. Elaborately sculpted white angels flanked the bronze double doors. Above the doorway, "Mason" had been engraved in large, gray letters.

Metal handles were set in the thick doors.

"Those doors looks heavy as hell," Jahlil said. "Hope they aren't locked."

David grabbed the handles. He leaned back, and pulled. At first, the doors did not budge. He tried again, and then they loosened, yet it still required help from Nia and Jahlil to force open the entrance.

Shadows congregated inside the vestibule. A musty odor hung in the still air.

David switched on a flashlight. He shone the beam within.

It was a spacious chamber, about the size of a large master bedroom. Six granite tombs stood on stone blocks in the center of the crypt, ranked in a line.

"Ed Mason's family was buried here," Nia said. "Him, his wife, and their three kids. After they died in the slave insurrection, their corpses were found and interred here, like he always wanted."

"Where's the door that goes to the underground place?" Jahlil said. "That's all I wanna know."

"It's hidden, I'm sure," David said. He stepped across the threshold. The others entered behind him.

"We'd better close these doors," Jahlil said. "The mutts are getting up."

Indeed, back in the cemetery, the vampiric hounds had begun to stir, like broken toys that had been repaired and gifted with new batteries.

David and Jahlil grabbed the interior door handles and

pulled the doors shut, cutting off the daylight. The flashlight was the only light source in the silent vestibule.

Nia ran her palms across the walls, searching for an indentation, or a lever. Jahlil began to do the same along the opposite wall. King sniffed curiously at the tombs.

Slowly, David walked, scanning the light beam around. He did not know what he was looking for. Anything out of the ordinary. As if walking inside a family mausoleum was an ordinary task.

"There's gotta be a door, somewhere," David said. He noticed King snuffling around a tomb against the far wall. "Wait a minute. King, move away from there."

Ears raised curiously, the dog edged aside.

David shone the flashlight across the lid of the stone coffin.

Large fingerprints were imprinted along the dusty edge.

Someone had recently opened the tomb.

David looked at Nia. "You said Mason, his wife, and their three kids were buried in here. But there are six graves, not five."

"You're right," Nia said. She came closer. "I didn't notice that."

David gave the flashlight to Nia. "Jahlil, help me open this, would you?"

Nia kept the light over them as they lifted the tomb's heavy lid. The thick cover raised like the hood of a car, attached to the granite casket via a set of steel hinges.

The tomb was empty.

A circular hole, large enough to admit a man, yawned in the center. The flashlight revealed a set of stone ladder rungs that began along the side of the opening, and dropped down into the darkness. David could not see the bottom of the shaft.

"You've got to be kidding me," Jahlil said, dusting his hands on his jeans. "We've got to go down there? Why can't we lob a bomb down there and call it a day?"

"That won't work," David said. "We have to be sure that he's gone."

"He's right," Nia said. She looked weary, and a pang of anxiety twisted through David. How much time did they have before the vampire poison worked its way through Nia and robbed her of consciousness? Most likely, not much time at all.

Jahlil groaned. "All right. This just keeps getting better, doesn't it?"

Nia peered over the lip of the hole, directing the flashlight down there.

"I can see the bottom, but barely," she said. "My guess is that it's a drop of about twenty, twenty-five feet."

David looked, too. "Yeah, something like that." He stepped back. "You don't all have to go, I can go by myself. You can wait up here."

"Negative, Hunter," Nia said. "How many times do I have to tell you that I'm with you all the way on this? I'm going, and you can't stop me."

"So am I," Jahlil said. He sighed. "I guess. Let's pray for God to stay with us on this, y'all."

David opened his mouth to argue about them following, then stopped, knowing that debating would be fruitless. Already, the three of them had endured so much together. He could not demand that they stand back and watch. Not now. They had already passed the point of no return.

"But you, King, you're staying up here," David said to the dog. "Unless you can climb down a ladder."

The dog wagged his tail eagerly, as though game for the challenge. But there was no way that David was carrying the dog down there. It was out of the question.

"Let's lighten our load, then," David said. "We need to bring only the essentials: guns and explosives."

They stuffed the remaining Molotov cocktails—they had only three left—into David's duffel bag. David carried the bag over his shoulder. Jahlil carried his shotgun, Nia wore her gun on her hip holster, and David had slid his own pistol at the back of his waist, where it was held snug by his belt.

"I'll go first," David said. "Nia comes after me, and Jahlil, you'll bring up the rear. Everyone ready?"

They nodded. David gazed into the shaft. It was like staring into the throat of a giant monster.

We're out of our minds for doing this, he thought. But the thought did not stop him. This had long since ceased to be a rational mission. They were fueled by faith alone. As he looked into the pit, he had an acute understanding of why his ancestor, William Hunter, had never been the same after confronting Diallo in the cave over a century ago. The man, operating on faith and courage, had looked Death in the face and survived, and there was little wonder why, afterward, William had become a legend who dedicated his life to saving others. Why fear man when you had conquered something greater than man?

If I live through this, everything is going to change for me, David thought. *I don't know how, but it will.*

He stashed the flashlight inside his shirt pocket, leaving the beam on. He gripped the edges of the tomb, slid his leg over the rim, and found a toehold on a ladder rung. He swung his other leg over, balanced that foot on the rung, too.

Then he clutched the ladder in both hands. The stone was cool and dry.

"It's steady," he said. "But take your time."

He began to descend. The sound of his breathing echoed in the shaft. The walls, revealed in the backsplash of the flashlight, were smooth, yet corroded in spots.

Above him, Nia positioned herself on the rungs and began to climb down. Jahlil came soon after.

The combined noise of their breathing was disturbingly loud. David had given up any hope that they would take Diallo by surprise, unless the beast slumbered in a sound-proof coffin.

Abruptly, one side of the shaft's wall ended. They were

nearing the bottom. After he passed the next rung, his foot touched solid ground.

He moved away from the ladder. He shone the flashlight around.

He was at the end of a long tunnel. It was about the width of a hallway in a large house, with a ceiling perhaps eight feet high. Several dark doorways branched off from the main corridor. The area reeked of damp earth, and old dust.

Nia, then Jahlil, pushed away from the ladder and joined him, their footsteps echoing in the passageway.

"Damn," Jahlil said, in a whisper. "So Ed Mason had his own little crib down here."

"Yeah," Nia whispered. "But which room will we find *him* in?"

"We're staying together," David said. "We'll check in each one. We can't risk being separated."

He was about to ask them to draw their weapons, but they automatically did so without him speaking a word.

David gripped the flashlight in his left hand. In his right, he held the .38.

It was so quiet in the tunnel that they might have been a thousand feet under the earth.

He was drenched in cold, sticky sweat. But his mouth was dry, and when he ran his tongue over his lips, it felt like steel wool scraping across his skin.

They crept down the corridor with the stealth of ghosts. He felt, rather than heard, Nia and Jahlil moving behind him.

Does Diallo feel us coming, too? Is he toying with us by allowing us to hunt him like this?

It was impossible to predict what their vampire nemesis had in store for them.

He swept the light beam into the first chamber. The room was full of old tables and chairs, and wooden crates that likely stored more comfort items. Edward Mason had planned to create a cozy home for himself down here.

But no living creature was inside. He shook his head to indicate to Nia and Jahlil that nothing important was in there.

Silently, he moved toward the next room.

Nia was determined to stay on her feet.

She did not tell David and Jahlil the degree of her pain. Her bitten leg throbbed, the bite burning as though the wound had been soaked in acid. Worse, a cold numbness had begun to spread throughout her thigh. She knew it would be only a matter of time before the numbness consumed her entire body and she lost consciousness, like the others who had fallen to the vampires.

I can't let that happen to me, she thought. *God, I can't let that happen. We've been through too much for me to fall before we reach the end.*

She gripped the revolver so tightly her flesh seemed to be fused to the metal. She kept the muzzle directed toward the ceiling, ready to bring it down and start shooting the instant she sensed danger.

David walked ahead of her. He had taken on a superhuman responsibility, and she admired and loved him for it. She would not let any harm come to him. She would sacrifice herself to protect this man, and she knew in her heart that he would do the same for her.

David directed the light inside the next room. He shook his head. Empty.

Pain sizzled through her leg. She winced, and continued forward.

Jahlil wanted for this to be over.

He hated that they had to climb down into this tunnel. He understood why it was necessary, but he hated it all the same. He hated those vampires. He hated what had happened to Dad. He hated everything that he had seen.

He didn't know what motivated David and Nia to keep going, but for him, it was simple: hate. Or maybe *anger* was more accurate. He didn't know. He couldn't identify his own emotions anymore. But it was easier for him to feed on anger, and hate, than it was for him to give in to the storm of other, more painful feelings that churned just below the surface of his thoughts. He could not afford to be weak.

His fingers tingled on his shotgun. Man, he wanted to blow away that bastard Diallo so bad. Diallo was the reason why all of this crap was happening. Nothing would please Jahlil more than seeing Diallo's lunatic brain splattered against the wall.

But where was he? They had checked two rooms so far, and all they had found was a bunch of old furniture and boxes.

Jahlil looked over his shoulder every few seconds, to make sure no one ambushed them from behind. He glanced at the ceiling, too. He had learned his lesson. They could be attacked from anywhere.

But the bloodsucker asshole had to know that they were down here searching for him. He had all those crazy powers and probably sensed them when they first came to the grave-yard. So where was he? What was he waiting for?

I've got something for you, Jahlil thought. *I don't care how powerful you are, I'm not going out without plugging some lead into your vampire ass.*

Shotgun ready, he pressed onward.

David flashed the wand of light inside the third room. Like the other chambers they had seen, it was full of only furniture and crates.

Don't drop your guard, he reminded himself. *Don't relax and get careless. There are a few more places for us to check out.*

He shook his head, signaling that there was nothing of in-terest inside. He turned back to the main passageway.

As though the corridor had suddenly become a wind tunnel, a blast of cold wind picked him up and hurtled him forward.

He shouted in surprise. He heard Nia and Jahlil yelling, too.

The roaring gale flung him into the chamber at the far end of the tunnel. He smacked against a wall, the impact cracking through his body. The flashlight fell out of his hand and rolled across the floor, the lens broken, but the yellow light still alive. He dropped the gun, too.

Nia and Jahlil tumbled on top of him in a tangled heap. Jahlil swore viciously, and Nia moaned in pain.

Desperate to get his hands on the firearm and the flashlight, David struggled from under their bodies. He crawled across the cold floor, grabbed the gun. Then he reached for the flashlight.

An invisible force snatched it away from him and threw it against the wall. Glass shattered. The light winked out.

Above him, an unearthly, blood-red glow blazed into life, like a crimson strobe light.

The strange luminescence brightened most of the vast room, which seemed to be the size of a high school gym.

Because of the ghostly light, the walls, floor, and ceiling appeared to be painted with blood.

Diallo stood in the middle of the chamber, face tilted upward, arms outspread. Basking in the crimson rays.

As David regarded the vampire, he questioned their sanity for ever thinking that they could defeat this monster. He was a giant whose powers defied explanation. What chance did they have against him?

Nia and Jahlil slowly got to their feet. They wore the same awestruck expression that David was certain was on his face, too.

Diallo lowered his head and glowered at them.

"All of you are brave," Diallo said. His deep, melodic voice reverberated through the room. "You have had assistance from Lisha, my former companion, as well. But that is not enough to save you."

Jahlil was the first to shake off the temporary paralysis that pinched the three of them, and attack. He jerked up his shotgun, aimed, and fired.

The boom of the gunshot echoed harshly.

Diallo took the hit in the chest. The giant rocked backward slightly, but he did not fall. A single shot would not be nearly enough to destroy him.

David did not plan to wait for Diallo to make the next move. Raising the .38, he squeezed off one, two, three shots.

Miraculously, each round hit the target, plowing into Diallo's chest.

In his peripheral vision, David spied Nia. She was shooting at Diallo. Jahlil had pumped the shotgun and begun to fire again, too.

The vampire quaked under the barrage of gunfire. Staggering, he brought up his arms to shield himself. He growled like a grizzly bear snared in a trap.

We're going to beat him, David thought, with a burst of giddy optimism. *It's not going to be as hard as we thought . . .*

Diallo vanished. One second, he cowered under the onslaught of bullets. The next instant, he was gone.

Acrid smoke, drifting from their hot firearms, curled through the air.

The blood-red orb that hovered above them continued to glow, like a monstrous heart.

We didn't kill him, David thought. Anxiety gnawed at his gut. He should have known better than to think finishing Diallo would be so easy.

"Where is he?" Jahlil said. "He's still here, somewhere, I can *feel* it."

Rich laughter thundered over them.

David spun around, searching. But he did not see Diallo. The laughter filled the room, as though rolling from surround-sound speakers hidden inside the walls.

"He's playing with us," Nia said. "We didn't hurt the bastard at all."

"He's not invincible," David said, desperately. He looked at Nia and Jahlil, their frightened faces washed in crimson light. If he could make them believe that they could win, maybe he could believe it, too. "Listen, we can kill him—"

In a dark flash, Diallo reappeared in front of Nia and Jahlil. He captured each of them in his gigantic hands, his fingers closing over their throats.

They screamed.

David whipped around the gun, but he was too slow to prevent what happened.

With the speed of a viper, Diallo bit each of them in the neck.

"No!" David fired. He struck Diallo's shoulder.

Diallo stumbled, then tossed Nia and Jahlil to the floor as if they were rag dummies.

Diallo smiled malevolently. "Sweet Nia had been bitten by one of my hounds, but the blood requires hours to work when delivered from them. When I deliver the bite myself, the life force travels rapidly, Hunter. Both the boy and the woman belong to me now."

Moaning, Nia and Jahlil writhed on the ground.

"No," David said. "It's not going to end like this."

He attempted to shoot the vampire again. Diallo knocked the weapon out of his hands. He seized David by the front of his shirt.

David punched him, but his fists were so useless against the monster that he might as well have been slugging an oak tree.

Diallo lifted him high in the air. The vampire's black eyes, laminated with red light, were bottomless pools of oblivion.

Terror made David so dizzy he almost passed out. He clenched his fists, digging his nails into his palms, and the sharp pain was enough to keep him focused.

The stench of death poured from Diallo's mouth, like flames from the lips of a dragon.

"Who are you to prevent the fulfillment of my destiny?" Diallo said. "You are the descendent of a courageous man, but he did not destroy me, and neither will you. Your family's legacy ends here, Hunter."

Diallo hurled David across the room. David cracked against the stone wall, and heard something in his body snap. Crying out, he slid to the floor.

It was his left arm. The bones were shattered.

Diallo bellowed victoriously.

Against the far wall, Jahlil and Nia were curled in a fetal position. Whimpering, they rolled back and forth, slowly, suffering the terrible metamorphosis to vampirism.

It's over, David thought, trembling in pain and anger. He tasted blood. He'd probably lost a tooth.

He spotted the duffel bag on the ground, only a few feet away. It contained explosives that they hadn't used. But what did it matter anymore? They had lost. Nia and Jahlil would become creatures of the night, and he was going to die.

Scalding tears coursed down his cheeks.

Fangs bared, Diallo strolled toward him, to finish him off.

It's over. Everything we did, it was all for nothing. I wasn't called here to finish an important duty, I was called here to die.

Closing in on him, Diallo hissed.

Suddenly, the red glow in the chamber brightened to a brilliant white.

Diallo stopped, grunting in confusion. He turned to face the light.

David, though he was blasted with agony, looked, too.

It was an apparition of a black woman. Ethereally beautiful, clothed in shimmering ivory garments, she floated beneath the orb of white light, like an angel.

David did not recognize the woman, but Diallo was stunned.

The vampire shuffled closer to the vision, and then dropped to his knees. In a voice full of reverence and awe, he uttered the name, *"Mariama."*

He had forgotten about David. It was the only opportunity David needed.

David log-rolled across the floor, forcing himself to endure the pain in his crushed arm. He snagged the duffel bag with his good hand, ripped down the zipper.

Diallo did not notice him. The vampire had his back to David as he bowed before the mysterious specter. He murmured words that David could not hear.

David dug inside the sack. He grasped a Molotov cocktail fashioned from a whiskey bottle.

He lit the cloth fuse with a cigarette lighter, and, praying that his aim would be true, flung the bottle at Diallo.

The bomb struck Diallo and exploded, and the vampire was suddenly on fire.

Mariama . . .

The sight of Mariama brought Diallo to his knees. He had waited so long to see her again, had long nurtured a naïve hope that he would be granted another chance to speak to her, and here she was, as the woman seer had foretold.

And how beautiful she was! She was like a goddess. Her luminescent beauty rendered him nearly speechless. Emotion lodged in his throat like a hot coal, and he found it difficult to even draw breath.

"Mariama," Diallo said, when he could at last speak clearly. "It's been so, so long."

Love shone in her angelic eyes. Yet sadness, too.

Why are you doing this, my love? she asked him. *You've caused so much pain since we have been apart. I remembered you as a kind, gentle man.*

"But I am not a man anymore," he said. "I am greater

than man. Man is responsible for my losing you. I will never forgive men for that transgression."

But you have no peace, Diallo. Your soul is like a turbulent sea.

He shook his head. "So it is, and so it will be, until my mission is done."

Please, come to me, my husband. Come into my arms and find peace.

Mariama's voice was like the sweetest honey, and her words conjured the dreams that he had been frightened to believe could ever come true. Dreams of a life of peace. Comfort. And a return to their long-lost home.

No, you romantic fool, he thought. *You can never go home again. Your home has been destroyed. By men. Destroy them, drench the world in their vile blood.*

But Mariama smiled at him, and her pure, glorious smile was like a promise of peace and everlasting happiness.

Did he dare to believe that his dreams could come true?

As he pondered the dilemma, teeth of fire tore into him.

Diallo howled. Mariama's body flickered, like a candle flame about to die.

No. He could not lose her. Not again. No.

In spite of the ravenous fire, he rushed toward Mariama, arms spread wide, to embrace her before he lost her again. He could not bear to lose her again. It would kill him.

But Mariama vanished.

Burning, wailing in anguish, Diallo crashed into the wall.

The fire devoured him, as he had devoured the lives of so many during his century-spanning rampage.

All for nothing. What I thought was my destiny to cleanse the world was only the demented mission of the mad.

Diallo gave up life, at last, and surrendered his soul to whatever fate awaited him in the Beyond.

* * *

The fire consumed the vampire.

As the creature died, the globe of bright light slowly faded, too.

Numb with pain, weary, David trudged to where Nia and Jahlil lay curled on the floor.

He was afraid of what he would find. Was it too late to save them?

Nia coughed. Her eyes opened, and they were honey-brown and blessedly normal.

"You're alive," he said. "And human."

"Better believe it, baby," she said. Her voice was raspy. "I was almost a goner, but then you did . . . something."

"Yeah," David said. He might never learn the identity of the ghost, and why seeing it had mesmerized Diallo. "Someone . . . did something. We're safe now."

Coughing, Jahlil sat up. "Hey, can we get out of here now? I'm serious, I can't take it down here anymore."

"I couldn't think of a better idea," David said. "Let's go."

Climbing the ladder out of the hideaway was a challenge for David, who had the use of only one arm. Nia wrapped her arm around him and assisted him. It was a tiring climb, but they had accomplished harder tasks lately.

King awaited them in the vestibule. The dog pounced on them ecstatically, wagging his tail.

"Easy, boy," David said. "Your daddy's got a bad arm here."

Nia and Jahlil pushed open the mausoleum doors. Sunlight flooded the room. They shuffled outside.

"Fresh air never tasted so good," Jahlil said.

A few feet away from the entrance, three mounds of ashes covered the ground. David instantly recognized them as the remains of the vampiric hounds.

"So it's true," Nia said. "Everyone that Diallo had infected with his life force . . . they're gone now."

"Yes," David said. "Everyone."

The three of them were silent. Then they came into one another's arms, and wept.

They walked to the Pathfinder. The vehicle had been undisturbed in their absence.

The raven stood in the same spot on the monument, as if it had not budged once while they were away.

"Thank you, Lisha," David said. "For everything."

The bird held his gaze for a beat. Then it uttered a shrill cry, leapt into the air, and soared away.

A breeze wafted through the cemetery. Golden sunlight warmed the morning.

David spotted a group of about a dozen people walking on the other side of the street. They looked as if they were surveying the town. A man appeared to be leading the crowd.

"That's Reverend Brown," David said.

"Sure is," Jahlil said. "Guess they were safe at the church last night."

The reverend waved at them. David lifted his good arm and waved back.

A service vehicle for a utility company rolled past, engine grumbling.

"Looks like people are here to clean up and put things back to normal," David said.

"You're right, they're here to clean up," Nia said. "But nothing will ever be normal in Dark Corner again."

In the End

Three weeks later, David, Nia, and Jahlil left Atlanta, where they had been staying in David's home, and returned to Dark Corner. They went to retrieve their belongings. And to pay their respects to the lost.

"The Lost" was how the news media had taken to describing the town residents who had mysteriously vanished over Labor Day weekend. Previously, Mason's Corner had been noteworthy only as the hometown of its famous native son, Richard Hunter. But the town gained a sudden, unwelcome notoriety when news of the "displaced" residents leaked out. Those who continued to live in Mason's Corner refused to discuss with the media what had happened, stating only that a terrible storm had come and wreaked havoc on their quiet hometown. They claimed that they did not know where "The Lost" had gone, and shut their doors when pressed to answer further questions.

David had followed the media coverage from Atlanta. After three weeks, when the media's interest in the taciturn residents waned and the news crews moved on to fresher stories elsewhere, he told Nia and Jahlil that it was time for them to go back.

Neither of them was surprised. They understood that they had unresolved business to handle there.

They drove back on an overcast Saturday. Nia drove, as David's arm was still healing. Throughout most of the drive, they were in good spirits, enjoying the familylike camaraderie they had developed. When they drew within ten miles of Mason's Corner, however, they grew quiet. When they entered the city limits, the only sound to be heard within the SUV was the music playing on the stereo.

This place looks a lot like it did when I first came here, David thought. Main Street had been cleaned up, the broken windows replaced. Cars and trucks drove back and forth along the road. People walked in and out of shops.

But there were differences, and they went beyond the orange-red autumn leaves. Everyone appeared to be in a hurry, as if afraid to meander outdoors for too long. Many of the storefronts had bars across the windows. And the residents who took note of them driving through town regarded them not with curiosity, but with quick, anxious glances.

"I could never live here again," Nia said in a brittle voice.

"Yeah," Jahlil mumbled. "Me neither."

Perched on the hill on the east side of the city, Jubilee gazed down on them, an ineradicable scar.

David's chest tightened. He looked away from the house.

They reached the park. The three of them, and King, climbed out.

With his left arm encased in a heavy cast, David grasped Nia's fingers with his right hand as they strolled along the grass. They had first met here; he would never forget that day. As he looked into her eyes, he knew she was thinking the same thoughts.

They stopped in a quiet corner of the park. Jahlil set down the potted magnolia sapling that he had been carrying.

They planted the magnolia there, in the rich soil. Finished, they formed a circle around the young tree. Jahlil had written a poem, entitled "Always," to dedicate the tree to those, friends and strangers alike, who had been lost when darkness had fallen over the town. He recited the bittersweet poem from memory; he had spent many hours preparing for this day.

By the time Jahlil finished speaking, tears trickled down his face. He lowered his head. David took him into his arms, and held him.

The next morning, after spending the night at a hotel in Southaven, they rented a U-Haul trailer, hooked it to the rear of the SUV, and went to each of their families' homes, to pick up the items they wanted to bring back to Atlanta. They visited Jahlil's place first, then Nia's. They arrived last at the Hunter family home.

David was crossing the sidewalk, lugging a suitcase packed with clothes to the trailer, when a champagne Lincoln limousine slid down the street and parked in front of the house.

Frowning, he placed the luggage on the ground.

A chauffeur, attired in a formal black suit and a cap, stepped outside the limousine. He nodded at David, strode to the rear passenger door, and pulled it open in a reverential manner, as though he were serving a member of royalty.

Two figures slipped out of the limo. The first was a tall, lean black man who wore shades, an elegant hat, and a fine dark suit. For a reason that David could not define, the man was familiar-looking.

But the second person was the stunner: an exquisitely beautiful black woman clothed in a midnight-blue dress and a matching, wide-brimmed hat. She wore a pair of tinted glasses, too.

After all that he had experienced, David had thought that it would be impossible for him to ever be shocked again, but he felt as though he had closed his hand over a live wire.

The woman's movements were so smooth that she appeared to glide across the distance between them.

"It's you," he said, breathlessly.

The ancient vampire, Lisha, smiled.

"I received word that you had returned," she said. "I had intended to visit the town, to see it with my own eyes, and what better time to come than when you would be present?"

His mouth was dry. "I . . . I don't know what to say. All I can say is, thank you for helping us. I don't know why you did it, but I'm glad that you did."

"Diallo was a cancer upon the earth," she said. "He would have consumed this world had I not intervened. In the process, his ill-advised actions would have drawn attention to our kind and brought destruction and misery upon us all. I could never allow such a disaster."

David nodded. "So you used me to save yourself. What about your son, Kyle?"

"Kyle had too much of his father in him. He would have become a problem in his own right, in time."

What kind of mother could so callously dismiss her own son? David comprehended how inhuman this creature really was. Although she looked like a woman, and had a woman's voice, and a sweet, feminine scent, too, there was nothing genuinely human about her. She was as alien as a species that might be found at the edge of the galaxy.

She appeared to sense his opinion of her, and looked amused. "You would have to live a millenia to understand, my child. Humans place their hope in heavenly salvation. But my only religion is self-preservation."

Alien. He would never understand her, and wasn't entirely sure he wanted to, either.

"Okay, can I ask you one thing?" David said. "The ghost that Diallo saw before he died, who was it?"

"That was not my doing, child," Lisha said. "Every soul has its hopes. Even the soul of a monster such as Diallo."

"I don't get it."

"It is not relevant for you to understand. You have fulfilled your family's legacy, David Hunter. Be proud of that.

Not all of those in your bloodline were quite as capable. You are very special."

David blushed. "Well, thank you."

Lisha reached forward and touched his cheek with her long, slender fingers. Her touch was warm.

"One day," she whispered, "perhaps we shall meet again. Until then, someone else would like to converse with you."

She smiled and, in a swirl of silk, whirled around and returned inside the limousine.

The curiously familiar man who had been waiting beside the vehicle approached David.

David's heart boomed. The man's walk, it was too familiar. His hands, too familiar. Then, when his lips broadened into a smile, recognition hit David like a club against his temple.

It was his father.

Richard Hunter removed his shades.

David stuttered, "What . . . what . . . what . . ."

"What am I doing with Lisha?" Richard said, his voice as suave as ever. "I'm her companion, of course."

"That can't be," David said. Certainly, his eyes were fooling him, or he was the victim of a cruel prank. "You died, at sea—"

"A disappearing act, son," his father said. "Madam Lisha has resources and connections that would boggle the mind."

"Bullshit. You're lying to me, like you always do."

Richard only smiled, characteristically impervious to insults. His eyes were familiar, yet strange. The irises were darker and deeper, it seemed, as if something cold and alien had taken residence in his body.

"I'm dismayed that you did not suspect it all along, David," his father said. "You found one of her letters to me, correct? It was underneath the nightstand drawer in the master bedroom."

"But that was written by someone named Elizabeth," David said. His head throbbed. This was really too much for him. This was it. He was going to lose it.

Richard smiled. "Come now, son. You're cleverer than that. Lisha . . . Elizabeth. She employed a childishly transparent nom de plume."

"What about the photo you took at the Mason place?"

"Merely a shot for an interview in a literary magazine, nothing of great importance; they wanted me to pose near a local landmark." Richard chuckled. "You made this much more complicated than you needed to, David. The truth was always simple."

"But *why* did you do it?" David said.

"Do you need to ask?" Richard said. "When I left behind my mortal life, I provided all of the financial benefits that you and your mother could ever wish for. And I get to enjoy everlasting life as the companion of a fabulously beautiful and wise creature. Do you think that was a difficult decision for me to make? You would have done the same thing if you were given the opportunity."

David shook his head. He felt ill. "So it was all about what you wanted for yourself, as always. Just so you know, I'm doing fine without your fortune. You can take it back. I don't want it."

"Dispose of it as you wish," Richard said. "It's no longer a concern of mine. I did not come here to revive old domestic squabbles. I only want to tell you that I'm proud of what you did." Richard paused. "You've grown into an admirable man, David. And . . . well, more of a man than I ever was."

David only stared at him.

His father awkwardly patted him on the shoulder. He replaced his shades and strolled to the limousine.

The driver closed the passenger door, then got behind the wheel. The limousine disappeared down the street.

David felt as though he had been punished by a boxer. His head hurt; his stomach ached. He wanted nothing more than to lie down, sleep for two days, and forget that this incident had ever happened.

Numb, he shuffled back to the house.

Nia stepped outside and met him on the porch.

"Who were those people?" she said. "I feel strange saying this, but that man . . . he kinda looked like your father."

"No," David said. He pulled Nia into his arms, desperately needing to feel someone who was indisputably real and lasting in his life. He held her so close that he felt the throbbing of her heart against his chest. "I thought it was my father. But my father is dead."

He kissed her, and they walked inside the house together.

He awoke in darkness.

His eyes were sore, his vision blurry, yet they adjusted sufficiently to the gloom for him to recognize his surroundings.

He was in the cave.

You will live, his father had promised him, implanting the thought in his soul, like a command. His consciousness hovered above his fire-ravaged corpse, as though he were the guardian spirit of his own body; he had watched his father carry him in his arms through the night. His father had brought him to the cave. His father had opened a cut in his own wrist and let the magical blood trickle into his ruined mouth.

You will live, his father promised. *But to live, you must Sleep.*

In the depths of the cave, his father dug a grave for him. Tenderly, he placed the body in the earthen pit, covering him with a blanket of raw earth.

Sleep, my son. And live.

So he had Slept. He did not know how long he had been Asleep. Not long enough, not yet. Although he had poked his head through the surface of the dirt, and his vision functioned, much of his physical body continued to slowly work through the regeneration process. No one had ever resurrected a vampire from death. His father had performed a miracle.

I will live, my father. I promise you.

His gaze traveled across the limestone walls. Above him, he discovered the inscription that his father had engraved in the rock, well over a century ago.

I will live . . . and . . . I shall rise again to slay my enemies.